A KING PENGUIN

TITUS ALONE

Mervyn Peake was born in China in 1911, and educated at Tientsin Grammar School, Eltham College, and the Royal Academy Schools. His first book of poems, *Shapes and Sounds*, was published in 1941. He also wrote *Rhymes Without Reason* (1944), *Captain Slaughterboard Drops Anchor* (1945), *The Craft of the Lead Pencil* and *Titus Groan* (1946), *Letters from a Lost Uncle* (1948), *Mr Pye* (1953), *The Wit to Woo*, a play (1957), and *The Rhyme of The Flying Bomb* (1962). For his poem *The Glassblowers* and his novel *Gormenghast* he was awarded the W. H. Heinemann Foundation Prize by the Royal Society of Literature in 1950. He also illustrated several classics, notably *The Ancient Mariner*, *Alice in Wonderland*, *Treasure Island*, and *The Hunting of the Snark*. He died in 1968.

MERVYN PEAKE

TITUS ALONE

A King Penguin

Published by
PENGUIN BOOKS

in association with
EYRE & SPOTTISWOODE

Penguin Books Ltd, Harmondsworth, Middlesex, England
Penguin Books, 625 Madison Avenue, New York,¦New York 10022, U.S.A.
Penguin Books Australia Ltd, Ringwood, Victoria, Australia
Penguin Books Canada Ltd, 2801 John Street, Markham, Ontario, Canada L3R 1B4
Penguin Books (N.Z.) Ltd, 182–190 Wairau Road, Auckland 10, New Zealand

—

First published by Eyre & Spottiswoode 1959
Revised edition simultaneously published in hardback by
Eyre & Spottiswoode and in paperback by
Penguin Books 1970
Reprinted in Penguin Books 1970, 1971, 1972, 1973, 1974,
1975, 1976, 1977, 1979, 1980
Reissued as a King Penguin 1981

—

—

Set, printed and bound in Great Britain by
Cox & Wyman Ltd, Reading
Set in Linotype Pilgrim

FOR MAEVE

TITUS ALONE

Publisher's Note

TITUS ALONE as originally published in 1959 was printed from
a typescript prepared from the notebooks in which Mervyn
Peake always wrote. Recent examination of the manuscripts
showed that the 1959 version was not complete and in this
revised edition various omissions have been restored. These
principally affect Chapters 24 (an entirely new episode), 77, 89,
and from Chapters 99 to the end where the original published
text has been considerably built up. In re-issuing this text the
publishers are pleased to be carrying out the author's intentions
and wish to join with Mrs Maeve Peake in recording their thanks
to Mr Langdon Jones for the long hours and meticulous care he
has spent on comparing the various versions and discovering the
author's real intentions.

Mr Langdon Jones writes:

When I came to the reconstruction of *Titus Alone* I was working
from three different versions. The most important was the first typescript. This was the version that had been first submitted for publica-
tion, and on which most of the alterations had been made. The first
third consisted of a carbon copy with no markings at all. The second
typescript was the version that had been prepared to the editor's
directions in his attempt to make the book coherent, for Mervyn
Peake was already suffering from his final illness at the time of sub-
mission. The first third of this consisted of the original sheets taken
from the first script, marked by Peake and the editor. The last two
thirds (in which the bulk of the modifications had occurred)
were re-typed according to the editor's specifications, although there
were sporadic corrections by Peake. The other script, to which re-
course was made to check illegibilities and for those sections which
had disappeared from the typescripts, was the first draft, which had
been handwritten in a variety of notebooks.

Thus while reconstructing this book I worked primarily from the
first typescript, constantly checking the second to ensure that I in-
corporated those alterations made by Peake, at a later date, to the
sections that had not been modified by the editor.

My aim has been to incorporate all Peake's own corrections while ignoring all other alterations. It has also been to try to make the book as consistent as possible with the minimum of my own alterations.

I have been forced to exercise my own judgement only in a few places, where normally one would have been obliged to consult the author. I have changed several inconsistencies, the only important alteration being the reluctant deletion of twenty-five words of Titus's delirium, in which he remembered characters whom only the reader, not he, had met.

Had Peake been able to continue there is no doubt that he would have polished the story still more. But I believe that in this version the factory has become a much more powerful expression of that evil which attained for Peake its supreme manifestations when, having been commissioned as a war artist, he entered Belsen at the end of the war. Peake seemed to regard evil and tragedy as a tangible force, and the book reflects a struggle that was taking place in reality, when Peake himself was facing a horror more dreadful and more protracted than that endured by Titus, and to which, after ten years, he succumbed.

ONE

To north, south, east or west, turning at will, it was not long before his landmarks fled him. Gone was the outline of his mountainous home. Gone that torn world of towers. Gone the grey lichen; gone the black ivy. Gone was the labyrinth that fed his dreams. Gone ritual, his marrow and his bane. Gone boyhood. Gone.

It was no more than a memory now; a slur of the tide; a reverie, or the sound of a key, turning.

From the gold shores to the cold shores: through regions thighbone-deep in sumptuous dust: through lands as harsh as metal, he made his way. Sometimes his footsteps were inaudible. Sometimes they clanged on stone. Sometimes an eagle watched him from a rock. Sometimes a lamb.

Where is he now? Titus the Abdicator? Come out of the shadows, traitor, and stand upon the wild brink of my brain!

He cannot know, wherever he may be, that through the worm-pocked doors and fractured walls, through windows bursted, gaping, soft with rot, a storm is pouring into Gormenghast. It scours the flagstones; churns the sullen moat; prises the long beams from their crumbling joists; and howls! He cannot know, as every moment passes, the multifarious action of his home.

A rocking-horse, festooned with spiders' rigging, sways where there's no one in a gusty loft.

He cannot know that as he turns his head, three armies of black ants, in battle order, are passing now like shades across the spines of a great library.

Has he forgotten where the breastplates burn like blood within the eyelids, and great domes reverberate to the coughing of a rat?

He only knows that he has left behind him, on the far side of the skyline, something inordinate; something brutal; something tender; something half real; something half dream; half of his heart; half of himself.

*

And all the while the far hyena laughter.

TWO

THE sun sank with a sob and darkness waded in from all horizons so that the sky contracted and there was no more light left in the world, when, at this very moment of annihilation, the moon, as though she had been waiting for her cue, sailed up the night.

Hardly knowing what he was doing, young Titus moored his small craft to the branch of a riverside tree and stumbled ashore. The margins of the river were husky with rushes, a great militia whose contagious whisperings suggested discontent, and with this sound in his ears he dragged his way through the reeds, his feet sinking ankle-deep in ooze.

It was his hazy plan to take advantage of the rising ground that was heaping itself up upon the right bank, and to climb its nearest spur, in order to gain a picture of what lay ahead of him, for he had lost his way.

But when he had fought his way up-hill through the vegetation, and by the time he had fallen in a series of mishaps and had added to the long tears in his clothes, so that it was a wonder that they held together at all – by this time, though he found himself at the crown of a blunt grass hill, he had no eyes for the landscape, but fell to the ground at the foot of what appeared to be a great boulder that swayed; but it was Titus who was swaying, and who fell exhausted with fatigue and hunger.

There he lay, curled up, and vulnerable it seemed in his sleep, and lovable also as are all sleepers by reason of their helplessness; their arms thrown wide, their heads turned to some curious angle that moves the heart.

But the wise are careful in their compassion, for sleep can be like snow on a harsh rock and melt away at the first fleck of sentience.

And so it was with Titus. Turning over to relieve his tingling arm he saw the moon and he hated it; hated its vile hypocrisy of light; hated its fatuous face; hated it with so real a revulsion that he spat at it and shouted, 'Liar!'

*

And then again, and not so far away, came the hyena laughter.

THREE

WITHIN a span of Titus's foot, a beetle, minute and heraldic, reflected the moonbeams from its glossy back. Its shadow, three times as long as itself, skirted a pebble and then climbed a grassblade.

Titus rose to his knees, the aftermath of a dream remaining like remorse, though he could remember nothing of it save that it was Gormenghast again. He picked up a stick and began to draw in the dust with the point of it, and the moonlight was so fierce that every line he drew was like a narrow trench filled up with ink.

Seeing that he had drawn a kind of tower he felt involuntarily in a pocket for that small knuckle of flint which he carried with him, as though to prove to himself that his boyhood was real, and that the Tower of Flints still stood as it had stood for centuries, out-topping all the masonry of his ancient home.

He lifted his head and his gaze wandered for the first time from all that was immediately at hand, wandered away to the north, across great phosphorescent slopes of oak and ilex until it came to rest upon a city.

*

It was a city asleep and deathly silent in the emptiness of the night and Titus rose to his feet and trembled as he saw it, not only with the cold but with astonishment that while he had slept, and while he had drawn the marks in the dust, and while he had watched the beetle, this city should have been there all the time and that a turn of his head might have filled his eyes with the domes and spires of silver; with shimmering slums; with parks and arches and a threading river. And all upon the flanks of a great mountain, hoary with forests.

But as he stared at the high slopes of the city his feelings were not those of a child or a youth, nor of an adult with romantic leanings. His responses were no longer clear and simple, for he had been through much since he had escaped from Ritual, and he was no longer child or youth, but by reason of his knowledge of tragedy, violence and the sense of his own perfidy, he was far more than these, though less than *man*.

Kneeling there he seemed most lost. Lost in the bright grey night. Lost in his separation. Lost in a swath of space in which the city lay like one-thing, secure in its cohesion, a great moon-bathed creature that throbbed in its sleep as from a single pulse.

FOUR

GETTING to his feet, Titus began to walk, not across the hills in the direction of the city, but down a steep decline to the river where his boat lay moored, and there in the dark of the wet flags he found her tethered and whispering at the water-line.

But as he stooped to slip the painter, two figures, drawing apart the tall rushes, stepped forward towards him, and the rushes closed behind them like a curtain. The sudden appearance of these men sent his heart careering and before he knew well what he was doing he had sprung into the air with a long backward bound and in another moment had half fallen into his boat, which pitched and rocked as though to throw him out.

They wore some kind of martial uniform, these two, though it was difficult to see the form it took, for their heads and bodies were striped with the shadows of the flags and streaked with slats of radiance. One of the heads was entirely moonlit save for an inch-thick striation which ran down the forehead and over one eye, which was drowned in the dark of it, then over the cheekbone and down to the man's long jaw.

The other figure had no face at all; it was part of the annihilating darkness. But his chest was aflame with limegreen fabric and one foot was like a thing of phosphorus.

On seeing Titus struggling with his long bow-oar they made no sound but stepped at once and without hesitation into the river and waded into the deepening bed, until only their plumed heads remained above the surface of the unreflecting water; and their heads appeared to Titus, even in the extremity of his escape, to be detached and floating on the surface as though they could be slid to and fro as kings and knights are slid across a chessboard.

This was not the first time that Titus had been suddenly accosted in regions as apparently remote. He had escaped before, and now, as his boat danced away on the water, he remembered how it was always the same – the sudden appearance, the leap of evasion, and the strange following silence as his would-be captors dwindled away into the distance, to vanish ... but not for ever.

FIVE

HE had seen, asleep in the bright grey air, a city, and he put aside the memories of his deserted home, and of his mother and the cry of a deserter in his heart; and for all his hunger and fatigue he grinned, for he was young as twenty years allowed, and as old as it could make him.

He grinned again, but lurched as he did so, and without realizing what he was doing he fell upon his side in a dead faint, and his grin lost focus and blurred his lips and the oar fell away from his grasp.

SIX

OF the bulk of the night he knew nothing; nothing of how his small boat twisted and turned; nothing of the city as it slid towards him. Nothing of the great trees that flanked the river on either side, with their marmoreal roots that coiled in and out of the water and shone wetly in the moonlight; nothing of how, in the half-darkness where the water-steps shelve to the stream, a humpbacked man turned from untangling a miserable net, and seeing an apparently empty boat bearing down upon him, stern first, splattered his way through the water and grabbed at the rowlocks and then, with amazement, at the boy, and dragged him from his moon-bright cradle so that the craft sped onward down the broad stream.

Titus knew nothing of all this; nor of how the man who had saved him stared blankly at the ragged vagrant beneath him on the shelving water-steps, for that is where he had laid the heap of weariness.

Had the old man bent down his head to listen he might have heard a faraway sound, and seen the trembling of Titus's lips, for the boy was muttering to himself:

'Wake up, you bloody city ... bang your bells!
I'm on my way to eat you!'

SEVEN

THE city was indeed beginning to turn in its sleep, and out of the half-darkness figures began to appear along the waterfront; some on foot hugging themselves in the cold; some in ramshackle mule-drawn carriages, the great beasts flaring their nostrils at the sharp air, their harsh bones stretching the coarse hide at hip and shoulder, their eyes evil and their breath sour.

And there were some, for the most part the old and the worn, who evolved out of the shades like beings spun from darkness. They made their way to the river in wheel-barrows, pushed by their sons and their sons' sons; or in carts, or donkey wagons. All with their nets or fishing-lines, the wheels rattling on the cobbled waterfront while the dawn strengthened; and a long shadowy car approached with a screech out of the gloom. Its bonnet was the colour of blood. Its water was boiling. It snorted like a horse and shook itself as though it were alive.

The driver, a great, gaunt, rudder-nosed man, square-jawed,

long-limbed, and muscular, appeared to be unaware of the condition of his car or of the danger to himself or to the conglomeration of characters who lay tangled among their nets in the rotting 'stern' of the dire machine.

He lay, rather than sat, his head below the level of his knees, his feet resting lazily on the clutch and the brake, and then, as though the snorting of a distant jackass were his clue, he rolled out of the driver's seat and on to his feet at the side of the hissing car, where he stretched himself, flinging his arms so wide apart in doing so that he appeared for a moment like some oracle, directing the sun and moon to keep their distance.

Why he should trouble so often to bring his car at dawn to the water-steps and so benefit whatever beggars wished to climb into the mouldering stern, it is not easy to fathom, for he was eminently a man of small compassion, a hurtful man, brazen and loveless, who would have no one beside him in the front of the car, save occasionally an old mandrill.

Nor did he fish. Nor had he any desire to watch the sun rising. He merely loomed out of the night-old shadows and lit an old black pipe, while the cold and hungry began to pour towards the bank of the river, a dark mass, as the first fleck of blood appeared on the skyline.

And it was while he stood this particular morning, with arms akimbo, and while he watched the boats being pushed out and the dark foam parting at the blunt prows, that he saw, kneeling on the water-steps, the humpbacked man with a youth lying prostrate below him.

EIGHT

THE old hunchback was obviously at a loss to know what to do with this sudden visitant from nowhere. The way he had clawed at Titus and dragged him from the sliding boat might well have suggested that he was, for all his age, a man of rapid wit and action. But no. What he had done was something which never afterwards failed to amaze him and amaze his friends, for they knew him to be clumsy and ignorant. And so, reverting to type, now the danger was over, he knelt and stared at Titus helplessly.

The torches further down the stream had been lit and the river was ruddy with reflected light. The cormorants, released from their wicker-work cages, slid into the water and dived. A mule, silhouetted against the torchlight, lifted its head and bared its disgusting teeth.

Muzzlehatch, the owner of the car, had wandered over to the hunchback and the youth and was now bending over Titus, not with any gentleness or concern, so it seemed, but with an air of detachment – proud, even in the face of another's plight.

'Into the chariot with it,' he muttered. 'What it *is* I have no idea, but it has a pulse.'

Muzzlehatch removed his finger and thumb from Titus's wrist and pointed to his long vibrating car with a massive index-finger.

Two beggars, pushing forward through the crowd that now surrounded the prostrate Titus, elbowed the old man out of their way and lifted the young Earl of Gormenghast, as ragged a creature as themselves, as though he were a sack of gravel, and shuffling to the car they laid him in the stern of the indescribable vehicle – that chaos of mildewed leather, sodden leaves, old cages, broken springs, rust and general squalor.

Muzzlehatch, following them with long, slow, arrogant strides, had reached about half-way to his diabolical car when a pelt of darkness shifted in the sky and the scarlet rim of an enormous sun began to cut its way up as though with a razor's edge, and immediately the boats and their crews and the cormoranteers and their bottle-necked birds, and the rushes and the muddy bank and the mules and the vehicles and the nets and the spears and the river itself, became ribbed and flecked with flame.

But Muzzlehatch had no eye for all this and it was well for Titus that this was so, for on turning his head from the daybreak as though it were about as interesting as an old sock, he saw, by the light of what he was dismissing, two men approaching smoothly and rapidly, with helmets on their identical heads and scrolls of parchment in their hands.

Muzzlehatch lifted his eyebrows so that his somewhat louring forehead became rucked up like the crumpled leather at the back of his car. Turning his eyes to the machine, as though to judge how far it was away, he continued walking towards it with a barely perceptible lengthening of his stride.

The two men who were approaching seemed to be not so much walking as gliding, so smoothly they advanced, and those fishers who were still left upon the cobbled waterfront parted at their approach, for they made their way unswervingly to where Titus lay.

How they could know that he was in the car at all is hard to conceive; but know it they did, and with helmets glittering in the dawn rays they bore down upon him with ghastly deliberation.

NINE

IT was then that Titus roused himself and lifted his face from his arms and saw nothing but the flush of the dawn sky above him and the profuse scattering of the stars.

What use were *they*? His stomach cried with hunger and he shook with the cold. He raised himself upon one elbow and moistened his lips. His wet clothes clung to him like seaweed. The acrid smell of the mouldering leather began to force itself upon his consciousness, and then, as though to offer him something different by way of a change, he found himself staring into the face of a large rudder-nosed man who at the next moment had vaulted into the front seat, where he slid into an all but horizontal position. Lying at this angle he began to press a number of buttons, each one of which, replying to his prodding finger, helped to create a tumult quite vile upon the eardrums. At the height of this cacophony the car backfired with such violence that a dog turned over in its sleep four miles away, and then, with an upheaval that lifted the bonnet of the car and brought it down again with a crash of metal, the wild thing shook itself as though bent upon its own destruction, shook itself, roared, and leapt forward and away down tortuous alleys still wet and black with the night shadows.

Street after street flew at them as they sped through the waking town; flew at them and broke apart at the prow-like bonnet. The streets, the houses, rushed by on either side, and Titus, clinging to an old brass railing, gasped at the air that ran into his lungs like icy water.

It was all that Titus could do to persuade himself that the impetuous vehicle was, in fact, being driven at all, for he could see nothing of the driver. It seemed that the car had an existence of its own and was making its own decisions. What Titus *could* see was that instead of a normal mascot, this stranger who was driving him (though why or where he did not know) had fixed along the brass cap of the radiator the sun-bleached skull of a crocodile. The cold air whistled between its teeth and the long crown of its skull was flushed with sunrise.

For now the sun was clear of the horizon, and as the world flew past, it climbed, so that for the first time Titus became aware of the nature of the city into which he had drifted like a dead branch.

A voice roared past his ears, 'Hold tight, you pauper!' and the sound flew away into the cold air as the car swerved in a sickening loop, and then again and again as the walls reared up before them, only to stream away in a high torrent of stone; and then, at last, diving beneath a low arch, the car, turning and slowing as it turned, came to rest in a walled-in courtyard.

The courtyard was cobbled and in between the cobbles the grass flourished.

TEN

AROUND three sides of the yard the walls of a massive stone-built building blocked the dawn away, save in one place where the slanting rays ran through a high eastern window and out of an even higher western window to end their journey in a pool of radiance upon a cold slate roof.

Ignorant of its setting and of the prodigious length of its shadow; ignorant that its drab little breast glowed in the sunrise, a sparrow pecked at its tinted wing. It was as though an urchin, scratching himself, absorbed in what he was doing, had become transfigured.

Meanwhile Muzzlehatch had rolled out of the driver's seat and lashed the car, as though it were an animal, to the mulberry tree which grew in the centre of the yard.

Then he meandered with long, lazy, loose-jointed strides towards the dark north-western corner of the yard and whistled between his teeth with the penetration of a steam whistle. A face appeared at a window above his head. And then another. And then another. There was then a great rattling to be heard of feet upon stairs, and the jangling of a bell, and behind these noises a further noise, more continuous and more diverse, for there was about it the suggestion of beasts and birds; of a howling and a coughing and a screaming and a kind of hooting

sound, but all of it in the distance and afar from the foreground noises, the feet loud upon the stairs and the jangling of
a near-by bell.

Then out of the shadows that hung like black water against
the walls of the great building a group of servants broke from
the house and ran towards their master, who had returned to
his car.

Titus was sitting up, with his face drawn, and as he sat there
facing the huge Muzzlehatch, he became, without thought,
without cognizance, irrationally savage, for at the back of his
mind was an earlier time when for all the horror and the
turmoil and the repetitive idiocy of his immemorial home, he
was in his own right the Lord of a Domain.

The hunger burned in his stomach but there was another
burn, the heartburn of the displaced; the unrecognized; the un-
recognizable.

Why did they not know of him? What right had any man to
touch him? To whirl him away on four mouldering wheels?
To abduct him and to force him to his courtyard? To lean
over him and stare at him with eyebrows raised? What right
had anyone to save him? He was no child! He had known horror. He had fought, and he had killed. He had lost his sister and
his father and the long man Flay, loyal as the stones of Gormenghast. And he had held an elf in his arms and seen her struck
by lightning to a cinder, when the sky fell in and the world
reeled. He was no child ... no child ... no child at all, and rising
shakily to his feet he stood swaying in his weakness as he
swung his fist at Muzzlehatch's face – a vast face that seemed
to disintegrate before him, only to clear again ... only to dis-
solve.

His fist was caught in the capacious paw of the rudder-nosed
man, who signed to his servants to carry Titus to a low room
where the walls from floor to ceiling were lined with glass
cases, where, beautifully pinned to sheets of cork, a thousand
moths spread out their wings in a great gesture of crucifixion.

It was in this room that Titus was given a bowl of soup
which, in his weakness, he kept spilling, until the spoon was
taken from him, and a small man with a chip out of his ear
fed him gently as he lay, half-reclined, on a long wicker chair.

Even before he was half-way through his bowl of soup he fell back on the cushions, and was within a moment or two drawn incontinently into the void of a deep sleep.

ELEVEN

WHEN he awoke the room was full of light. A blanket was up to his chin. On a barrel by his side was his only possession, an egg-shaped flint from the Tower of Gormenghast.

The chip-eared man came in.

'Hullo there, you ruffian,' he said. 'Are you awake?'

Titus nodded his head.

'Never known a scarecrow to sleep so long.'

'*How* long?' said Titus, raising himself on one elbow.

'Nineteen hours,' said the man. 'Here's your breakfast.' He deposited a loaded tray at the side of the couch and then he turned away, but stopped at the door.

'What's your name, boy?' he said.

'Titus Groan.'

'And where d'you come from?'

'Gormenghast.'

'*That's* the word. *That's* the word indeed. "Gormenghast." If you said it once you said it twenty times.'

'What! In my sleep?'

'In your sleep. Over and over. Where is it, boy? This place. This Gormenghast.'

'I don't know,' said Titus.

'Ah,' said the little man with the chip out of his ear, and he squinted at Titus sideways from under his eyebrows. 'You don't know, don't you? That's peculiar, now. But eat your breakfast. You must be hollow as a kettledrum.'

Titus sat up and began to eat, and as he ate he reached for the flint and moved his hand over its familiar contours. It was his only anchor. It was, for him, in microcosm, his home.

And while he gripped it, not in weakness or sentiment but for the sake of its density, and proof of its presence, and while the midday sunlight sifted itself to and fro across the room, a dreadful sound erupted in the courtyard and the open door of his room was all at once darkened, not by the chip-eared man but, more effectively, by the hindquarters of an enormous mule.

TWELVE

TITUS, sitting bolt upright, stared incredulously at the rear of this great bristling beast whose tail was mercilessly thrashing its own body. A group of improbable muscles seldom brought into play started, now here, now there, across its shuddering rump. It fought *in situ* with something on the other side of the door until it forced its way inch by inch out into the courtyard again, taking a great piece of the wall with it. And all the time the hideous, sickening sound of hate; for there is something stirred up in the breasts of mules and camels when they have the scent of one another which darkens the imagination.

Jumping to his feet, Titus crossed the room and gazed with awe at the antagonists. He was no stranger to violence, but there was something peculiarly horrible about this duel. There they were, not thirty feet away, locked in deadly grapple, a conflict without scale.

In that camel were all the camels that had ever been. Blind with a hatred far beyond its own power to invent, it fought a world of mules; of mules that since the dawn of time have bared their teeth at their intrinsic foe.

What a setting was that cobbled yard, now warm and golden in the sunlight, the gutter of the building thronged with sparrows; the mulberry tree basking in the sunbeams, its leaves hanging quietly while the two beasts fought to kill.

By now the courtyard was agog with servants and there were shouts and countershouts and then a horrible quiet, for it could be seen that the mule's teeth had met in the camel's throat. Then came a wheeze like the sound of a tide sucked out of a cave; a shuffle of shingle, and the rattle of pebbles.

And yet that bite that would have killed a score of men appeared to be no more than an incident in this battle, for now it was the mule who lay beneath the weight of its enemy, and suffered great pain, for its jaw had been broken by a slam of the hoof and a paralysing butt of the head.

Sickened but thrilled, Titus took a step into the courtyard, and the first thing he saw was Muzzlehatch. This gentleman was giving orders with a peculiar detachment, mindless that he was stark naked except for a fireman's helmet. A number of servants were unwinding an old but powerful-looking hose, one end of which had already been screwed into a vast brass hydrant. The other end was gurgling and spluttering in Muzzlehatch's arms.

Its nozzle trained at the double-creature, the hose-pipe squirmed and jumped like a conger, and suddenly a long, flexible jet of ice-cold water leapt across the quadrangle.

This white jet, like a knife, pierced here and there, until, as though the bonfire of their hatred had been doused, the camel and the mule, relaxing their grips, got slowly to their feet, bleeding horribly, a cloud of animal heat rising around them.

Then every eye was turned to Muzzlehatch, who took off his brass helmet and placed it over his heart.

As though this were not peculiar enough, Titus was next to witness how Muzzlehatch ordered his servants to turn off the water, to seat themselves on the floor of the wet courtyard, and to keep silent, and all by the language of his expressive eyebrows alone. Then, more peculiar still, he was surprised to hear the naked man address the shuddering beasts from whose backs great clouds of steam were rising.

'My atavistic, my inordinate friends,' whispered Muzzlehatch in a voice like sandpaper, 'I know full well that when you smell one another, then you grow restless, then you grow thoughtless, then you go ... too far. I concede the ripe condition of your blood; the darkness of your native anger; the gulches of your ire. But listen to me with those ears of yours and fix your eyes upon me. Whatever your temptation, whatever your primordial hankering, yet' (he addressed the camel), 'yet you have no excuse in the world grown sick of excuses. It was not for you to charge the iron rails of your cage, nor, having broken them down, to vent your spleen upon this mule of ours. And it was not for you' (he addressed the mule), 'to

23

seek this rough-and-tumble nor to scream with such unholy lust for battle. I will have no more of it, my friends! Let this be trouble enough. What, after all, have you done for me? Very little, if anything. But I – I have fed you on fruit and onions, scraped your backs with bill-hooks, cleaned out your cages with pearl-handled spades, and kept you safe from the carnivores and the bow-legged eagle. O, the ingratitude! Unregenerate and vile! So you broke loose on me, did you – and *reverted*!'

The two beasts began to shuffle to and fro, one on its hassock-sized pads and the other on its horny hooves.

'Back to your cages with you! Or by the yellow light in your wicked eyes I will have you shaved and salted.' He pointed to the archway through which they had fought their way into the courtyard – an archway that linked the yard in which they stood to the twelve square acres where animals of all kinds paced their narrow dens or squatted on long branches in the sun.

THIRTEEN

THE camel and the mule lowered their terrible heads and began their way back to the arch, through which they shuffled side by side.

What was going on in those two skulls? Perhaps some kind of pleasure that after so many years of incarceration they had at last been able to vent their ancient malice, and plunge their teeth into the enemy. Perhaps, also, they felt some kind of pleasure in sensing the bitterness they were arousing in the breasts of the other animals.

They stepped out of the tunnel, or long archway, on the southern side, and were at once in full view of at least a score of cages.

The sunlight lay like a gold gauze over the zoo. The bars of the cages were like rods of gold, and the animals and birds were flattened by the bright slanting rays, so that they seemed cut out of coloured cardboard or from the pages of some book of beasts.

Every head was turned towards the wicked pair; heads furred and heads naked; heads with beaks and heads with horns; heads with scales and heads with plumes. They were all turned, and being so, made not the slightest movement.

But the camel and the mule were anything but embarrassed. They had tasted freedom and they had tasted blood, and it was with a quite indescribable arrogance that they swaggered towards the cages, their thick, blue lips curled back over their disgusting teeth; their nostrils dilated and their eyes yellow with pride.

If hatred could have killed them they would have expired a hundred times on the way to their cages. The silence was like breath held at the ribs.

And then it broke, for a shrill scream pierced the air like a splinter, and the monkey, whose voice it was, shook the bars of its cage with hands and feet in an access of jealousy so that the iron rattled as the scream went on and on and on, while other voices joined it and reverberated through the prisons so that every kind of animal became a part of bedlam.

The tropics burned and broke in ancient loins. Phantom lianas sagged and dripped with poison. The jungle howled and every howl howled back.

FOURTEEN

TITUS followed a group of servants through the archway and into the open on the other side where the din became all but unbearable.

Not fifty feet from where he stood was Muzzlehatch astride a mottled stag, a creature as powerful and gaunt as its rider. He was grasping the beast's antlers in one hand, and with the other he was gesticulating to some men who were already, under his guidance, beginning to mend the buckled cages, at the back of which sat the miscreants licking their wounds and grinning horribly.

Very gradually the noise subsided and Muzzlehatch, turning from the scene, saw Titus, and with a peremptory gesture

25

beckoned him. But Titus, who had been about to greet the intellectual ruffian who sat astride the stag like some ravaged god, stayed where he was, for he saw no reason why he should obey, like a dog to the whistle.

Seeing how the young vagrant made no response Muzzlehatch grinned, and turning the stag about he made to pass his guest as though he were not there, when Titus, remembering how his host-of-one-night had saved him from capture and had fed him and slept him, lifted his hand as though to halt the stag. Staring at the stag-rider, Titus realized that he had never really seen that face before, for he was no longer tired nor were his eyes blurred, and the head had come into a startling focus – a focus that seemed to enlarge rather than contract, a head of great scale with its crop of black hair, its nose like a rudder, and its eyes all broken up with little flecks and lights, like diamonds or fractured glass, and its mouth, wide, tough, lipless, almost blasphemously mobile, for no one with such a mouth could pray aloud to any god at all, for the mouth was wrong for prayer. This head was like a challenge or a threat to all decent citizens.

Titus was about to thank this Muzzlehatch, but on gazing at the craggy face he saw that his thanks would find no answer, and it was Muzzlehatch himself who volunteered the information that he considered Titus to be a soft and rancid egg if he imagined that he, Muzzlehatch, had ever lifted a finger to help anyone in his life, let alone a bunch of rags out of the river.

If he had helped Titus it was only to amuse himself and to pass the time, for life can be a bore without action, which in its turn can be a bore without danger.

'Besides,' he continued, gazing over Titus's shoulder at a distant baboon, 'I dislike the police. I dislike their feet. I dislike that whiff of leather, oil and fur, camphor and blood. I dislike officials, who are nothing, my dear boy, but the pip-headed, trash-bellied putrid scrannel of earth. Out of darkness it is born.'

'What is?' said Titus.

'There is no point in erecting a structure,' said Muzzlehatch, taking no notice of Titus's question, 'unless someone else pulls it down. There is no value in a rule until it is broken.

26

There is nothing in life unless there is death at the back of it. Death, dear boy, leaning over the edge of the world and grinning like a boneyard.'

He swung his gaze from the distant baboon and pulled back the antlers of the mottled stag until the creature's head pointed at the sky. Then he stared at Titus.

'Don't burden me with gratitude, dear boy. I have no time for – '

'Don't bother,' said Titus. 'I will never thank you.'

'Then go,' said Muzzlehatch.

The blood ran into Titus's face and his eyes shone.

'Who do you think you are talking to?' he whispered.

Muzzlehatch looked up sharply. 'Well,' he said, 'who *am* I talking to? Your eyes blaze like the eyes of a beggar – or of a lord.'

'Why not?' said Titus. 'That is what I am.'

FIFTEEN

HE made his way back through the tunnel and across the quadrangle and so out of the grounds until he came to a spider's web of tortuous lanes, and walking on and on, found himself at last upon a wide stone highway.

From there he saw the river far below and smoke rising in rosy plumes from countless chimneys.

But Titus turned his back on the vista and, as he climbed, two long cars, side by side, flashed by without a sound. There could have been no more than an inch of space between them as they sped.

At the back of the cars, one in each, and very upright, sat two dark, be-jewelled, deep-bosomed women who had no eyes for the flying landscape but smiled at each other with unhealthy concentration.

Far behind in the wake of the cars and farther with every passing moment, a small ugly black dog with its legs far too short for its body, tore with a ridiculous concentration of purpose down the centre of the long winding road.

As Titus climbed and as the trees closed in on either side, he wondered at a change that had come over him. The remorse that had filled him lately with so black a cloud had spent itself and there was a ripple in his blood and a spring in his step. He knew himself to be a deserter; a traitor to his birthright, the 'shame' of Gormenghast. He knew how he had wounded the castle, wounded the very stones of his home; wounded his mother ... all this he knew in his head, but it did not affect him.

He could only see now the truth of it – that he could never turn back the pages.

He was Lord Titus, Seventy-Seventh Lord of Gormenghast, but he was also a limb of life, a sprig, an adventurer, ready for love or hate; ready to use his wits in a foreign world; ready for anything.

This was what lay beyond those far horizons. This was the pith of it. New cities and new mountains; new rivers and new creatures. New men and new women.

But then a shadow came over his face. How was it that they were so self-sufficient, those women in their cars, or Muzzlehatch with his zoo – having no knowledge of Gormenghast, which was of course the heart of everything?

He climbed on, his shadow climbing beside him on the beautiful white stone of which the road was built, until he had almost reached a dividing of the highway, the eastern arm, an aisle of great oaks, and the western ... but Titus was not able to fix his attention upon the trees nor upon anything else, for moving out of the shade into the sunlight, with a dreadful unhurried pace, were the two tall figures, identical in every way, their helmets casting a deep shade across their eyes, their bodies moving smoothly across the ground.

SIXTEEN

WITHOUT waiting for any orders from the brain a demon in his feet had already carried Titus deep into the flanking trees, and through the great park-like forest he ran and ran and ran, turning now this way and now that way until one would say he was irrevocably lost, were it not that he was always so.

But when, having fallen exhausted, he got to his knees and parted some branches, he found himself gazing at the very road from which he had fled. But there was no one there and after some while he walked out boldly and stood in the centre of the road as though to say, 'Do your worst.' But nothing happened except that what Titus had taken to be an old thorn bush got to its feet and shambled its way towards him, its shadow like a crab on the white stone highway. When it had come so close to Titus that he could have touched it with an outstretched foot the thorn bush spoke.

'I am a beggar,' it said, and the soft grit of its dreadful voice sent Titus's heart into his mouth. 'That is why I am stretching out my withered arm. Do you see it? Eh? Would you call it beautiful with that claw at the end of it – can you see it?'

The beggar stared at Titus through the red circles of his eyelids, and alternately shook his old knuckly fist and opened it out with the palm upwards.

The palm of that hand was like the delta of some foul dried-up river. At its centre was a kind of callus or horny disc, a tell-tale shape that argued the receipt and passage of many coins.

'What do you want?' said Titus. 'I have no money for you. I thought you were a thorn bush.'

'I'll *thorn* you!' said the beggar. 'How dare you refuse me! Me! An emperor! Dog! Whelp! Cur! Empty your gold into my sacred throat.'

'Sacred throat! What does he mean by that?' thought Titus, but only for a moment, for suddenly the beggar was no longer there but was twenty feet away and was staring down the white highway looking more like a thorn bush than ever. One of his arms, like a branch, was crook'd so that the claw at the end of it was conveniently cupped at the ear.

Then Titus heard it – the distant whirring sound of a fast machine, and a moment later a yellow car the shape of a shark sped from the south.

It seemed that the cantankerous old mendicant was about to be run down, for he stood on the crown of the road with his arms out like a scarecrow, but the yellow shark swerved past him, and as it did so a coin was tossed into the air by the driver, or by the shape that could only *be* the driver, for there was nothing else at the wheel but something in a sheet.

It was gone as quietly as it had arrived and Titus turned his face to the beggar, who had retrieved the coin. Seeing that he was being scrutinized the beggar leered at Titus and threw out his tongue like the mildewed tongue of a boot. Then to Titus's amazement the foul old man swung back his head and, dropping the silver coin into his mouth, swallowed it at a gulp.

'Tell me, you dirty old man,' said Titus softly, for a kind of hot anger filled him and a desire to squash the creature beneath his feet, 'why do you eat money?' And Titus picked up a rock from beside the road.

'Whelp!' said the beggar at last. 'Do you think I'd *waste* my wealth? Coins are too big, you dog, to sidle through me. Too small to kill me. Too heavy to be lost! I am a beggar.'

'You are a travesty,' said Titus, 'and when you die the earth will breathe again.'

Titus dropped the heavy stone he had lifted in anger, and with not a backward glance made for the right-hand fork where, with a prodigious sigh, an avenue of cedars inhaled him, as though he were a gnat.

SEVENTEEN

TREE after tree slid by to the pace of his footsteps. In the gloom of the cedars his heart was happy. Happy in the chill of the tunnel. Happy in the danger of it all. Happy to remember his own childhood and how he had acquitted himself in a tract of ivy. Happy in spite of the helmeted spies, though they awoke within him a dark alarm.

He had lived on his wits for what seemed so long a while that he was very different now from the youth who had ridden away.

It had seemed that the avenue was endless, but suddenly and unexpectedly the last of the cedars floated away behind him as though from a laying-on of hands, and the wide sky looked down, and there before him was the first of the *structures*.

He had heard of them but had not expected anything quite so far removed from the buildings he had known, let alone the architecture of Gormenghast.

The first to catch his eye was a pale-green edifice, very elegant, but so simple in design that Titus's gaze could find no resting place upon its slippery surface.

Next to this building was a copper dome the shape of an igloo but ninety feet in height, with a tapering mast, spider-frail and glinting in the sunlight. An ugly crow was sitting on the cross-tree and fouling from time to time the bright dome beneath.

Titus sat down by the side of the road and frowned. He had been born and bred to the assumption that buildings were ancient by nature, and were and always had been in the process of crumbling away. The white dust lolling between the gaping bricks; the worm in the wood. The weed dislodging the stone; corrosion and mildew; the crumbling patina; the fading shades; the beauty of decay.

Unable to remain seated, for his curiosity was stronger than his longing to rest, he got to his feet and, wondering why there was no one about, began to make his way to whatever lay beyond the dome, for the buildings curved away as though to obscure some great circle or arena. And indeed it was something of this kind that broke upon his view as he rounded the dome, and he came to a halt through sheer amazement; for it was *vast*. Vast as a grey desert, its marble surface glowing with a dull opaque light. The only thing that could be said to break the emptiness was the reflection of the structures that surrounded it.

The farthest away of these buildings, in other words those that fanned out in a glittering arc on the opposite side of the arena, were, to Titus's gaze, no larger than stamps, thorns, nails, acorns, or tiny crystals, save for one gigantic edifice outtopping all the rest, which was like an azure match-box on its end.

EIGHTEEN

HAD Titus come across a world of dragons he could hardly have been more amazed than by these fantasies of glass and metal; and he turned himself about more than once as though it were possible to catch a last glimpse of the tortuous, poverty-stricken town he had left behind him, but the district of Muzzlehatch was hidden away by a fold in the hills and the ruins of Gormenghast were afloat in a haze of time and space.

And yet, though his eyes shone with the thrill of his discovery, he suffered at the same time a pang of resentment – a resentment that this alien realm should be able to exist in a world that appeared to have no reference to his home and which seemed, in fact, supremely self-sufficient. A region that had never heard of Fuchsia and her death, nor of her father, the melancholy earl, nor of his mother the countess with her strange liquid whistle that brought wild birds to her from distant spinneys.

Were they coeval; were they simultaneous? These worlds; these realms – could they *both* be true? Were there no bridges?

Was there no common land? Did the same sun shine upon them? Had they the constellations of the night in common?

When the storm came down upon these crystal structures, and the sky was black with rain, what of Gormenghast? Was Gormenghast dry? And when the thunder growled in his ancient home was there never any echo hereabouts?

What of the rivers? Were they separate? Was there no tributary, even, to feel its way into another world?

Where lay the long horizons? Where throbbed the frontiers? O terrible division! The near and the far. The night and the day. The yes and the no.

A VOICE. 'O Titus, can't you remember?'

TITUS. 'I can remember everything except . . .'

VOICE. 'Except . . .?'

TITUS. 'Except the way.'

VOICE. 'The way where?'

TITUS. 'The way home.'

VOICE. 'Home?'

TITUS. 'Home. Home where the dust gathers and the legends are. But I have lost my bearings.'

VOICE. 'You have the sun and the North Star.'

TITUS. 'But is it the same sun? And are the stars the stars of Gormenghast?'

He looked up and was surprised to find himself alone. His hands were cold with sweat, and the dread of being lost and having no proof of his own identity filled him with a sudden stabbing terror.

He looked about him at this sheer and foreign land, and then, all in a breath, something fled across the sky. It made no sound other than the slither of a finger across a slate, though it seemed to have passed as close as a scythe.

By now it was settling, a speck of crimson on the far side of the marble desert where the furthest mansions glinted. It had seemed to have no wings but an incredible purpose and beauty, like a stiletto or a needle, and as Titus fixed his eyes upon the building in whose shadow it lay, he thought he could see not one, but a swarm.

33

And this was so. Not only was there already quite a fleet of fish-shaped, needle-shaped, knife-shaped, shark-shaped, splinter-shaped devices, but all kinds of land-machines of curious design.

NINETEEN

BEFORE him lay stretched the grey marble, a thousand acres of it, with its margins filled with the reflections of the mansions.

To walk alone across it, in view of all the distant windows, terraces, and roof-gardens was to proclaim arrogance, naked and culpable. But this is what he did, and when he had been walk-ing for some while a small green dart detached itself from the planes on the far side of the arena and sped towards him, its glass-green belly skimming the marble, and an instant later it was upon him, only to veer at the last moment and sing away into the stratosphere, only to plunge, only to circle Titus's head in narrowing gyres, only to return like a whippet of the air to the black mansion.

Bewildered, startled as he was, Titus began to laugh, though his laughter was not altogether without a touch of hysteria.

This exquisite beast of the air; this wingless swallow; this aerial leopard; this fish of the water-sky; this threader of moon-beams; this dandy of the dawn; this metal play-boy; this wan-derer in black spaces; this flash in the night; this drinker of its own speed; this godlike child of a diseased brain – what did it do?

What did it do but act like any other petty snooper, prying upon man and child, sucking information as a bat sucks blood; amoral; mindless; sent out on empty missions, acting as its maker would act, its narrow-headed maker – so that its beauty was a thing on its own, beautiful only because its function shapes it so; and having no heart it becomes fatuous – a fat-uous reflection of a fatuous concept – so that it is incongruous, or gobbles incongruity to such an outlandish degree that laughter is the only way out.

And so Titus laughed, and as he laughed, high-pitched and

34

uncontrolled (for at the back of it all he was scared and little relished the idea of being singled out, pin-pointed, and examined by a mechanical brain), while he laughed, he began at the same time to run, for there was something ominous in the air, ominous and ludicrous – something that told him that to stay any longer on this marble tract was to court trouble, to be held a vagrant, a spy, or a madman.

Indeed the sky was beginning to fill with every shape of craft, and little clusters of people were spreading out across the arena like a stain.

TWENTY

SEEN from above Titus must have appeared very small as he ran on and on. Seen from above, it could also be realized how isolated in the wide world was the arena with its bright circumference of crystal buildings: how bizarre and ingenious it was, and how unrelated it was to the bone-white, cavepocked, barren mountains, the fever-swamps and jungles to the south, the thirsty lands, the hungry cities, and the tracts beyond of the wolf and the outlaw.

It was when Titus was within a hundred yards of the olive palace, and as the princes of maintenance turned or paused in their work to stare at the ragged youth, that a gun boomed, and for a few minutes there was a complete silence, for everyone stopped talking and the engines were shut off in every craft.

This gun-boom had come just in time, for had it been delayed a moment longer Titus must surely have been grabbed and questioned. Two men, halted in their tracks by the detonation, drew back their lips from their teeth and scowled with frustration, their hands halted in mid-air.

On every side of him were faces; faces for the most part turned towards him. Malignant faces, speculative faces, empty faces, ingenuous faces – faces of all kinds. It was quite obvious that he would never pass unnoticed. From being lost and obscure he was the focus of attention. Now, as they posed at every

35

angle, as stiff as scarecrows caught in the full flight of living, their half-way gestures frozen – now was his time to escape.

He had no idea of the significance which was presumably attached to the firing of the cannon. As it was he was served well by his own ignorance and with a pounding heart he ran like a deer, dodging this way and that way through the crowd until he came to the most majestic of the palaces. Racing up the shallow glass pavements and into the weird and lucent gloom of the great halls, it was not long before he had left the custom-shackled hierophants behind him. It is true that there was a great number of persons scattered about the floor of the building who stared at Titus whenever he came into their range of vision. They could not turn their heads to follow him, nor even their eyes because the cannon had boomed, but when he passed across their vision they knew at once he was not one of them and that he had no right to be in the olive palace. And then as he ran on and on the cannon boomed again and at once Titus knew that the world was after him, for the air became torn with cries and counter-cries, and suddenly four men turned a corner of the long glass corridor, their reflections in the glazed floor as detailed and as crisp as their true selves.

'There he goes,' cried a voice. 'There go the rags!' But when they reached the spot where Titus had halted for a moment they found he was indeed gone and all they had to stare at were the closed doors of a lift shaft.

Titus, who had found himself cornered, had turned to the vast, purring, topaz-studded lift not knowing exactly what it was. That its elegant jaws should have been open and ready was his salvation. He sprang inside and the gates, drawing themselves together, closed as though they ran through butter.

The interior of the lift was like an underwater grotto, filled with subdued lights. Something hazy and voluptuous seemed to hover in the air. But Titus was in no mood for subtleties. He was a fugitive. And then he saw that wavering in his underwater world were rows of ivory buttons, each button carved into some flower, face, or skull.

He could hear the sound of footsteps running and angry voices outside the door and he jabbed indiscriminately among the buttons, and immediately soaring through floor after

36

floor in a whirl of steel the lift all at once inhaled its own speed and the doors slid open of their own accord.

How quiet it was and cool. There was no furniture, only a single palm tree growing out of the floor. A small red parrot sat on one of the upper branches and pecked itself. When it saw Titus it cocked its head on one side and then with great rapidity it kept repeating, 'Bloody corker told me so!' This phrase was reiterated a dozen times at least before the bird continued pecking at its wing.

There were four doors in this cool upper hall. Three led to corridors but the last one, when Titus opened it, let in the sky. There, before and slightly below him, lay spread the roof.

TWENTY-ONE

No one found him all that sun-scorched evening and when the twilight came and the shadows withered he was able to steal to and fro across the wide glass roofscape and see what was going on in the rooms below.

For the most part the glass was too thick for Titus to see more than a blur of coloured shapes and shadows but he came at last to an open skylight through which he could see without obstruction a scene of great diversity and splendour.

To say a party was in progress would be a mean and cheese-paring way of putting it. The long sitting-room or salon, no more than twelve or fifteen feet below him, was in the throes of it. Life, of a kind, was in spate.

Music leaped from the long room and swarmed out of the skylight while Titus lay on his stomach on the warm glass roof, his eyes wide with conjecture. The sunken sun had left behind it a dim red weight of air. The stars were growing fiercer every moment, when the music suddenly ended in a string of notes like coloured bubbles and to take their place a hundred tongues began to wag at once.

Titus half closed his eyes at the effulgence of a forest of candles, the sparkle of glass and mirrors, and the leaping reflections of light from polished wood and silver. It was so close

37

to him that had he coughed a dozen faces would, for all the noise in the room, have turned at once to the skylight and discovered him. It was like nothing else he had seen, and even from the first glimpse, it appeared as much like a gathering of creatures, of birds and beasts and flowers, as a gathering of humans.

They were all there. The giraffe-men and the hippopotamus-men. The serpent-ladies and the heron-ladies. The aspens and the oaks: the thistles and the ferns – the beetles and the moths – the crocodiles and the parrots: the tigers and the lambs: vultures with pearls around their necks and bison in tails.

But this was only for a flash, for as Titus, drawing a deep breath, stared again, the distortions, the extremes, appeared to crumble, to slip away from the surge of heads below him, and he was again among his own species.

Titus could feel the heat rising from the long dazzling room so close below him – yet distant as a rainbow. The hot air as it rose was impregnated with scent; a dozen of the most expensive perfumes were fighting for survival. Everything was fighting for survival – with lungs, and credulity.

There were limbs and heads and bodies everywhere: and there were *faces!* There were the foreground faces; the middle distance faces; and the faces far away. And in the irregular gaps *between* the faces were *parts* of faces, and halves and quarters at every tilt and angle.

This panorama in depth was on the move, whole heads turning, now here, now there, while all the while a counterpoint of tadpole quickness, something in the nature of a widespread agitation, was going on, because, for every head or body that changed its position in space there would be a hundred flickering eyelids; a hundred fluttering lips, a fluctuating arabesque of hands. The whole effect had something in the nature of foliage about it, as when green breezes flirt in poplar trees.

Commanding as was Titus's view of the human sea below him, yet however hard he tried he could not discover who the hosts might be. Presumably an hour or two earlier when even a deep breath was possible without adding to the discomfort of some shoulder or adjacent bosom – presumably the ornate flunkey (now pinned against a marble statue) had announced the names of the guests as they arrived; but all that was over. The flunkey, whose head, much to his embarrassment, was wedged between the ample breasts of the marble statue, could no longer even see the door through which the guests arrived, let alone draw breath enough to announce them.

Titus, watching from above, marvelled at the spectacle and while he lay there on the roof, a half-moon above him, with its chill and greenish light, and the warm glow of the party below him, was able not only to take in the diversity of the guests but, in regard to those who stood immediately below him, to overhear their conversation . . .

TWENTY-TWO

'THANK heavens it's all over now.'

'What is?'

'My youth. It took too long and got in my way.'

'In your *way* Mr Thirst? How do you mean?'

'It went on for so *long*,' said Thirst. 'I had about thirty years of it. You know what I mean. Experiment, experiment, experiment. And now . . .'

'Ah!' whispered someone.

'I used to write poems,' said Thirst, a pale man. He made as if to place his hands upon the shoulder of his confidant, but the crush was too great. 'It passed the time away.'

'Poems,' said a pontifical voice from just behind their shoulders, '. . . should make time stand *still*.'

The pale man, who had jumped a little, merely muttered, 'Mine didn't,' before he turned to observe the gentleman who had interpolated. The stranger's face was quite inexpressive and it was hard to believe that he had opened his mouth. But now there was another tongue at large.

'Talking of poems,' it said, and it belonged to a dark, cadaverous, over-distinguished nostril-flaring man with a long blue jaw and chronic eyestrain, 'reminds me of a poem.'

'I wonder why,' said Thirst irritably, for he had been on the brink of expansion.

39

The man with eyestrain took no notice of the remark.

'The poem which I am reminded of is one which I wrote myself.'

A bald man knitted his brows; the pontifical gentleman lit a cigar, his face as expressionless as ever; and a lady, the lobes of whose ears had been ruined by the weight of two gigantic sapphires, half opened her mouth with an inane smirk of anticipation.

The dark man with eyestrain folded his hands before him.

'It didn't come off,' he said, ' – although it had *something* – ' (he twisted his lips). 'Sixty-four stanzas in fact.' (He raised his eyes.) ' – Yes, yes – it was very, very long and ambitious – but it didn't come off. And why ...?'

He paused, not because he wanted any suggestions, but in order to take a deep, meditative breath.

'I will tell you why, my friends. It didn't come off because you see, it was *verse* all the time.'

'*Blank* verse?' inquired the lady, whose head was bent forward by the weight of the sapphires. She was eager to be helpful. 'Was it *blank* verse?'

'It went like this,' said the dark man, unclasping his hands before him and clasping them behind him, and at the same time placing the heel of his left shoe immediately in front of the toe of his right shoe so that the two feet formed a single and unbroken line of leather. 'It went like this.' He lifted his head. 'But do not forget it is *not* Poetry – except perhaps for three *singing* lines at the outside.'

'Well, for the love of Parnassus – let's *have* it,' broke in the petulant voice of Mr Thirst who, finding his thunder stolen, was no longer interested in good manners.

'A-l-t-h-o-u-g-h,' mused the man with the long blue jaw, who seemed to consider other people's time and patience as inexhaustible commodities like air, or water, 'a-l-t-h-o-u-g-h,' (he lingered over the word like a nurse over a sick child), 'there *were* those who said the whole thing *sang*; who hailed it as the purest poetry of our generation – "incandescent stuff" as one gentleman put it – but there you are – there you are – how is one to tell?'

'Ah,' whispered a voice of curds and whey. And a man with

gold teeth turned his eyes to the lady with the sapphires, and they exchanged the arch expression of those who find themselves, however unworthily, to be witnesses at an historic moment.

'Quiet please,' said the poet. 'And listen carefully.'

> A mule at prayer! Ignore him: turn to me
> Until the gold contraption of our love
> Rattles its seven biscuit boxes, and the sea
> Withdraws its combers from the rhubarb-grove.
>
> This is no place for maudlin-headed fays
> To smirk behind their mushrooms! 't is a shore
> For gaping daemons: it is such a place,
> As I, my love, have long been looking for.
>
> Here, where the rhubarb-grove into the wave
> Throws down its rueful image, we can fly
> Our kites of love, above the sandy grave,
> Of those long lost in ambiguity.
>
> For love is ripest in a rhubarb-grove
> Where weird reflections glimmer through the dawn:
> O vivid essence vegetably wove
> Of hues that die, the moment they are born.
>
> Lost in the venal void our dreams deflate
> By easy stages through green atmosphere:
> Imagination's bright balloon is late,
> Like the blue whale, in coming up for air.
>
> It is not known what genus of the wild
> Black plums of thought best wrinkle, twitch and flow
> Into sweet wisdom's prune – for in the mild
> Orchards of love there is no need to know.
>
> What use to cry for Capricorn? It sails
> Across the heart's red atlas: it is found
> Only within the ribs, where all the tails
> The tempest has are whisking it around.
>
> No time for tears: it is enough, today,
> That we, meandering these granular shores
> Should watch the ponderous billows at their play
> Like midnight beasts with garlands in their jaws . . .

41

It was obvious that the poem was still in its early stages. The novelty of seeing so distinguished-looking a man behave in a manner so blatant, so self-centred, so withdrawn at one and the same time had intrigued Titus so keenly that he had outlasted at least thirty guests since the poem started. The lady with the sapphires and Mr Thirst had long since edged away, but a floating population surrounded the poet who had become sightless as he declaimed, and it would have been all the same to him if he had been alone in the room.

Titus turned his head away, his brain jumping in his skull with words and images.

TWENTY-THREE

Now that the poem was gone, and gone with it the poet, for truly he seemed to follow in the wake of something greater than himself, Titus became aware of a strange condition, a quality of flux, an agitation; a weaving or a *threading* motion – and then, all at once, one of those tidal movements that occur from time to time at crowded parties, began to manifest itself. There is nothing that can be done about them. They move to a rhythm of their own.

The first sensation perceived by the guest was that he or she was off-balance. There was a lot of elbow-jogging and spirit-spilling. As the pressure increased a kind of delicate stampeding began. Apologies broke loose on every side. Those by the walls were seriously crushed, while those in the centre leaned across one another at intimate angles. Tiny, idiotic footsteps were taken by everyone as the crowd began to surge meaninglessly, uncontrollably, round and round the room. Those who were talking together at one moment saw no sign of one another a few seconds later, for underwater currents and cross-eddies took their toll.

And yet the guests were still arriving. They entered through the doorway, were caught up in the scented air, wavered like ghosts and, hovering for a moment on the coiling fumes, were drawn into the slow but invincible maelstrom.

Titus, who had not been able to foresee what was about to happen, was now able to appreciate in retrospect the actions of a couple of old roués whom he had observed a few minutes earlier, seated by the refreshment table.

Long versed in the vicissitudes of party phenomena, they had put down their glasses and, leaning back, as it were, in the arms of the current, had given themselves up to the flow, and were now to be seen conversing at an incredible angle as they circled the room, their feet no longer touching the floor.

By the time some balance was restored it was nearly midnight, and there was a general pulling down of cuffs, straightening of garments, fingering of coifs and toupees, a straightening of ties, a scrutiny of mouths and eyebrows and a general state of salvage.

TWENTY-FOUR

AND so, by a whim of chance, yet another group of guests stood there beneath him. Some had limped and some had slid away. Some had been boisterous: some had been aloof.

This particular group were neither and both, as the offshoots of their brain-play merited. Tall guests they were, and witless that through the accident of their height and slenderness they were creating between them a grove – a human grove. They turned, this group, this grove of guests, turned as a newcomer, moving sideways an inch at a time, joined them. He was short, thick and sapless, and was most inappropriate in that lofty copse, where he gave the appearance of being pollarded.

One of this group, a slender creature, thin as a switch, swathed in black, her hair as black as her dress and her eyes as black as her hair, turned to the newcomer.

'Do join us,' she said. 'Do talk to us. We need your steady brain. We are so pitifully emotional. *Such* babies.'

'Well I would hardly – '

'Be quiet, Leonard. You have been talking quite enough,' said the slender, doe-eyed Mrs Grass to her fourth husband. 'It is

43

Mr Acreblade or nothing. Come along dear Mr Acreblade. There ... we are ... there ... we are.'

The sapless Mr Acreblade thrust his jaw forward, a sight to be wondered at, for even when relaxed his chin gave the impression of a battering ram; something to prod with; in fact a *weapon*.

'Dear Mrs Grass,' he said, 'you are always so unaccountably kind.'

The attenuate Mr Spill had been beckoning a waiter, but now he suddenly crouched down so that his ear was level with Acreblade's mouth. He did not face Mr Acreblade as he crouched there, but swivelling his eyes to their eastern extremes, he obtained a very good view of Acreblade's profile.

'I'm a bit deaf,' he said. 'Will you repeat yourself? Did you say "unaccountably kind"? How droll.'

'Don't be a bore,' said Mrs Grass.

Mr Spill rose to his full working height, which might have been even more impressive were his shoulders not so bent.

'Dear lady,' he said. 'If I am a bore, who made me so?'

'Well who *did* darling?'

'It's a long story – '

'Then we'll skip it, shall we?'

She turned herself slowly, swivelling on her pelvis until her small conical breasts, directed at Mr Kestrel, were for all the world like some kind of delicious *threat*. Her husband, Mr Grass, who had seen this manoeuvre at least a hundred times, yawned horribly.

'Tell me,' said Mrs Grass, as she let loose upon Mr Kestrel a fresh broadside of naked eroticism, 'tell me, dear Mr Acreblade, all about *yourself*.'

Mr Acreblade, not really enjoying being addressed in this off-hand manner by Mrs Grass, turned to her husband.

'Your wife is very special. Very rare. Conducive to speculation. She talks to me through the back of her head, staring at Kestrel the while.'

'But that is as it should be!' cried Kestrel, his eyes swimming over with excitement, 'for life must be various, incongruous, vile and electric. Life must be ruthless and as full of love as may be found in a jaguar's fang.'

44

'I like the way you talk, young man,' said Grass, 'but I don't know *what* you're saying.'

'What are you mumbling about?' said the lofty Spill, bending one of his arms like the branch of a tree and cupping his ear with a bunch of twigs.

'You are somewhat divine,' whispered Kestrel, addressing Mrs Grass.

'I think I spoke to you, dear,' said Mrs Grass over her shoulder to Mr Acreblade.

'Your wife is talking to me again,' said Acreblade to Mr Grass. 'Let's hear what she has to say.'

'You talk about my wife in a very peculiar way,' said Grass. 'Does she annoy you?'

'She would if I lived with her,' said Acreblade. 'What about you?'

'O, but my dear chap, how naïve you are! Being *married* to her I seldom *see* her. What is the point of getting married if one is always bumping into one's wife? One might as well not be married. Oh no dear fellow, she does what she wants. It is quite a coincidence that we found each other here tonight. You see? And we enjoy it – it's like first love all over again without the heartache – without the *heart* in fact. Cold love's the loveliest love of all. So clear, so crisp, so empty. In short, so civilized.'

'You are out of a legend,' said Kestrel, in a voice that was so muffled with passion that Mrs Grass was quite unaware that she had been addressed.

'I'm as hot as a boiled turnip,' said Mr Spill.

'But tell me, you horrid man, how do I feel?' cried Mrs Grass as she saw a newcomer, lacerating her beauty with the edge of her voice. 'I'm looking so well these days, even my husband said so, and you know what husbands are.'

'I have no idea what they *are*,' said the fox-like man newly arrived at her elbow, 'but you must tell me. What are they? I only know what they become . . . and perhaps . . . what drove them to it.'

'Oh, but you are *clever*. Wickedly clever. But you must tell me all. How *am* I, darling?'

The fox-like man (a narrow-chested creature with reddish

hair above his ears, a very sharp nose and a brain far too large
for him to manage with comfort) replied:

'You are feeling, my dear Mrs Grass, in need of something
sweet. Sugar, bad music, or something of that kind might do
for a start.'

The black-eyed creature, her lips half open, her teeth shining
like pearls, her eyes fixed with excited animation on the foxy
face before her, clasped her delicate hands together at her
conical breasts.

'You're quite right! O, but *quite!*' she said breathlessly. 'So
absolutely and miraculously *right*, you brilliant, *brilliant* little
man; something sweet is what I *need!*'

Meanwhile Mr Acreblade was making room for a long-faced
character dressed in a lion's pelt. Over his head and shoulders
was a black mane.

'Isn't it a bit hot in there?' said young Kestrel.

'I am in agony,' said the man in the tawny skin.

'Then why?' said Mrs Grass.

'I thought it was Fancy Dress,' said the skin, 'but I mustn't
complain. Everyone has been most kind.'

'That doesn't help the heat you're generating in there,' said
Mr Acreblade. 'Why don't you just whip it off?'

'It is all I have on,' said the lion's pelt.

'How delicious,' cried Mrs Grass, 'you thrill me utterly. Who
are you?'

'But my *dear*,' said the lion, looking at Mrs Grass, 'surely
you . . .'

'What is it, O King of Beasts?'

'Can't you remember me?'

'Your nose seems to ring a bell,' said Mrs Grass.

Mr Spill lowered his head out of the clouds of smoke. Then
he swivelled it until it lay alongside Mr Kestrel. 'What did she
say?' he asked.

'She's worth a million,' said Kestrel. 'Lively, luscious, what
a plaything!'

'Plaything?' said Mr Spill. 'How do you mean?'

'You wouldn't understand,' said Kestrel.

The lion scratched himself with a certain charm. Then he
addressed Mrs Grass.

46

'So my nose rings a bell – is that all? Have you forgotten me? *Me!* Your one-time Harry?'

'Harry? What . . . my . . . ?'

'Yes, your Second. Way back in time. We were married, you remember, in Tyson Street.'

'Lovebird!' cried Mrs Grass. 'So we *were*. But take that foul mane off and let me see you. Where have you been all these years?'

'In the wilderness,' said the lion, tossing back his mane and twitching it over his shoulder.

'What sort of wilderness, darling? Moral? Spiritual? O but tell us about it!' Mrs Grass reached forward with her breasts and clenched her little fists at her sides, which attitude she imagined would have appeal. She was not far wrong, and young Kestrel took a step to the left which put him close beside her.

'I believe you said "wilderness",' said Kestrel. 'Tell me, how wild *is* it? Or isn't it? One is so at the mercy of words. And would you say, sir, that what is wilderness for one might be a field of corn to another with little streams and bushes?'

'What sort of bushes?' said the elongated Mr Spill.

'What does that matter?' said Kestrel.

'*Everything* matters,' said Mr Spill. '*Everything*. That is part of the pattern. The world is bedevilled by people thinking that some things matter and some things don't. Everything is of equal importance. The wheel must be complete. And the stars. They *look* small. But are they? No. They are large. Some are very large. Why, I remember – '

'Mr Kestrel,' said Mrs Grass.

'Yes, my dear lady?'

'You have a vile habit, dear.'

'What is it, for heaven's sake? Tell me about it that I may crush it.'

'You are too *close*, my pet. But *too* close. We have our little areas you know. Like the home waters, dear, or fishing rights. Don't trespass, dear. Withdraw a little. You know what I mean, don't you? Privacy is *so* important.'

Young Kestrel turned the colour of a boiled lobster and retreated from Mrs Grass who, turning her head to him, by way of forgiveness switched on a light in her face, or so it seemed to Kestrel, a light that inflamed the air about them with a smile like an eruption. This had the effect of drawing the dazzled Kestrel back to her side, where he stayed, bathing himself in her beauty.

'Cosy again,' she whispered.

Kestrel nodded his head and trembled with excitement until Mr Grass, forcing his way through a wall of guests, brought his foot down sharply upon Kestrel's instep. With a gasp of pain, young Kestrel turned for sympathy to the peerless lady at his side, only to find that her radiant smile was now directed at her own husband where it remained for a few moments before she turned her back on them both and, switching off the current, she gazed across the room with an aspect quite drained of animation.

'On the other hand,' said the tall Spill, addressing the man in the lion's pelt, 'there is something in the young man's question. This wilderness of yours. Will you tell us more about it?'

'But oh! But do!' rang out the voice of Mrs Grass, as she gripped the lion's pelt cruelly.

'When I say "wilderness",' said the lion, 'I only speak of the heart. It is Mr Acreblade that you should ask. His wasteland is the very earth itself.'

'Ah me, that Wasteland,' said Acreblade, jutting out his chin, 'knuckled with ferrous mountains. Peopled with termites, jackals, and to the north-west – hermits.'

'And what were *you* doing out there?' said Mr Spill.

'I shadowed a suspect. A youth not known in these parts. He stumbled ahead of me in the sandstorm, a vague shape. Sometimes I lost him altogether. Sometimes I all but found myself beside him, and was forced to retreat a little way. Sometimes I heard his singing, mad, wild, inconsequential songs. Sometimes he shouted out as though he were delirious – words that sounded like "Fuchsia", "Flay" and other names. Sometimes he cried out "Mother!" and once he fell on his knees and cried, "Gormenghast, Gormenghast, come back to me again!"

'It was not for me to arrest him – but to follow him, for my superiors informed me his papers were not in order, or even in *existence*.

'But on the second evening the dust rose up more terribly

than ever, and as it rose it blinded me so that I lost him in a red and gritty cloud. I could not find him, and I never found him again.'

'Darling.'

'What is it?'

'Look at Gumshaw.'

'Why?'

'His polished pate reflects a brace of candles.'

'Not from where I am.'

'No?'

'No. But look – to the left of centre I see a tiny image, one might almost say of a boy's face, were it not that faces are unlikely things to grow on ceilings.'

'Dreams. One always comes back to dreams.'

'But the silver whip RK 2053722220 – the moon circles, first of the new –'

'Yes, I know all about that.'

'But love was nowhere near.'

'The sky was smothered with planes. Some of them, though pilotless, were bleeding.'

'Ah, Mr Flax, how is your son?'

'He died last Wednesday.'

'Forgive me, I am so sorry.'

'Are you? I'm not. I never liked him. But mark you – an excellent swimmer. He was captain of his school.'

'This heat is horrible.'

'Ah, Lady Crowgather, let me present the Duke of Crowgather; but perhaps you have met already?'

'Many times. Where are the cucumber sandwiches?'

'Allow me –'

'Oh I beg your pardon. I mistook your foot for a tortoise. What is happening?'

'No, indeed, I do not like it.'

'Art should be artless, not heartless.'

'I am a great one for beauty.'

'Beauty, that obsolete word.'

'You beg the question, Professor Salvage.'

'I beg nothing. Not even your pardon. I do not even beg to differ. I differ without begging, and would rather beg from an ancient, rib-staring, sightless groveller at the foot of a column than beg from you, sir. The truth is not in you, and your feet smell.'

'Take that ... and that,' muttered the insultee, tearing off one button after another from his opponent's jacket.

'What fun we do have,' said the button-loser, standing on tip-toe and kissing his friend's chin: 'Parties would be unbearable without abuse, so don't go away Harold. You sicken me. What is that?'

'It is only Marblecrust making his bird noises.'

'Yes, but ...'

'Always, somehow ...'

'O no ... no ... and yet I like it.'

'And so the young man escaped me without knowing,' said Acreblade, 'and judging by the hardship he must have undergone he must surely be somewhere in the City ... where else could he be? Has he stolen a plane? Has he fled down the ... ?'

TWENTY-FIVE

THEN came the stroke of midnight, and for a few moments gooseflesh ran up every leg in Lady Cusp-Canine's party, swarmed up the thighs and mustered its hideous forces at the base of every backbone, sending forth grisly outriders through-out the lumbar landscape. Then up the spine itself, coiling like lethal ivy, fanning out, eventually, from the cervicals, draping like icy muslin across the breasts and belly. Midnight. As the last cold crash resounds, Titus, alone on the rooftop, easing the cramp in his arm, shifting the weight of his elbow, smashes suddenly the skylight and with no time to recover, falls through the glass roof in a shower of splinters.

TWENTY-SIX

IT was very lucky for all concerned that no one was seriously hurt. Titus himself was cut in a few places but the wounds were superficial and as far as the actual fall was concerned, he was particularly fortunate in that a dome-shouldered, snow-ball-breasted lady was immediately below him as he fell.

They capsized together, and lay for a moment alongside one another on the thickly carpeted floor. All about them glittered fragments of broken glass, but for Juno, lying at Titus's side, and for the others who had been affected by his sudden appearance in mid-air and later on the floor, the overriding sensation was not pain but shock.

For there was something that was shocking in more than one sense in the almost biblical visitation of a youth in rags.

Titus withdrew his face, which had been crushed against a naked shoulder, and got dizzily to his feet, and as he did so he saw that the lady's eyes were fixed upon him. Even in her horizontal position she was superb. Her dignity was unimpaired. When Titus reached down to her with his hand to help her she touched his finger-tips and rose at once and with no apparent effort to her feet, which were small and very beautiful. Between these little feet of hers and her noble, Roman head, lay, as though between the poles, a golden world of spices.

Someone bent over the boy. It was the Fox.

'Who the devil are you?' he said.

'What does that matter?' said Juno. 'Keep your distance. He is bleeding.... Isn't that enough?' and with quite indescribable *élan* she tore a strip from her dress and began to bind up Titus's hand, which was bleeding steadily.

'You are very kind,' said Titus.

Juno softly shook her head from side to side, and a little smile evolved out of the corner of her generous lips.

'I must have startled you,' said Titus.

'It was a rapid introduction,' said Juno. She arched one of her eyebrows. It rose like a raven's wing.

51

'Did you hear what he said?' snarled a vile voice. ' *"I must have startled you."* Why, you mongrel-pup, you might have killed the lady!'

An angry buzz of voices suddenly began and scores of faces raised themselves to the shattered skylight. At the same time a nearby section of the crowd, which until a few moments ago had appeared to be full of friendly flippancy, was now wearing a very different aspect.

'Which one of you,' said Titus, whose face had gone white, 'which one of you called me a mongrel-pup?' In the pocket of his ragged trousers his hand clutched the knuckle of flint from the high towers of Gormenghast.

'Who was it?' he yelled, for all at once rage boiled up in him, and jumping forward he caught the nearest figure by the throat. But no sooner had he done so than he was himself hauled back to his position at Juno's side. Then Titus saw before him the back of a great angular man, on whose shoulder sat a small ape. This figure whose proportions were unmistakably those of Muzzlehatch now moved very slowly along the half-circle of angry faces and as he did so he smiled with a smile that had no love in it. It was a wide smile. It was a lipless smile. It was made up of nothing but anatomy.

Muzzlehatch stretched out his big arm: his hand hovered and then took hold of the man who had insulted Titus, picked him up, and raised him through the hot and coiling air to the level of his shoulder, where he was received by the ape who kissed him upon the back of his neck in such a way that the poor man collapsed in a dead faint, and then, since the ape had already lost interest in him, he slid to the carpeted floor.

Muzzlehatch turned to the gaping circle of faces and whispered 'Little children. Listen to Oracle. Because Oracle loves you,' and Muzzlehatch drew a wicked-looking penknife from his pocket, flicked it open and began to strop it upon the ball of his thumb.

'He is not pleased with you. Not so much because you have

done anything wicked but because your Soul smells – your collective *Soul* – your little dried-up turd of a Soul. Is it not so? Little Ones?'

The ape began to scratch itself with slow relish and its eyelids trembled.

'So you would *menace* him, would you?' said Muzzlehatch. 'Menace him with your dirty little brains, and horrid little noises. And you, ladies, with your false bosoms and ignorant mouths. You also have menaced him?'

There was a good deal of shuffling and coughing; and those who were able to do so without being seen began to retreat into the crowded body of the room.

'Little children,' he went on, the blade of his knife moving to and fro across his thumb, 'pick up your colleague from the floor and learn from him to keep your hands off this pip-squeak of a boy.'

'He is no pip-squeak,' said Acreblade. 'That is the youth I have been trailing. He escaped me. He crossed the wilderness. He has no passport. He is wanted. Come here, young man.'

There was a hush that spread all over the room.

'What nonsense,' said a deep voice at last. It was Juno. 'He is my friend. As for the wilderness – good Heavens – you misconstrue the rags. He is in fancy dress.'

'Move aside, madam. I have a warrant for his arrest as a vagrant; an alien; an undesirable.'

Then he moved forward, did this Acreblade, out of the crowd of guests, forward towards where Titus, Juno, Muzzlehatch and the ape waited silently.

'Beautiful policeman,' said Muzzlehatch. 'You are exceeding your duty. This is a party – or it was – but you are making something vile out of it.'

Muzzlehatch worked his shoulders to and fro and shut his eyes.

'Don't you ever have a holiday from crime? Do you never pick up the world as a child picks up a crystal globe – a thing of many colours? Do you never love this ridiculous world of ours? The wicked and the good of it? The thieves and angels of it? The all of it? Throbbing, dear policeman, in your hand? And knowing how all this is inevitably so, and that without the dark of life you would be out on your ear? Yet see how you take it. Passports, visas, identification papers – does all this mean so much to your official mind that you must needs bring the filthy stink of it to a party? Open up the gates of your brain then, policeman dear, and let a small sprat through.'

'He is my friend,' said Juno again, in a voice as ripe and deep as some underwater grotto, some foliage of the sea-bed. 'He is in fancy dress. He is as nothing to you. What was it you said? "Across the wilderness?" Oh ha ha ha ha ha,' and Juno, having received a cue from Muzzlehatch, moved forward and in a moment had blocked Mr Acreblade's vision, and as she did this she saw away to her left, their heads a little above the heads of the crowd, two men in helmets who appeared to slide rather than walk. To Juno they were merely two of the guests and meant nothing more, but when Muzzlehatch saw them he gripped Titus by the arm just above the elbow and made for the door, leaving behind him a channel among the guests like the channel left on a field of ripe corn where a file of children has followed its leader.

Inspector Acreblade was trying very hard to follow them but every time he turned or made a few steps his passage was blocked by the generous Juno, a lady with such a superb car- riage and such noble proportions, that to push past her was out of the question.

'Please allow me – ' he said. 'I must follow them at once.'

'But your tie, you cannot go about like that. Let me adjust it for you. No ... no ... don't move. Th-ere we are. ... There ... we ... are ...'

TWENTY-EIGHT

MEANWHILE Titus and Muzzlehatch were turning to left and right at will, for the place was honeycombed with rooms and corridors.

Muzzlehatch, as he ran, a few feet ahead of Titus, looked like some kind of war-horse, with his great rough head thrown back, and his chest forward.

He did not look round to see whether Titus could keep up with his trampling pace. With his dark-red rudder of a nose pointing to the ceiling he galloped on with the small ape, now wide awake, clinging to his shoulder, its topaz-coloured eyes fixed upon Titus, a few feet behind. Every now and again it cried out only to cling the tighter to its master's neck as though frightened of its own voice.

Covering the ground at speed Muzzlehatch retained a monumental self-assurance – almost a dignity. It was not mere flight. It was a thing in itself, as a dance must be, a dance of ritual.

'Are you there?' he suddenly muttered over his shoulder. 'Eh? Are you there? Young Rag'n'bone! Fetch up alongside.'

'I'm here,' panted Titus. 'But how much longer?'

Muzzlehatch took no notice but pranced around a corner to the left and then left again, and right, and left again, and then gradually slackening pace they ambled at last into a dimly-lit hall surrounded by seven doors. Opening one at random the fugitives found themselves in an empty room.

TWENTY-NINE

MUZZLEHATCH and Titus stood still for a few moments until their eyes became adjusted to the darkness.

Then they saw, at the far end of the apartment, a dull grey rectangle that stood on end in the darkness. It was the night.

There were no stars and the moon was on the other side of the building. Somewhere far below they could hear the whisper of a plane as it took off. All at once it came into view, a slim, wingless thing, sliding through the night, seemingly unhurried, save that suddenly, where was it?

Titus and Muzzlehatch stood at the window and for a long while neither of them spoke. At last Titus turned to the dimly outlined shape of his companion.

'What are you doing here?' he said. 'You seem out of place.'

'God's geese! You startled me,' said Muzzlehatch, raising his hand as though to guard himself from attack. 'I'd forgotten you

55

were here. I was brooding, boy. Than which there is no richer pastime. It muffles one with rotting plumes. It gives forth sullen music. It is the smell of home.'

'Home?' said Titus.

'Home,' said Muzzlehatch. He took out a pipe from his pocket, and filled it with a great fistful of tobacco; lit it, drew at it; filled his lungs with acrid fumes, and exhaled them, while the bowl burned in the darkness like a wound.

'You ask me why I am here – here among an alien people. It is a good question. Almost as good as for me to ask you the same thing. But don't tell me, dear boy, not yet. I would rather guess.'

'I know nothing about you,' said Titus. 'You are someone to me who appears, and disappears. A rough man: a shadow-man: a creature who plucks me out of danger. Who are you? Tell me.... You do not seem to be part of this – this glassy region.'

'It is not glassy where I come from, boy. Have you forgotten the slums that crawl up to my courtyard? Have you forgotten the crowds by the river? Have you forgotten the stink?'

'I remember the stink of your car,' said Titus, ' – sharp as acid; thick as gruel.'

'She's a bitch,' said Muzzlehatch, ' – and smells like one.'

'I am ignorant of you,' said Titus. 'You with your acres of great cages, your savage cats; your wolves and your birds of prey. I have seen them, but they tell me little. What are you thinking of? Why do you flaunt this monkey on your shoulder as though it were a foreign flag – some emblem of defiance? I have no more access to your brain than I have to this little skull,' and Titus fumbling in the dark stroked the small ape with his forefinger. Then he stared at the darkness, part of which was Muzzlehatch. The night seemed thicker than ever.

'Are you still there?' said Titus.

It was twelve long seconds before Muzzlehatch replied.

'I am. I am still here, or some of me is. The rest of me is leaning on the rails of a ship. The air is full of spices and the deep salt water shines with phosphorus. I am alone on deck and there is no one else to see the moon float out of a cloud so that a string of palms is lit like a procession. I can see the dark-white surf as it beats upon the shore; and I see, and I remember, how a figure ran along the strip of moonlit sand, with his arms raised high above his head, and his shadow ran beside him and jerked as it sped, for the beach was uneven; and then the moon slid into the clouds again and the world went black.'

'Who was he?' said Titus.

'How should I know?' said Muzzlehatch. 'It might have been anyone. It might have been me.'

'Why are you telling me all this?' said Titus.

'I am not telling *you* anything. I am telling myself. My voice, strident to others, is music to me.'

'You have a rough manner,' said Titus. 'But you have saved me twice. Why are you helping me?'

'I have no idea,' said Muzzlehatch. 'There must be something wrong with my brain.'

THIRTY

ALTHOUGH there was no sound, yet the opening of the door produced a change in the room behind them; a change sufficient to awake in Titus and his companion an awareness of which their conscious minds knew nothing.

No, not the breath of a sound; not a flicker of light. Yet the black room at their backs was alive.

Muzzlehatch and Titus had turned at the same time and as far as they knew they turned for no more reason than to ease a muscle.

In fact they hardly knew that they *had* turned. They could see very little of the night-filled room, but when a moment later a lady stepped forward, she brought with her a little light from the hall beyond. It was not much of an illumination but it was strong enough to show Titus and his companion that immediately to their left was a striped couch and on the other side of the room, down-stage as it were, supposing the night to be the auditorium, was a tall screen.

At the sight of the door opening Muzzlehatch plucked the small ape from Titus's shoulder and muzzling it with his right hand and holding its four feet together in his left, he moved silently through the shadows until he was hidden behind the tall screen. Titus, with no ape to deal with, was beside him in a moment.

Then came the click and the room was immediately filled with coral-coloured light. The lady who had opened the door stepped forward without a sound. Daintily, for all her weight, she moved to the centre of the room, where she cocked her head on one side as though waiting for something peculiar to happen. Then she sat down on the striped couch, crossing her splendid legs with a hiss of silk.

'He must be hungry,' she whispered, 'the roof-swarmer, the skylight-burster ... the ragged boy from nowhere. He must be very hungry and very lost. Where would he be, I wonder? Behind that screen for instance, with his friend, the wicked Muzzlehatch?' There was a rather silly silence.

THIRTY-ONE

WHILE sitting there Juno had opened a hamper which she had filled at the party before following the boy and Muzzlehatch.

'Are you hungry?' said Juno, as they emerged.

'Very hungry,' said Titus.

'Then eat,' said Juno.

'O my sweet flame! My mulcted one. What are you thinking of?' asked Muzzlehatch, but in a voice so bored that it was almost an insult. 'Can you imagine how I found him, love-pot?'

'Who?' said Juno.

'This boy,' said Muzzlehatch. 'This ravenous boy.'

'Tell me.'

'Washed up, he was,' said Muzzlehatch, ' – at dawn. Ain't that poetic? There he lay, stranded on the water-steps – sprawled out like a dead fish. So I drove him home. Why? Because I had never seen anything so unlikely. Next day I shoo'd him off. He was no part of me. No part of my absurd life, and away he went, a creature out of nowhere, redundant as a candle in the sun. Quite laughable – a thing to be forgotten – but what *happens?*'

'I'm listening,' said Juno.

'I'll tell you,' continued Muzzlehatch. 'He takes it upon himself to fall through a skylight and bears to the ground one of the few women who ever interested me. O yes. I saw it all. His head lay sidelong on your splendid bosom and for a little while he was Lord of that tropical ravine between your midnight breasts: that home of moss and verdure: that sumptuous cleft. But enough of this. I am too old for gulches. How did you find us? What with our twistings and turnings and doubling back – we should by rights have shaken off the devil himself – but then you wander in as though you'd been a-riding on my tail. How did you find me?'

'I will tell you, Muzzle-dove, how I found you. There was nothing miraculous about it. My intuition is as non-existent as the smell of marble. It was the boy who gave you both away. His feet were wet and still are. They left a glister down the corridors.'

'A glister, what's a glister?' said Muzzlehatch.

'It's what his wet feet left behind them – the merest film. I had only to follow it. Where are your shoes, pilgrim-child?'

'My shoes?' said Titus, with a chicken bone in his hand. 'Why, somewhere in the river, I suppose.'

'Well then; now that you've found us, Juno, my love-trap – what do you want of us? Alone or separately? I, after all, though unpopular, am no fugitive. So there's no need for me to hide. But young Titus here (Lord of somewhere or other – with an altogether most unlikely name) – he, we must admit, is on the run. Why, I'm not quite sure. As for myself, there is nothing I want more than to wash my two hands of both of you. One reason is the way you haven't my marrow. I yell for nothing but solitude, Juno, and the beasts I brood on. Another is this young man – the Earl of Gorgon-paste or whatever he calls himself – I must wash my hands of him also, for I have no desire to be involved with yet another human being – especially one in the shape of an enigma. Life is too brief for such diversions and I cannot bring myself to scrape up any interest in the problems of his breast.'

59

The small ape on Muzzlehatch's shoulder nodded its head and then began to fish about in the depth of its master's hair; its wrinkled, yet delicate, fingers probing here and there were as tender yet as inquisitive as any lover's.

'You're almost as rude as I was hungry,' said Titus. 'As for the workings of my heart, and my lineage, you are as ignorant as that monkey on your shoulder. As far as I am concerned you will remain so. But get me out of here. It is a swine of a building and smells like a hospital. You have been good to me, Mr Marrow-patch, but I long to see the last of you. Where can I go, where can I hide?'

'You must come with me,' said Juno. 'You must have clean clothes, food, and shelter.' She turned her splendid head to Muzzlehatch. 'How are we going to leave without being seen?'

'One move at a time,' said Muzzlehatch. 'Our first is to find the nearest lift-shaft. The whole place ought to be asleep by now.' He strode to the door and, opening it quietly, discovered a young man bent double. He had been given no time to rise from the keyhole, let alone escape.

'But my dearest essence of stoat' – said Muzzlehatch, gradually drawing the man forward into the room by his lemon-yellow lapels (for he was a flunkey of the household – 'you are most welcome. Now, Juno dear, take Gorgon-paste with you and lean with him over the balustrade and stare down into the darkness. It will not be for long.'

Titus and Juno, obeying his curiously authoritative voice, for it had power however ridiculous its burden, heard a peculiar shuffling sound, and then a moment later – 'Now then, Gorgon-blast, leave the lovely lady in charge of the night and come here.'

Titus turned and saw that the flunkey was practically naked. Muzzlehatch had stripped him as an autumn tree is stripped of its gold leaves.

'Off with your rags and into the livery,' said Muzzlehatch to Titus. He turned to the flunkey, 'I do hope you're not too chilly. I have nothing against you, friend, but I have no option. This young gentleman must escape, you see.'

'Hurry, now, "Gorgon",' he shouted. 'I have the car waiting and she is restless.'

He did not know that as he spoke the first strands of dawn were threading their way through the low clouds and lighting not only the few aeroplanes that shone like spectres, but also that monstrous creature, Muzzlehatch's car. Naked as the flunkey, naked in the early sunbeams, it was like an oath, or a jeer, its nose directed at the elegant planes; its shape, its colour, its skeleton, its tendons, its skull, its muscles of leather – its low and rakish belly, and its general air of blood and mutiny on the high seas. There she waited far below the room where her captain stood.

'Change clothes,' said Muzzlehatch. 'We can't wait all night for you.'

Something began to burn in Titus's stomach. He could feel the blood draining from his face.

'So you can't wait all night for me,' he said in a voice he hardly recognized as his own. 'Muzzlehatch, the zoo-man, is in a hurry. But does he know who he is talking to? Do you?'

'What is it, Titus?' said Juno, who had turned from the window at the sound of his voice.

'What is it?' cried Titus. 'I will tell you, madam. It is this bully's ignorance. Does he know who I am?'

'How can we know about you, dear, if you won't tell us? There, there, stop shaking.'

'He wants to run away,' said Muzzlehatch. 'But you don't want to be jailed, do you now? Eh? You want to get free of this building, surely.'

'Not with *your* help,' shouted Titus, though he knew as he shouted that he was being mean. He looked up at the big cross-hatched face with its proud rudder of a nose and the living light in its eye and a flicker of recognition seemed to pass between them. But it was too late.

'Then to hell with you, child,' said Muzzlehatch.

'I will take him,' said Juno.

'No,' said Muzzlehatch. 'Let him go. He must learn.'

'Learn, be damned!' said Titus, all the pent-up emotion breaking through. 'What do you know of life, of violence and guile? Of madmen and subterfuge and treachery? My treachery. My hands have been sticky with blood. I have loved and I have killed in my kingdom.'

'Kingdom?' said Juno. 'Your *kingdom*?'

A kind of fearful love brimmed in her eyes. 'I will take care of you,' she said.

'No,' said Muzzlehatch, 'let him find his way. He will never forgive you if you take him now. Let him be a man, Juno dear – or what he thinks to be a man. Don't suck his blood, dear. Don't pounce too soon. Remember how you killed our love with spices – eh? My pretty vampire.'

Titus, white with indecision, for to him Juno and Muzzlehatch seemed to talk a private language, took a step nearer to the smiling man who had turned his head across his shoulder so that the little ape was able to rest its furry cheek along its master's.

'Did you call this lady a vampire?' he whispered.

Muzzlehatch nodded his smiling head slowly.

'That is so,' he said.

'He meant nothing,' said Juno. 'Titus! O, darling ... O ...'

For Titus had whipped out his fist with such speed that it was a wonder it did not find its mark. This it failed to do, for Muzzlehatch, catching Titus's fist as though it were a flung stone, held it in a vice and then, with no apparent effort, propelled Titus slowly to the doorway, through which he pushed the boy before closing the door and turning the key.

For a few minutes Titus, shocked at his own impotence, beat upon the door, yelling 'Let me in, you coward! Let me in! Let me in!' until the noise he made brought servants from all quarters of the great mansion of olive-green glass.

While they took Titus away struggling and shouting, Muzzlehatch held Juno firmly by her elbow, for she longed to be with the sudden young man dressed half in rags and half in livery, but she said nothing as she strained against the grip of her one-time lover.

THIRTY-TWO

The day broke wild and shaggy. What light there was seeped
into the great glass buildings as though ashamed. All but a
fraction of the guests who had attended the Cusp-Canines'
party lay like fossils in their separate beds, or, for various sunken causes, tossed and turned in seas of dream.

Of those who were awake and on their feet, at least half
were servants of the House. It was from among these few that
a posse of retainers (on hearing the shindy) converged upon the
room, switching on lights as they ran, until they found Titus
striking upon the outside of the door.

It was no good for him to struggle. Their clumsy hands
caught hold of him and hustled him away and down seven
flights into the servants' quarters. There he was kept prisoner
for the best part of the day, the time being punctuated by visits
from the Law and the Police and towards evening by some kind
of a brain-specialist who gazed at Titus for minutes on end
from under his eyebrows and asked peculiar questions which
Titus took no trouble to answer, for he was very tired.

Lady Cusp-Canine herself appeared for one fleeting minute.
She had not been down to the kitchens for thirty years and was
accompanied by an Inspector, who kept his head tilted on one
side as he talked to her Ladyship while keeping his eyes on the
captive. The effect of this was to suggest that Titus was some
kind of caged animal.

'An enigma,' said the Inspector.

'I don't agree,' said Lady Cusp-Canine. 'He is only a boy.'

'Ah,' said the Inspector.

'And I like his face, too,' said Lady Cusp-Canine.

'Ah,' said the Inspector.

'He has splendid eyes.'

'But has he splendid habits, your Ladyship?'

'I don't know,' said Lady Cusp-Canine. 'Why? Have you?'

The Inspector shrugged his shoulders.

'There is nothing to shrug about,' said Lady Cusp-Canine.
'Nothing at all. Where is my Chef?'

This gentleman had been hovering at her side ever since she had entered the kitchen. He now presented himself.

'Madam?'

'Have you fed the boy?'

'Yes, my Lady.'

'Have you given him the best? The most nutritious? Have you given him a breakfast to remember?'

'Not yet, your Ladyship.'

'Then what are you waiting for!' Her voice rose. 'He is hungry. He is despondent, he is young!'

'Yes, your Ladyship.'

'Don't say "yes" to me!' She rose on tip-toe to her full height, which did not take her long for she was minute. 'Feed him and let him go,' and with that she skimmed across the room on tiny septuagenarian feet, her plumed hat swaying dangerously among the loins and briskets.

THIRTY-THREE

MEANWHILE, the powerful Muzzlehatch had escorted Juno out of the building and had helped her into his hideous car. It was his intention to take her to her house above the river and then to race for home, for even Muzzlehatch was weary. But, as usual when he was at the wheel, whatever plans had been formulated were soon to be no more than chaff in the wind, and within half a minute of his starting he had changed his mind and was now heading for that wide and sandy stretch of the river where the banks shelved gently into the shallow water.

The sky was no longer very dark, though one or two stars were still to be seen, when Muzzlehatch, having taken a long and quite unnecessary curve to the west, careered off the road and, turning left and right to avoid the juniper bushes that littered the upper banks, swept all of a sudden into the shallows of the broad stream. Once in the water he accelerated and great arcs of brine spurted from the wheels to port and starboard.

As for Juno, she leaned forward a little; her elbow rested on the door of the car, and her face lay sideways in the gloved palm of her hand. As far as could be seen she was quite oblivious of the speed of the car, let alone the spray: nor did she take any notice of Muzzlehatch, who, in his favourite position, was practically lying on the floor of the machine, one eye above the 'bulwarks' from whence came forth a sort of song:

'I have my price: it's rather high –
(About the level of your eye),
But if you're nice to me, I'll try
To lower it for you –
To lower it; to lower it;
Upon the kind of rope they knit
From yellow grass and purple hay
When knitting is taboo –'

A touch of the wheel and the car sped deeper into the river so that the water was not far from brimming over, but another movement brought her out again while the steam hissed like a thousand cats.

'Some knit them pearl,' roared Muzzlehatch,

'Some knit them plain –
Some knit their brows of pearl in vain
Some are so plain they try again
To tease the wool of love!
But ah! the palms of yesterday –
There's not a soul from yesterday
Who's worth the dreaming of – they say –
Who's worth the dreaming of . . .'

As Muzzlehatch's voice wandered off the sun began to rise out of the river.

'Have you finished?' said Juno. Her eyes were half closed.

'I have given my *all*,' said Muzzlehatch.

'Then listen please!' – her eyes were a little wider but their expression was still faraway.

'What is it, Juno love?'

'I am thinking of that boy. What will they do to him?'

'They'll find him difficult,' said Muzzlehatch, 'very difficult. Rather like a form of me. It is more a case of what will he do to *them*. But why? Has he set a sparrow twittering in your breast? Or woken up a predatory condor?'

But there was no reply, for at that moment he drew up at the front door of Juno's house, with a great cry of metal. It was a tall building, dusty pink in colour, and was backed by a small hill or knoll surmounted by a marble man. Immediately behind the knoll was a loop of the river. On either side of Juno's house were two somewhat similar houses but these were forsaken. The windows were smashed. The doors were gone and the rooms let in the rain.

But Juno's house was in perfect repair and when the door was opened by a servant in a yellow gown it was possible to see how daringly yet carefully the hall was furnished. Lit up in the darkness, it presented a colour scheme of ivory, ash, and coral red.

'Are you coming in?' said Juno. 'Do mushrooms tempt you – or plovers' eggs? Or coffee?'

'No my love!'

'As you wish.'

They sat without moving for a little while.

'Where do you think the boy is? 'she said at last.

'I have no idea,' said Muzzlehatch.

Juno climbed out of the car. It was like a faultless disembarkation. Whatever she did had style.

'Good night then,' she said, 'and sweet dreams.'

Muzzlehatch gazed at her as she made her way through the dark garden to the lighted hall. Her shadow cast by the light reached out behind her, almost to the car, and as she moved away step by long smooth step, Muzzlehatch felt a twitch of the heart, for it seemed that he saw in the slow leisure of her stride something, at the moment, that he was loth to forgo.

It was as if those faraway days when they were lovers came flooding back, image upon image, shade upon shade, unsolicited, unbidden, each one challenging the strength of the dykes which they had built against one another. For they knew that beyond the dykes heaved the great seas of sentiment on whose bosom they had lost their way.

How often had he stared at her in anger or in boisterous

66

love! How often had he admired her. How often had he seen her leave him, but never quite like this. The light from the hall where the servant stood came flooding across the garden and Juno was a silhouette against the lighted entrance. From the full, rounded, and bell-shaped hips which swayed imperceptibly as she moved, arose the column of her almost military back; and from her shoulders sprang her neck, perfectly cylindrical, surmounted by her classic head.

As Muzzlehatch gazed at her he seemed to see, in some strange way, himself. He saw her as his failure – and he knew himself to be hers. For they had each received all that the other could provide. What had gone wrong? Was it that they need no longer try because they could see through one another? What was the trouble? A hundred things. His unfaithfulness; his egotism; his eternal play-acting; his gigantic pride; his lack of tenderness; his deafening exuberance; his selfishness.

But she had run out of love; or it had been battered out of her. Only a friendship remained: ambient and unbreakable.

So it was strange, this twitch of the heart, strange that he should follow her with his eyes; strange that he should turn the car about so slowly, and it was strange also (when he arrived in the courtyard of his home) to see how ruminative was the look upon his face as he tied his car to the mulberry tree.

THIRTY-FOUR

In the late afternoon of the next day they took Titus and they put him in a cell. It was a small place with a barred window to the south-west.

When Titus entered the cell this rectangle was filled with a golden light. The black bars that divided the window into a dozen upright sections were silhouetted against the sunset.

In one corner there was a rough trestle bed with a dark-red blanket spread over it. Taking up most of the space in the middle of the cell was a table that stood up on three legs only, for the stone floor was uneven. On the table were a few candles, a box of matches and a cup of water. By the side of the table stood a chair, a flimsy-looking thing which someone had once started to paint: but they (whoever they may have been) had grown tired of the work so that the chair was piebald black and yellow.

As Titus stood there taking in the features of the room the jailer closed the door behind him and he heard the key turn in the lock. But the sunbeams were there, the low, slanting beams of honey-coloured light; they flooded through the bars and gave a kind of welcome to the prisoner – so that he made, without a pause, for the big window, where, holding an iron bar with either hand, he stared across a landscape.

It seemed it was transfigured. So ethereal was the light that great cedars floated upon it and hilltops seemed to wander through the gold.

In the far distance Titus could see what looked like the incrustation of a city, and as though the sun were striking it obliquely there came the golden flash of windows, now here, now there, like sparks from a flint.

Suddenly, out of the gilded evening a bird flew directly towards the window where Titus stood staring through the bars. It approached rapidly, looping its airborne way, was all at once standing on the window-ledge.

By the way its head moved rapidly to and fro upon its neck it seemed it was looking for something. It was evident that the last occupant of the cell had shared his crumbs with the piebald bird – but today there were no crumbs and the magpie at last began to peck at its feathers as though in lieu of better fare.

Then out of the golden atmosphere: out of the stones of the cell: out of the cedars: out of a flutter of the magpie's wing, came a long waft of memory so that images swam up before his eyes and he saw, more vividly than the sunset or the forested hills, the long coruscated outline of Gormenghast and the stones of his home where the lizards lazed, and there, blotting out all else, his mother as he had last seen her at the door of the shanty, the great dripping castle drawn up like a backcloth behind her.

'You will come back,' she had said. 'All roads lead back to Gormenghast'; and he yearned suddenly for his home, for the bad of it no less than for the good of it – yearned for the smell of it and the taste of the bitter ivy.

Titus turned from the window as though to dispel the nostalgia, but the mere movement of his body through space was no help to him, and he sat down on the edge of the bed.

From far below the window came the fluting of a blackbird; the golden light had begun to darken and he became conscious of a loneliness he had never felt before.

He leaned forward pressing the tightened muscles below his ribs and then began to rock back and forth, like a pendulum. So regular was the rocking that it would seem that no assuagement of grief could result from so mechanical a rhythm.

But there was a kind of comfort to be had, for while his brain wept, his body went on swaying.

An aching to be once again in the land from which he grew gave him no rest. There is no calm for those who are uprooted. They are wanderers, homesick and defiant. Love itself is helpless to heal them though the dust rises with every footfall – drifts down the corridors – settles on branch or cornice – each breath an inhalation from the past so that the lungs, like a miner's, are dark with bygone times.

Whatever they eat, whatever they drink, is never the bread of home or the corn of their own valleys. It is never the wine of their own vineyards. It is a foreign brew.

So Titus rocked himself in grief's cradle to and fro, to and fro, while the cell darkened, and at some time during the night he fell asleep.

THIRTY-FIVE

WHAT was it? He sat bolt upright and stared about him. It was very cold but it was not this that woke him. It was a little sound. He could hear it now quite clearly. It came from within a few feet of where he sat. It was a kind of tapping, but it did not seem to come from the wall. It came from beneath the bed.

Then it stopped for a little and when it returned it seemed as though it bore some kind of message, for there was a pattern or rhythm in it: something that sounded like a question. 'Tap–Tap... Tap–Tap–Tap.' Are ... yóu ... thére ...? Are ... yóu ... thére ...?'

This tapping, sinister as it was, had the effect, at least, of turning Titus's mind from the almost unbearable nostalgia that had oppressed it.

Edging himself silently from the flimsy bed, he stood beside it, his heart beating, and then he lifted it bodily from where it stood and set it down in the centre of the cell.

Remembering the candles on the table, he fumbled for one, lit it, and then tip-toed back to where the bed had stood, and then moved the small flame to and fro along the flagstones. As he did so the tapping started again.

'Are ... yóu ... thére ...?' it seemed to say – 'Are ... yóu ... thére ...?'

Titus knelt down and shone the candle flame full upon the stone from immediately below which the tapping appeared to proceed.

It seemed quite ordinary, at first, this flagstone, but under scrutiny Titus could see that the thin fissure that surrounded it was sharper and deeper than was the case with the adjacent stones. The candlelight showed up what the daylight would have hidden.

Again the knocking started and Titus, taking the knuckle of flint from his pocket, waited for the next lull. Then, with a trembling hand, he struck the stone slab twice.

For a moment there was no reply and then the answer came – 'One ... two ...'

It was a brisk 'one – two', quite unlike the tentative tapping which had preceded it.

It was as though, whoever or whatever stood or lay or crawled beneath the flagstone, the *mood* of the enigma had changed. The 'being', whatever it was, had gained in confidence.

What happened next was stranger and more fearful. Something more startling than the tapping had taken its place. This time it was the eyes that were assailed. What did they see that made his whole body shake? Peering at the candle-lit flagstone below him, he saw it move.

Titus jumped back from the oscillating stone and, lifting

his candle high in the air, he looked about him wildly for some
kind of weapon. His eyes returned to the stone which was
now an inch above the ground.

From where Titus stood in the centre of the cell he could
not see that the stone was supported by a pair of hands that
trembled with its weight. All he saw was a part of the floor
rising up with a kind of slow purpose.

Woken out of his sleep to find himself in a prison – and then
to hear a knocking in the darkness – and then to be faced with
something phantasmagoric – a stone, apparently alive, raising
itself in secret in order to survey the supine vaults – all this
and the depth of his homesickness – what could all this lead to
but a lightness in the head? But this lightness, though it all but
brought a kind of mad laughter in its train, did not prevent him
seeing in the half-painted chair a possible weapon. Grabbing it,
with his eyes fixed upon the flagstone, he wrenched the chair
to pieces, this way and that, until he had pulled free from the
skeleton one of its front legs. With this in his hand he began
to laugh silently as he crept towards his enemy, the stone.

But as he crept forward he saw before the flagstone, which
was by now five inches up in the air, two thick grey wrists.

They were trembling with the weight of the stone slab, and
as Titus watched, his eyes wide with conjecture, he saw the
thick slab begin to tilt and edge itself over the adjacent stone
until, by degrees, the whole weight was transferred and there
was a square hole in the floor.

The thick grey hands had withdrawn, taking their fingers
with them – but a moment later something arose to take their
place. It was the head of a man.

THIRTY-SIX

LITTLE did he know – this riser-out-of-flagstones – that his head
was that of a batter'd god – nor that with such a visage, he
was, when he spoke, undermining his own grandeur, for no
voice could be tremendous enough for such a face.

'Be not startled,' he whined, and his accents were as soft as dough. 'All is well; all is lovely; all is as it should be. Accept me. That is all I ask you. Accept me. Old Crime they call me. They *will* have their little jokes. Dear boys, they are. Ha ha! That I have come to you through a hole in the floor is nothing. Put down that chair-leg, friend.'

'What do you want?' said Titus.

'Listen to him,' replied the soft voice. "What do you want?" he says. I want nothing, dear child. Nothing but friendship. Sweet friendship. That is why I have come to see you. To initiate you. One must help the helpless, mustn't one? And pour out balm, you know: and bathe all kinds of bruises.'

'I wish to hell you had left me alone,' said Titus savagely. 'You can keep your balm.'

'Now is that *nice?*' said Old Crime. 'Is that *kind?* But I understand. You are not used to it: are you? It takes some time to love the Honeycomb.'

Titus stared at the leonine head.

The voice had robbed it of all grandeur, and he placed the chair leg on the table within reach.

'The Honeycomb? What's that?' said Titus at last. The man had been staring at him intently.

'It is the name we give, dear boy, to what some would call a prison. But we know better. To us it is a world within a world – and *I* should know, shouldn't I? I've been here all my life – or nearly all. For the first few years I lived in luxury. There were tiger-skins on the scented floor-boards of our houses: and golden cutlery and golden plates. Money was like the sands of the sea. For I come from a great line. You have probably heard of us. We are the oldest family in the world – we are the originals.' He edged forward, out of the hole.

'Do you think that because I am here, in the Honeycomb, I am missing anything? Do you think I am jealous of my family? Do you think I miss the golden plates and the tiger-skins? No! Nor the reflections in the polished floor. I have found my luxury *here*. This is my joy. To be a prisoner in the Honeycomb. So, my dear child, be not startled. I came to tell you there's a friend below you. You can always tap to me. Tap out your thoughts. Tap out your joys and sorrows. Tap out your love. We will grow old together.'

72

Titus turned his face sharply. What did he mean, this vile, unhealthy creature.

'Leave me alone,' cried Titus, ' – leave me alone!'

The man from the cell below stared at Titus. Then he began to tremble.

'This used to be *my* cell,' he said. 'Years and years ago. I was a fire-raiser. "Arson" they called it. I did so love a fire. The flames make up for everything.

'Bring on the rats and mice! Bring on my skinning-knife. Bring on the New Boys.'

He moved a step towards Titus who, in his turn, moved a little nearer to the chair-leg weapon.

'This is a good cell. I had it once,' whined Old Crime. 'I made something out of it, I can tell you. I learned the nature of it. I was sad to leave it. This window is the finest in the prison. But who cares about it now? Where are the frescoes gone? My yellow frescoes. Drawings, you understand. Drawings of fairies. Now they have been covered up and nothing is left of all my work. Not a trace.'

He lifted his proud head and but for the shortness of his legs he might well have been Isaiah.

'Put that chair-leg on the table, boy. Forget yourself. Eat up your crumbs.'

Titus looked down at the old lag and the craggy grandeur of his upturned face.

'You've come to the right place,' said Old Crime. 'Away from the filthy thing called Life. Join us, dear boy. You would be an asset. My friends are unique. Grow old with us.'

'You talk too much,' said Titus.

The man from below stretched out his strong arm slowly. His right hand fastened upon Titus's biceps and as it tightened Titus could feel an evil strength, a sense that Old Crime's power was limitless and that, had he wanted to, he could have torn the arm away with ease.

As it was he brought Titus to his side with a single pull, and far back in the sham nobility of his countenance Titus could see two little fires no bigger than pin-heads burning.

'I was going to do so much for you,' said the man from below. 'I was going to introduce you to my colleagues. I was going to show you all the escape routes – should you want them – I was going to tell you about my poetry and where the harlots prowl. After all one mustn't become ill, must we? That wouldn't do at all.

'But you have told me I talk too much, so I will do something quite different and crack your skull like an egg-shell.'

All in a breath the dreadful man let go of Titus, wheeled in his tracks, and lifting the table above his head he flung it, with all the force he could command, at Titus. But he was too late, for all his speed. Directly Titus saw the man reach for the table he sprang to one side, and the heavy piece of furniture crashed against the wall at his back.

Turning now upon the massive-chested and muscular creature, he was surprised to hear the sound of sobbing. His adversary was now upon his knees, his huge archaic face buried in his hands.

Not knowing what to do, Titus re-lit one of the candles which had been on the table and then sat down on his trestle bed, the only piece of furniture left in the cell that hadn't been smashed.

'Why did you have to say it? Why did you have to? O why? Why?' sobbed the man.

'O God,' said Titus to himself, 'what have I done?'

'So I talk too much? O God, I talk too much.'

A shadow passed over Old Crime's face. At the same moment there was a heavy sound of feet beyond the door and then after a rattling of keys the sound of one turning in the lock. Old Crime was by this time on the move and by the time the door began to open he had disappeared down the hole in the floor.

Hardly knowing what he was doing, Titus dragged the trestle bed over the hole and then lay down on it as the door opened.

A warder came in with a torch. He flashed it around the cell, the beam of light lingering on the broken table, the broken chair, and the supposedly sleeping boy.

Four strides took him to Titus, whom he pulled from his bed only to beat him back again with a vicious clout on the head.

'Let that last you till the morning, you bloody whelp!' shouted the warder. 'I'll teach you to keep your temper! I'll teach you to smash things.' He glowered at Titus. 'Who were you talking to?' he shouted, but Titus, being half stunned, could hardly answer.

In the very early morning when he awoke he thought it had all been a dream. But the dream was so vivid that he could not refrain from rolling to the floor and peering in the half-darkness beneath the trestle bed.

It had been no dream, for there it was, that heavy slab of stone, and he immediately began to shift it inch by inch and it fell into its former place. But just before the hole was finally closed he heard the old man's voice, soft as gruel, in the darkness below.

'Grow old with me . . . ,' it said. 'Grow old with me.'

THIRTY-SEVEN

A DIM light shone above his Worship's head. In the hollow of the Court someone could be heard sharpening a pencil. A chair creaked, and Titus, standing upright at the bar, began to bang his hands together, for it was a bitter cold morning.

'Who is applauding what?' said the Magistrate, recovering from a reverie. 'Have I said something profound?'

'No, not at all, your Worship,' said the large, pock-marked Clerk of the Court. 'That is, sir, you made no remark.'

'Silence can be profound, Mr Drugg. Very much so.'

'Yes, your Worship.'

'What *was* it then?'

'It was the young man, your Worship; clapping his hands, to warm them, I imagine.'

'Ah, yes. The young man. Which young man? Where is he?'

'In the dock, your Worship.'

The Magistrate, frowning a little, pushed his wig to one side and then drew it back again.

'I seem to know his face,' said the Magistrate.

'Quite so, your Worship,' said Mr Drugg. 'This prisoner has been before you several times.'

75

'That accounts for it,' said the Magistrate. 'And what has he been up to now?'

'If I may remind your Worship,' said the large pock-marked Clerk of the Court, not without a note of peevishness in his voice, ' – you were dealing with this case only this morning.'

'And so I was. It is returning to me. I have always had an excellent memory. Think of a Magistrate with no memory.'

'I am thinking of it, your Worship,' said Mr Drugg as, with a gesture of irritation, he thumbed through a sheaf of irrelevant papers.

'Vagrancy. Wasn't *that* it, Mr Drugg?'

'It *was*,' said the Clerk of the Court. 'Vagrancy, damage, and trespass' – and he turned his big greyish-coloured face to Titus and lifted a corner of his top lip away from his teeth like a dog. And then, as though upon their own volition, his hands slid down into the depths of his trouser pockets as though two foxes had all of a sudden gone to earth. A smothered sound of keys and coins being jangled together gave the momentary impression that there was about Mr Drugg something frisky, something of the playboy. But this impression was gone as soon as it was born. There was nothing in Mr Drugg's dark, heavy features, nothing about his stance, nothing about his voice to give colour to the thought. Only the noise of coins.

But the jangling, half smothered as it was, reminded Titus of something half forgotten, a dreadful, yet intimate music; of a cold kingdom; of bolts and flag-stoned corridors; of intricate gates of corroded iron; of flints and visors and the beaks of birds.

' "Vagrancy", "damage", and "trespass",' repeated the Magistrate, 'yes, yes, I remember. Fell through someone else's roof. Was that it?'

'Exactly, sir,' said the Clerk of the Court.

'No visible means of support?'

'That is so, your Worship.'

'Homeless?'

'Yes, and no, your Worship,' said the Clerk. 'He talks of – '

'Yes, yes, yes, yes. I have it now. A trying case and a trying young man – I had begun to tire, I remember, of his obscurity.'

The Magistrate leaned forward on his elbows and rested his

76

long, bony chin upon the knuckles of his interlocked fingers.

'This is the fourth time that I have had you before me at the bar, and as far as I can judge, the whole thing has been a waste of time to the Court and nothing but a nuisance to myself. Your answers, when they have been forthcoming, have been either idiotic, nebulous, or fantastic. This cannot be allowed to go on. Your youth is no excuse. Do you like stamps?'

'Stamps, your Worship?'

'Do you collect them?'

'No.'

'A pity. I have a rare collection rotting daily. Now listen to me. You have already spent a week in prison – but it is not your vagrancy that troubles me. That is straightforward, though culpable. It is that you are rootless and obtuse. It seems you have some knowledge hidden from us. Your ways are curious, your terms are meaningless. I will ask you once again. What is this Gormenghast? What does it mean?'

Titus turned his face to the Bench. If ever there was a man to be trusted, his Worship was that man.

Ancient, wrinkled, like a tortoise, but with eyes as candid as grey glass.

But Titus made no answer, only brushing his forehead with the sleeve of his coat.

'Have you heard his Worship's question?' said a voice at his side. It was Mr Drugg.

'I do not know,' said Titus, 'what is meant by such a question. You might just as well ask me what is this hand of mine? What does it mean?' And he raised it in the air with the fingers spread out like a starfish. 'Or what is this leg?' And he stood on one foot in the box and shook the other as though it were loose. 'Forgive me, your Worship, I cannot understand.'

'It is a *place*, your Worship,' said the Clerk of the Court. 'The prisoner has insisted that it is a *place*.'

'Yes, yes,' said the Magistrate. 'But where is it? Is it north, south, east, or west, young man? Help *me* to help *you*. I take it you do not want to spend the rest of your life sleeping on the roofs of foreign towns. What is it, boy? What is the matter with you?'

A ray of light slid through a high window of the Courtroom

and hit the back of Mr Drugg's short neck as though it were revealing something of mystical significance. Mr Drugg drew back his head and the light moved forward and settled on his ear. Titus watched it as he spoke.

'I would tell you, if I could, sir,' he said. 'I only know that I have lost my way. It is not that I want to return to my home – I do not; it is that even if I wished to do so I could not. It is not that I have travelled very far; it is that I have lost my bearings, sir.'

'Did you run away, young man?'

'I rode away,' said Titus.

'From . . . Gormenghast?'

'Yes, your Worship.'

'Leaving your mother . . . ?'

'Yes.'

'And your father . . . ?'

'No, not my father . . .'

'Ah . . . is he dead, my boy?'

'Yes, your Worship. He was eaten by owls.'

The Magistrate raised an eyebrow and began to write upon a piece of paper.

THIRTY-EIGHT

THIS note, which was obviously intended for some important person, probably someone in charge of the local Asylum, or home for delinquent youths – this note fell foul of the Magistrate's intentions, and after being dropped and trodden on, was recovered and passed from hand to hand until it came to rest for a little while in the wrinkled paw of a half-wit, who eventually, after trying to read it, made a dart out of it, and set it sailing out of the shadows and into a less murky quarter of the Court.

A little behind the half-wit was a figure almost completely lost in the shadows. In his pocket lay curled a salamander. His eyes were closed and his nose, like a large rudder, pointed at the ceiling.

On his left sat Mrs Grass with a hat like a yellow cabbage. She had made several attempts to whisper in Muzzlehatch's ear, but had received no response.

Some distance to the left of these two sat half a dozen strong men, husky and very upright. They had followed the proceedings with strict, if frowning, attention. In their view the Magistrate was being too lenient. After all the young man in the dock had proved himself no gentleman. One had only to look at his clothes. Apart from this, the way he had broken into Lady Cusp-Canine's party was unforgivable.

Lady Cusp-Canine sat with her little chin propped up by her little index finger. Her hat, unlike Mrs Grass's cabbage-like creation, was black as night and rather like a crow's nest. From under the multiform brim of twigs her little made-up face was mushroom-white save where her mouth was like a small red wound. Her head remained motionless but her small, black, button eyes darted here and there so that nothing should be missed.

Very little *was*, when she was around, and it was she who first saw the dart soar out of the gloom at the back of the Court and take a long leisurely half-circle through the dim air.

The Magistrate, his eyelids dropping heavily over his innocent eyeballs, began to slip forward in his high chair until he assumed the kind of position that reminded one of Muzzlehatch at the wheel of his car. But there the similarity ended, for the fact that they had both, even now, closed their eyes meant little. What was important was that the Magistrate was half asleep while Muzzlehatch was very wide awake.

He had noticed, in spite of his seeming torpor, that in an alcove, half hidden by a pillar, were two figures who sat very still and very upright; with an elasticity of articulation; an imperceptible vibrance of the spine. They were upright to the point of unnaturalness. They did not move. Even the plumes on their helmets were motionless, and were in every way identical.

He, Muzzlehatch, had also picked out Inspector Acreblade (a pleasant change from the tall enigmas), for there could be nothing more earthy than the Inspector, who believed in nothing so much as his hound-like job, the spoor and gristle of it: the dry bones of his trade. Within his head there was always a quarry. Ugly or beautiful; a quarry. High morals took no part in his career. He was a hunter and that was all. His aggressive chin prodded the air. His stocky frame had about it something dauntless.

Muzzlehatch watched him through eyelids that were no more than a thread apart. There were not many people in Court that were *not* being watched by Muzzlehatch. In fact there was only one. She sat quite still and unobserved in the shade of a pillar and watched Titus as he stood in the dock, the Magistrate looming above him, like some kind of a cloud. His forgetful face was quite invisible but the crown of his wig was illumined by the lamp that hung above his head. And as Juno stared, she frowned a little and the frown was as much an expression of kindness as the warm quizzical smile that usually hovered on her lips.

THIRTY-NINE

WHAT was it about this stripling at the bar? Why did he touch her so? Why was she frightened for him? 'My father is dead,' he had answered. 'He was eaten by owls.'

A group of elderly men, their legs and arms draped around the backs and elbow-rests of pew-like settees, made between them a noisy corner. The Clerk of the Court had brought them to order more than once but their age had made them impervious to criticism, their old jaws rattling on without a break.

At that moment the paper dart began to loop downward in a gracile curve so that the central figure of the elderly group – the poet himself – jumped to his feet and cried out 'Armageddon!' in so loud a voice that the Magistrate opened his eyes.

'What's this!' he muttered, the dart trailing across his line of vision. There was no answer, for at that moment the rain came down. At first it had been the merest patter; but then it had thickened into a throbbing of water, only to give way after a little while to a protracted *hissing*.

This hissing filled the whole Court. The very stones hissed and with the rain came a premature darkness which thickened the already murky Court.

'More candles!' someone cried. 'More lanterns! Brands and torches, electricity, gas and glow-worms!'

By now it was impossible to recognize anyone save by their silhouettes, for what lights had begun to appear were sucked in by the quenching effect of the darkness.

It was then that someone pulled down a small emergency lever at the back of the Court, and the whole place was jerked into a spasm of naked brilliance.

For a while the Magistrate, the Clerk, the witnesses, the public, sat blinded. Scores of eyelids closed: scores of pupils began to contract. And everything was changed save for the roaring of the rain upon the roof. While this noise made it impossible to be *heard*, yet every detail had become important to the *eye*.

There was nothing mysterious left; all was made naked. The Magistrate had never before suffered such excruciating limelight. The very essence of his vocation was 'removedness'; how could he be 'removed' with the harsh unscrupulous light revealing him as a *particular* man? He was a symbol. He was the Law. He was Justice. He was the wig he wore. Once the wig was gone then he was gone with it. He became a little man among little men. A little man with rather weak eyes; that they were blue and candid argued a quality of magnanimity, when in Court; but they became irritatingly weak and empty directly he removed his wig and returned to his home. But now the unnatural light was upon him, cold and merciless: the kind of light by which vile deeds are done.

With this fierce radiance on his face it was not hard for him to imagine that *he* was the prisoner.

He opened his mouth to speak but not a word could be heard, for the rain was thrashing the roof.

The gaggle of old men, now that their voices were drowned, had gone into their shells, their old tortoise faces turned from the violence of the light.

Following Titus's gaze, Muzzlehatch could see that he was staring at the Helmeted Pair and that the Helmeted Pair were staring at Titus. The young man's hands were shaking on the rail of the bar.

One of the group of six had picked up the paper dart and

smoothed it out with the flat of his big insensitive hand.
He frowned as he read and then shot a glance at the young
man at the bar. Spill, the tall deaf gentleman, was peering over
the man's shoulder. His deafness made him wonder at the lack
of conversation in the Court. He could not know that a black
sky was crashing down upon the roof nor that the light flooding the walnut-panelled Court was so incongruously coinciding
with the black downpour of the outer world.

But he could read, and what he read caused him to dart a
glance at Titus, who, turning his head at last from the Helmeted
Pair, saw Muzzlehatch. The blinding light had plucked him

from the shadows. What was he doing? He was making some kind of sign. Then Titus saw Juno, and for a moment he felt a kind of warmth both for and *from* her. Then he saw Spill and Kestrel. Then he saw Mrs Grass and then the poet.

Everything was horribly close and vivid. Muzzlehatch, looking about nine foot high, had reached the middle of the Court, and choosing the right moment he relieved the man of the crinkled note.

As he read, the rain slackened, and by the time he had finished, the black sky, as though it were a solid, had moved away, all in one piece, and could be heard trundling away into another region.

There was a hush in the Court until an anonymous voice cried out – 'Switch off this fiendish light!'

This peremptory order was obeyed by someone equally anonymous, and the lanterns and the lamps came into their own again: the shadows spread themselves. The Magistrate leaned forward.

'What are you reading, my friend?' he said to Muzzlehatch. 'If the furrow between your eyes spells anything, I should guess it spells news.'

'Why, yes, your Worship, why, yes, indeed. Dire news,' said Muzzlehatch.

'That scrap of paper in your hands,' continued the Magistrate, 'looks remarkably like a note I handed down to my Clerk, creased though it is and filthy as it has become. Would it be?'

'It would,' said Muzzlehatch, 'and it *is*. But you are wrong; he isn't. No more than I am.'

'No?'

'No!'

'Isn't what?'

'Can you not remember what you wrote, your Worship?'

'Remind me.'

Muzzlehatch, instead of reading out the contents of the note, slouched up to the Magistrate's bench and handed him the grubby paper.

'This is what you wrote,' he said. 'It is not for the public. Nor for the young prisoner.'

'No?' said the Magistrate.

'No,' said Muzzlehatch.

'Let me see. . . . Let me see . . .' said the Magistrate, pursing his mouth as he took the note from Muzzlehatch and read to himself.

Ref.: No. 1721536217

My dear Filby,

I have before me a young man, a vagrant, a trespasser, a quite peculiar youth, hailing from Gorgonblast, or some such improbable place, and bound for nowhere. By name he admits to 'Titus', and sometimes to 'Groan', though whether Groan is his real name or an invention it is hard to say.

It is quite clear in my mind that this young man is suffering from delusions of grandeur and should be kept under close observation – in other words, Filby, my dear old chap, the boy, to put it bluntly, is *dotty*. Have you room for him? He can, of course, pay nothing, but he may be of interest to you and even find a place in the treatise you are working on. What was it you were calling it? 'Among the Emperors'?

O dear, what it is to be a Magistrate! Sometimes I wonder what it is all about. The human heart is too much. Things go too far. They become unhealthy. But I'd rather be me than you. You are in the entrails of it all. I asked the young man if his father were alive. 'No,' he said, '*he was eaten by owls*.' What do you make of that? I will have him sent over. How is your neuritis? Let me hear from you, old man.

Yours ever,

Willy.

The Magistrate looked up from his note and stared at the boy. 'That seems to cover it,' he said. 'And yet . . . you look all right. I wish I could help you. I will try once more – because I may be wrong.'

'In what way?' said Titus; his eyes were fixed on Acreblade, who had changed his seat in the Court and was now very close indeed.

'What is wrong with me, your Worship? Why do you peer at me like that?' said Titus. 'I am lost – that is all.'

The Magistrate leaned forward. 'Tell me, Titus – tell me about your home. You have told us of your father's death. What of your mother?'

'She was a woman.'

This answer raised a guffaw in the Court.

'Silence,' shouted the Clerk of the Court.

'I would not like to feel that you are showing contempt of Court,' said the Magistrate, 'but if this goes on any longer I will have to pass you on to Mr Acreblade. Is your mother alive?'

'Yes, your Worship,' said Titus, 'unless she has died.'

'When did you last see her?'

'Long ago.'

'Were you not happy with her? – You have told us that you ran away from home.'

'I would like to see her again,' said Titus. 'I did not see very much of her; she was too vast for me. But I did not flee from *her*.'

'What *did* you flee from?'

'From my duty.'

'Your duty?'

'Yes, your Worship.'

'What kind of duty?'

'My hereditary duty. I have told you. I am the last of the Line. I have betrayed my birthright. I have betrayed my home. I have run like a rat from Gormenghast. God have mercy on me.

'What do you want of me? I am sick of it all! Sick of being followed. What have I done wrong – save to myself? So my papers are out of order, are they? So is my brain and heart. One day I'll do some shadowing myself!'

Titus, his hands gripping the sides of the box, turned his full face to the Magistrate.

'Why was I put in jail, your Worship,' he whispered, 'as though I were a criminal? Me! Seventy-Seventh Earl and heir to that name.'

'Gormenghast,' murmured the Magistrate. 'Tell us more, dear boy.'

'What can I tell you? It spreads in all directions. There is no end to it. Yet it seems to me now to have boundaries. It has the sunlight and the moonlight on its walls just like this country. There are rats and moths – and herons. It has bells that chime. It has forests and it has lakes and it is full of people.'

'What kind of people, dear boy?'

'They had two legs each, your Worship, and when they sang they opened their mouths and when they cried the water fell out of their eyes. Forgive me, your Worship, I do not wish to be facetious. But what can I say? I am in a foreign city; in a foreign land; let me go free. I could not bear that prison any more.

'Gormenghast was a kind of jail. A place of ritual. But suddenly and under my breath I had to say good-bye.'

'Yes, my boy. Please go on.'

'There had been a flood, your Worship. A great flood. So that the castle seemed to float upon it. When the sun at last came out the whole place dripped and shone. . . . I had a horse, your Worship. . . . I dug my heels into her flank and I galloped into perdition. I wanted to *know*, you see.'

'What did you want to know, my young friend?'

'I wanted to know,' said Titus, 'whether there was any other place.'

'Any other place . . .?'

'Yes.'

'Have you written to your mother?'

'I have written to her. But every time my letters are returned. Address unknown.'

'What was this address?'

'I have only one address,' said Titus.

'It is odd that you should have recovered your letters.'

'Why?' said Titus.

'Because your name is hardly probable. Now is it?'

'It is my name,' said Titus.

'What, Titus Groan, Seventy-Seventh Lord?'

'Why not?'

'It is unlikely. That sort of title belongs to another age. Do you dream at night? Have you lapses of memory? Are you a poet? Or is it all, in fact, an elaborate joke?'

'A joke? O God!' said Titus.

So passionate was his outcry that the Court fell silent. That was not the voice of a hoaxer. It was the voice of someone quite convinced of his own truth – the truth in his head.

FORTY

MUZZLEHATCH watched the boy and wondered why he had felt a compulsion to attend the Court. Why should he be interested in the comings and goings of this young vagabond? He had never from the first supposed the boy to be insane: though there were some in the Court who were convinced that Titus was mad as a bird, and had come for no other reason than to indulge a morbid curiosity.

No; Muzzlehatch had attended the Court because, although he would never have admitted it, he had become interested in the fate and future of the enigmatic creature he had found half drowned on the water-steps. That he *was* interested annoyed him for he knew, as he sat there, that his small brown bear would be pining for him and that every one of his animals was at that moment peering through the bars, fretful for his approach.

While such thoughts were in his head, a voice broke the stillness of the Court, asking permission to address the Magistrate.

Wearily, his Worship nodded his head, and then seeing who it was who had addressed him, he sat up and adjusted his wig. For it was Juno.

'Let me take him,' she said, her eloquent and engulfing eyes fixed upon his Worship's face. 'He is alone and resentful. Perhaps I could find out how best he could be helped. In the meantime, your Worship, he is hungry, travel-stained, and tired.'

'I object, your Worship,' said Inspector Acreblade. 'All that this lady says is true. But he is here on account of serious infringement of the Law. We cannot afford to be sentimental.'

'Why not?' said the Magistrate. 'His sins are not serious.'

He turned to her with a note almost of excitement in his tired old voice. 'Do you wish to be responsible,' he said, 'both to me and for him?'

'I take full responsibility,' said Juno.

'And you will keep in touch with me?'

'Certainly, your Worship – but there's another thing.'

'What is that, madam?'

'The young man's attitude. I will not take him with me un-less he wishes it. Indeed I *cannot*.'

The Magistrate turned to Titus and was about to speak when he seemed to change his mind. He returned his gaze to her.

'Are you married, madam?'

'I am not,' said Juno.

There was a pause before the Magistrate spoke again.

'Young man,' he said, 'this lady has offered to act as your guardian until you are well again ... what do you say?'

All that was weak in Titus rose like oil to the surface of deep water. 'Thank you,' he said. 'Thank you, madam. Thank you.'

FORTY-ONE

AT first what was it but an apprehension sweet as far bird-song – a tremulous thing – an awareness that fate had thrown them together; a world had been brought into being – had been discovered? A world, a universe over whose boundaries and into whose forests they had not dared to venture. A world to be glimpsed, not from some crest of the imagination, but through simple words, empty in themselves as air, and sen-tences quite colourless and void; save that they set their pulses racing.

Theirs was a small talk – that evoked the measureless avenues of the night, and the green glades of noonday. When they said 'Hullo!' new stars appeared in the sky; when they laughed, this wild world split its sides, though what was so funny neither of them knew. It was a game of the fantastic senses; febrile; tender, tip-tilted. They would lean on the win-dow-sill of Juno's beautiful room and gaze for hours on end at the far hills where the trees and buildings were so close to-gether, so interwoven, that it was impossible to say whether it was a city in a forest or a forest in a city. There they leaned in the golden light, sometimes happy to talk – sometimes bask-ing in a miraculous silence.

Was Titus in love with his guardian, and was she in love with him? How could it be otherwise? Before either of them had formed the remotest knowledge of one another's characters, they were already, after a few days, trembling at the sound of each other's footsteps.

But at night, when she lay awake, she cursed her age. She was forty. A little more than twice as old as Titus. Next to others of her age, or even younger, she still appeared unparalleled, with a head like a female warrior in a legend – but with Titus beside her she had no choice but to come to terms with nature, and she felt an angry and mutinous pain in her bosom. She thought of Muzzlehatch and how he had swept her off her feet twenty years earlier and of their voyagings to outlandish islands, and of how his ebullience became maddening and of how they were equally strong-headed, equally wilful, and of how their travels together became an agony for them both, for they broke against one another like waves breaking against headlands.

But with Titus it was so different. Titus from nowhere – a youth with an air about him: carrying over his shoulders a private world like a cloak, and from whose lips fell such strange tales of his boyhood days, that she was drawn to the very outskirts of that shadowland. 'Perhaps,' she thought, 'I am in love with something as mysterious and elusive as a ghost. A ghost never to be held at the breast. Something that will always melt away.'

And then she would remember how happy they sometimes were; and how every day they leaned on the sill together, not touching one another, but tasting the rarest fruit of all – the sharp fruit of suspense.

But there were also times when she cried out in the darkness biting her lips – cried out against the substance of her age: for it was *now* that she should be young; *now* above all other times, with the wisdom in her, the wisdom that was frittered away in her 'teens', set aside in her twenties, now, lying there, palpable and with forty summers gone. She clenched her hands together. What good was wisdom; what good was anything when the fawn is fled from the grove?

'God!' she whispered. ' – Where is the youth that I *feel*?' And then she would heave a long shuddering sigh and toss her head on the pillow and gather her strength together and laugh; for she was, in her own way, undefeatable.

She lifted herself on her elbow, taking deep draughts of the night air.

'He needs me,' she would mutter in a kind of golden growl. 'It is for me to give him joy – to give him direction – to give him love. Let the world say what it likes – he is my mission. I will be always at his side. He may not know it, but I will be there. In body or in spirit always, near him when he most needs me. My child from Gormenghast. My Titus Groan.'

And then, at that moment, the light across her features would darken, and a shadow of doubt would take its place – for who was this youth? What was he? Why was he? What was it about him? Who were those people he spoke of? This inner world? Those memories? Were they true? Was he a liar – a cunning child? Some kind of wild misfit? Or was he mad? No! No! It couldn't be. It mustn't be.

FORTY-TWO

IT was now four months since Titus first set foot in Juno's house. A watery light filled the sky. There were voices in the distance. A rustle of leaves – an acorn falling – the barking of a distant hound.

Juno leaned her superb, tropical head against the window in her sitting-room and gazed at the falling leaves or to speak more truly, she gazed *through* them, as they fell, fluttering and twisting, for her mind was elsewhere. Behind her in her elegant room a fire burned and cast a red glow across the marble cheek of a small head on a pedestal.

Then, all at once, there he was! A creature far from marble, waving to her from the statue'd garden, and the sight of him swept cogitation from her face as though a web were snatched from her features.

Seeing this happen, this change in her aspect, and the movement of her marvellous bosom, young Titus experienced, all in a flash, a number of simultaneous emotions. A pang of greed, green-carnal to the quick, sang, rang like a bell, his scrotum tightening; skidaddled through his loins and qualming tissues and began to burn like ice, the trembling fig on fire. And yet at the same time there was an aloofness in him – even a kind of suspicion, a perversity quite uncalled for. Something that Juno had always felt was there – something she feared beyond failure; this thing she could not compass with her arms.

Yet even worse than this, there was mixed up in him a pity for her. Pity that punctures love. She had given him everything, and he pitied her for it. He did not know that this was lethal and infinitely sad.

And there was the fear in him of being caught – caught in the generous folds of her love – her helpless love: fierce and loyal.

They gazed at one another. Juno with a quite incredible tenderness, something not easily associated with a lady in the height of fashion, and Titus with his greed returning as he watched her, flung out his arms in a wild, expansive gesture, quite false; quite melodramatic; and he knew it to be so, and so did she; but it was right at the moment, for his lust was real enough and lust is an arrogant and haughty beast and far from subtle.

So quickly did they flow one into another, these sensations of pity, physical greed, revulsion, excitement and tenderness, that they became blurred in an overriding impetus, a desire to hold all this in his outflung arms; to bring the total of their relationship to a burning focus. To bring it all to an *end*. That was the sadness of it. Not to create the deed that should set glory in motion but to bring glory to an end – to stab sweet love: to stab it to death. To be free of it.

None of this was in his mind. It was far away, in another pocket of his being. What was important, now, with her eyes bent upon him, and the shadow of a branch trembling across her breast, was the immemorial game of love: no less a game for being grave. No less grave for being wild. Grave as a great green sky. Grave as a surgeon's knife.

'So you thought you'd come back, my wicked one. Where have you been?'

'In hell,' said Titus. 'Swigging blood and munching scorpions.'

'That must have been great fun, my darling.'

'Not so,' said Titus, 'hell is overrated.'

'But you escaped?'

'I caught a plane. The slenderest thing you ever saw. A million years slid by in half a minute. I sliced the sky in half. And all for what?'

'Well . . . what?'

'To batten on you.'

'What of the slender plane?'

'I pressed a button and away she flew.'

'Is that good or bad?'

'It is very good. We don't want to be watched, *do* we? Machines are so inquisitive. You're rather far away. May I come up?'

'Of course, or you'll disjoint yourself.'

'Stay, stay where you are. Don't go – I'm on my way,' and with a mad and curious tilt of the head he disappeared from the statue'd garden and a few minutes later Juno could hear his feet on the stairs.

He was no longer entangled in a maze of moods. Whatever was happening to his subconscious, it made no attempt to break surface. His mind fell asleep. His wits fell awake. His cock trembled like a harp-string.

As he flung open the door of her room he saw her at once; proud, monumental, relaxed; one elbow on the mantelpiece, a smile on her lips, an eyebrow raised a little. His eyes were so fixed upon her that it was not surprising that he tripped up on a footstool that stood directly in his path, and trying to recover his balance tripped again and fell headlong.

Before he could recover she was already sitting on the floor beside him.

'This is your second time to crash at my feet. Have you hurt yourself, darling? Is it symbolic?' said Juno.

'Bound to be,' said Titus – 'absolutely *bound* to be.'

Had he known her less well this absurd fall might well have distracted him from his somewhat unoriginal purpose, but with Juno hovering above him and smelling like Paradise, his passion, far from being quenched, took on a strange quality

– something ridiculous and lovable – so that to laugh became a part of their tenderness.

When Juno laughed the process began like a child's gurgle. As for Titus he shouted his laughter.

It was the death-knell of false sentiment and of any cliché, or recognized behaviour. This was a thing of their own invention. A new compound.

A spasm caught hold of him. It sidled across his diaphragm and skidded through his entrails. It shot up like a rocket to the back of his throat; it radiated into separate turnings. It converged again, and capsized through him, cart-wheeled into a land of near-lunacy, where Juno joined him. What they were laughing at they had no idea, which is more shattering than a world of wit.

Titus, turning over with a shout, flung out his hand and a moment later found it resting upon Juno's thigh, and suddenly his laughter left him, and hers also, so that she rose to her feet and when he had done so also they put their arms around one another and they wandered away to the doorway and up the stairs and along a corridor and into a room whose walls were filled with books and pictures, suffused with the light of the autumn sun.

There was a sense of peace in this remote room, with the long shafts of sunlight a-swim with motes. Without any form of untidiness, this library was strangely informal. There was the remoteness of a ship at sea – a removal from normal life about it, as though it had never been put together by carpenters and masons, but was a projection of Juno's mind.

'Why?' said Titus.

'Why what, my sweet?'

'This unexpected room?'

'You like it?'

'Of course, but why the secrecy?'

'Secrecy?'

'I never knew it existed.'

'It doesn't really, not when it's empty. It only comes to life when we are in it.'

'Too glib, my sweet.'

'Brute.'

'Yes; but don't look sad. Who lit the fire? And don't say the goblins, will you?'

'I will never mention goblins again. I lit it.'

'How sure you are of me!'

'Not really. I feel a nearness, that's all. Something holds us together. In spite of our ages. In spite of everything.'

'O, age doesn't matter,' said Titus, taking hold of her arms.

'Thank you,' said Juno. A wry little smile came to her lips and then withered away. Her sculptured head remained. The lovely room grew soft with evening light as Juno and Titus slid from their clothes, and, trembling, sank to the floor together and began to drown.

The firelight flickered and grew dim; danced and died again. Their bodies sent one shadow through the room. It swarmed across the carpet; climbed a wall of books, and shook with joy across the solemn ceiling.

FORTY-THREE

A LONG while later when the moon had risen and while Juno and Titus were asleep in each other's arms by the dying fire, Muzzlehatch, in roguish mood, having found no answer to his knocking, had climbed the chestnut tree whose high branches brushed the library window, and had, at great risk to life and limb, made a lateral leap in the dark and had landed on the window-sill of Juno's room, catching hold, as he did so, of the open frame.

More by luck than skill he had managed to keep his balance and in doing so had made no noise at all save for the swish of the returning leaves and a faint rattle of the window-sash.

For some while now, he had seen little of Juno. It is true that for a few days following the unforeseen twinge of heart, when he had watched her move away from him down the drive of her home, he had seen something of her; he had realized that the past can never be recaptured, even if he had wished it, and he turned his life away from her, as a man turns his back upon his own youth.

Why then this visitation late at night to his one-time love? Why was he standing on the sill, blocking out the moon and staring at the embers of the fire? Because he longed to talk. To talk like a torrent. To put into words the scores of strange ideas that had been clamouring for release; clamouring to set his tongue on fire. All day he had longed for it.

The morning, afternoon and evening had been spent in moving from cage to cage in his inordinate zoo.

But love them as he did, he was not with his animals tonight. He wanted something else. He wanted words, and in his wish, he realized as the sun went down, was the image of the only person in the wide world at the foot of whose bed he could sit; bolt upright, his head held very high, his jaw thrust forward, his face alight with an endless sequence of ideas. Who else but Juno?

He had thought he had had from her all that she had to give. They had grown tired of each other. They knew too much about each other; but now, quite unexpectedly, he needed her again. There were the stars to talk about, and the fishes of the sea. There were demons and there were the wisps of down that cling to the breasts of the seraphim. There were old clothes to ponder and terrible diseases. There were the flying missiles and the weird workings of the heart. There was *all* ... *all* to be chosen from. It was talking for its own mad, golden sake.

So Muzzlehatch, ignoring his ancient car, chose from his animals a great smelling llama; saddled it and cantered from his courtyard and away across the hills to Juno's house, singing as he went.

He had no wish to disturb the other sleepers, but, as there was no reply to the pebbles he flung up at her window he was forced to knock upon the door. As this bore no results, and as he had no intention of bashing his way in, or of prising a window open, he decided to climb the chestnut tree whose branches fingered the windows on the second floor. He tethered the llama to the foot of the chestnut and began to climb and eventually to make the jump.

Standing on the sill, with a thirty-foot drop below him, he continued to stare for some while at the glow of embers in the grate, before he climbed carefully at last over the sash and down into the darkness of the room.

He had been in this room before, several times, but long ago, and it seemed very different tonight. He knew that Juno's bedroom was immediately below and he started to make for the shadowy door.

He grinned to think what a surprise it would be for her. She was wonderful in the way she took surprises. She never *looked* surprised. She just looked happy to see you – almost as though she had been waiting for you. Waking out of a deep sleep she had often surprised Muzzlehatch by turning her head to him and smiling with almost unbearable sweetness before she had even opened her eyes. It was this that he wished to see again before the burning words came tumbling out.

It was when he was but a few steps from the door that he heard the first sound. With a reflex stemming from far earlier times his hand moved immediately to his hip pocket. But there was no revolver there and he brought back his empty hand to his side. He had swung in his tracks at the sound and he faced the last few vermilion embers in the grate.

What he had heard exactly he did not know, but it might have been a sigh. Or it might have been the leaves of the tree at the window except that the sound seemed to have come from near the fireplace.

And then it came again: this time it was a voice.

'Sweet love . . . O, sweet, sweet love . . .'

The words were so soft that had they not been whispered in the profound silence of the night they would never have been heard.

Muzzlehatch, motionless in the seemingly haunted room, waited for several long minutes, but there were no more words and no sound save for a long sigh like the sigh of the sea.

Moving silently forward and a little to the right Muzzlehatch became almost immediately aware of a blot of darkness more intense than the surrounding shades and he bent forward with his hands raised as though ready for action.

What kind of a creature would lie on the floor and whisper? What kind of monster was luring him forward?

And then there was a movement in the darkness by the dulling embers and then silence again and no more stirrings.

The moon broke free of the clouds and shone into the library, lighting up a wall of books – lighting up four pictures: lighting up a patch of carpet and the sleeping heads of Juno and the boy.

Walking with slow, silent strides to the window; climbing through; jumping for the chestnut tree; lowering himself branch by branch; slipping and bruising his knee; reaching the ground; untying the llama and riding home – all this was a dream. The reality was in himself – a dull and sombre pain.

FORTY-FOUR

THE days moved by in a long, sweet sequence of light and air. Each day an original thing. Yet behind all this there was something else. Something ominous. Juno had noticed it. Her lover was restless.

'Titus!'

His name sprang up the stairs to where he lay.

'Titus!'

Was it an echo, or a second cry? Whichever one it was it failed to wake him. There was no movement – save in his dream, where, tumbling from a tower, a skewbald beast fell headlong.

The voice was twelve treads closer.

'Titus! My sweet!'

His eyelid moved but the dream fought on for life, the blotched beast plunging and wheeling through sky after sky.

The voice had reached the landing –

'My mad one! My bad one! Where are you, poppet?'

Through the curtained windows of the bedroom, a flight of sunbeams, traversing the warm, dark air, forced a pool of light on the pillow. And beside that pool of light, in the ash-grey, linen shadow, his head lay, as a boulder might lie, or a heavy book might lie; motionless; undecipherable – a foreign language.

The voice was in the doorway; a cloud moved over the sun; and the sunbeams died from the pillow.

But the rich voice was still a part of his dream, though his eyes were open. It was blended with that rush of images and sounds which swarmed and expanded as the creature of his nightmare, falling at length into a lake of pale rainwater, vanished in a spurt of steam.

And as it sank, fathom by darkening fathom, a great host of heads, foreign yet familiar, arose from the deep and bobbed upon the water – and a hundred strange yet reminiscent voices began to call across the waves until from horizon to horizon he was filled with a great turbulence of sight and sound.

Then, suddenly, his eyes were wide open –

Where was he?

The empty darkness of the wall which faced him gave him no answer. He touched it with his hand.

Who was he? There was no knowing. He shut his eyes again. In a few moments there was no noise at all, and then the scuffling sound of a bird in the ivy outside the tall window recalled the world that was outside himself – something apart from this frightful zoneless nullity.

As he lifted himself up on one elbow, his memory returning in small waves, he could not know that a figure filled the doorway of his room – not so much in bulk as in the intensity of her presence – filled it as a tigress fills the opening of her cave.

And like a tigress she was striped: yellow and black: and because of the dark shadows behind her, only the yellow bands were visible, so that she appeared to be cut in pieces by the horizontal sweeps of a sword. And so she was like some demonstration of magic – a 'severed woman' – quite extraordinary and wonderful to see. But there was no one to see her, for Titus had his back to her.

And Titus could not see that her hat, plumed and piratical, sprouted as naturally from her head as the green fronds from the masthead of a date-palm.

She raised her hand to her breast. Not nervously; but with a kind of tense and tender purpose.

Propped upon his elbow with his back to her, his aloneness touched her sharply. It was wrong that he should be so single; so contained, so little merged into her own existence.

He was an island surrounded by deep water. There was no

98

isthmus leading to her bounty; no causeway to her continent of love.

There are times when the air that floats between mortals becomes, in its stillness and silence, as cruel as the edge of a scythe.

'O Titus! Titus, my darling!' she cried. 'What are you thinking of?'

He did not turn his head immediately, although at the first sound of her voice he was instantaneously aware of his surroundings. He knew that he was being watched – that Juno was very close indeed.

When at last he turned, she took a step towards the bed and she smiled with genuine pleasure to see his face. It was not a particularly striking face. With the best will in the world it could not be said that the brow or the chin or the nose or the cheek bones were *chiselled*. Rather, it seemed, the features of his head had, like the blurred irregularities of a boulder, been blunted by the wash of many tides. Youth and time were indissolubly fused.

She smiled to see the disarray of his brown hair and the lift of his eyebrows and the half-smile on his lips that seemed to have no more pigment in them than the warm sandy colour of his skin.

Only his eyes denied to his head the absolute simplicity of a monochrome. They were the colour of smoke.

'What a time of day to sleep!' said Juno, seating herself on the edge of the bed.

She took a mirror from her bag and bared her teeth for a moment as she scrutinized the line of her top lip, as though it were not hers but something which she might or might not purchase. It was perfectly drawn – a single sweep of carmine.

She put her mirror away and stretched her strong arms. The yellow stripes of her costume gleamed in a midday dusk.

'What a time to sleep!' she repeated. 'Were you *so* anxious to escape, my chicken-child? So determined to evade me that you sneak upstairs and waste a summer afternoon? But you know you are free in my house to do exactly what you please, don't you? To live as you please, how you please, where you please, you know this don't you, my spoiled one?'

99

'Yes,' said Titus, 'I remember you saying so.'

'And you will, won't you?'

'O yes, I will,' said Titus, 'I will.'

'Darling, you look so adorable.'

Titus took a deep breath. How sumptuous, how monumental and enormous she was as she sat there close to him,
her wonderful hat almost touching, so it seemed, the ceiling.
Her scent hung in the air between them. Her soft, yet strong
white hand lay on his knee – but something was wrong – or
lost; because his thoughts were of how his responses to her
magnetism grew vaguer and something had changed or was
changing with every passing day and he could only think of
how he longed to be alone again in this great tree-filled city of
the river – alone to wander listless through the sunbeams.

FORTY-FIVE

'You are a strange young man,' said Juno. 'I can't quite make
you out. Sometimes I wonder why I take so much trouble
over you, dear. But then of course I know, a moment later,
that I have no choice. Now have I? You touch me so, my cruel
one. You know it, don't you?'

'You say I do,' said Titus '– though *why* God only knows.'

'Fishing?' said Juno. 'Fishing again? Shall I tell you what I
mean?'

'Not now,' said Titus, *'please.'*

'Am I boring you? Just tell me if I am. Always tell me. And
if you are angry with me, don't hide it. Just shout at me. I will
understand. I want you to be yourself – only yourself. That's
how you flower best. O my mad one! My bad one!'

The plume of her hat swayed in the golden darkness. Her
proud black eyes shone wetly.

'You have done so much for me,' said Titus. 'Don't think I
am callous. But perhaps I must go. You give me too much. It
makes me ill.'

There was a sudden silence as though the house had stopped
breathing.

'Where could you go? You do not belong outside. You are my own, my discovery, my ... my ... can't you understand, I love you darling. I know I'm twice your – O Titus, I adore you. You are my mystery.'

Outside her window the sun shone fiercely on the honey-coloured stone of the tall house. The wall fell featurelessly down to a swift river.

On the other side of the house was the great quadrangle of prawn-coloured bricks and the hideous moss-covered statues of naked athletes and broken horses.

'There is nothing I can say,' said Titus.

'Of course there is nothing you can say. I understand. Some things can never be expressed. They lie too deep.'

She rose from beside him and turning away, tossed her proud handsome head. Her eyes were shut.

Something fell and struck the floor with a faint sound. It was her right earring, and she knew that the proud flinging gesture of her head had dislodged it, but she also knew that this was not the moment to pay any attention to so trivial a disturbance. Her eyes remained shut and her nostrils remained dilated.

Her hands came slowly together and then she lifted them to her up-flung chin.

'Titus,' she said, and her voice was little more than a whisper, a whisper less affected than one would expect to emerge from a lady in the stance she was adopting, with the plumes of her hat reaching down between her shoulder blades.

'Yes,' said Titus, 'What is it?'

'I am losing you, Titus. You are dissolving away. What is it I am doing wrong?'

At a bound Titus was off the bed and with his hands grasping her elbows had turned her about so that they faced one another in the warm dust of the high room. And then his heart grew sick, for he saw that her cheeks were wet and there in the wetness that wandered down her cheek a stain from her lashes appeared to float and thinly spread so that her heart became naked to him.

'Juno! Juno! This is too much for me. I cannot bear it.'

'There is no need to, Titus – please turn your head away.'

But Titus, taking no notice, held her closer than ever while her cheek-bones swam with tears. But her voice was steady.

'Leave me, Titus. I would rather be alone,' she said.

'I will never forget you,' said Titus, his hands trembling. 'But I must go. Our love is too intense. I am a coward. I cannot take it. I am selfish but not ungrateful. Forgive me, Juno – and say good-bye.'

But Juno, directly he released her, turned from him and, walking to the window, took out a mirror from her handbag.

'Good-bye,' said Titus.

Again there was no reply.

The blood rushed into the boy's head, and hardly knowing what he was doing he ran from the room and down the stairs and out into a winter afternoon.

FORTY-SIX

So Titus fled from Juno. Out of the garden and down the riverside road he kept on running. A sense of both shame and liberation filled him as he ran. Shame that he had deserted his mistress after all the kindness and love she had showered on him; and liberation in finding himself alone, with no one to weigh him down with affection.

But after a little while, his sense of aloneness was not altogether pleasurable. He was aware that something was missing. Something that he had half forgotten during his stay at Juno's house. It was nothing to do with Juno. It was a feeling that in leaving her he had once again to face the problem of his own identity. He was a part of something bigger than himself. He was a chip of stone, but where was the mountain from which it had broken away? He was the leaf but where was the tree? Where was his home? Where was his home?

Hardly knowing where he was going, he found after a long while that he was drawing near to that network of streets that surrounded Muzzlehatch's house and zoo; but before he reached that tortuous quarter he became aware of something else.

The road down which he stumbled was long and straight

with high, windowless walls. The lines of perspective converged not many degrees from the skyline.

There was no one ahead of him in spite of the length of the road, but it seemed that he was no longer alone. Something had joined him. He turned as he ran, and at first saw nothing, for he had focused his eyes upon the distance. Then all at once he halted, for he became aware of something floating beside him, at the height of his shoulders.

It was a sphere no bigger than the clenched fist of a child, and was composed of some transparent substance, so pellucid that it was only visible in certain lights, so that it seemed to come and go.

Dumbfounded, Titus drew aside from the centre of the road until he could feel the northern wall at his back. For a few moments he leaned there seeing no sign of the glassy sphere, until suddenly, there it was again, hovering above him.

This time as Titus watched it he could see that it was filled with glittering wires, an incredible filigree like frost on a pane; and then as a cloud moved over the sun, and a dim, sullen light filled the windowless street, the little hovering globe began to throb with a strange light like a glow-worm.

At first, Titus had been more amazed than frightened by the mobile globe which had appeared out of nowhere, and followed or seemed to follow every movement he made; but then fear began to make his legs feel weak, for he realized that he was being watched not by the globe itself, for the globe was only an agent, but by some remote informer who was at this very moment receiving messages. It was this that turned Titus's fear into anger, and he swung back his arms as though to strike the elusive thing which hovered like a bird of paradise.

At the moment that Titus raised his hand, the sun came out again, and the little glittering globe with its coloured entrails of exquisite wire slid out of range, and hovered again as though it were an eyeball watching every move.

Then, as though restless, it sped, revolving on its axis, to the far end of the street where it turned about immediately and sang its way back to where it hung again five feet from Titus, who, fishing his knuckle of flint from his pocket, slung it at the hovering ball, which broke in a cascade of dazzling splinters, and as it broke there was a kind of gasp, as though the globe had given up its silvery ghost ... as though it had a sentience of its own, or a state of perfection so acute that it entered, for the split second, the land of the living.

Leaving the broken thing behind him he began to run again. Fear had returned, and it was not until he found himself in Muzzlehatch's courtyard that he came to a halt.

FORTY-SEVEN

LONG before Titus could see Muzzlehatch he could hear him. That great rusty voice of his was enough to split the ear-drums of a deaf-mute. It thudded through the house, stamping itself upstairs and down again, in and out of half-deserted rooms and through the open windows so that the beasts and the birds lifted up their heads, or tilted them upon one side as though to savour the echoes.

Muzzlehatch lay stretched at length upon a low couch, and gazed directly down through the lower panes of a wide french window on the third floor. It gave him an unimpeded view of the long line of cages below him, where his animals lay drowsing in the pale sunlight.

This was a favourite room and a favourite view of his. On the floor at his side were books and bottles. His small ape sat at the far end of the couch. It had wrapped itself up in a piece of cloth and gazed sadly at its master, who had only a few moments ago been mouthing a black dirge of his own concoction.

Suddenly the small ape sprang to its feet and swung its long arms to and fro in a strangely jointless way, for it had heard a foot on the stairs two floors beneath.

Muzzlehatch lifted himself on to one elbow and listened. At first he could hear nothing, but then he also became aware of footsteps.

At last the door opened and an old bearded servant put his head around the corner.

'Well, well,' said Muzzlehatch. 'By the grey fibres of the

xadnos tree, you look splendid, my friend. Your beard has never looked more authentic. What do you want?'

'There is a young man here sir, who would like to see you.'

'Really? What appallingly low taste. That can only be young Titus.'

'Yes, it's me,' said Titus, taking a step into the room. 'Can I come in?'

'Of course you can, sweet rebus. Should I be getting to my palsied feet? What with you in a suit like migraine, and a spotted tie, and co-respondent shoes, you humble me. But swish as a willow-switch you look indeed! There's been some scissor flashing, not a doubt.'

'Can I sit down?'

'Sit down, of course you can. The whole floor is yours. Now then,' muttered Muzzlehatch, as the ape leapt upon his shoulder, 'mind my bloody eyes, boy, I'll be needing them later,' and then, turning to Titus –

'Well, what do you want?' he said.

'I want to talk,' said Titus.

'What about, boy?'

Titus looked up. The huge, craggy head was tilted on one side. The light coming through the window surrounded it with a kind of frosty nimbus. Remote and baleful, it put Titus in mind of the inordinate moon with its pits and craters. It was a domain of leather, rock and bone.

'What about, boy?' he said again.

'First of all, my fear,' said Titus. 'Believe me, sir, I didn't like it.'

'What are you talking about?'

'I am afraid of the globe. It followed me until I broke it. And when I broke it, it sighed. And I forgot my flint. And without my flint I am lost ... even more lost than before. For I have nothing else to prove where I come from, or that I ever had a native land. And the proof of it is only proof for me. It is no proof of anything to anyone but me. I have nothing to hold in my hand. Nothing to convince myself that it is not a dream. Nothing to prove my actuality. Nothing to prove that we are talking together here, in this room of yours. Nothing to prove my hands, nothing to prove my voice. And the globe! That intellectual globe! Why was it following me? What did it want? Was it spying on me? Is it magic, or is it science? Will they know who broke it? Will they be after me?'

'Have a brandy,' said Muzzlehatch.

Titus nodded his head.

'Have you seen them, Mr Muzzlehatch? What are they?'

'Just toys, boy, just toys. They can be simple as an infant's rattle, or complex as the brain of man. Toys, toys, toys, to be played with. As for the one you chose to smash, number LKZoo572 ARG 39 576 Aij9843K2532 if I remember rightly, I have already read about it and how it is reputed to be almost human. Not quite, but *almost*. So *THAT* is what has happened? You have broken something quite hideously efficient. You have blasphemed against the spirit of the age. You have shattered the very spear-head of advancement. Having committed this reactionary crime, you come to me. Me! This being so, let me peer out of the window. It is always well to be watchful. These globes have origins. Somewhere or other there's a backroom boy, his soul working in the primordial dark of a diseased yet sixty horse-power brain.'

'There's something else, Mr Muzzlehatch.'

'I'm sure there is. In fact there is everything else.'

'You belittle me,' said Titus, turning suddenly upon him, 'by your way of talking. It is serious to me.'

'Everything is serious or not according to the colour of one's brain.'

'My brain is black,' said Titus, 'if that's a colour.'

'Well? Spit it out. The core of it.'

'I have deserted Juno.'

'Deserted her?'

'Yes.'

'It had to happen. She is too good for males.'

'I thought you would hate me.'

'Hate you? Why?'

'Well, sir, wasn't she your ... your ...'

'She was my everything. But like the damned creature that I inescapably am, I swapped her for the freedom of my limbs. For solitude which I eat as though it were food. And if you like, for animals. I have erred. Why? Because I long for her and am too proud to admit it. So she slipped away from me like a ship on the ebb tide.'

'I loved her too,' said Titus: 'If you can believe it.'

'To be sure you did, my pretty cutlet. And you still do. But you are young and prickly: passionate and callow: so you deserted her.'

'Oh God!' said Titus. 'Talk sir, with fewer words. I am sick of language.'

'I will try to,' said Muzzlehatch. 'Habits are hard to break.'

'Oh, sir, have I hurt your feelings?'

Muzzlehatch turned away and stared through the window. Almost immediately below him, he could see, through the bars of a domed roof, a family of leopards.

'Hurt my feelings! Ha ha! Ha ha! I am a kind of crocodile on end. I have no feelings. As for you. Get on with life. Eat it up. Travel. Make journeys in your mind. Make journeys on your feet. To prison with you in a filthy garb! To glory with you in a golden car! Revel in loneliness. This is only a city. This is no place to halt.'

Muzzlehatch was still turned away.

'What of the castle that you talk about – that crepuscular myth? Would you return after so short a journey? No, you must go on. Juno is part of your journey. So am I. Wade on, child. Before you lie the hills, and their reflections. Listen! Did you hear that?'

'What?' said Titus.

Muzzlehatch did not trouble to answer as he raised himself on one elbow, and peered out of the window.

There away to the east, he saw a column of scientists marching, and almost at the same moment the beasts of the zoo began to lift their heads, and stare all in the same direction.

'What is it?' said Titus.

Muzzlehatch again took no notice, but this time Titus did not wait for an answer, but moved to the window, and stared down, with Muzzlehatch, cheek by cheek, at the panorama spread out below him.

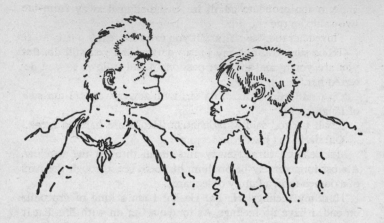

Then came the music: the sound of trumpets as from another world: the distant throbbing of the drums; and then, shattering the distance, the raw immoderate yell of a lion.

'They are after us,' said Muzzlehatch. 'They are after our guts.'

'Why?' said Titus. 'What have I done?'

'You have only destroyed a miracle,' said Muzzlehatch. 'Who knows how pregnant with possibilities that globe could be? Why, you dunderhead, a thing like that could wipe out half the world. Now, they'll have to start again. You were observed. They were on their toes. Perhaps they found your flint. Perhaps they have seen us together. Perhaps this ... perhaps that. One thing is certain. You must disappear. Come here.'

Titus frowned, and then straightened himself. Then he took a step towards the big man.

'Have you heard of the Under-River?' asked Muzzlehatch.

Titus shook his head.

'This badge will take you there.' Muzzlehatch folded back his cuff, and tore away a bit of fabric from the lining. On the small cloth badge was printed the sign

'What is that supposed to mean?' said Titus.

'Keep quiet. Time is on the slide. The drums are twice as loud. Listen.'

'I can hear them. What do they want? What about your . . .?'

'My animals? Let them but try to touch them. I'll loose the white gorilla on the sods. Put away the badge, my dear. Never lose it. It will take you down.'

'Down?' said Titus.

'Down. Down into an order of darkness. Waste no time.'

'I don't understand,' said Titus.

'This is no time for comprehension. This is a great moment for the legs.'

Then suddenly a screaming of monkeys filled the room, and even Muzzlehatch with his stentorian throat was forced to raise his voice to a shout.

'Down the stairs with you, and into the wine cellars. Turn left immediately at the foot of the flight, and mind the nails on the hand-rail. Left again, and you will see ahead of you, dimly, a tunnel, vaulted and hung with filthy webs as thick as blankets. Press on for an hour at least. Go carefully. Beware of the ground at your feet. It is littered with the relics of another age. There is a stillness down there that is not to be dwelt upon. Here, cram these in your pockets.'

Muzzlehatch strode across the room, and pulling open a drawer in an old cabinet he took a fistful of candles.

'Where are we? Ah yes. Listen. By now you will be under the city at the northern end, and the darkness will be intense. The walls of the tunnel will be closing in. There will not be much room above your head. You will have to move doubled up. Easier for you than for me. Are you listening? If not, I'll blast you, child. This is no game.'

'O sir,' said Titus, 'that is why I cannot keep still. Listen to the trumpets! Listen to the beasts!'

'Listen to me instead! You have your candle raised; but in place of hollow darkness you have before you a gate. At the foot of the gate is a black dish, upside down. Underneath it you will find a key. It may not be the key to your miserable life, but it will open the gate for you. Once through, and you have before you a long, narrow gradient that stretches at average pace for forty minutes. If you whisper the world sighs and sighs again. If you shout the earth reverberates.'

'Oh sir,' said Titus, 'don't be poetic, I can't bear it. The zoo is going mad. And the scientists . . . the scientists . . .'

'Fugger the scientists!' said Muzzlehatch. 'Now listen like a fox. I said a gradient. I said echoes. But now another thing. The sound of water . . .'

'Water,' said Titus, 'I'm damned if I'll drown.'

'Pull your miserable self together, Lord Titus Groan. You will come, inevitably, to where suddenly, on turning a corner, there is a noise above you, like distant thunder, for you will be under the river itself . . . the same river that brought you to the city months ago. Ahead of you will spread a half-lit field of flagstones, at the far end of which you will see the glow of a green lantern. This lantern is set upon a table. Seated at this table, his face reflecting the light, you will see a man. Show him the badge I have given you. He will scrutinize it through a glass, then look up at you with an eye as yellow as lemon peel, whistle softly through a gap in his teeth until a child comes trotting through the shadows and beckons you to follow to the north.'

FORTY-EIGHT

For all the noise of water overhead, there was silence also. For all the murk there were the shreds of light. For all the jostling and squalor, there were also the great spaces and a profound withdrawal.

Long fleets of tables were like rafts with legs, or like a market, for there were figures seated at these tables with crates and sacks before them or at their sides or heaped together upon the damp ground . . . a sodden and pathetic salvage, telling of other days in other lands. Days when hope's bubble, bobbing in their breasts, forgot, or had not heard of dissolution. Days of bravado. Gold days and green days. Days half forgotten. Days with a dew upon them. And here they were, the hundreds of them, at their stalls, awaiting, or so it seemed, the hour that never came, the hour for the market to open and the bells to ring. But there was no merchandise. Nothing to buy or sell. What they had left was what they meant to keep. There was also something of a dreadful ward, for throughout the dripping halls that led in all directions there were beds and berths of every description, pallets, litters and mattresses of straw.

But there were no doctors and there was no authority: and the sick were free to leap among the shadows and soar with their own fever. And the hale were free to spend their days in bed, curled up like cats, or at full stretch, rigid as men in armour.

A world of sound and silence stitched together. A habitation under the earth ... under the river: a kingdom of the outcasts; the fugitives; the failures; the mendicants; the plotters; a secret world with a roof that leaked eternally, so that wide skirts of water reflected the beds and the tables, and the denizens who leaned against pit-props or pillars, and who long ago had been forced to form themselves into ragged groups so that it seemed that the dark scene was seismic and had thrown up islands of wood and iron. All was reflected here in the dim glazes. If a hand moved, or a head was flung back, or if anyone stumbled the reflection stumbled with him, or gestured in the depths of the sheen. It did not seem to brighten but rather to intensify the darkness that there were hundreds of lamps and that many of them were reflected in the 'lakes'. It was so vast a district that there were of necessity deep swaths of darkness hanging beyond reach of brand or lantern, dire volumes at whose centres the air was thick with dark, and smelt of desolation. The candles guttered even at the verge of these deadly pockets, guttered and failed as though from a failure of the candle's nerve.

A wilderness of tables, beds and benches. The stoves and curious ranges. The figures moving by at various levels, with various distinctness, some silhouetted, sharp and edged like insects, some pale and luminous against the gloom. And the 'lakes' changing their very nature: now ankle-deep, the clear water showing the pocked and cheesy bricks beneath and then, a moment later, at a shift of the head, revealing a world in so profound and so meticulous an inversion as to swallow up the eye that gazed upon it and drag it down, out-fathoming invention.

III

And overhead the eternal roar of the river: a voice, a turmoil, a lunatic wrestling of waters, whose muffled reverberations were a background to all that ever happened in the Under-River.

To those ignorant of extreme poverty and of its degradations; of pursuit and the attendant horrors; of the crazed extremes of love and hate; for those ignorant of such, there was no cause to suffer such a place. It was enough for the great city to know and to have heard of it by echo or by rumour and to maintain a tacit silence as dreadful as it was accepted. Whether it was through shame or fear or a determination to ignore, or even to disbelieve what they knew to be true, it was, for whatever reason, an unheard of thing for the outrageous place to be mentioned by those who, being less desperate, were able to live out their lives in either of the two great cities that faced one another across the river.

And so the halls and tunnels of the cold sub-river life where it throbbed beneath the angry water were, to the populace on the opposing banks, in the nature of a bad dream, both too bizarre to be taken seriously, yet horrid enough to speculate upon, only to recoil, only to speculate again, and recoil again, and tear the clinging cobwebs from the brain.

What were the thoughts of those who lived and slept in the fastness beneath the water? Were these thieves and broken poets, these fugitives affected by some stigma; were they jealous or afraid of the world? How had they all foregathered in this crepuscular region? What had they so much in common that they needed each other's presences? Nothing but hope. Hope like a wavering marsh-light: hope like a pale sun: hope like a floating leaf.

All at once and very close a harsh and unexpected noise of metal being sharpened was in horrid contrast to the soft drip . . . drip . . . drip . . . of water from above.

Far away there was an angry sound that broke into fragments that echoed for a while in hollow dungeons.

Somewhere, someone was adjusting the shutter of a lantern so that for a little while a shaft of light played erratically to and fro across the darkness, picking out groups of figures at varying distances, groups like hummocks of varying sizes, some pyramidal, some irregular, each with a life and shape of its own.

Before the door of the lantern was finally fastened the thread of light had come to rest upon a group of them. For a long while they had been silent; beneath the light the colour of a bruise. It hung above them, casting the kind of glow that suggested crime. Even the kindest smile appeared ghastly.

FORTY-NINE

MR CRABCALF lay upon a trestle bed, his brow creased with hours of semi-thought: his flat and speculative face was directed at the dark yet glistening ceiling where the moisture collected and hung in beads that grew and grew like fruit, and fell, when water-ripe, to the ground.

What did he see among the overhead shadows? Some, in his place, must surely have seen battle or the great jaws of carnivores or landscapes of infinite mystery and invention complete with bridges and deep chasms, forests and craters. But Crabcalf saw none of these. He saw nothing in the shadows but great profiles of himself, one after the other.

He lay quietly, his arms outside the thick red blanket that covered him. To his left sat Slingshott on the edge of a crate, his knees drawn up to his chin, his long jaw resting on his kneecap. He wore a woollen cap, and like Mr Crabcalf had lapsed for the while into silence.

At the foot of the bed, crouched like a condor over its young, was Carrow cooking a meal over a stove, and stirring what looked like a mass of horrible green fibre in a wide-necked pot. As he stirred he whistled between his teeth. The sound of this meditative occupation could be heard for a minute or two, echoing faintly in far quarters before a hundred other sounds slid back to hush it.

Mr Crabcalf was propped up, not against pillows or a bolster of straw, but by books; and every book was the same book with its dark grey spine. There at his back, banked up like a wall of bricks, were the so-called 'remainders' of an epic, long

113

ago written, long ago forgotten, except by its author, for his lifework lay at his shoulder blades.

Out of the five hundred copies printed thirty years ago by a publisher long since bankrupt, only twelve copies had been sold.

Around his bed, three hundred identical volumes were erected ... like walls or ramparts, protecting him from – what? There was also a cache beneath the bed that gathered dust and silver-fish.

He lay with his past beside him, beneath him, and at his head: his past, five hundred times repeated, covered with dust and silver-fish. His head, like Jacob's on the famous stone, rested against the volumes of lost breath. The ladder from his miserable bed reached up to heaven. But there were no angels.

FIFTY

'WHAT on earth are you doing?' said Crabcalf in a deep voice (a voice so very much more impressive than anything it ever had to say). 'I have seen some pretty revolting things in my time, but the meal that you are preparing, Mr Carrow, is the most nauseating affair that I ever remember.'

Mr Carrow hardly troubled to look up. It was all part of the day. There would have been something missing if Crabcalf had forgotten to insult his crouching and angular friend, who went on stirring the contents of a copper bowl.

'How many of us have you killed in your time, I wonder?' muttered Crabcalf, allowing his head to fall back on the pillow of books, so that a little whiff of dust rose into the lamplight, new heavens being formed, new constellations, as the motes wavered.

'Eh? Eh? How many have you sent to their deathbeds through hapless poisoning?'

Even Crabcalf was apt to become tired of his own heavy banter, and he shut his eyes. Carrow as usual made no answer. But Crabcalf was content. Even more than most he felt a great need for companionship, and he spoke only to prove to himself that his friendships were real.

Carrow knew all about this, and from time to time he turned his hawk-like features towards the one-time poet and lifted the dry corner of his lipless mouth in a dry smile. This arid salutation meant much to Crabcalf. It was part of the day.

'O, Carrow,' murmured the recumbent Crabcalf, 'your desiccation is like juice to me. I love you better than a ship's biscuit. You have no green emotions. You are dry, my dear Carrow: so dry, you pucker me. Never desert me, old friend.'

Carrow turned his eyes to the bed, but never ceased in his stirring of the grey broth.

'You are talkative today,' he said. 'Don't overdo it.'

The third of the trio, Slingshott, rose to his feet.

'I don't know about you,' he said, addressing the space half-way between Carrow and Crabcalf, 'but speaking for myself I'm hand in hand with grief.'

'You always are,' said Crabcalf. 'At this time of day. And so am I. It is the eternal problem. Is one to be hungry, or is one to eat old Carrow's gruel?'

'No, no, I'm not talking about food,' said Slingshott. 'It's worse than that. You see, I lost my wife. I left her behind. *Was* I wrong?' He lifted his face to the dripping ceiling. No one answered.

'When I escaped from the merciless mines,' he said, folding his arms. 'When the days and the nights were salt, and my lips were cracked and split with it, and the taste of that vile chemical was like knives in my mouth and a white death more terrible than any darkness of the spirit ... when ... I escaped I swore ...'

'That whatever happened you would never again complain of anything whatever, for nothing could be as terrible as the mines,' said Crabcalf.

'Why, how do you know all this? Who has been ...?'

'We have all heard it many times before. You tell us too often,' said Carrow.

'It is always in my head, and I forget.'

'But you escaped. Why fret about your deliverance?'

'I am so happy that they cannot take me. O never let them take me to the salt mines. There was a time when I collected eggs: and butterflies ... and moths ...'

'I am growing hungry,' said Crabcalf.

'I used to dread the nights I spent alone: but after a while, when for various reasons I was forced to quit the house, and had to spend my evenings with the others, I looked back upon those solitary evenings as times of excitement. It has always been my longing to be alone again and drink the silence.'

'I wouldn't care to live *alone* in this place,' said Crabcalf.

'It's not a nice place, that is very true,' said Slingshott, 'but I have been living here for twelve years and it is my only home.'

'Home,' said Carrow. 'What does that mean? I have heard the word somewhere. Wait . . . it is coming back. . . .' He had ceased to stir the bowl. 'Yes, it is coming back. . . .' (His voice was sharp and crisp.)

'Well, let's have it then,' said Crabcalf.

'I'll tell you,' said Carrow. 'Home is a room dappled with firelight: there are pictures and books. And when the rain sighs, and the acorns fall, there are patterns of leaves against the drawn curtains. Home is where I was safe. Home is what I fled from. Who mentioned home? Who mentioned home?'

The tight-lipped Carrow, who prided himself on his control and who loathed emotionalism, sprang to his feet in a fury of self-disgust, and stumbling away, upset the grey soup so that it spread itself sluggishly beneath Crabcalf's bed.

This disturbance caused two passers-by to stop and stare. They had heard Carrow's outburst.

One of the two men cocked his scorbutic head on one side like a bird and then nudged his companion with such zest as to fracture one of the smaller ribs.

'You have hurt me bad, you have,' growled his comrade.

'Forget it!' said his irritating friend. He turned his gaze to where Crabcalf and Slingshott sat with frowns like birds' nests on their brows.

Slingshott got to his feet and took a few paces towards the newcomers. Then he lifted his face to the dark ceiling.

'When I escaped from the merciless mines,' he said, 'when the days and the nights were salt, and my lips were cracked and split with it and the taste of that damn chemical . . .'

'Yes, old man, we know all about that,' said Crabcalf. 'Sit

down and keep quiet. Now let me ask these two gentlemen whether they are interested in literature.'

The taller of the two, a long-limbed, crop-headed man with a grass-green handkerchief, rose to tiptoe.

'Interested!' he cried. 'I'm practically literature myself. But surely you know that? After all, my family is not exactly devoid of lustre. We are patrons, as you know, of the arts, and have been so for hundreds of years. In fact, it is doubtful whether the literature of our time could come into being without the inspired guidance of the Foux-Foux family. Think of the great works that would never have been born without the patronage of my grandfather. Think of the works of Morzch in general, and of his masterpiece "Pssss" in particular: and think how my mother nursed him back out of chaos to the limpid vision of . . .'

'Oh, shut up,' said a voice. 'You and your family make me sick.'

It was Crabcalf who, surrounded and walled in by the hundreds of unsold copies of his ill-fated novel, felt that he if anyone should be the judge not only of literature, but of all that went on behind the sordid scenes.

'Foux-Foux indeed,' he continued. 'Why you and your family are nothing but jackals of art.'

'Well really,' said Foux-Foux. 'That's hardly fair, you know. We cannot all be creative, but the Foux-Foux family have always . . .'

'Who's your friend?' said Crabcalf, interrupting. 'Is he a jackal too? Never mind. Carrow has flown. He helped me in his day to kill emotion. But now he vanishes on an up-draught of the stuff. He has failed me. I need a cynic for a friend, old man. A cynic to steady me. Sit down, indeed. Is your friend a Foux-Foux too? I soften, as you see. I can't make enemies: not for long. It is only when I look at my books that I get angry. After all, that's where my heart's blood is. But who reads them? Who cares about them? Answer me that!'

Slingshott rose to his feet, as though it were he who had been addressed.

'I left my wife behind,' he said. 'On the fringe of the ice-cap. Did I do right?' He brought his heel down to the wet brick floor with a click and a spurt of spray.

But as no one was watching him his posture faded out. He turned and addressed the author.

'Shall I continue with the broth?' he said.

'Yes, if that's what it is,' said Crabcalf. 'By all means do. As for you, gentlemen, join us ... eat with us ... suffer acute bellyache with us ... and then, if needs be, die with us as friends.'

FIFTY-ONE

AT that very moment, with Crabcalf about to expand ... Carrow gone ... Slingshott about to dilate upon the salt mines, and Foux-Foux on the point of withdrawing a long eating-knife from his belt, and his friend about to stir what was left of the sluggish grey fibre in the pot ... at that very moment there was a pause, a silence, and in the pregnant heart of that silence another sound could be heard, the quick muffled fly-away thudding of hounds' feet.

The sound came from the black and hollow land that spread to the south in a honeycomb of under-river masonry: the sound grew louder.

'Here they come again,' said Crabcalf. 'What dandy boys they are, and no mistake.'

The others made no reply, but remained motionless, waiting for the appearance of the hounds.

'It is later than I thought,' said Foux-Foux ... 'but look, look...'

But there was nothing to see. It was only the shifting of a long shadow and a glimmer across the saturated bricks. The hounds were still a league or more away.

Why were these men with their heads cocked upon one side so anxious to see the entrance of the hounds? Why were they so intent?

It was always like this in the Under-River, for the days and nights could be so unbearably monotonous: so long: so featureless, that whenever anything really happened, even when it was expected, the darkness appeared to be momentarily pierced, as though by a thought in a dead skull, and the most trivial happening took on prodigious proportions.

But now, as other figures emerged out of the semi-darkness, there appeared out of the shadowy south seven loping hounds. They were exceptionally lean, their ribs showing, but were by no means ill. Their heads were held high as though to remind the world of a proud lineage, and their teeth were bared as a reminder of something less noble. Their tongues lolled out of the sides of their mouths. Their skulls were chiselled. They panted as they passed: their nostrils dilated; their eyes shone. There were seven of them, and now they were gone, even the sound of them, and the night welled up again.

Where are they now, those hot-breath'd lopers? They have veered away through colonnades a-drip. They have reached a lake four inches deep and a mile across where their feet splash in the shallow, sombre water. The spray surrounds them as they gallop in a pack so tight, that it seems they are one creature.

On the far side of the broad-skirted water-sheen the floor rose a little, and the ground was comparatively dry. Here, pranked across the lamp-lit slope were small communities similar to the group that had for its recumbent centre the bedridden Crabcalf. Similar, but different, for in every head are disparate dreams.

And so, at speed, threading the groups lit here and there with lamps, the dog-pack all of a sudden and seemingly with no warning doubled its speed until it reached a district where there was more light than is common beneath the river. Scores of lamps hung from nails in the great props or stood on ledge or shelf, and it was beneath a circle of these that the hounds drew up and lifted their heads to the dripping ceiling, and gave one single simultaneous howl. At the sound of this a tall spare man with a minute fleshless head, like the head of a bird, came out of the lamp-stained gloom, his white apron stained with blood, for in his arms he held seven hunks of crimson horse-flesh. As he approached them, the hounds quivered.

But he did not give them to the dogs at once. He lifted the dripping things above his head, where they shone with a ghostly, almost luminous red. Then forming his mouth into a perfect circle he hooted, and in the silence the echoes replied, and it was at the sound of the fourth echo that he tossed the crimson steaks high into the air. The hounds, taking their turn, one after the other, leaped at the falling meat, gripped it between their teeth, and then, turning in their tracks, galloped, with their heads held high, across the great sheet of water where they disappeared into the wet darkness.

The man with the bird-like head wiped his hand on his apron'd hips and plunged his long arms up to the elbows in a tub of tepid water. Beyond the tub, twenty feet to the west was a wall, covered with rank ferns, and in this wall was an arched doorway. On the other side of this door was a room lit by six lamps.

FIFTY-TWO

HERE, in this fern-hung chamber, set about with cracked and broken mirrors to reflect the light of the lamps, are a group of characters. Some lie reclined upon mildewed couches: some sit upright on wickerwork chairs: some are gathered about a central table.

They are talking in a desultory way, but when they hear the bird-headed man begin his hooting, the sound of their conversation subsides. They have heard it a thousand times and are blunted to the strangeness of it, yet they listen as though every time were the first.

At one end of a rotting couch, with his great bearded chin propped up by knuckly fists, sits an ancient man. At the other end sits his equally ancient wife with her feet tucked up beneath her. The three of them (man, wife, and couch) present a picture of venerable decrepitude.

The ancient man sits very still, occasionally lifting his hand and staring at something that is crawling across his wrist.

His wife is busier than this, for here, there and everywhere run endless threads of coloured wool, until it seems she is festooned with it. The old lady, whose eyes are sore and red, has long since given up any idea of knitting but spends her time in trying to disentangle the knots in the wool. There were days, long ago, when she knew what she was making, and yet earlier days, when she was actually known by the clickety-clack of her needles. They had been a part, a tiny part of the Under-River.

But not so, now. Entanglement, for her, is everything. Occasionally she looks up and catches her husband's eye, and they exchange smiles, pathetically sweet. Her little mouth moves, as though it is forming a word; but it is no word but a movement of her withered lips. For his part, there is no seeing through the long, hairy fog of his beard; no mouth is locatable . . . but all his love finds outlet through his eyes. He takes no part in the disentangling, knowing that this is her only joy, and that the knots and interweavings must outlive her.

But tonight, at the sound of the hooting she lifts her head from her work.

'Dear Jonah,' she says. 'Are you there?'

'Of course I am, my love. What is it?' says the old man.

'My mind was roving back to a time . . . a time . . . almost before I . . . almost as though . . . what was it I used to do? I can't remember . . . I can't remember at all . . .'

'To be sure, my squirrel; it was a long while ago.'

'One thing I *do* remember, Jonah, dear, though whether we were together . . . oh but we *must* have been. For we ran away, didn't we, and floated like two feathers from our foes? How beautiful we were, Jonah, my own, and you rode with me beside you into the forest . . . are you listening, dearest?'

'Of course, of course . . .'

'You were my prince.'

'Yes, my little squirrel, that is so.'

'I am tired, Jonah . . . tired.'

'Lean back, my dear.' He tries to sit forward so that he can touch her, but is forced to desist, for the movement has brought with it a jab of pain.

One of the four men, who are playing cards on the marble table, turns round at the sound of a little gasp, but cannot make out where the sound comes from. He turns back to a perusal of his hand. Another to have heard the sound, is an all-but-naked infant who crawls towards the rotting couple dragging its left

leg after it, as though it were some kind of dead and worth-
less attachment.

When the infant reaches the couch where the old couple sit
silent again, it stares at them in turn with a concentration that
would have been embarrassing in a grown-up. There it heaves
itself up and keeps its balance by grasping the edge of the
couch. In the eyes of the ragged infant there seems to be an
innocence quite moving to behold. A final innocence that
has survived in spite of a world of evil.

Or was it, as some might think, mere emptiness? A sky-blue
vacancy? Would it be too cynical to believe that the little child
was without a thought in its head and without a flicker of light
in its soul? For otherwise why should the infant turn on, at the
most sentimental moment, his tiny waterworks, and flick an
arc of gold across the gloom?

Having piddled with an incongruous mixture of nonchalance
and solemnity the infant catches sight of a spoon shining in the
shadows beneath the couch and dropping to his little naked
haunches he rights himself and crawls in search of treasure. He
is the essence of purpose. His minute appendage is forgotten:
it dangles like a slug. He has lost interest in it. The spoon is *all*.

But the dangler's done its worst . . . in all innocence, and in
all ignorance, for it has saturated a phalanx of warrior ants who,
little guessing that a cloudburst was imminent, were making
their way across difficult country.

FIFTY-THREE

THE child, and now the father and mother, refugees from
the Iron Coast, sit opposite one another at the table. The father
plays his cards with a mere fraction of his brain. The rest of
it, a scythe-like instrument, is far away in realms of white
equations.

His wife, a heavy-jaw'd woman, scowls at him out of habit.
As usual he has won enough token money to correspond to a
dozen fortunes. But there is no money down here in the
Under-River, nor anywhere else for them, as far as she can see.

Everything has gone wrong. Her uncle had been a general long ago; and her brother had been presented to a duke. But what was that to them now? They were real men. But her husband was only a brain. They should never have tried to escape from the Iron Coast. They should never have married, and as for their son ... he would have been better unborn. She turns her heavy-jaw-boned head to her husband. How aloof he seems: how sexless!

She rises to her feet. 'Are you a man?' she shouts.

'Delicious query!' cries a voice, like a cracked bell. ' "Are you a man?" she says. What fun! What roguery! Well, Mr Zed? Are you?'

The brilliant, articulate, white-eyelashed Mr Zed turns his eyes to his wife and sees nothing but $Tx\frac{1}{4} \ p\frac{3}{4} = \frac{1}{2}-prx\frac{1}{4}$ (inverted). Then he turns them on the willowy man with the cracked voice, and he realizes all in an instant that his last three years of constructive thought have been wasted. His premises have failed him. He had been assuming that Space was intrinsically modelled.

Realizing that this gentleman is way over the horizon, Crack-Bell tosses his hair from his forehead, laughs like a carillon, gesticulates freely to his partners across the table, in such a way as to say 'O, isn't it marvellous?'

But his partner, the sober Carter sees nothing marvellous about it, and leans back in his chair with his eyes half-closed. He is a massive, thoughtful man, not given to extravagance either in thought or deed. He keeps his partner under observation, for Crack-Bell is apt to become too much of a good thing.

Yes, Crack-Bell is happy. Life to him is a case of 'now' and nothing but 'now'. He forgets the past as soon as it has happened and he ignores the whole concept of a future. But he is full of the sliding moment. He has a habit of shaking his head, not because he disagrees with anything, but through the sheer spice of living. He tosses it to and fro, and sends the locks cavorting.

'He's a card he is, that husband of yours,' cries Crack-Bell leaning across the table and tapping Mrs Zed on her freckle-mottled wrist. 'He's an undeniable one, eh? Eh? Eh? But oh so *dark.* . . . Why don't he laugh and play?'

'I hate men,' says Mrs Zed. 'You included.'

FIFTY-FOUR

'JONAH dear, are you all right?' said the old, old lady.

'Of course I am. What is it squirrel?' The old man smoothed his beard.

'I must have dropped off to sleep.'

'I wondered ... I wondered ...'

'I dreamed a dream,' said the old lady.

'What was it about?'

'I don't remember ... something about the sun.'

'The sun?'

'The great round sun that warmed us long ago.'

'Yes, I remember it.'

'And the rays of it? The long, sweet rays ...'

'Where were we then ...?'

'Somewhere in the south of the world.'

The old lady pursed her lips. Her eyes were very tired. Her hands went on and on with their disentangling of the wool, and the old man watched her as though she were of all things the most lovely.

FIFTY-FIVE

'HA, ha, ha, ha, ha, ha, ha, ha, ha, ha, ha, ha!' cried Crack-Bell, throwing his head back and laughing like crockery.

'Steady on,' said Sober-Carter, the heavy man. 'You would do well to keep quiet. Life may be hilarious to you, but They are on your trail.'

'But I haven't got a trail,' said Crack-Bell. 'It petered out long ago. Don't let's think about it. I am happy in half-light. I have always loved the damp. I can't help it. It suits me. Ha, ha!'

'That laugh of yours,' said Carter, 'will be the death of you, one day.'

'Not it,' said Crack-Bell. 'I'm as safe down here as a fig in a

fog. To hell with the fourth dimension. It's *now* that matters!'
He tossed a mop of hair out of his eyes and, turning on a gay
heel he pointed to a figure in the shades. 'Look at her,' he cried,
'why don't she move? Why don't she laugh and sing?'

The shadow was a girl. She stood motionless. Her huge black
eyes suggested illness. A man came through the door. Looking
to neither right nor left he made for the dark girl where she
stood.

She gazed expressionlessly over the shoulder of the man
as he approached her with long, spindly strides. It seemed as
though, knowing his features as she did, his high flinty cheekbones, his pale skin, his glinting eyes, his cleft chin, she saw no
reason to focus her sight. When he reached her, he stood aggressively, like a mantis, his knee bent a little, his long-fingered
hands clasped together in a bunch of bones.

'How much longer?' she said.

'Soon. Soon.'

'Soon? What sort of word is that? Soon! Ten hours? Ten
days? Ten years? Did you find the tunnel?'

Veil turned his eyes from her, and rested them for a moment
on each of the others in turn.

'What did you find?' repeated the girl, still looking over his
shoulder.

'Quiet, curse you!' said the man Veil, raising his arm.

The Black Rose stood unflinchingly upright, but with all the
coil and re-coil of the flesh gone out of her. She had been
through too much, and all resilience had gone. She stood there,
upright but broken. Three revolutions had rocked over her. She
had heard the screaming. Sometimes she did not know whether
it was herself or someone else who screamed. The cry of children who have lost their mother.

One night they took her naked from her bed. They shot her
lover. They left him in a pool of blood. They took her to a
prison camp, and then her beauty began to thicken and to
leave her.

Then she had seen him: Veil, one of the guards. A tall and
spindly figure, with a lipless mouth, and eyes like beads of glass.
He tempted her to run away with him. At first she believed this
to be a ruse, but as time elapsed the Black Rose realized that

he had other plans in life, and was determined to escape the camp. It was part of his plan to have a decoy with him.

So they escaped, he from the cramping life of official cruelty; she from the pain of whips and burning stubs.

Then came their wanderings. Then came a time of cruelty worse than behind the barbed wire. Then came her degradation. Seven times she tried to escape. But he always found her. Veil. The man with the small head.

FIFTY-SIX

ONE day he slew a beggar as though he were so much pork, and stole from his blood-stained pocket the secret sign of the Under-River. The police were in the next street. He crouched with the Black Rose in the lee of a statue, and when the moon dipped behind a cloud he dragged her to the river-side. There in the deep shadows he found at last what he was looking for, an entrance to the secret tunnel; for with a cunning mixture of guile and fortune he had learned much in the camp.

But that was a year ago. A year of semi-darkness. And now she stood there silently in the small room, very upright, her eyes staring into space.

For the first time the Black Rose turned her head to the man standing before her.

'I'd almost rather be a slave again,' she whispered, 'than have this kind of freedom. Why do you follow me? I am losing my life. What have you found?'

Yet again the man cast his eyes about the small, silent assembly, before he turned once more to the girl. From where she stood she could only see the man in silhouette.

'Tell me,' said the Black Rose. Her voice, as it had been throughout, was almost meaninglessly flat. 'Have you found it? The tunnel?'

The bony man rubbed his hands together with a sound like sandpaper. Then he nodded his small head.

'A mile away. No more. Its entrance dense with ferns. Out

of them came a boy. Come close to me; I do not care to be overheard. You remember the whip?'

'The whip? Why do you ask me that?'

Before answering, the silhouette took hold of the Black Rose, and a few seconds later they were out of the lamp-lit chamber. Turning left and left again they came to a corner of stones, like the corner of a street. A streak of light fell across the wet floor. Her arms were rigid in his vice-like grip.

'Now we can talk,' he said.

'Let go my arm, or I will scream for God.'

'He never helped you. Have you forgotten?'

'Forgotten what, you skull? you filthy stalk-head! I have forgotten nothing. I can remember all your dirty games. And the stench of your fingers.'

'Can you remember the whip at Kar and the hunger? How I gave you extra bread! Yes, and fed you through the bars. And how you barked for more.'

'O slime of the slime-pit!'

'I could see for all your coupling, your indiscriminate whoredom that you had been splendid once. I could see why you were given such a name. Black Rose. You were famous. You were desirable. But when revolution came your beauty counted for nothing. And so they whipped you, and they broke your pride. You grew thinner and thinner. Your limbs became tubes. Your head was shaved. You did not look like a woman. You were more like a . . .'

'I do not want to think of that again . . . leave me alone.'

'Do you remember what you promised me?'

'No.'

'And then how I saved you again; and helped you to escape?'

'No! No! No!'

'Do you remember how you prayed to me for mercy? You prayed on your knees, your cropped head bent as at an execution. And mercy I gave you, didn't I?'

'Yes, oh yes.'

'In exchange, as you promised, for your body.'

'No!'

'Escape with me or rot in lamplight.'

Again he grasped her savagely, so that she cried out in agony. But there was at the same time another sound that went unheard . . . the sound of light footsteps.

'Lift up your head! Why all this nicety? You are a whore.'

'I am no whore, you festering length of bone. I would as much have you touch me as a running sore.'

Then the man with the small skull-like head lifted his fist, and struck her across the mouth. It was a mouth that had once been soft and red: lovely to look upon: thrilling to kiss. But now it seemed to have no shape, for the blood ran all over it. In jerking back her head she struck it on the wall at her back, and immediately her eyes closed with sickness; those eyes of hers, those irises, as black, it seemed, as their pupils so that they merged and became like a great wide well that swallowed what they gazed upon. But before they closed a kind of ghost appeared to hover in the eyes. It was no reflection, but a terrible and mournful thing . . . the ghost of unbearable disillusion.

The footsteps had stopped at the sound of her cry, but now, as she began to sink to her knees a figure began to run, his steps sounding louder and louder every moment.

The small-skull'd man with his long spindly limbs, cocked his head on one side and ran his tongue to and fro along his fleshless lips with a deliberate stropping motion. This tongue was like the tongue of a boot, as long, as broad and as thin.

Then as though he had come to a decision he picked the Black Rose up in his arms and took a dozen steps to where the darkness was thickest, and there he dropped her as though she were a sack, to the ground. But as he turned to retrace his steps, he saw that someone was waiting for him.

FIFTY-SEVEN

FOR as long as a man can hold his breath, there was no sound; not one. Their eyes were fixed upon one another, until at last the voice of Veil broke the wet silence.

'Who are you?' he said, 'and what do you want?'

He drew back his leather lips as he spoke, but the new-comer instead of answering took a step forward, and peered through the gloom on every side as though he were looking for something.

'I questioned you I think! Who are you? You do not belong here. This is not your quarter. You are trespassing. Get to the north with you or I will . . .'

'I heard a cry,' said Titus. 'What was it?'

'A cry? There are always cries.'

'What are you doing here in the dark? What are you hiding?'

'Hiding, you pup? Hiding? Who are you to cross-question me? By God, who are you anyway? Where do you come from?'

'Why?'

The mantis man was suddenly upon the youth and though he did not actually *touch* Titus, at any point, yet he seemed to encircle and to threaten with his nails, his joints, his teeth, and with his sour and horrible breathing.

'I will ask you again,' said the man. 'Where do you come from?'

Titus, his eyes narrowed, his fists clenched, felt his mouth go suddenly dry.

'You wouldn't understand,' he whispered.

At this Mr Veil threw back his bony head to laugh. The sound was intolerably cold and cruel.

The man was deadly enough without his laugh but with it he became deadly in another way. For there was no humour in it. It was a noise that came out of a hole in the man's face. A sound that left Titus under no illusion as to the man's intrinsic evil. His body, limbs and organs and even his head could hardly be said to be any fault of his, for this was the way in which he had been made; but his laughter was of his own making.

As the blood ran into Titus's face there was a movement in the darkness, and the boy turned his head at once.

'Who's there?' he cried, and as he cried, the thin man Veil took a spidery step towards him.

'Come back, pup!'

The menace in the voice was so horrible that Titus jumped

ahead into the darkness, and immediately his foot struck something that yielded, and at the same time there was a sob from immediately below him.

As he knelt down he could see the faint pattern of a human face in the gloom. The eyes were open.

'Who are you?' whispered Titus. 'What has happened to you?'

'No . . . no,' said the voice.

'Raise your head,' said Titus, but as he began to lift the vague body, a hand fixed its fingers, like pincers, into his shoulder, and with one movement, not only jerked Titus to his feet, but sent him spinning against the wall, where a slant of pale, wet light illumined his face.

Written across his young features was something not so young; something as ancient as the stones of his home. Something uncompromising. The gaze of civility was torn from his face as the shrouding flesh can be torn from the bone. A primordial love for his birth-place, a love which survived and grew, for all that he had left his home, for all that he was a traitor, burned in him with a ferocity that he could not understand. All he knew was that as he stared at the spider-man, he, Titus, began to age. A cloud had passed over his heart. He was not so much in the thick of an adventure as alone with something that smelt of death.

Where Titus leaned against the wall the cold brick ran with moisture. It ran through his hair and spread out over his brows and cheekbones. It gathered about his lips and chin and then fell to the ground in a string of water-beads.

His heart pounded. His hands and knees shook, and then, out of the gloom the Black Rose re-appeared.

'No, no, no! Keep to the darkness, whoever you are!'

At these words the Black Rose swayed and sank again to the floor, and then with a great effort she raised herself on her elbow and whispered, 'Kill the beast.'

The spider had turned his small, bony head in her direction and in an instant Titus (with no weapons to slice or stab, and with no scruples, for he knew that within a minute he would be fighting for his life) brought up his knee with all the force he could muster. As he did this the spider leaned forward so that the full force of the blow was driven immediately below the ribs; but the only sound to be heard was that of a rush of air as it sped hissing from between his jaws. This was the only sound. He made no kind of groan: he merely brought his hands together, the fingers making a kind of grid to protect the solar-plexus, as he bent himself double.

This was Titus's moment. He stumbled his way to the Black Rose: lifted her, and panting as he ran, he made for a blur of light which seemed to hang in the air some distance to the west where the wet floor, the walls and the ceiling were suffused with a vaporous, slug-coloured glow.

As he ran he saw (although he hardly knew he had seen it) a family move by, then stop, and draw itself together, and stare: then came another group and then another, as though the very walls exuded them. Figures of all kinds, from all directions. They saw the boy stumbling with his burden, and paused.

Veil, meanwhile, had all but recovered from the knee-stab, and was following Titus with merciless deliberation. But for all the speed of his spindly legs he was not in time to see Titus kneel down and lay the Black Rose on the ground where a shadow cast by a hoary pyramid of decomposing books hid her from view.

Immediately he had done this he turned about on his heel and saw his foe. He also saw how great a crowd had congregated. An alarm had been sounded. An alarm that had no need of words or voices. Something that travelled from region to region until the air was filled as though with a soundless sound like a giant bellowing behind a sound-proof wall of glass, or the yelling of a chordless throat.

FIFTY-EIGHT

So the grey arena formed itself and the crowd grew, while the domed ceiling of the dark place dripped, and the lamps were re-filled and some held candles, some torches, while others had brought mirrors to reflect the light, until the whole place swam like a miasma.

Were his shoulder not hurting from the grip it had sustained Titus might well have wondered whether he was asleep and dreaming.

Around him, tier upon tier (for the centre of the arena was appreciably lower than the margin, and there was about the place almost the feeling of a dark circus) were standing or were seated the failures of earth. The beggars, the harlots, the cheats, the refugees, the scatterlings, the wasters, the loafers, the bohemians, the black sheep, the chaff, the poets, the riff-raff, the small fry, the misfits, the conversationalists, the human oysters, the vermin, the innocent, the snobs and the men of straw, the pariahs, the outcasts, rag-pickers, the rascals, the rake-hells, the fallen angels, the sad-dogs, the castaways, the prodigals, the defaulters, the dreamers and the scum of the earth.

Not one of the great conclave of the displaced had ever seen Titus before. Each one supposed this ignorance of the young man to be peculiar to himself, for the population was so dense and so far-flung.

As for Veil, there were many who knew his face: they recognized that horrible spidery walk; that bullet head; that lip-less mouth. There was about him something indestructible; as though his body were made of a substance that did not understand the sensation of pain.

As he advanced, a hush as palpable as any sound descended and lay thick in the air. Even the most flippant and insensitive of the characters took on another colour. Knowing no reason for the conflict they trembled, nevertheless, to see the distance narrow between the two.

How the news of the impending battle had reached the outlying districts and brought back, almost on the wings of the returning echoes, such a multitude, it is hard to understand. But there was now no part of the Under-River ignorant of the scene.

Head after head in long lines, thick and multitudinous and cohesive as grains of honey-coloured sugar, each grain a face, the audience sat or stood without a movement.

To shift the gaze from any one of the faces was to lose it forever. It was a delirium of heads: an endless profligacy. There was no end to it. The inventiveness of it was so rapid, various, profluent. Each movement sank away, sank with a smoulder-ing fist-feel of raw plunder: sank into nullity.

And all was lit by the lamps; reflected by the mirrors. A shallow pool of water at the centre of the circle reflected the long cross beams; reflected a paddling rat as it climbed a high slippery prop, reflected the glint of its teeth and the stiffness of its ghastly tail.

Somewhere in the heart of this sat Slingshott. For a little while he had forgotten to be sorry for himself, so vivid was the plight of the youth.

His hands were clasped together in the depths of his pockets as he stared down into the wet ring. Within a few feet (though they had lost sight of one another) crouched Carrow. Biting his knuckles he kept his eyes fixed upon Titus, and wondered what, without a weapon, the youth could do.

Thirty to forty feet away from Carrow and Slingshott stood Sober-Carter, and on the far side of the open space the old couple, Jonah and his 'squirrel' grasped one another's hands.

Crack-Bell, usually so irritatingly cheerful, sat with his shoulders hunched up rather like some kind of cold bird. His face had sagged: his mouth hung open. He clasped his hands, and for all that he had no part in the conflict they were cold and moist, and his pulse uneven.

Crabcalf, imprisoned by his books, had been carried to the arena in his bed. This bed, on being lifted from the floor had disclosed a rectangle of deep and sumptuous dust.

In the silence was the voice of the river, a muted sound, all but inaudible, yet ubiquitous and dangerous as the ocean. It was not so much a sound as a warning of the world above.

FIFTY-NINE

TITUS had come to a halt in the centre of the 'ring', and had then turned his face to his foe, the execrable Veil. He had little hope, for the man appeared to be composed of nothing but bone and whipcord, and he remembered how quick had been the creature's recovery from the stomach-jab. It was not just that Titus was frightened: he was also awed by what he saw approaching; this Thing of scarecrow proportions: this Thing that seemed larger than life.

It was as though he were faced with a machine: something without a nervous system, heart, kidney, or any other vulnerable organ.

His clothes were black and clung to him as though they were wet, and this accentuated the length of his bones. About his skeleton waist he wore a wide leather belt; the brass of the buckle twinkled in the firelight.

As he drew close to Titus, the boy saw that he had contracted his mouth so that his lips, which were thin enough on their own account, were now no more than a thread of bloodless cotton. This in its turn had tightened the skin above, so that the cheekbones stood out like small rocks. The eyes glinted from between the eyelids, and the effect was that of a concentration fierce enough to argue insanity.

For a moment only, this concentration slackened, and in that moment he swept his eyes across the terraced hordes: but there was no sign of Black Rose. As he returned his gaze to Titus he lifted his face and saw the great beams that swept across the dim and upper air: he saw the high props, green and slimy with moss, and as his eyes travelled down the rotting pillar he saw the rat.

Now, with a corner of his gaze fixed upon Titus, and with the rat in the tail of his other eye, the spiderman moved unexpectedly, and with a sidling motion, to the left, until he was within reaching distance of the sweating pillar.

A kind of indrawn gasp of relief came from the surrounding audience. Any unforeseen action was preferable to the ineluctable drawing together of the incongruous pair.

But this relief was short lived, for something worse than the horror of the silence brought every one of them to his feet, as with a movement too quick to follow, like the flick of a cobra's tongue, or the spurt of a squid's tentacle, Veil shot out his long left arm and plucked the crouching rat from where it lurked, and crunched with his long fingers the life out of the creature. There had been a scream and then a silence more terrible, for Veil had turned upon Titus.

'And now, you,' he said.

As Titus bent down to be sick, Veil tossed the dead animal in his direction. It fell a few paces from him with a thud. Without knowing what he was doing Titus, in a fever of fear and hatred, tore away a piece of his own shirt, folded it, and dropping on to his knees, spread it over the lifeless rodent.

Then as he knelt, he saw a shadow move and he jumped back with a cry for Veil was all but upon him. Not only this but there was a knife in his hand.

SIXTY

BLACK ROSE on the far side of the ring had seen the flash of Veil's knife. She knew he kept it whetted like a razor. She saw that the young man had no weapon, and gathering her strength together she cried out, 'Give him your knives ... your knives! The beast will kill him.'

As though the assemblage had come out of some nightmare or trance, a hundred hands slid into a hundred belts and then for a dozen seconds the air was alight with steel, the great place echoing with the clang of metal and stone. Weapons of all kinds lay scattered like stars across the floor. Some on dry ground, and some gleaming in the pools of water.

But there was one, a long, slender weapon, half-way between a knife and a sword, which, because it hurtled past Titus's head and fell with a splash some distance from Veil, forced him immediately into action. Turning, he ran to where it lay, and as he plucked it out of the shallow water, he gave a great laugh, not of joy, but of relief that he could hold something tight in his grasp, something with an edge, something fiercer, keener and more deadly than his bare hands.

Two-handed at the hilt he held it before him like a brand. The water was over his ankles, and to the minutest detail he was mirrored upside down.

Now that Veil was so close to Titus that a mere ten feet divided them it might have been thought that someone out of the great assembly would have raced to the young man's rescue. But not a finger stirred. The brigands no less than the weaklings stared at the scene in a kind of universal trance. They watched but they could not move.

The mantis-man drew closer, and as he did so, Titus drew back a pace. He was shaking with fear. Veil's face seemed to expose itself as though it were vile as a sore: it swam before his eyes like the shiftings of the grey slime of the pit. It was indecent. Indecent not for reason of its ugliness, or even the cruelty that was part of it, but in the way that it was a perpetual reminder of death.

For an instant there rushed through Titus's mind an understanding. For a moment he lost his hatred. He abhorred nothing. The man had been born with his bones and his bowels. He could not help them. He had been born with a skull so shaped that only evil could inhabit it.

But the thought flashed and fell away for Titus had no time for anything but to remain alive.

SIXTY-ONE

WHAT is it threads the inflamed brain of the one-time killer? Fear? No, not so much as would fill the socket of a fly's eye. Remorse? He has never heard of it. It is loyalty that fills him, as he lifts his long right arm. Loyalty to the child, the long scab-legged child, who tore the wings off sparrows long ago. Loyalty to his aloneness. Loyalty to his own evil, for only through this evil has he climbed the foul stairways to the lofts of hell. Had he wished to do so, he could never have withdrawn from the conflict, for to do so would have been to have denied Satan the suzerainty of pain.

Titus had lifted his sword high in the air, and at that instant, his enemy slung his blade in the direction of the youth. It ran through the air with the speed of a stone from a sling and struck Titus's sword immediately below the handle, and sent it hurtling from his grasp.

The force of this had Titus on his back. It was as though he himself had been struck. His arms and empty hands shook and buzzed with the shock.

As he lay there he saw two things. The first thing he saw was that Veil had picked up a couple of knives from the wet ground, and was coming towards him, his neck and head craned forward, like a hen's when it runs for food, his dagger'd fists uplifted to the level of his ears. For a moment as Titus gazed spellbound the mean mouth opened and the purplish tongue sped from one corner to the other. Titus stared, all initiative, all power drained out of him, but even as he lay sprawling helplessly something moved in the tail of his eye, something above his head so that for an involuntary second he found himself staring wide-lidded at a long slippery beam, a beam that seemed to float across the semi-darkness.

But what Titus saw, and what set his pulses racing, was not the beam itself, but something that crawled along it: something massive yet absolutely silent: something that moved inexorably forward inch by inch. What it was he could not quite make out. All he could tell was that it was heavy, agile and alive.

But Mr Veil, the breaker of lives, observing how Titus had, for a fraction of a second, lifted his eyes to the shadows above, stopped for a moment his advance upon the spreadeagled youth and turned his face to the rafters. What he saw at that moment was something that brought forth from the very entrails of the vast audience, an intake of terrified breath, for the figure, huge it seemed in that wavering light, rose to its feet upon the beam, and a moment later leaped into space.

There was no computing the weight and speed of Muzzle-hatch as he crushed the 'Mantis' to the slippery ground. The victim's face had been lifted so that the jaw, the clavicles, the shoulder blades and five ribs were the first to go down like dead sticks in a storm.

And yet he made no sound, this devil, this 'Mantis', this Mr Veil. Crushed and prostrate, he rose again, and to Titus's horror it seemed as though the features of his face had all changed places.

It could also be seen that there was damage to his limbs. In trying to move away he was forced to trail a broken leg which

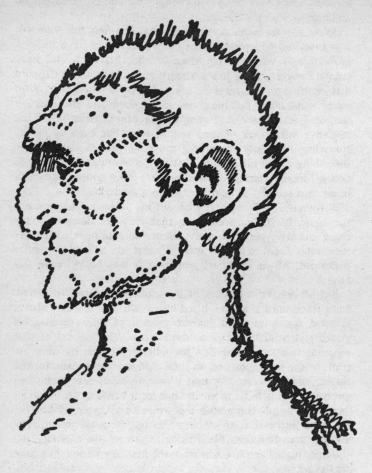

followed him like something tied to his hip: a length of drift-wood. All he could do was to hop away from Muzzlehatch with that assortment of features clustered upon his neck like a horrible nest.

But he did not go far. Titus, Muzzlehatch and the great awe-struck audience realized suddenly that the knives were still in his hands, and that his hands and arms alone had escaped the destruction. There, in his fists, they sparkled.

But he could no longer see his enemies. His face had capsized. Yet his brain had not been damaged.

'Black Rose!' he cried into the dreadful silence. 'Take your last look at me,' and he plunged the two knives, through the ribs, in the region of his heart. He left them there, withdrawing his hands from the hilts.

Out of the silence that followed, the horrible sound of his laughter began to grow, and as it grew in volume, the blood poured out the quicker, until there came the moment when, with a final convulsion of his long bones, he fell upon his dislocated, meaningless face, twitched for the last time, and died.

SIXTY-TWO

TITUS got to his feet and turned to Muzzlehatch. He saw at once by the distant look in his friend's eye that he was in no talking mood. He seemed to have forgotten the long shattered man at his feet, and to be brooding on some other matter. When Black Rose came stumbling up, her hands clasped, he took no notice of her. She turned to Titus.

At once, Titus drew back. Not because she repelled him, for even in the drawn and sunken condition she was in, she was still beautiful. But now, she had no option but to arouse pity: she could not help it. It was a beauty to beware of. Her enormous eyes so often big with fear were now big with hope ... and Titus knew that he must get away. He could see at once that she was predatory. She did not know it, but she was.

'She goes through hell,' muttered Titus. 'She wades in it, and the thicker and deeper it is, the more I long to escape. Grief can be boring.' Titus was immediately sickened by his own words. They tasted foul on the tongue.

He turned to her and was held again by the gaping tragedy of her eyes. Whatever she said could be nothing but mere corroboration. It could merely repeat or embroider the reality of her eloquent eyes. The trembling of her hands, and the wetness of her cheekbones. These and other signs were redundant. He knew that were he to let fall the smallest seed of kindness, then that seed would inevitably grow into some kind of weird relationship. A smile might set the avalanche moving.

'I can't, I can't,' he thought. 'I can't sustain her. I can't comfort her. I can't love her. Her suffering is far too clear to see. There is no veil across it: no mystery: no romance. Nothing but a factual pain, like the pain of a nagging tooth.'

Again he turned his eyes to her as though to verify what he had been thinking, and at once he was ashamed.

She had become emptied. Pain had emptied her. There was nothing left. What could he do?

He turned to Muzzlehatch: there was something about him that baffled the boy. For the first time it seemed as though his friend had a weakness: some vulnerable spot. Somebody or something had searched it out. As Titus watched, and as Black Rose stood with her eyes fixed upon him, Muzzlehatch turned to the great crowd.

He had heard without knowing it the first murmur, and he now became aware of a widespread stirring, as gradually the crowd began to crumble, grain by grain, making its way to the arena, gradually as though a great hill of sugar were on the move.

But what was more important, the incredulous population appeared to be drifting in the direction of the three. Within a minute, they (the Black Rose, Titus and Muzzlehatch) would, if they stayed where they were, be caught up in an insufferable press.

Before them, inexorably, came spilling out the tide. The tide of the unwanted, the dispossessed: the dross of the Under-River. Among them came Crabcalf and the bird-headed man who fed the hounds; came the old man, and his squirrel: came Crack-Bell: came Sober-Carter.

There was no time to lose. 'This way,' said Muzzlehatch, and Titus with the Black Rose clinging to his arm hurried after him, as the gaunt man strode into a blanket of darkness. Not a lantern burned: not a candle even. Only by the sound of his footsteps was Titus able to keep contact with his friend.

After what seemed an hour or more, they turned to the

south. He seemed to have eyes like a cat's, this silent Muzzle-hatch; for dark as it was, he never faltered.

Then, after yet an hour or more of walking, this time with the Black Rose slung over his shoulders, Muzzlehatch at last came to a long flight of steps. As they climbed, they became aware, momently, of a percolation of faint light, and then, all at once, of a small white opening in the darkness, the size of a coin. When at last they reached it, they found it to be an entrance, or for themselves an egress. They had reached one of the secret mouths of the under-river world, and Titus was amazed to see, on wriggling himself out into the air, that they were in the silent heart of a forest.

SIXTY-THREE

THEY had to wait until dark before they dared to venture to Juno's house. What else could they do with the Black Rose but take her there? As they waited the tension became almost unbearable. Nobody spoke. Muzzlehatch's eyes had a far-away look, which Titus had seldom seen before.

It was a rocky place, and over the rocks the trees spread out their branches. At last Titus walked over to where Muzzlehatch lay on his back on a great grey stone. Black Rose followed him with her eyes.

'I can't bear this any longer,' said Titus, 'what in hell is it? Why are you so different? Is it because . . . ?'

'Boy,' said Muzzlehatch, 'I will tell you. It will keep you quiet.' He paused for a long while. Then he said, 'My animals are dead.'

At the end of the forest silence that followed, Titus knelt down beside his friend. All he could say was, 'What happened?'

'The dedicated men,' said Muzzlehatch, 'sometimes known as scientists: they were after me. Someone is always after me. As usual I escaped them. I know many ways of disappearing. But what use are they now, my dear chap? My animals are dead.'

'But . . .'

'Baffled because they could not find me ... no, not even with their latest device, that is no bigger than a needle, and threads a keyhole with the speed of light ... baffled, I say, they turned from hunting me, and killed my animals.'

'How?'

Muzzlehatch rose to his feet on the rock, and lifting his arm caught hold of a thick branch that hung above him, and broke it off. A muscle in his jawbone ticked endlessly like a clock.

'Some kind of ray, it was,' he said at last. 'Some kind of ray. A pretty notion, prettily executed.'

'And yet you had the heart to rescue me,' said Titus, 'from the thin man.'

'Did I?' muttered Muzzlehatch. 'I was in a dream. Think no more of it. I had no choice but to make for the Under-River. The scientists were converging. They were after you, boy: they were after us both.'

'But you remembered me,' said Titus. 'You crawled along the beam.'

'Did I? Good! And so I crushed him? I was far away ... I was among my creatures. I saw them die ... I saw them roll over. I heard their breath blow bleakly from their ribs. I saw my zoo become an abattoir. My creatures! Vital as fire. Sensuous and terrible. There they lay. There they lay – for ever and ever.'

He turned his face to Titus. The abstracted look had gone and in its place was something as cold and pitiless as ice.

SIXTY-FOUR

CURSING the moon, for it was full, Titus and his two companions were forced to make a long detour, and to keep as far as possible in the shadows that skirted the woods, or lay beneath the walls of the city. To have taken the shorter path across the moonlit woods would have invited trouble.

As they made their way, their pace conditioned by the weary steps of the Black Rose, Titus, perhaps for reason of his supreme indebtedness to Muzzlehatch felt an almost ungovernable desire to shake this from him as though he were a ponderous weight. He longed for isolation, and in his longing he recognized that same canker of selfishness that had made itself manifest in his attitude towards the Black Rose in her pain.

What kind of brute was he? Was he destined to destroy both love and friendship? What of Juno? Had he not the courage or the loyalty to hold fast to his friends? Or the courage to speak up? Perhaps not. He had, after all, deserted his home.

Forcing himself to frame the words, he turned his head to Muzzlehatch, 'I want to get away from you,' he said. 'From you and everyone. I want to start again, when but for you, I would be dead! Is this vile of me? I cannot help it. You are too vast and craggy. Your features are the mountains of the moon. Lions and tigers lie bleeding in your brain. Revenge is in your belly. You are too vast and remote. Your predicament burns. It makes me hanker for release. I am too near you. I long to be alone. What shall I do?'

'Do what you like, boy,' said Muzzlehatch, 'skidaddle to the pole, for all I care, or scorch your bottom on the red equator. As for this lady? She is ill. *Ill*, you numbskull! Ill as they take them on this side of breath.'

The Black Rose turned to Muzzlehatch, and her pupils gaped like well-heads.

'He wants to get away from me, too,' she said. 'He is disgusted by my poverty. I wish you could have seen me years ago, when I was young and fair.'

'You are still beautiful,' said Titus.

'I don't care, any more,' said the Black Rose. 'It no longer matters. All I want is to lie down quietly forever, on linen. Oh God, white linen, before I die.'

'You shall have your linen,' said Muzzlehatch. 'White as a seraph's underwing. We're not far away.'

'Where are you taking me?'

'To a home by a river, where you can rest.'

'But Veil will find me.'

'Veil is dead,' said Titus. 'Dead as dead.'

'His ghost will strike me then. His ghost will twist my arm.'

'Ghosts are fools,' said Muzzlehatch, 'and much overrated. Juno will care for you. As for this young Titus Groan: he can

143

do as he pleases. If I were in his shoes I would cut adrift and vanish. The world is wide. Follow your instinct and get rid of us. That was why you left your so-called Gormenghast, wasn't it? Eh? To find out what lay beyond the skyline. Eh? And as you once said ...'

'I think you said, "your so-called Gormenghast". God damn you for that phrase. For *you* to say it! You! For you to be a thing of disbelief! *You!* You've been a kind of God to me. A rough-hewn God. I hated you at times, but mostly I loved you. I have told you of my home; of my family; of our ritual; of my childhood; of the flood; of Fuchsia, of Steerpike and how I killed him; of my escape. Do you think I have invented it all? Do you think I have been deceiving you? You have failed me. Let me go!'

'What are you waiting for,' said Muzzlehatch, turning his back on the boy. His heart was pounding.

Titus stamped his foot with anger, but he did not move away. A moment later, the Black Rose began to give at the knees, but Muzzlehatch was in time to catch her up in his powerful arms, as though she were a tattered doll.

They had come to an open space, and stopped where the shadows ended.

'Do you see that cloud?' said Muzzlehatch, in a curiously loud voice. 'The one like a curled-up cat. No, there, you chicken, beyond that green dome. Can't you see it? With the moon on its back.'

'What about it?' said Titus in an irritable whisper.

'That is your direction,' said Muzzlehatch. 'Make for it. Then on and beyond for a month's march, and you will be in comparative freedom. Freedom from the swarms of pilotless planes: freedom from bureaucracy: freedom from the police. And freedom of movement. It is largely unexplored. They are ill-equipped. No squadron for the water, sea, or sky. It is as it should be. A region where no one can remember who is in power. But there are forests like the Garden of Eden where you can lie on your belly and write bad verse. There will be nymphs for your ravishing, and flutes for your delectation. A land where youths lean backwards in their tracks, and piss the moon, as though to put it out.'

'I am tired of your words,' said Titus.

'I use them as a kind of lattice-work,' said Muzzlehatch. 'They hide me away from me ... let alone from you. Words can be tiresome as a swarm of insects. They can prick and buzz! Words can be no more than a series of farts; or on the other hand they can be adamantine, obdurate, inviolable, stone upon stone. Rather like your "so-called Gormenghast" (you notice that I use the same phrase again. The phrase that makes you cross?). For although you have learned, it seems, the art of making enemies (and this is indeed good for the soul), yet you are blind, deaf, and dumb when it comes to another language. Stark: dry: unequivocal: and cryptic: a thing of crusts and water. If you ask for flattery.... Remember this in your travels. Now go ... for God's sake. ... GO!'

Titus lifted his eyes to his companion. Then he took three steps towards him. The scar on his cheekbone shone like silk in the moonlight.

'Mr Muzzlehatch,' he said.

'What is it boy?'

'I grieve for you.'

'Grieve for this broken creature,' said Muzzlehatch. 'She is the weak of the world.'

Out of the silence came the far-away voice of the Black Rose. 'Linen,' it cried in a voice both peevish and beautiful. 'Linen ... white linen.'

'She is as hot as fever can make her,' muttered Muzzlehatch. 'It is like holding embers in my arms. But there is Juno for a refuge, and a cat for your bearing; and beyond, to the world's end.

'The sleeping cat,' he muttered with a catch in his throat, 'did you ever see it ... my little civet? They silenced him with all the rest. He moved like a wave of the sea. Next to my wolves, I loved him, Titus child. You have never seen such eyes.'

'Hit me,' cried Titus, 'I've been a dog to you.'

'Globules to that!' said Muzzlehatch. 'It's time the Black Rose was in Juno's hands.'

'Ah, Juno; give her my love,' said Titus.

'Why?' said Muzzlehatch. 'You've only just retracted it! That's no way to treat a lady. By hell it ain't. Giving your love; taking your love; secreting it; exposing it ... as though it were a game of hide and seek.'

'But you have been in love with her yourself and have lost her. And now *you* are returning to her again.'

'True,' said Muzzlehatch. 'Touché, indeed. She has, after all, a haze about her. She is an orchard ... a golden thing is Juno. Generous as the milky way, or the source of a great river. What would you say? Is she not wonderful?'

Titus turned his head quickly to the sky.

'Wonderful? She *must* have been.'

'Must she?' said Muzzlehatch.

There was a curious silence, and in this silence a cloud began to pass over the moon. It was not a large cloud so that there was little time to waste, and in the half-darkness the two friends moved away from one another, and began to hurry into the darkness as though they needed it, one in the direction of Juno's home, the Black Rose in his arms, and the other moving rapidly to the north.

But before they became lost to one another in the final murk Titus stopped and looked back. The cloud had passed and he could see Muzzlehatch standing at the corner of the sleeping square. His shadow, and the shadow of the Black Rose in his arms, lay at his feet, and it was as though he was standing in a pool of black water. His head, rock-like, was bent over the poor frail creature in his arms. Then Titus saw him turn on his heel, and walk with long strides, his shadow skimming the ground beneath him, and then the moon disappeared and the silence was as intense as ever.

In this thick silence, the boy waited: for what he did not know: he just waited while a great unhappiness filled him; only to be dispersed, immediately, for a far-away voice cried out in the darkness:

'Hullo there, Titus Groan! Prop up your chin, boy! We'll meet again; no doubt of it – one day.'

'Why not!' cried Titus. 'Thank you forever ...'

But the sentence was broken by Muzzlehatch with another great shout, 'Farewell Titus. ... Farewell my cocky boy! Farewell ... farewell.'

SIXTY-FIVE

AT first there was no sign of a head but after a while an acute observer might have concentrated his attention more and more upon a particular congestion of branches, and eventually discovered, deep in the interplay of leaf or tendril, a line that could be one thing only ... the profile of Juno.

She had been sitting in her vine-arbour for a long while, hardly moving. Her servants had called her, but she had not heard them: or if she had, she made no response.

Three days ago her one-time lover, Muzzlehatch, had been hidden in her attic. Now, he was gone again. The wraith he had brought with him had been washed and put to bed, but had died the moment her head had touched the snowy pillow.

There had been the funeral; there had been questions to answer. Her lovely house had been filled by a swarm of officials, including Acreblade, the detective. Where was Titus? he had asked. Where was Muzzlehatch? She shook her head for hour after hour.

Now she sat immobile in her arbour, and her bosom ached. She was seeing herself as a girl. She was remembering the gallant days. The days when the young men longed for her: risking their leaping lives for her: daring one another to swing among the high cedar branches in the dark grove near her home, and others to swim the barbarous bay when the lightning flashed above it. And those who were not so young, but whose wit and suavity beguiled her ... the gentlemen in their forties, hiding their love away from public view, nursing it like a wound or a bruise, only to burst the stronger out of darkness.

And the elderly for whom she was the unobtainable, a will-o'-the-wisp, a marsh-light, waking their lust to life, or waking something rarer, a chaos of poetry, the scent of a rose.

Before her, through the vine leaves was a daisy'd slope that led down to a high box hedge, clipped into peacocks, heraldic against the sky. And the sky itself to which she now lifted her gaze, was filled with little clouds.

It was a favourite place of Juno's, this tangled arbour, and she had many a time found solace in its seclusion. But today was different from all other times, for a remote sense of being imprisoned by the interwoven branches began to trouble her, though she had no idea what it was that she was feeling.

Nor did she ever know for her body, working independently from the brain, rose and moved out of the arbour like a ship leaving harbour.

Now she was on the daisy'd lawn: now she was leaving the shear'd box behind: now she was meandering into pastures where dragonflies hovered and darted.

On and on she wandered, hardly taking in her surroundings, until she came to the dark cedar grove. She had not noticed it approaching for her eyes were all but sightless as she moved. But when she was within a short distance of the dark grove she found the verge of a wide glaze of dew.

Now fully awake, she stared into the depths and saw, inverted, a haunt of her girlhood – the almost legendary cedar grove.

Her first sensation was that she was upside down: but this belief was shattered when she raised her head. But before she raised it she saw someone lounging, upside-down on the underside of a great cedar-bough and defying, as he did so, the law of gravity. But when Juno raised her head and tried to locate the man on his branch, it was not so easy. At first she could see nothing but the green terraces of foliage, but suddenly she saw the man again. He was nearer to where she stood than she had expected.

Directly the man realized he had been noticed he dropped to the ground and bowed, his dark red hair falling over his eyes like a mop.

'What are you doing in my cedar grove?' she said.

'Trespassing,' said the man.

Juno shielded her eyes and gazed steadily at the man – with his dark red hair and his boxer's nose.

'Well, "trespasser": what do you want?' she said at last. 'Is this a favourite haunt of yours or am I being ambushed?'

'You are being ambushed. If I have startled you, I am profoundly sorry. I would not have you startled. No, not by so much as an ant on your wrist, or the buzz of a bee.'

'I see,' said Juno.

'But I have waited for the devil of a long while,' said the man, screwing up his forehead, 'Great Heaven, I have indeed.'

'Who have you waited for?' said Juno.

'For this moment,' said the man.

Juno lifted an eyebrow.

'I have waited for you to be deserted. And alone. As you are now.'

'What has my life to do with you?' said Juno.

'Everything and nothing,' said the tousled man. 'It is your own of course. So is your unhappiness. Titus is gone. Muzzle-hatch is gone. Not for ever perhaps, but for a long while. Your house by the river, fine as it is, is now a place of echoes and of shades.'

Juno joined her hands together at her breast. There was something in his voice that belied his mop of dark red hair and general air of brigandage. It was deep, husky – and unbeliev-ably gentle.

'Who are you?' she said at last, 'and what do you know of Titus?'

'My name is of no account. As for Titus, I know very little. Very little. But enough. Enough to know that he left the city out of hunger.'

'Hunger?'

'The hunger to be always somewhere else. This and the pull of his home, or what he thinks of as his ancestral home (if he ever had one). I have seen him in this cedar grove, alone. Beat-ing the great branches with his fists. Beating the boughs as though to let his soul out.'

The Trespasser stepped forward for the first time, his feet breaking the mirror of green dew.

'You cannot sit and wait for either of them. Neither for Titus nor for Muzzlehatch. You have a life of your own, lady. Something that starts from now. I have watched you long before this Titus ever came upon the scene. I watched you from the shadows. Were it not that "Muzzle" whipped your heart away, I would have trailed you to the ends of the earth. But you loved him. And you loved Titus. As for me, now, you can see I'm no ladies' man – I'm a rough and ready one – but give me half a hint and I'll companion you. Companion you until the doors swing open – door after door from dawn till dusk and each fresh day will be a new invention!

'If you want me I will be here, somewhere among these cedars.'

He turned upon his heel, walked quickly away, and a few moments later he was lost in the forest and all that was left of him by way of proof were his footsteps like black smudges in the dazzling dew.

SIXTY-SIX

So Juno returned to her home, and it was true that it had already become a place of echoes, shadows, voices; moments of pause and suspense; moments of vague suffering or dwindling laughter, where the staircase curved from sight; moments of acute nostalgia where she stood all unwittingly at a window in a haze of stars; or of sweetness hardly to be borne when the shadow of Titus came between her and the sun as it rose through the slanting rain.

And while she lay stretched upon her bed one silent afternoon her hands behind her head, her eyes closed, her thoughts following one another in a sad cavalcade, Muzzlehatch, by now a hundred miles from Juno, was sitting at a rickety, three-legged table in another shaft of the same hot, ambient sun.

To right and left of him lay stretched the straggling street. Street? It was more of a track, for in keeping with everything else within Muzzlehatch's range of vision, it was half-finished and forsaken. Abandoned projects littered the land. Never reaching completion, it is never doomed. This gimcrack village that might have been a township ten times over. It had never had a past, nor could ever have a future. But it was full of happenings. The sliding moment blossomed febrile at one extreme and, at the other, was thick with human sleep. Bells rang, and were quickly stifled.

Children and dogs squatted hip-bone deep in the white dust. Elaborate trenches that were once the foundation of envisaged theatres, markets or churches, had become, for the children of this place, a battleground beyond the dreams of normal childhood.

The day was drowsy. It was a day of tacit somnolence. To work on such a day would be an insult to the sun.

The coffee tables curved away to the north, and to the south, as rickety a line of perspective as can well be imagined, and at these tables sat groups of multifarious face, frame and gesture. Yet there was a common denominator that strung these groups together. Of all the outspread company there was not one member who did not look as though he had just got out of bed.

Some had shoes, but no shirts; others had no shoes but wore hats of endless variety, at endless angles. Bygone headgear, bygone capes and jerkins and nightgowns drawn together at the waist with leather belts. In this company Muzzlehatch was very much at home, and sat at a table beneath a half-finished monument.

Hundreds of sparrows twittered and flapped their wings in the dust, the boldest of them hopping about on the coffee tables where the traditional handleless coffee cups and saucers gleamed vermilion in the sun.

Muzzlehatch was not alone at his table. Apart from a dozen sparrows, which he brushed clear of the table top from time to time, with the back of his hand, as though he were brushing away crumbs ... apart from these there was a crowd of human stragglers. A crowd divided loosely into three. The first of these segregations loitered about the person of Muzzlehatch himself, for they had never seen a man so relaxed, or so indifferent to their stares; a man so sprawled in his chair, and at such an indolent state of supreme collapse.

Masters as they were in the art of doing nothing, they had seen, nevertheless, nothing in their lives to compare with the scale on which this huge vagrant deported himself. He was, it seemed, a symbol of all that they unconsciously believed in and they stared at him, as though at a prototype of themselves.

They noted that great rudder of a nose: that arrogant head. But they had no notion that it was filled with a ghost. The ghost of Juno. And so it was his gaze was far away.

Next to Muzzlehatch, as magnet in the soft, hot light, was his car. The same, recalcitrant, hot-blooded beast. As was his custom he had tied her up, for she was apt at unforeseeable moments to leap a yard or so in a kind of reflex, the water bubbling in her rusty guts. Today he had for bollard the unfinished monument half-erected to some all but forgotten anarchist. And there she stood lash'd and twitching. The very personification of irritability.

The third of the three centres of interest was at the back of the car, where Muzzlehatch's small ape lay asleep in the sun. No one hereabouts had ever seen an ape before and it was with the wildest speculation, not without fear, that they boggled at the creature.

This animal had become, since the tragedy, a companion closer than ever, and had indeed become a symbol of all he had lost. Not only this but it kept doubly alive in a bitter region of the mind, the memory of that ghastly holocaust when the cages buckled, and his birds and animals cried out for the last time.

Who would have guessed that behind the formidable brow of his, which appeared to be made of some kind of rock, there lay so strange a mixture of memories and thoughts? For he lay sprawling in such a way as to suggest that nothing whatever was taking place in his head. Yet there, in the cerebral gloom, held in by the meridian of the skull, his Juno wandered in the cedar grove: his Titus moving by night, sleeping by day, made his way ... where ...? His ape lay coiled asleep, with one eye open, and scratched his ear. The silence droned like a bee in the heart of a flower.

The small ape gazers: the car gazers: and those that peered from short range at Muzzlehatch himself now turned their united attention to the lounging stranger; for Muzzlehatch, gripping the sides of his chair, all but bursting it, levered himself into an upright position.

Then, very slowly, he tilted back his head, until his face was level with the sky. But his eyes, as though to prove that they were not to be gainsaid by the angle of the face that lodged them, were downward cast, their line of vision grazing like a scythe the pale field of hair that made of his cheekbone, what would be for a gnat, a barley field.

Yet what he saw was not the scene before him with all its detail, but a memory of other days, no less vivid, no less real.

He saw, afloat, as it were, in the whorls of his boyhood, a string of irrelevant images; the days before he had ever heard of Juno, let alone a hundred others. Days flamboyant; days at large, and days in hiding, when he lay stretched on his back upon the high rocks, or lolled in glades until he took their colour; his arrogant nose, like a rudder, pointing at the sky. And as he lounged there, leaning precariously backwards in his chair, surrounded by a horde of ragged gapers, as might well have unnerved friend Satan himself, an old voice cried . . .

'Buy up the sunset! Buy it up! Buy it up! Buy . . . buy . . . buy. A copper for a seat, sirs. A copper for the view.' The croaking of the voice seemed to hack its way out of the arid throat of the ticket vendor, a diminutive figure dressed in non-descript black. His head protruded out of his torn collar much as the head of the tortoise protrudes from its shell, the throat unwrinkling, the eyes like beads, or pips of jet.

SIXTY-SEVEN

BETWEEN each strangulated cry the old man turned his head, and spat, swivelled his eyes, threw back his little bony head and barked at the sky like a dog.

'Buy it! Buy it! A seat for the sunset. Take your pick of 'em! every one. They say it will be coral, green and grey. Twenty coppers! Only twenty coppers.'

Threading his way through the tables, it was not long before he came upon Muzzlehatch. The old man paused, his jaws apart, but no sound came for some little while, so sharply was his attention taken by the sight of a new face at the tables.

The shadows of leaves and branches lay upon the table like grey lace and moved imperceptibly to and fro. The delicate shadow of an acacia frond fluctuated as it lay like a living thing upon Muzzlehatch's bony brow.

At last the old ticket vendor closed his jaws and then started again.

'A seat for the sunset, coral, green and grey. Two coppers for the standing! Three coppers for the sitting! A copper in the trees. The sunset at your bloody doorstep, friends! Buy it up! Buy! Buy! Buy!'

As Muzzlehatch stared through half-closed eyes at the old man the silence came down again, warm and thick with the sweetness of death in it.

At last Muzzlehatch muttered softly, 'What does he mean, in the name of mortality and all her brood . . . what does he mean?'

There was no answer. The silence settled down again, and seemed appalled at the notion that anyone could be ignorant of what the old man meant.

'Coral, green and grey,' continued Muzzlehatch as though mumbling to himself. 'Are these the colours of the sky tonight? Do you *pay*, my dears, to see the sunset? Ain't the sunset free? Good God, ain't even the *sunset* free?'

'It's all we have,' said a voice, 'that, and the dawn.'

'You can't trust the dawn,' said another, with such pathos that it seemed he held a personal grudge against tinted atmosphere.

The ticket seller leaned over and peered at Muzzlehatch from closer range.

'Free, did you say?' he said. 'How could it be free? With colours like the jewelled breasts of queens. Free indeed! Isn't there nothing sacred? Buy a chair, Mr Giant, and see it comfortable – they say there may be strokes of puce as well, and curdled salmon in the upper ranges. All for a copper! Buy! Buy! Buy! Thank you sir, thank you. For you, the *cedar benches*, sir. Hell, bless you.'

'What happens if the wind decides to veer?' said Muzzlehatch. 'What happens to your green and coral, then? Do I get my coppers back? What if it rains? Eh? What if it pours?'

Someone spat at Muzzlehatch, but he took no notice beyond smiling at the man with such a curious angle of the lips that the spitter felt his spine grow cold as death.

'Tonight there is no wind,' said a third voice. 'A puff or two. The green will be like glass. Maybe a slaughtered tiger will float southwards. Maybe his wounds will drip across the sky . . . but no . . .'

'No! Not tonight! Not tonight! Green, coral, grey.'

'I have seen sunsets black like soot, awash in the western spaces, stirred with cats' bood. I have seen sunsets like a flock of roses: drifting they were ... their pretty bums afloat. And once I saw the nipple of a queen ... the sun it was ... as pink as ...'

SIXTY-EIGHT

LATER that evening, Muzzlehatch and the small ape shook themselves free of the gaping crowd and drove the car, slowly at the tail of a ragged cavalcade that, winding this way and that, finally disappeared into a birdless forest. On the other side of these woods lay stretched a grass terrace, if such a word can be used to describe the rank earthwork upon whose western side the land dropped sheer away for a thousand feet to where the tops of miniature trees, no longer than lashes, hovered in the evening mist.

When the two of them had reached the terrace with its swathing vistas spreading like sections of the globe itself away and away into a great hush of silence and distance mixed, as though to form a new element, they left their car, and took their seats on one of the cedar benches. These benches, forming a long line, from north to south, were placed within a few feet of the edge of the precipice. Indeed there were those whose legs were on the long side and whose feet, as a result, hung loosely over the edge of the terrifying drop.

The small ape must have sensed something of the danger for it stayed no more than a few moments before leaping from its seat on to Muzzlehatch's lap, where it made faces at the sunset.

No one noticed this. And no one noticed Muzzlehatch's strong-fingered hand as it caressed the little ape beneath its jaw. All the attention and interest these ragged people had lavished upon the stranger and his ape was now a thing of the past. Every face was tinted with an omnipresent hue. Every eye was the eye of a connoisseur. A hush as of the world ceasing to breathe came down upon the company, and Muzzlehatch tossed his head in the silence, for something had touched him; some inner thing that he could not understand. An irritant ... a catch of the heat ... a bubble of air in a vast aorta ... for he found himself, all of a sudden, spellbound by what he saw above him. A coloured circus caught in a whirl of air had disintegrated and in its place a thousand animals of cloud streamed through the west.

At the backs of the watchers, and very close stood up the flanks of the high woods lit up by the evening sun, save where the shadows of the watchers were ranged against it. Before the watchers and below them the faraway valley had drawn across itself another veil of cold. Above, the sunset-watchers saw the beasts: all with their streaming manes, whatever the species: great whales no less than lions with their manes; tigers no less than fawns.

The sky was animals from north to south. Beasts of the earth and air, lifting their heads to cry ... to howl ... to scream, but they had no voices, and their jaws remained apart, gulping the fast air.

And it was then that Muzzlehatch rose to his feet. His face was dark with a sudden pain, a pain he was only half able to understand.

He stood at his full height in the spellbound silence, his whole body trembling. For some while, his eyes were fixed upon the sky where the animals changed shape before his gaze, melting from species to species but always with the manes propelling them.

A few feet to Muzzlehatch's side a great dusty bush of juniper clung on the verge of the precipice. One step took Muzzlehatch to this solitary object and he wrenched it free of the earth, and, raising it above his head, slung it out into the emptiness of the air where it fell and went on falling.

Now every head was turned to him. Every head from near or far away: they all turned. When they saw him there, standing trembling, they could not understand that he was looking through these animals of clouds to another time and another place: to a zoo of flesh and blood. Nor did they know that the gaunt visitor was feeling for the first time the utmost agony of their death. Beast after beast of the upper air recalled some most particular one of feather, scale or claw, some most particular one of beauty or of strength . . . some symbol of the unutterable wilds.

They had been his joy in a world gone joyless. Now they were not even mouldering, these beasts of his. Nor were they turned into ash, nor any part of earth. Science had eliminated them, and there was no trace. His brindled heron with its broken foot: where was he now? And the lemur, five months gone, yet with so wistful a face, and a jaw so full of needles. O liquidation! And for every one his own particular story. For each the divers capture: and as the cloudscape thronged itself with figures: with humps: with fins: with horns, and his mind with the images of mortality, so he trembled the more, for Muzzlehatch knew that the time had come for him to return to the scene of supreme wickedness, foul play, and death. For it was there that they lived or partly lived in cells, sealed from the light of day.

The small ape began to cry with a thin, sad, far-away sound and its master shifted it from one shoulder to the other.

Dazed by the enormity of his loss, he had for a time refused to believe; despite all evidence; had refused to consider the brutal reality of such a thing. But all the while a dreadful seed was gathering itself together beneath his ribs and on his tongue was a taste quite indescribably horrible.

But the moment came, when despite the nightmare of it all, he realized that his life, as he knew it, had snapped in half. He was no longer balanced or entire. There had been a time when he was lord of the fauna. Muzzlehatch, in his house by the mulberry tree, supremely at large among the iron cages. And there was the second, the present Muzzlehatch, vague yet menacing, lord of nothing.

Yet in this nothing, and ever since, though he did not know it, so obscure was the ghastly growth in his brain, there had been growing an implacable substance: an inner predicament from which he had no right, no wish to escape the disgusting world itself across whose body he must now retrace his way into the camp of the enemy.

And then it broke out like an asp from its shell ... a venomous creature, growing larger every moment as the vile scene took shape.

The clouds were gone, and the prophesied colours hung in the air like sheets. He turned his back on the sky and stared up at the trees that towered above the overgrown terrace. And as he did so his hatred oozed out of him and everything clarified. The chaos of his belated anger became congealed into a carbuncle. There was no longer any need for ferocity, or the brandishing of bushes. Were he able to, he would have restored the juniper to its precipitous perch. And when he turned back his big head to the silent lines of beggars his face was quite expressionless.

'Have any of you,' he bellowed, 'seen Gormenghast?'

The heads of the sunset-gazers made no movement. Their bodies remained half turned to him. Their eyes were fixed upon the biggest man they had ever seen. Not a sound came from the long, long lines of throats.

'Forget your bloody clouds,' he cried again. 'Have you seen a boy ... lord of a region? Have any strangers passed this way before?' He tossed his big head. 'Am I the only one?'

No sound but the faint rustling of leaves in the forest behind him. An unhappy silence, an ugly, fatuous silence. In this silence, Muzzlehatch's temper rose again. His loved zoo, dead by the hand of science, sprang before his eyes. Titus lost. Everything lost, except to find the lost realm of Gormenghast. And then to guide young Titus to his home. But why? And what to prove? Only to prove the boy was not a madman. A madman? He strode to the forest verge, his head in his hands, then raised his eyes, and pondered on the bulk and weight of his crazy car. He released the brake, and brought her to life, so that she sobbed, like a child pleading. He turned her to the precipice, and with a great heave sent her running upon her way. As she ran, the small ape leaped from his shoulders to the driver's seat, and riding her like a little horseman plunged down the abyss.

Ape gone. Car gone. All gone?

Muzzlehatch felt nothing; only a sense of incredulity that a fragment of his life should be so vividly hung up before him like a picture on the wall of the dark sky. He felt no anguish. All he could feel was a sense of liberation. What burdens had he left upon him, and within him? Nothing but love and vengeance.

These two precluded suicide, though for a moment the lines of watchers stared as Muzzlehatch stood looking down, his feet within an inch or two of the swallowing edge. Suddenly, turning his back upon the precipice and the shadowy congregation he made his way on foot into the birdless forest, and as he strode on and on in the tracks of his out-bound journey, retracing his route, he sang in the knowledge that he would come in the course of time to a region he had left where the scientists worked, like drones, to the glory of science and in praise of death.

Were Titus to have seen him now and noted the wry smile on the face of his friend and the unusual light in his eye, he would surely have been afraid.

SIXTY-NINE

MEANWHILE Titus, whose journeyings in search of his home and of himself had taken him through many climates, was now at rest in a cool grey house in the quiet of whose protecting walls he lay in fever.

His face, vivid and animate for all its stillness, lay half submerged in the white pillow. His eyes were shut: his cheeks flushed and his forehead hot and wet. The room about him was high, green, dusky and silent. The blinds were drawn and a sense of an underwater world wavered through the room.

Beyond the windows lay stretched a great park, in whose south-east corner a lake (for all its distance) stabbed the eye with a wild dazzle of water. Beyond the lake, almost on the horizon, arose a factory. It took the sky in its stride, its outline cruising across a hundred degrees, a masterpiece of design. Of all this Titus knew nothing, for his room was his world.

Nor did he know that sitting at the foot of his bed with her eyebrows raised was the scientist's daughter.

It was well for Titus that he was unable to see her through the hot haze of his fever. For hers was a presence not easily forgotten. Her body was exquisite. Her face indescribably quizzical. She was a modern. She had a new kind of beauty. Everything about her face was perfect in itself, yet curiously (from the normal point of view) misplaced. Her eyes were large and stormy grey, but were set a thought too far apart; yet not so far as to be immediately recognized. Her cheekbones were taut and beautifully carved, and her nose, straight as it was, yet gave the impression of verging, now on the retroussé side, now on the aquiline. As for the curl of her lips, it was like a creature half asleep, something that like a chameleon could change its colour (if not at will, at any rate at a minute's notice). Her mouth, today, was the colour of lilac blossom, very pale. When she spoke, her pale lips drew themselves back from her small white teeth, and allowed a word or two to wander like a petal that is blown listlessly away. Her chin was rounded like the smaller end of a hen's egg, and in profile it seemed deliciously small and vulnerable. Her head was balanced upon her neck, and her neck on her shoulders like a balancing act, and the bizarre diversity of her features, incongruous in themselves, came together and fused into a face quite irresistible.

From far below were cries and counter-cries, for the house was full of guests.

'Cheeta,' they shouted, 'where are you? We're going riding.'

'Then go!' said Cheeta, between her pretty teeth.

Great blond men were draped over the banisters, two floors below.

'Come on, Cheeta,' they yelled. 'We've got your pony ready.'

'Then shoot the brute,' she muttered.

She turned her head from Titus for a moment, and all her features, orientated thus, provoked a new relationship . . . another beauty.

'Leave her alone,' cried the young ladies, who knew that with Cheeta alongside there would be no fun for them. 'She doesn't want to come . . . she *told* us so,' they squealed.

Nor did she. She sat quite upright, her eyes fixed upon the young man.

SEVENTY

HE had been found lying asleep in an outhouse several days previously by one of the servants on his midnight round. His clothing was drenched, and he was shivering and babbling to himself. The servant, amazed, had been on his way to his master, but had been stopped in his tracks by Cheeta on her way to bed. Being asked why he was running, the servant told Miss Cheeta of the trespasser and together they made their way to the outhouse and there he was, to be sure, curled up and shuddering.

For a long while, she had done nothing but stare at the profile of the young man. It was, taken all in all, a young face, even a boyish face, but there had been something else about it not easy to understand. It was a face that had looked out on many a scene. It was as though the gauze of youth had been plucked away to discover something rougher, something nearer the bone. It seemed that a sort of shade passed to and fro over his face; an emanation of all he had been. In short, his face had the substance out of which his life was composed. It was nothing to do with the shadowy hollow beneath his cheekbones or the minute hieroglyphics that surrounded his eyes; it was to her as though his face was his life . . .

But also, she had felt something else. An instantaneous attraction.

'Say nothing of this,' she had said, 'do you understand? Nothing. Unless you wish to be dismissed.'

'Yes, madam.'

'Can you lift him?'

'I think so, madam.'

'Try.'

With difficulty he had raised Titus in his arms and together the three of them made their midnight journey to the green room at the end of the east wing. There, in this remote corner of the house, they laid him on a bed.

'That will be all,' said the scientist's daughter.

SEVENTY-ONE

THREE days had passed since that night when she had tended him. One would have thought that he must surely have opened his eyes if only because of his nearness to her peculiar beauty, but no, his eyes remained shut, or if not, then they *saw* nothing.

With an efficiency almost unattractive in a woman so compelling, she dealt with the situation, as though she were doing no more than pencilling her eyebrows.

It is true that on the second day of her patient's fever she was amazed at the farrago of his outpourings, for he had struggled in bed and cried out again and again, in a language made almost foreign by the number of places and of people; words she had never heard of, with one out-topping all . . . Gormenghast.

'Gormenghast.' That was the core and gist of it. At first Cheeta could make nothing of it, but gradually in between the feverish repetition of the word, were names and phrases that slowly fell into place and made for her some kind of picture.

Cheeta, the sophisticate, found herself, as she listened, drawn into a zone, a layer of people and happenings, that twisted about, inverted themselves, moved in spirals, yet were nevertheless consistent within their own confines. From the cold centre of elegance and a life of scheduled pleasure she was now being shown the gulches of a barbarous region. A world of capture and escape. Of violence and fear. Of love and hate. Yet above all, of an underlying calm. A calm built upon a rock-like certainty and belief in some immemorial tradition.

Here, tossing and sweating on the bed below her, lay a fragment, so it seemed, of a great tradition: for all the outward movement utterly still in the confidence of its own hereditary truth. Cheeta, for the first time in her life, felt in the presence of blood so much bluer than her own. She ran her little tongue along her lips.

There he lay in the dusk of the green room, while the voices of the house below him rang faintly down the corridors, and the riding horses stamped in their impatience.

'Can you hear me . . . O can you hear me . . . Can you . . . ?'
'Is that my son . . . ? Where are you . . . child?'
'Where are you, mother . . . ?'
'Where I always am . . .'
'At your high window, mother, a-swarm with birds?'
'Where else?'
'Can no one tell me . . . ?'
'Tell you what . . . ?'
'Where in the world I am . . .'
'Not easily . . . not easily.'
'You were never easy with your sums, young man. Never.'
'O fold me in the foul folds of your gown, O Mr Bellgrove, sir.'
'Why did you do it, boy? Why did you run away?
'Why did you . . . ?
'Why . . . why . . . ?
'Why . . . ?
'Listen . . . listen . . .'
'Why are your shoulders turned away from me?'
'The birds are perched upon her head like leaves.'
'And the cats like a white tide?'
'The cats are loyal in a traitors' world.'
'Steerpike . . . ?'
'O no !'
'Barquentine . . . ?'
'O no !'
'I cannot stand it . . . O my doctor dear.'
'I have missed you Titus . . . O very much so . . . by all that abdicates you take the cake.'
'But where have you gone to . . . love?'
'Why did you do it . . . why?'
'Why did you?'
'Why . . . why . . . ?
'Why . . .
'Your father . . . and your sister and now . . . you . . .'
'Fuchsia. . . . Fuchsia . . .'

163

'What was that?'

'I heard nothing.'

'O Dr Prune ... I love you, Dr Prune ...'

'I heard a footfall.'

'I heard a cry.'

'Ahoy there Urchin! Titus the flyblown ...'

'Hell how you've wandered! Who were you talking to?'

'Who was it Titus?'

'You wouldn't understand. He is different.'

'He drinks the red sky for his evening wine. He loved her.'

'Juno?'

'Juno.'

'He saved my life. He saved it many times.'

'Enough. Cut out the woman in you with a jack-knife.'

'God save the sweetness of your iron heart.'

'So they all died ... all ... fish, flesh and fowl.'

'Ha ha ha ha ha! They were only caged-up creatures after all. Look at that lion. That's all it is. Four legs ... two ears ... one nose ... one belly.'

'But they killed the zoo! Muzzlehatch's zoo! Plumes; horns; and beaks compounded all together. A slice of living over. The lion's mane, clotted with blood, creaking as it crumbles.'

'I love you, child. Where are you? Am I worrying you?'

'He's been away so long.'

'So long ... What were you doing in that part of the world that you could get so wet with the rain?'

'I was lost. I have always been lost; Fuchsia and I were always lost. Lost in our great house where the lizards crawled and the weeds made their way up the stairs and blossomed on the landings. Who is that? Why don't you open the door? Why do you keep fidgeting? Have you not the courage to open the door? Are you afraid of wood? Don't worry, I can see you through the door. Don't worry. Your name is Acreblade. King of the police. I hate your face. It is made of tin-tacks. Your arms are fixed with nails ... but Juno is with me. The castle is afloat. Steerpike my enemy swims under water, a dagger between his teeth. Yet I killed him. I killed him dead.

'Come here and we will dance together on the battlements. The turrets are white with bird-lime. It is like phosphorus. Join

hands with me, Muzzlehatch, and Juno, loveliest of all, and step
out into space. We will not fall alone for as we pass window
after window, a score of heads will bob along beside us, grin-
ning like ten-to-three. Veil and the Black Rose: Cusp-Canine and
the Grasses ... and close to me, all the way as we fell, was
the head of Fuchsia; her black hair in my eyes, but I could not
wait for there was the Thing to seek. The Thing. She lived in
the bole of a tree. The walls were honeycombs and the bole
droned, but never a bee would sting us. She leapt from branch
to branch until the schoolmasters came, Bellgrove, Cutflower,
and the rest; their mortar-boards slanting through the shadows.
Dig a great pit for them: sing to them. Make flower fairies out
of hollyhocks. Throw down the bean-pods like dove-green
canoes. That ought to keep them happy through the winter.
Happy? Happy? Ha, ha, ha, ha, ha. The owls are on their way
from Gormenghast. Ha, ha, ha! The ravenous owls ... the
owls ... the little owls.'

SEVENTY-TWO

WHEN Titus saw her first he imagined her to be yet another of
the crowding images, but as he continued to stare at her he
knew that this was no face in the clouds.

She had not seen him open his eyes, and so Titus was afforded
the opportunity of watching, for a moment or two, the ice in
her features. When she turned her head and saw him staring at
her she made no effort to soften her expression, knowing
that he had taken her unawares. Instead, she stared at Titus
in return, until the moment came when, as though they had
been playing the game of staring-one-another-out, she made
as though she could keep her features set no longer and the
ice melted away and her face broke into an expression that
was a mixture of the sophisticated, the bizarre, and the
exquisite.

'You win,' she said. Her voice was as light and as listless as
thistledown.

'Who are you?' said Titus.

165

'It doesn't matter,' she said. 'As long as I know who you are
... or does it?'

'Who am I then?'

'Lord Titus of Gormenghast, Seventy-Seventh Earl.' The
words fluttered like autumn leaves.

Titus shut his eyes.

'Thank God,' he said.

'For what?' said Cheeta.

'For knowing. I'd grown to almost doubt the bloody place.
Where am I? My body's on fire.'

'The worst is over,' said Cheeta.

'Is it? What kind of worst?'

'The search. Drink this and lie back.'

'What a face you have,' said Titus. 'It's paradise on edge.
Who are you? Eh? Don't answer, I know it all. You are a woman! That's what you are. So let me suck your breasts, like
little apples, and play upon your nipples with my tongue.'

'You are obviously feeling better,' said the scientist's daughter.

SEVENTY-THREE

ONE morning, not very long after he had fully recovered from
his fever, Titus rose early, and dressed himself with a kind of
gaiety. It was a sensation somewhat foreign to his heart. There
had been a time, and not so long ago, when a whim of ludicrous
thought could bend him double; when he could laugh at everything and anything as though it were nothing ... for all the
darkness of his early days. But now it seemed had come a time
when there was more darkness than light.

But a time had been reached in his life when he found him-
self laughing in a different kind of way and at different things.
He no longer yelled his laughter. He no longer shouted his joy.
Something had left him.

Yet on this particular morning, something of his younger self
seemed to be with him as he rolled out of bed and on to his
feet. An inexplicable bubble; a twinge of joy.

As he let fly the blinds, and disclosed a landscape, he screwed up his face with pleasure, stretched his arms and legs. Yet there was nothing for him to be so pleased about. In fact it was more the other way. He was entangled. He had made new enemies. He had compromised himself irremediably with Cheeta who was dangerous as black water.

Yet this morning Titus was happy. It was as though nothing could touch him. As though he bore a charmed life. Almost as though he lived in another dimension, un-enterable to others, so that he could risk anything, dare everything. Just as he had revelled in his shame and felt no fear on that day when he lay recovering from his fever . . . so now he was in a world equally on his side.

So he ran down the elegant stairs this early morning, and galloped to the stables as though he were himself one of the ponies. In a few moments she was saddled and away . . . the grey mare, away to the lake in whose motionless expanse lay the reflection of the factory.

Out of the slender, tapering chimneys arose, like incense, thin columns of green smoke. Beyond these chimneys the dawn sky lay like an expanse of crumpled linen. As she galloped, the lake growing closer and closer with each stride, he did not know that there was someone following him. Someone else had woken early. Someone else had been to the stables, saddled a pony and raced away. Had Titus turned his head he would have seen as lovely a sight as could be encountered. For the scientist's daughter could ride like a leaf in the wind.

When Titus reached the shore of the lake he made no effort to rein in his grey, who, plunging ever deeper into the lake, sent up great spurts of water, so that the perfect reflection of the factory was set in motion, wave following wave, until there was no part of the lake that was not rippled.

From the motionless building there came a kind of rumour; an endless impalpable sound that, had it been translated into a world of odours, might have been likened to the smell of death: a kind of sweet decay.

When the water had climbed to the throat of the grey horse, and had all but brought the animal to a standstill, Titus lifted his head, and in the softness of the dawn he heard for the first time the full, vile softness of the sound.

167

Yet, for all this it looked anything but mysterious and Titus ran his eye along the great façade, as though it were the flank of a colossal liner, alive with countless portholes.

Letting his eye dwell for a moment on a particular window, he gave a start of surprise, for in its minute centre was a face; a face that stared out across the lake. It was no larger than the head of a pin.

Turning his eyes on the next of the windows, he saw, as before, a minute face. A chill ran up his spine and he shut his eyes, but this did not help him, for the soft, sick, sound seemed louder in his ears, and the far musty smell of death filled his nostrils. He opened his eyes again. Every window was filled with a face, and every face was staring at him, and most dreadful of all else, every face was the same.

It was then that from far away there came the faint sound of a whistle. At the sound of it the thousands of windows were suddenly emptied of their heads.

All the joy had gone from the day. Something ghastly had taken its place. He turned the grey horse round slowly, and came face to face with Cheeta. Whether it was because her image followed so hard upon that of the factory so that it became tainted in his mind, or whether for some more obscure cause, one cannot tell, but for one reason or another, he was instantaneously sickened at the sight of her. His joy was now finally gone. There was no adventure in his bones. All about him the dawn was like a sickness. He sat on horseback, between an evil edifice, and someone who seemed to think that to be exquisite was enough. Why was she curling the upper petal of her mouth? Could she not smell the foul air? Could she not hear the beastliness of that slow regurgitation?

'So it's you,' he said at last.

'It's me,' said Cheeta, 'why not?'

'Why do you follow me?'

'I can't imagine,' answered Cheeta, in so laconic a voice, that Titus was forced to smile in spite of himself.

'I think I hate you,' he said. 'I don't quite know why. I also hate that stinking factory. Did your father build it – this edifice?'

'They say so,' said Cheeta. 'But then they say anything, don't they?'

168

'Who?' said Titus.

'Ask me another, darling. And don't go scampering off. After all I love you all I dare.'

'All you dare! That is very good.'

'It is indeed *very* good, when you think of the fools I have sent packing.'

Titus turned his head to her, nauseated by the self-sufficiency in her voice, but directly he focused his gaze upon her his armour began to crack, and he saw her this time in the way he had first seen her, as something infinitely desirable. That he abhorred her brain seemed almost to add to his lust for her body.

Perched aloft her horse, she was there it seemed for the taking. It was for her to remain exactly as she was, her profile motionless against the sky; small, delicate and perhaps vicious. Titus did not *know*. He could only sense it.

'As for you,' she said. 'You're different, aren't you? You can behave yourself.'

The smugness of this remark was almost too much, but before Titus could say a word, she had flicked her reins, and trotted out of the hem of the lake.

Titus followed her, and when they were on dry ground, she called to him.

'Come along, Titus Groan. I know you think you hate me. So try and catch me. Chase me, you villain.'

Her eyes shone with a new light, her body trim as the last word in virgins. Her little riding-habit beautifully cut and moulded as though for a doll. Her tiny body horribly wise, horribly irritating. But O how desirable! Her face lit up as though with an inner light, so clear and radiant was her complexion.

'Chase me,' she cried again, but it was the strangest cry ... a cry that seemed to be directed at no one, a distant, floating sound.

With her listless voice in his head, the factory was forgotten and Titus, taking up the challenge, was in a few moments in hot pursuit.

Around them on three sides were distant mountains, with their crests shining wanly in the dawn's rays.

Set against these mountains, like stage properties, glimmering in the low beams were a number of houses, one of which was the property of Cheeta's father, the scientist. To the south of this house was a great airfield, shimmering; a base for all kinds of aircraft. To the south again was a belt of trees from the dark interior of which came the intermittent cries of forest creatures.

All this was on the skyline. Far away from Cheeta as she sped, irrational, irritating, a flying virgin, with her lipstick gleaming with a wet, pink light on her half-open mouth; her hair bobbing like a living animal as she rode to the rhythm of the horse's stride.

As Titus thundered in pursuit, he suddenly felt foolish. Normally he would have brushed the feeling to one side, but today it was different. It was not that he cared about behaving foolishly. That was in key with the rest of his nature, and he would have ignored or retained the whim, according to his mood. No. This was something more peculiar. There was something incurably obvious about it all. Something puerile. They were riding on the wings of a cliché. Man pursues woman at dawn! Man has got to consummate his lust! Woman gallops like mad on the rim of the near future. And rich! As rich as her father's factory can make her. And he? He is heir to a kingdom. But where is it? Where is it?

To his left was a small copse and Titus made for it, throwing the reins across the horse's neck. Immediately he reached the limes he knelt down with an acid smile on his lips, thinking he had evaded her, and her designs. He shut his eyes, but only for a moment, for the air became full of a perfume both dry and fresh, and opening his eyes again he found himself looking up at the scientist's daughter.

SEVENTY-FOUR

HE started to his feet.

'O hell!' he cried. 'Do you have to keep on hopping out of nothing? Like that damn' Phoenix bird. Half blood, half ashes.

I don't like it. I'm tired of it. Tired of opening my eyes to find odd women peering at me from a great height. How did you get here? How did you know? I thought I'd slipped you.'

Cheeta ignored his questions.

'Did you say "women"?' she whispered. Her voice was like dry leaves in a tree.

'I did,' said Titus. 'There was Juno.'

'I am not interested in Juno,' said Cheeta. 'I've heard all about her . . . too often.'

'You have?'

'I have.'

'How foolish of me,' said Titus, curling his lip. 'Great God, you must have plundered my subconscious. Entrails 'n all. What'll you do with such a foul cargo? How far did I go? What did I tell you? Of how I raped her in a bed of parsley?'

'Who?' said the scientist's daughter.

'My great grand-dam. The one with pointed teeth.'

'Now that,' said Cheeta, 'I *don't* remember!'

'Your face,' said Titus, 'is quite wonderful. But it spells disaster. To have you would be like holding a time bomb. Not that you mean to be dangerous. Oh no! But your features carry a danger of their own. You cannot help it, nor can they.'

Cheeta stared at her companion for a long time. At last she said . . .

'What is it, Titus, that isolates us? You seem to do all you can to belittle our friendship. You are so very difficult. I could be happy talking to you, hour after hour, but you are never serious, never. Heaven knows, I am no talker. But a word here and there would be something. All you seem to think of is either to make love to me, or to be facetious.'

'I know what you mean,' said Titus. 'I know *exactly* what you mean.'

'Then . . . why . . .?'

'It is more difficult than I can tell you. I have to form a barrier against you. A barrier of foolery. I cannot, I *must* not take it seriously, this land of yours, this land of factories, this *you*. I have been here long enough to know it is not for me. You are no help with your peculiar wealth and beauty. It leads nowhere. It keeps me like a dancing bear on the end of a rope.

Ah ... you are a rare one. You spend your time with me, showing me off to your father. But why? Why? To shock him and his friends. You throw off your suitors one by one, and leave them hopping mad. This jealousy whipped up is like a stink. What is it?'

Titus, reaching out for her hand as she stood above him, pulled her down to the ground.

'Careful,' she said. Her eyebrows were raised as she lay beside him.

A dragonfly cruised above them with a thin vibration of transparent wings, and then the silence settled again.

'Take your hand away,' said Cheeta. 'I don't like it. To be touched makes me sick. You understand, don't you?'

'No, I bloody well don't,' said Titus, jumping to his feet. 'You're as cold as meat.'

'Do you mean that it has always been my body and only my body that has attracted you? Do you mean that there is no other reason why you should want to be near me?'

Her voice took on a new tone. It was dry and remote but it carried with it an edge.

'The strange thing is,' she said, 'that I should love you. You. A young man who has harboured nothing but lust for me. An enigmatic creature from somewhere that is not to be found in an atlas. Can't you understand? You are my mystery. Sex would spoil it. There's nothing mysterious about sex. It is your mind that matters, and your stories, Titus, and the way you are different from any other man I have ever seen. But you are cruel, Titus, cruel.'

'Then the sooner I'm gone, the better,' he shouted, and as he swung round upon her, he found himself closer than he imagined himself to be, for he was staring down at a little face, bizarre, utterly feminine, and delicious. His arms were at once about her, and he drew her to him. There was no response. As for her head it was turned away so that he could not kiss her.

'Hello, hello!' he shouted, letting her go. 'This is the end.'

He let her go and she at once began to brush her riding clothes.

'I'm finished with you,' said Titus. 'Finished with your marvellous face and your warped brain. Go back to your clutch of virgins and forget me as I shall forget you.'

'You *beast*,' she cried. 'You ungrateful *beast*. Am I nothing in myself that you desert me? Is coupling so important? There are a million lovers making love in a million ways, but there is only one of me.' Her hands trembled. 'You have disappointed me. You're cheap. You're shoddy. You're weak. You're probably mad. You and your Gormenghast! You make me sick.'

'I make myself sick,' said Titus.

'I'm glad,' said the scientist's daughter, 'long may you remain so.'

Now that Cheeta knew that she was in no way loved by Titus, the harshness that had crept into her voice was transferring itself to her thoughts. Never before in her life had she been thwarted. There was not one of all her panting admirers who had ever dared to talk to her in the way that Titus had talked. They were prepared to wait a hundred years for a smile from those lips of hers, or the lift of an eyebrow. She stared at him now, as though for the first time, and she hated him. In some peculiar way she had been humbled by him, although it was Titus who had been stopped short in his advances. The harshness that had crept into her voice and mind was turning into native cunning. She had given herself to him in every way short of the actual act of love and she had been flouted; brushed aside.

What did she care whether or not he was Lord of Gormenghast? Whether he was sane or deranged? All she knew was that something miraculous had been snatched from her grasp, and that she would stop at nothing short of absolute revenge.

SEVENTY-FIVE

THE violent death of Veil in the Under-River was cause for endless speculation and wonderment, not for a day or two, but for months on end. Who was the boy who had made so miraculous an escape? Who was the rangy stranger who had saved him? (There were some to be sure who had seen Muzzlehatch from time to time over the last decade, but even to those he was more of a ghost than a reality and the stories that were told of him were all but legends.)

There were those who remembered Muzzlehatch on the run, and how the dripping gates had opened to him with as great a sigh as ever haunted the dream of a melancholic.

Here, long ago, in his enormous hideout he would sing until the bells gave in, or sit for hours brooding, like a monarch, sometimes covered in brambles, or daubed with earth according to the country through which he had been stealing. And there was the time, on a never-to-be-forgotten day, when he was seen immaculately clad from head to toe, striding down a seemingly endless corridor, complete with a top hat on his head, a cane in his hand (which he twirled like a juggler) and an air of indescribable hauteur.

But for the most part he was known for the shameful negligence with which he kept his garments.

But he never lived there, with the denizens. The Under-River was a refuge and nothing more to him, and so he was as much a mystery to them as to the sophisticates who lived in the great houses above the river banks.

But where had they disappeared to, these two figures, the gaunt and self-sufficient Muzzlehatch, and the young man he saved? How could they ever know, these self-incarcerated rebels; these thieves and refugees? Yet they talked of little else but the flight and where they might be. Their talk was nothing but conjecture, and could get them nowhere, yet it provided almost a reason for living. For all, except three. Three, and a most unlikely three. It seems that they had been awakened in their different ways, by the horror of the ghastly incident. They were shocked, but they did not remain so. All they wanted now was to escape, at any risk, from the thronged emptiness of the place.

Superficially unadventurous, yet restless to quit that saturated morgue: superficially inactive yet ready now to take the risk of escape. For the police were after all three.

Crabcalf, with his pale pushed-in face and his general air of martyrdom. Self-centred, if not to the point of megalomania, then very near it. What of the fact that he was bed-ridden?

And what of the heavy 'remainder' of identical volumes that had once propped up his pillow and surrounded his bed for so many years?

His bed, thanks to his friend Slingshott, and one or two others, had been exchanged for an upright chair on wheels. On the back of this chair was hung a great sack. It was filled with his books, and a great weight it was. Poor Slingshott, whose duty it was to push the chair, books, Crabcalf and all, from district to district, found little pleasure in the occupation. Not only had Slingshott the lowest opinion of Literature as a whole, he had even more a distaste for this particular book in so far as it was repeated so many times, and every time a strain upon the heart.

But though it was a long book and heavy, in spite of Crab-calf having jettisoned the bulk of it, and though it was dupli-cated scores of times, yet Slingshott never dreamed of rebel-lion, or queried his rights. He knew that without Crabcalf he would be lost.

As for Crabcalf, he was so absorbed in shallow speculations, that the fact that Slingshott was in any way suffering never occurred to him.

To be sure he heard from time to time the sound of wailing, but it might just have well been the scraping together of branches for all he knew or cared.

SEVENTY-SIX

IT was on a moonless, starless night that they escaped from the Under-River and headed north by east. Within a month they were on foreign soil.

It was under a bald hill that they picked up Crack-Bell as planned. He was, for all his idiocy, the only one of the three who had any money. Not much, as they soon found out, but enough to last them for a month or two. This money was trans-ferred to Crabcalf's pocket, where, as he said, it would be safer. When it came to money Crabcalf's vagueness seemed to desert him.

Crack-Bell had no objections. Nothing happened. He had been rich. Now he was poor. What did it matter? His laugh was as shrill, as penetrating as it always was. His smile just as fatuous. His responses just as quick. Compared with his two companions, Crack-Bell was intensely alive, like a monkey.

'Here we are,' he cried. 'Bang in the middle of somewhere. Don't ask me where, but somewhere. Ha, ha, ha.' His crockery laughter rattled down the hill in broken pieces.

'Mr Crabcalf, sir,' said Slingshott.

'Yes?' said Crabcalf, raising an eyebrow. 'What do you want this time? Another rest, I suppose.'

'We have covered a lot of heavy ground today,' said Slingshott, 'and I am tired. Indeed I am. It reminds me of those . . .'

'Years in the salt mines. Yes, yes. We know all about them,' said Crabcalf. 'And would you care to be a little more careful with my volumes? You handle that sack as though it were full of potatoes.'

'If I may get a tiny word in edgeways,' trilled Crack-Bell. 'I would put it like this . . .'

'Unstrap my volumes,' said Crabcalf. 'All of them. Dust them down with a dry cloth. Then count them.'

'When I was in the mines you know, I had time to think . . .' said Slingshott, obeying Crabcalf mechanically.

'Oh la! And did you then? And what did you think of? Women? Women! Ha, ha, ha. Women. Ha, ha, ha, ha.'

'Oh no. Oh no indeed. I know nothing of women,' said Slingshott.

'Did you hear that, Crabcalf? What an extraordinary statement to have made. It is like saying "I know nothing of the moon".'

'Well, what *do* you know of it?' said Crabcalf.

'As much as I know of *you*, my dear fellow. The moon is arid. And so are you. But what does all this matter? We are alive. We are at large. To hell with the moon. It's a coward anyway. Only comes out at night! Ha, ha, ha, ha!'

'The moon figures in my book,' said Crabcalf. 'I can't remember quite where . . . but it figures quite a lot. I talk, or rather, I dilate you know, on the change that has come over the moon.

Ever since Molusk circled it, it has been quite a different thing. It has lost its mystery. Are you listening, Slingshott?'

'Yes, and no,' said Slingshott. 'I was really thinking about our next encampment. It was different in the mines. There was no ...'

'Forget the mines,' said Crabcalf. 'And mind your clumsy elbow on my manuscript. Oh my friends, my friends, is it nothing that we have escaped from that pernicious place? That we are all three together as we had planned? That we are here at peace on the lee side of a bald hill?'

'Yet even here one cannot help remembering that beastly grapple. It quite turns me up,' said Slingshott.

'Oh my. It was a scrap indeed! Bones, muscles, tendons, organs, 'n all sorts, scattered this way and that, but what does it matter now? The evening is fine; there are two stars. Life is ahead of us ... or some of it is. Ha! ha! ha!'

'Yes, yes, yes. I know all about that Crack-Bell, but I can't help wondering ...'

'Wondering?'

'Yes, about that boy. He sticks in my mind,' said Slingshott.

'I didn't see much of him. I was some way down the hill. But from what I saw, and from what I know of life, I should say he was well reared.'

'Well reared! Ha, ha, ha, ha, ha! That's very spicy.'

'Spicy! You fool! Do you think I've spent my life in the Under-River? I was a valet once.'

Slingshott rose to his feet.

'The dew is rising,' he said. 'I must build the fire. As for the young man, I would give much to see him.'

'Obviously,' said Crabcalf. 'He had an air about him. Yet, why should we want to ...?'

'To see him?' cried Crack-Bell. 'Why should we? Oh la! He and his crocodile friend. Oh la! What food for conjecture.'

'Leave that to me,' said Crabcalf. 'I have a head like a compass, and a nose like a bloodhound. For you dear Slingshott, the encampments and the care of the volumes ... Crack-Bell, for forage and the wringing of hens' necks. Oh my dear, how neatly and fleetly you move when the moon gloats on farms and the yards are black and silver. How neatly and fleetly you stalk

177

the livestock. If ever we catch up with the boy we will have wine and turkey.'

'I don't drink,' said Slingshot.

'Hush!'

'What is it?'

'Did you not hear the laughter?'

'Sh ... sh ...'

SEVENTY-SEVEN

THERE was a sound; and their heads turned together to the west flank of the bald hill.

Came slithering through the dusk the entrail gobblers: the belly-brained, agog for carrion. The jackals and the foxes. What are they digging for? The scrabbling of their horn-grey nails proceeds. Their eyes start like jellies. Their ears, the twitching spades of playing-cards. Ahoy! scavengers! The moon's retching.

As Slingshott, Crack-Bell and Crabcalf crouched trembling (for at first it might have been anything, so curiously repellent was the noise) another kind of sound caused them to turn their heads again, and this time it was towards the sky.

Out of the blind space, sunless and terrible, like coloured gnats emerging from the night, a squadron of lime-green needles, peeling at speed, made for the earth.

The jackals lifted their vile muzzles. Slingshott, Crabcalf, and Crack-Bell lifted theirs.

There was no time for fear or understanding. They were gone no sooner than they appeared. But, fast as they travelled, there was something more than speed for its own sake. *It seemed they were looking for someone.*

The jackals and the foxes returned to their carcase on the other side of the bald hill, and in doing so they were unable to see the helmeted figures, who now stood against the sky like tall carvings, identical in every particular.

They wore a kind of armour, yet were free to move with absolute ease. When one of them took a step forward, the other

178

took a similar step at the same moment. When one of them shielded his huge hollow eyes from the moon, his companion followed suit.

Had they been guiding those soundless aerial darts? It did not seem so, for their heads were bowed a little.

Around their column-like necks were tiny boxes, suspended from metal threads. What were they? Could it be that they were receiving messages from some remote headquarters? But no! Surely not. They were not the sort of mortals to obey. Their silence in itself was hostile and proud.

Only once did they turn their gaze upon the three vagrants, and in that double gaze was such a world of scorn that Crabcalf and his two trembling pards felt an icy blast against their bodies. It was not for them that the helmeted pair were searching.

Then came a growl as the teeth of one of the jackals met in the centre of some dead brute's intestines, and at that sound the tall pair turned upon their heels, and moved away with a strange and gliding action that was more terrible than any strut or stride.

Now *they* were gone the jackals followed suit, for nothing was left on the bones of the poor dead beast. Like a canopy the countless flies hung over the skeleton as though to form a veil or shawl of mourning.

The three from the Under-River climbed at last to the crest of the hill, and saw spread out in the moonlight, on every side, a lunar landscape, infinitely brittle. But they were in no mood for pulchritude.

'No sleep for us tonight,' said Crabcalf. 'I don't like the place one little bit. My thighs are as wet as turbots.'

The other two agreed that it was no place for sleep, though it fell upon Slingshott, as always, to push the wheeled chair up and down the slopes of this horrible terrain, with not only Crabcalf himself on board, but his 'remainder' of sixty-one volumes.

Crack-Bell (who, over and above the blanching effect of the moon on his face was, in his own right, as white as a sheet) walked a little behind the other two, and in an attempt to appear courageous, whistled an air both shrill and out of key.

SEVENTY-EIGHT

AND so they moved in a single file across the white landscape, and encountered no sign of a living creature. Crabcalf was seated in his high-backed chair on wheels; his sack of identical books in his lap. Slingshott, his retainer, pushed his master, laboriously, down narrow defiles, along cold ridges, across deserts of shale. As for Crack-Bell, he had long ago given up whistling, saving his breath for the thankless task of hauling an old cooking stove, some camping gear, and a stolen turkey. Staggering along in the rear of this three-piece cavalcade, with nothing but a cold night ahead, Crack-Bell, by his very nature, could not help the irritating grin that hovered over the lower regions of his face, nor the mad twinkle in his empty eyes. 'Life is good,' they seemed to say ... 'Life is very good.'

Had it not been that he took up the rearguard station his facial fatuities must surely have maddened his two companions. As it was, he trudged along unseen.

SEVENTY-NINE

SHE sat motionlessly at her peerless mirror, gazing not *at*, but *through* herself, for her meditation was deep and bitter, and her eyes had lost their sense of sight. Had she been aware of her own reflection and freed her eyes of the veil that lay like a cataract across them, she would have seen, first of all, the unnatural rigidity of her body, and she would have relaxed not only the muscles of her spine, but those of her face.

For there was, in spite of her beauty, something macabre about her head; something she would certainly have attempted to disguise had she known it permeated her features. But she knew nothing of this, and so she sat there, bolt upright, staring, with her eyes out of focus, while the blank reflections of her orbs stared back.

The stillness was horrible, especially when, like something

palpable, it coagulated and seemed almost to drown the only authentic sound, that of a dry leaf as it fluttered from time to time against the glass of a distant window.

The very atmosphere of Cheeta's dressing-room was in itself enough to chill the blood, so austere and loveless it was. And yet, although it sent a vile chill up the spine, it was not, on that account, a place of ugliness. On the contrary, it was majestic in its proportions and superb in its economy.

The floor, to begin with, was spread from corner to distant corner with a tundra of white camel skins, pale as white sand and soft as wool.

The walls were hung with tapestries that glowed with a sullen, prawn-coloured luminosity ... a system of concealed lighting that gave the impression that the muted light was not so much falling upon the tapestries, as emerging from them. As though they were themselves effulgent, and burned their lives away.

EIGHTY

NOT so many years ago she had cried out, 'Oh how I hate you all.' The elders shook their heads. 'What does she mean?' they said. 'Has she not everything that money can buy? Is she not the scientist's daughter?'

But she was restless, was Cheeta. Would she care for this? Would she care for that? No. Would she accept the Greeziorthspis Tapestries? She would accept them.

They were bought for her, thus denuding a small country of its only treasure.

So here they hung in the great room that was designed to take them, lovelier than ever, burning away in dusty pinks and golds, but with no one to see them, for Cheeta had deserted what was once her joy.

They had gone dead on her; or she on them. The unicorns leapt unseen. The crags that blushed in the sun's rays, meant nothing now. The perilous combers were now no longer perilous.

The floor of camel-hair; the walls of tapestry; the dressing-table. It was carved from a single hunk of granite. Upon its surface were laid out, as usual, the articles of her toilet.

The surface of the black granite was peerlessly smooth, yet thrillingly uneven to the palm of the hand, appearing to bulge, or sway, and the reflections of the various instruments were as sharp as the instruments themselves, yet wavered. For all the multiplicity of her toilet, the coloured objects took up the merest fraction of the surface. To right and left of them, the granite fanned out in adamantine yet sumptuous undulations.

But Cheeta who sat upright on the camel-hair seat of her chair was today in no frame of mind to run the palms of her hands in silent and sensuous delight. Something had happened to her. Something that had never happened before. She knew now for the first time that she was unnecessary. Titus Groan had found that he could do without her.

Beneath the rigidity of her small, slender, military spine was a writhing serpent. Beyond the blankness of her seemingly dead eyes was a world of febrile horror, for she now knew that she hated him. Hated his self-sufficiency. Hated a quality that he had, which she lacked. She lifted her glazed eyes to the sky beyond the mirror. It swam with little clouds, and her sight cleared at last, and her eyelids fell.

Her thoughts like scales began to shed themselves until there was an absolute nothingness in her head, a nothingness made necessary, for the intensity of her dark thoughts had been horrible and could not be kept up forever, short of madness.

Beyond the mirror, scissoring its way across the sky, was her father's pride. The latest of all his factories. Even as she watched, a plume of smoke spiralled its way out of one of the chimneys.

Rigid as herself in her agony, her implements were drawn up in battle array. A militant array of eccentrics; instruments of beauty; coloured like the rainbow; shining like steel or wax; the unguent vases carved in alabaster; the Kohl; the nard.

The fragrance from the onyx and the porphyry pots, the elusive aromatic spikenard ... olive and almond and the sesame oil. The powdery perfumes, ground for her alone; rose, almond, quince. The rouges, the spices and the gums. The eyebrow pencils, and the coloured cyeline; mascara and the powder brush. The eyebrow tweezers and the eyelash curlers. The tissues, the crêpes and several little sponges. Each in its place before the perfect mirror.

Then there was a sound. At first it was so faint it was impossible to make out what was being said, or whether indeed it was her voice at all. Had it not been that there was no one else in the room one would not have guessed the sound to come from such pretty lips as Cheeta's. But now the sound grew louder and louder until she beat upon her granite dressing-table with her minute fists and called out, 'Beast, beast, beast! Go back to your filthy den. Go back to your Gormenghast!' and rising to her feet she swept the granite table with her arm so that everything that had been set out so beautifully was sent hurtling through the air to smash itself and waste itself upon the white camel skins of the carpet and the dusky red of the tapestries.

EIGHTY-ONE

OUT of the bitterness that was now a part of her, like an allergy, *something* had begun to arise to the surface of her conscious mind; something that might be likened to a sea monster rising from the depths of the ocean; scaled and repulsive. At first she did not know or feel any kind of contraction, but gradually as the days went by, the nebulous ponderings began to find focus. Something harsher took their place until she realized that what she craved was the knowledge not just of *how* to hurt but *when*. So that at last, a fortnight after her argument with Titus she realized that she was actively plotting the downfall of the boy, and that her whole being was diverted to that end.

In sweeping her make-up to the floor she had swept away all that was blurred in her mind and passion. This left her not only more venomous but icy-headed, so that when she next saw Titus her behaviour was the very heart of poise.

EIGHTY-TWO

'Is that the boy?' asked Cheeta's father, the merest wisp of a man.

'Yes father, that is he.' His voice had been utterly empty. His presence was a kind of subtraction. He was nondescript to the point of embarrassment. Only his cranium was positive – a lard-coloured hummock.

His features, if described piecemeal, would amount to nothing, and it was hard to believe that the same blood ran through Cheeta's body. Yet there was something – an emanation that linked the father and daughter. A kind of atmosphere that was entirely their own; although their features had no part in it. For he was *nothing*: a creature of solitary intellect, unaware of the fact that, humanly speaking, he was a kind of vacuum for all that there was genius in his skull. He thought of nothing but his factory.

Cheeta, following his gaze, could see Titus quite clearly.

'Pull up,' she said, in a voice as laconic as a gull's.

Her father touched a button, and at once the car sighed to a halt.

At the far end of an overhung carriage-way was Titus, apparently talking to himself, but just as Cheeta and her father were about to suppose that he had lost his senses, three beggars emerged out of the distant tangle of leaves, at Titus's side.

This group of four had apparently not heard or seen the approach of the car.

The long drive was dappled with soft autumnal light.

'We have been following you,' said Crack-Bell. 'Ha, ha, ha! In and out of your footsteps as you might say.'

'Following me? What for? I don't even know you,' said Titus.

'Don't you remember, young man?' said Crabcalf. 'In the Under-River? When Muzzlchatch saved you?'

'Yes, yes,' said Titus, 'but I don't remember *you*. There were thousands of you ... and besides ... have you seen him?'

'Muzzlehatch?'

'Muzzlehatch.'

'Not so,' said Slingshott.

There was a pause.

'My dear boy,' said Crack-Bell –

'Yes?' said Titus.

'How elegant you are. Just as I used to be. You were a beggar when we saw you last. Like us, you were. Ha, ha, ha! A mouldering mendicant. But look at you now. O la la!'

'Shut up,' said Titus.

He stared at them again. Three failures. Pompous as only failures can be.

'What do you want with me?' said Titus. 'I have nothing to give you.'

'You have everything,' said Crabcalf. 'That's why we follow you. You are different, my lord.'

'Who called me that?' whispered Titus. 'How did you know?'

'But everybody knows,' cried Crack-Bell, in a voice that carried to where Cheeta and her father watched every move.

'How did you know where to find me?'

'We have kept our ears to the ground, and our eyes skinned, and we used what wits God gave us.'

'After all you have been watched. You are not unknown.'

'Unknown!' cried Crack-Bell. 'Ha, ha, ha! That's good!'

'What's in the sack?' said Titus, turning away.

'My lifework,' said Crabcalf. 'Books, scores of them, but every one the same.' He lifted his head in pride, and tossed it to and fro. 'These are my "remainders". They are my centre. Please take one, my lord. Take one with you back to Gormenghast. Look. I will dip for you.'

Crabcalf, brushing Slingshott aside from the wheel-chair tore open the sack, and plunging his arm down its throat, drew forth a copy from the darkness. He took a pace towards Titus, and offered him the enigmatic volume.

'What's it about?' said Titus.

'Everything,' said Crabcalf. 'Everything I know of life and death.'

'I'm not much of a reader,' said Titus.

'There's no hurry,' said Crabcalf. 'Read it at your leisure.'

'Thanks very much,' said Titus. He turned over a few pages at random. 'There are poems too, are there?'

'Interlarded,' said Crabcalf. 'That is very true; there are poems *interlarded*. Shall I read you one ... my lord?'

'Well ...'

'Ah, here we are ... mm ... mm. A thought ... just a passing thought. Where are we? Are you ready sir?'

'Is it very long?' said Titus.

'It is very short,' said Crabcalf, shutting his eyes. 'It goes thus . . .

> 'How fly the birds of heaven save by their wings?
> How tread the stags, those huge and hairy kings
> Save by their feet? How do the fishes turn
> In their wet purlieus where the mermaids yearn
> Save by their tails? How does the plantain sprout
> Save by that root it cannot do without?'

Crabcalf opened his eyes. 'Do you see what I mean?' he said.

'What is your name?' said Titus.

'Crabcalf.'

'And your friends?'

'Crack-Bell and Slingshott.'

'You escaped from the Under-River?'

'We did.'

'And have you been searching for me a long while?'

'We have.'

'For what reason?'

'Because you need us. You see . . . we believe you to be what you say you are.'

'What do I say I am?'

The three took a simultaneous step forward. They lifted their rugged faces to the leaves above them and spoke together . . .

'You are Titus, the Seventy-Seventh Earl of Groan, and Lord of Gormenghast. So help us God.'

'We are your bodyguard,' said Slingshott in a voice so weak and fatuous that the very tone of it negated whatever confidence the words were intended to convey.

'I do not want a bodyguard,' said Titus. 'Thank you all the same.'

'That is what I used to say when I was a young man,' said Slingshott. 'I thought as you did . . . that to be *alone* was everything. That is before they sent me to the salt mines . . . since then, I . . .'

'Forgive me,' said Titus, 'but I cannot stay. I appreciate your selflessness in searching for me, and your idea of protecting me from this and that ... but no. I am, or I'm *becoming*, one of those damnable selfish so-and-sos, forever biting at the hand that feeds them.'

'We will follow you, nevertheless,' said Crack-Bell. 'We will be, if you like, out of sight. We have no pretensions. We are not easily dissuaded.'

'And there will be others,' said Slingshott. 'Men of spleen and lads of high romance. As time goes on, you'll have an army, my lord. An invisible army. Ready eternally for the note.'

'What note?' said Titus.

'This one of course,' cried Crack-Bell, pursing his lips and expelling a note as shrill as a curlew's. 'The danger note. Ha, ha, ha, ha! Oh no. You needn't fear a thing. Your viewless army will be with you, everywhere, save in your sight.'

'Leave me!' cried Titus. 'Go! You are over-reaching yourselves. There is only one thing you can do for me.'

For a while the three sat glumly, staring at Titus. Then Crabcalf said ...

'What is it we can do?'

'Scour the world for Muzzlehatch. Bring news of him, or bring the man himself. Do that, and you can share my wanderings. But for now, please GO, GO, GO!'

EIGHTY-THREE

THE three from the Under-River melted into the woods, and Titus was left alone, or so he thought. He broke and re-broke a small branch in his hands, and then turned away and began to retrace his steps in the direction of the scientist's daughter. It was then that he suddenly saw her.

A few minutes earlier Cheeta had stepped from the car, and her father had turned it about and slid silently away, so that Titus and Cheeta found themselves drawing closer to one another with every step they took.

Anyone standing half-way between the approaching figures would have seen, as he turned his head this way and that, how similar were their backgrounds; for the tree-walled avenue was flecked with gold and green, and Cheeta and Titus were themselves flecked also, and floated, it almost seemed, on the slanting rays of the low sun.

Their past which made them what they were and nothing else, moved with them, adding at each footfall a new accretion. Two figures: two creatures: two humans: two worlds of loneliness. Their lives up to this moment contrasted, and what was amorphous became like a heavy boulder in their breasts.

Yet in Cheeta's bearing, as she moved down the avenue, there was no sign of passion or of the ice in her heart and Titus could only marvel at the way she moved, inevitably, smoothly, like the approach of a phantom.

The merest shred she was: slender as an eyelash, erect as a little soldier. But O the danger of it! To fill her clay with something that leaps higher and throws its wild and flickering shadow further than the blood's wisdom knows. How dangerous, how desperate and how explosive for such a little vessel.

As for Titus, she held him steadily in her eye. She saw it all and at once, his somewhat arrogant, loose-jointed walk, his way of tossing his nondescript hair out of his eyes, his bloody-mindedness, implicit in the slouch of his shoulders, and that general air of detachment which had been so great a stumbling block to the young ladies in his past, who saw no fun in the way he could become abstracted at the oddest moments. That was the irritating thing about him. He could not force a feeling, or bring himself to love. His love was always elsewhere. His thoughts were fastidious. Only his body was indiscriminate.

Behind him, whenever he stood, or slept, were the legions of Gormenghast ... tier upon cloudy tier, with the owls calling through the rain, and the ringing of the rust-red bells.

EIGHTY-FOUR

WHEN Cheeta and Titus came abreast, they stopped dead, for the idea of cutting one another would have been ludicrously dramatic. In any event, as far as Cheeta was concerned, there was never any question of letting the young man go by like a cloud, never to return. She was not finished with him. She had hardly started. She recognized in the sliding moments, a quality that set this day apart from others. It was a febrile day, not to be gainsaid; a day, perhaps of insight and heightened apprehension.

Any yet at the same time there was, in spite of the tension, a feeling in both of them that there was nothing new in what was happening; that they had shared in years gone by, an identical situation, and that there was no escape from the fate that overhung them.

'Thank you for stopping,' said Cheeta, in her slow and listless way. (Titus was always reminded when she spoke of dry leaves rustling.)

'What else could I do?' said Titus. 'After all, we know each other.'

'Do you think so?' said Cheeta. 'Perhaps that would be a good reason to *avoid* one another.'

'Perhaps,' said Titus. The avenue hummed with silence.

'Who were they?' said Cheeta at last. The three short syllables of her question drifted away one by one.

'Who do you mean?' said Titus. 'I'm in no mood for riddles.'

'The three beggars.'

'Oh them! Old friends of mine.'

'Friends?' whispered Cheeta, as though to herself. 'What are they doing in Father's grounds?'

'They came to save me,' said Titus.

'From what?'

'From myself I suppose. And from women. They are wise. Wise men are the beggars. They think you are too luscious for me. Ha, ha, ha, ha! But I told them not to worry. I told them you were frozen at the very tap-root. That your sex is bolted from the inside; that you are as prim as the mantis, that gobbles up the heads of her admirers. Love's so disgusting, isn't it?'

Had Titus not been ranting with his head thrown back, he might for a split second have seen, between the narrowing eyelids of the scientist's daughter, a fleck of terrible light.

But he did not see it. All he saw when he looked down at her was something rare and flawless, as a rose or a bird.

The eyes that had blazed for a moment were now as luminous with love as the eyes of a monkey-eating eagle.

'And yet you said you loved me. That is the spice of it.'

'Of course I love you,' said Cheeta, throwing the words away like dead petals. 'Of course I do, and I always will. That is why you must go.' She drew her pencilled eyebrows together, and at once became another creature, a creature in every way as unique and bizarre as before. She turned her head away, and there she was again, or was she someone else?

'Because I love you, Titus; so much, I can hardly bear it.'

'Then tell me something,' said Titus in so casual a voice that it was all that Cheeta could do to control a spurt of rage, which, had she given vent to it, might have ruined her carefully laid plans. For above all Titus must not be allowed to leave as he intended on the evening of this very day.

'What is it you want to ask me?' She drew herself close to him.

'Your father . . .'

'What about him?'

'Why does he dress like a mute? Why is he so dreary? What's in his factory? Why is his brow like a melon? Are you sure he *is* your father? Whose are those faces that I saw? Thousands of them, and all of them the same, staring like waxworks? What was that stink that crept across the lake? What is it he's making there? For, by God, the very look of the place turns me up. Why is it surrounded by guards?'

'I never asked him. Why should I?' said Cheeta.

'Has he not told you anything at all? And what about your mother?'

'She's . . . What's that?'

There was a faint sound of footsteps, and they drew into the hem of the woods together, and were only just in time, for as they moved, two figures lifted their heads in perfect yet unaffected unison, and slid over the soft turf. On their heads they wore helmets that smouldered in the low rays of the sun.

As they passed, there was yet another sound, apart from the whisper of their feet on the grass. Titus (whose heart was thudding, for he recognized the enigmatic pair) was able for the first time to hear yet *another* noise. It was a low and horrible hissing. It seemed as though a deep-seated anger had at last found vent for itself through the teeth of these identical figures. Their faces showed no sign of excitement. Their bodies were as unhurried as ever. They had control of every muscle. But they could do nothing about the tell-tale hissing which argued so palpably the anger, the ferment and the pain that was twisted up inside them.

They passed by, and the hissing died away, and all that could be seen were the sunbeams glancing from their studded helmets.

As soon as they were far enough away, the fauna of the woods crept out from their hiding places in the boles of trees, or in among the roots and borrows, clustered together on the dappled ride, their private enmities forgotten as they stared at the retreating figures.

'Who were they?'

'Were?' said Titus. 'They're in the present tense, God help me.'

'Who *are* they, then?'

'They sleuth me. I must *go*.'

Cheeta turned to look at him. 'Not yet,' she said.

'At once,' said Titus.

'Impossible,' said Cheeta. 'All is ready.'

The shadow of a leaf trembled on her cheekbones. Her eyes were huge; as though they were sunk for one purpose only ... to drown the unwary ... to gulp him down to where the wet ferns drip ... a world away; down, down into the cold. She hated him because she could not love him. He was unattainable. His love was somewhere else, where dust blossomed.

Cheeta bit her pretty lips. In her head was malice, like a growth. In her heart was a kind of yearning, because passion was not part of her life. Even as she stared she could see the lust in his eyes; that stupid male lust that cheapened everything.

Titus leant forward suddenly, and caught her lower lip between his own.

'You are almost without substance,' he said, 'save for the bits of you that you call your body. I'm off.' As he raised his head he ran his tongue along her throat, and cupped her perfect little breast in his left hand. 'I'm away,' he whispered. 'Away for good.'

'You cannot go,' she said. 'Everything is ready ... for you.'

'Me? What do you mean? Everything is ready for what?'

'Take your hand away.' She turned at the sound of her own words so that Titus could not see an expression pass across her face. It was lethal.

'They will all be there,' she said.

'Who, in God's name?'

'Your friends. Your early friends.'

'Who? Who? What early friends?'

'That would be telling, wouldn't it?'

There was something sickening about the way this glib childish phrase was delivered in that same laconic drawl. 'But it is all for you.'

'*What* is? O jumping hell!'

'I'll tell you,' said Cheeta, 'and then you'll have no option. It's only one night, and there's only a little time to wait for it. A night in your honour. A farewell party. A feast. Something for you to remember as long as you live.'

'I don't want a party,' said Titus. 'I want . . .'

'I know,' said Cheeta. 'I do indeed know. You are eager to forget me. To forget that I found you destitute and nursed you back to health. You have forgotten all this. What did you do for me, except be horrible to my friends? Now you are strong again, you think you'll go. But there is one thing that you must not forget, and that is that I worship you.'

'Spare me that,' said Titus.

'Yes, worship you, my darling.'

'I am going to be sick,' said Titus.

'Why should you not be? I am also sick. To the very roots of myself. But can I help it? Can I? When I love you without hope?'

Mixed with her loathing of what she was saying was a shred of truth, that, small as it was, was yet enough to make her hands tremble, like the wings of humming-birds.

'You cannot desert me, Titus. Not now, when all is prepared

for you. We will laugh and sing, and drink and dance, and go mad with all that one night can give us.'

'Why?'

'Because a chapter will be over. Let us end it in a flourish. Let us end it not with a full stop, dead as death, but with an exclamation mark . . . a leaping thing.'

'Or a question mark?' said Titus.

'No. All questions will be over. There will be only the facts. The mean, sharp, brittle facts, like the wild bits of bone, and us, the two of us, riding the human storm. I know you cannot stand it any longer. This house of my father's. This way of living. But let me have one last night with you, Titus; not in some dusky arbour where all the ritual of love drags out for hours, and there is nothing new; but in the bright invention of the night, our egos naked and our wits on fire.'

Titus, who had never heard her say so much in so short a time, turned to her.

'Our star has been unlucky,' she said. 'We were doomed from the beginning. We were born in different worlds. You with your dreams . . .'

'My dreams?' cried Titus. 'I have no dreams! O God! I have no dreams! It is you who are unreal. You and your father and your factory.'

'I will be real for you, Titus. I will be real on that night, when the world pours through the halls. Let us drain it dry at a gulp and then turn our backs on one another, forever. Titus, oh Titus, come to the barbecue. *Your* barbecue. Tell me that you'll be there. If for no other reason than that I would follow your tousled head to the ends of the earth.'

Titus pulled her towards him gently, and she became like a doll in his arms, tiny, exquisite, fragrant, infinitely rare.

'I will be there,' he whispered, 'never fear.'

The great dreaming trees of the ride stretched away into the distance, sighing; and as he held her to him a spasm passed across her perfect features.

EIGHTY-FIVE

WHEN at last they parted, Cheeta making her way down the aisle of oak trees, and Titus slanting obliquely through the body of the forest, the three vagrants, Crack-Bell, Slingshott, and Crabcalf got to their feet, and followed at once, and were now no more than forty feet from their quarry.

It was no easy task for them to keep track of him, for Crabcalf's books weighed heavily.

As they stole through the shadows they were halted by a sound. At first the three vagrants were unable to locate it; they stared all about them. Sometimes the noise came from here, sometimes from there. It was not the kind of noise they understood, although the three of them were quick in the ways of the woods, and could decipher a hundred sounds, from the rubbing together of branches to the voice of a shrew.

And then, all at once, the three heads turned simultaneously in the same direction, the direction of Titus, and they realized that he was muttering to himself.

Crouching down together, they saw him, ringed by leaves. He was wandering listlessly in the half-darkness and, as they watched, they saw him press his head against the hard bole of a tree. As he pressed his head he whispered passionately to himself, and then he raised his voice and cried out to the whole forest . . .

'O traitor! Traitor! What is it all about? Where can I find me? Where is the road home? Who are these people? What are these happenings? Who is this Cheeta, this Muzzlehatch? I don't belong. All I want is the smell of home, and the breath of the castle in my lungs. Give me some proof of me! Give me the death of Steerpike; the nettles; give me the corridors. Give me my mother! Give me my sister's grave. Give me the nest; give me my secrets back . . . for this is foreign soil. O give me back the kingdom in my head.'

EIGHTY-SIX

JUNO has left her house by the river. She has left the town once haunted by Muzzlehatch. She is driving in a fast car along the rim of a valley. Her quiet companion sits beside her. He looks like a brigand. A hank of dark red hair blows to and fro across his forehead.

'It is an odd thing,' says Juno, 'that I still don't know your name. And somehow or other I don't want to. So I must call you something of my own invention.'

'You do that,' says Juno's companion, in a gentle growl of such depth and cultivation that it is hard to believe that it could ever issue from so piratical a head.

'What shall it be?'

'Ah, there I can't help you.'

'No?'

'No.'

'Then I must help myself. I think I will call you my "Anchor",' says Juno. 'You give me so deep a sense of safety.'

Turning to look at him she takes a corner at unnecessary speed, all but overturning the car.

'Your driving is unique,' says Anchor. 'But I cannot say it gives me confidence. We will change places.'

Juno draws in to the side of the road. The car is like a sword-fish. Beyond it the long erratic line of the amethyst-coloured mountains. The sky overhanging everything is cloudless save for a wisp way down in the far south.

'How glad I am that you waited for me,' says Juno. 'All those long years in the cedar grove.'

'Ah,' says the Anchor.

'You saved me from being a sentimental old bore. I can just see myself with my tear-stained face pressed against the window-panes ... weeping for the days long gone. Thank you, Mr Anchor, for showing me the way. The past is over. My home is a memory. I will never see it again. For look, I have these sun-beams and these colours. A new life lies ahead.'

'Do not expect too much,' says the Anchor. 'The sun can be snuffed without warning.'

'I know, I know. Perhaps I am being too simple.'

'No,' says the Anchor. 'That is hardly the word for an uprooting. Shall we go on?'

'Let us stay a little longer. It is so lovely here. Then drive. Drive like the wind . . . into another country.'

There is a long silence. They are completely relaxed; their heads thrown back. Around them lies the coloured country. The golden cornfields; the amethyst mountains.

'Anchor, my friend,' says Juno in a whisper.

'Yes, what is it?'

His face is in profile. Juno has never seen a face so completely relaxed, and without strain.

'I am so happy,' says Juno, 'although there is so much to be sad about. It will take its turn, I suppose . . . the sadness. But *now* . . . in this very *now*. I am floating with love.'

'Love?'

'Love. Love for everything. Love for those purple hills; love for your rusty forelock.'

She sinks back against the cushions and closes her eyes, and as she does so the Anchor turns his lolling head in her direction. She is indeed handsome with a handsomeness beyond the scope of her wisdom. Majestic beyond the range of her knowledge.

'The world goes by,' says Juno, 'and we go with it. Yet I feel young today; young in spite of everything. In spite of my mistakes. In spite of my age.' She turns to the Anchor . . . 'I'm over forty,' she whispers. 'Oh my dear friend, I'm over forty!'

'So am I,' says the Anchor.

'What shall we do?' says Juno. She clutches his forearm with her jewelled hands, and squeezes him.

'There is nothing we can do, except live.'

'Is that why you thought I should leave my home? My possessions? My memories? Everything? Is that why?'

'I have told you so.'

'Yes, yes. Tell me again.'

'We are beginning. Incongruous as we are. You with your mellow beauty that out-glows a hundred damsels, and me with . . .'

'With what?'

'With a kind of happiness.'

Juno turns to him but she says nothing. The only movement comes from the black silk at her bosom where a great ruby rises and sinks like a buoy on a midnight bay.

At last Juno says, 'The sunlight's lovelier than it's ever been, because we have decided to begin. We will pass the days together as they pass. But . . . Oh . . .'

'What is it?'

'It's Titus.'

'What about him?'

'He is gone. Gone. I disappointed him.'

The Anchor moving with a kind of slow, lazy deliberation takes his place at the wheel. But before the swordfish whips away he says . . .

'I thought it was the *future* we were after.'

'But O, but O, it *is*,' cries Juno. 'Oh my dear Anchor, it is indeed.'

'Then let us catch it by its tail and fly!'

Juno, her face radiant, leans forward in the padded swordfish, and away they go, soundless save for the breath of their own speed.

EIGHTY-SEVEN

SHAMBLING his way from the west, came Muzzlehatch. Once upon a time there was no shambling in his gait or in his mind. Now it was different. The arrogance was still there, redolent in every gesture, but added to it was something more bizarre. The rangy body was now a butt for boys to copy. His rangy mind played tricks with him. He moved as though oblivious of the world. And so he was, save for one particular. Just as Titus ached for Gormenghast, ached to embrace its crumbling walls, so Muzzlehatch had set himself the task of discovering the centre of destruction.

Always his brain returned to that mere experiment; the liquidation of his zoo. There was no shape in all that surrounded him, whether branch or boulder, but revived in him the memory of one or other of his beloved creatures. Their death had quickened in him something which he had never felt in early days; the slow-burning, unquenchable lust for revenge.

Somewhere he would find it; the ghastly hive of horror; a hive whose honey was the grey and ultimate slime of the pit. Day after day he slouched from dawn until dusk. Day after day he turned this way and that.

It was as though his obsession had in some strange manner directed his feet. It was as though it followed a path known only to itself.

EIGHTY-EIGHT

OUT of the fermentations of her brain; out of the chronic hatred she bore him, Cheeta, the virgin, slick as a needle to the outward eye, foul in the inward, had at last conceived a way to bring young Titus to the dust; a way to hurt him.

That there was some part of her which could not do without him, she refused to believe. What might once upon a time have turned to some sort of love, was now an abhorrence. How could a wisp contain such a gall as this? She smarted beneath the humiliation of his obvious boredom . . . his casual evasion. What did he want from her? The act and nothing else? Her tiny figure trembled with detestation.

Yet her voice was as listless as ever. Her words wandered away. She was all sophistication; desirable, intelligent, remote. Who could have told that joined in deadly grapple beneath her ribs were the powers of fear and evil?

Out of all this, and because of this, she had framed a plan; a terrible and twisted thing, that proved, if it did nothing else, the quality of her inventive brain.

A cold fever of concentration propelled her. It was a state more readily associated with a man's than with a woman's mentality. And yet, a sexless thing, it was more dreadful than either.

She had told Titus of the farewell party she was preparing in his honour. She had pleaded with him; she had made her eyes to shine; her lips to pout; her breasts to tremble. Bludgeoned by sex he had said he would be there. Very well, then, her decks were cleared for action. Hers was the flying start; the initiative; the act of surprise; the choice of weapons.

But to put her plan into action necessitated the co-operation of a hundred or more of their guests, besides scores of workmen. The activity was prodigious, yet secret. There was co-operation, yet no one knew they were co-operating; or if they did, who, where, why, or in what way. They only knew their own particular roles.

She had in some magnetic way convinced each particular man and woman that he or she was at the centre of the whole affair. She had flattered them grotesquely, from the lowest to the highest; and such were the varieties of her approach, that no dupe among them but found her orders unique.

At the back of it all was a nebulous, accumulative foreboding; a gathering together in the cumulus sky; a mounting excitement in the heart of secrecy; a thing like a honeycomb which Cheeta alone apprehended in its entirety, for she was no drone, but author and soul of the hive. The insects, though they worked themselves to death, saw nothing but their own particular cells.

Even Cheeta's enigmatic father, the wisp, with his dreadful skull the colour of lard, knew nothing except that on the fateful night it was for him to take his place in some charade.

It might be thought that with everyone seemingly working at cross purposes it was merely a matter of time before the whole intricate structure irrevocably collapsed. But Cheeta, moving from one end of the domain to the other, so synchronized the activities of the guests and workmen (carpenters, masons, electricians, steeple-jacks, and so on) that, unknown to themselves, they and their work began to coalesce.

What was it all about? Nothing of its kind had ever happened before. Speculation was outlandish. It knew no end. Fabrication grew out of fabrication. To every inquiry there was one reply from Cheeta.

'If I should tell you, there'd be no surprise.'

To those prickly young men who saw no reason why so much expenditure and attention should be lavished upon Titus

Groan, she winked in such a way as to suggest a conspiracy between her critics and herself.

Here, there and everywhere she flitted like a shadow; leaving behind her instructions, now in this room, now in that, now in the great timber-yard; now in the kitchen; now where the seamstresses were huddled like bats; or in the private homes of her friends.

But a great deal of her time was spent elsewhere.

From then on, Titus was shadowed unknowingly, wherever he went.

But those who shadowed him were in their turn shadowed, by Crabcalf, Slingshott and Crack-Bell.

Full of old crimes, they had learned the value of silence, and if a branch stirred or a twig snapped one can be sure that none of these gentlemen was responsible.

EIGHTY-NINE

CHEETA, when she had first conceived her plan, had assumed that her party would take place in the great studio that covered the whole of the top floor of her father's mansion. It was a studio indeed, lovely in its lighting, bland in its floorboards, vast in its perpectives (the easel no larger than a ninepin when seen from the door, reared up like a tall insect).

But it was wrong, fatally wrong, for it had an air about it ... almost of that kind of innocence that nothing can eradicate. Innocence was no part of Cheeta's plan.

Yet there was no other room in the building, large though it was, that suited her purpose. She had flirted with the idea of knocking down a long wall in the southern wing which would have opened up a long and ponderous hall; but there again, the 'feel' would have been wrong; as was the longest of the twelve high barns, those rotting structures on the northern boundaries.

As the days went by, the situation became more and more peculiar. It was not that there was any slackening of vitality among the friends and labourers; rather that the sight of scores upon scores of seemingly incongruous objects under construction inflamed the general speculation to an almost unbearable degree.

And then, one overcast morning as Cheeta was about to make a tour of the workshops, she stopped suddenly dead, as though she had been struck. Something she had seen or heard had wakened a memory. All in a flash came the answer.

It had been a long time ago, when Cheeta was a mere child, that an expedition had been mounted, the main purpose of which had been to establish the exact boundaries of that great tract of land, as yet but vaguely charted, that lay, a shadowy enigma, to the south-west.

This excursion proved to be abortive, for the area covered was treacherous marshland, along whose sluggish flanks great trees knelt down to drink.

Young as she had been, yet Cheeta, by a superb imitation of hysteria, eventually forced her parents to allow her to join the expedition. The extra responsibility involved in having to take a child on such a mission was maddening, to put it at its mildest, and there were those on the return journey who were openly against the intractable child, and fully believed their failure to be due to her presence.

But this was long ago, and had been all but forgotten: all save for one thing, and this itself had been smothered away in her unconscious mind until now. Like something long subdued, it had broken free and leapt out of the shadows of her mind in devastating clarity.

It was hard for Cheeta, all at once, to be sure whether it was a valid memory of something that was really there, a hundred miles from her home, or whether it was a startling dream, for she had no recollection of the finding of the place, nor of leaving it. But she was not long in doubt. Image after image returned to her as she stood, the pupils of her eyes dilated. There could be no doubt about it. She saw it with a mounting vividness. *The Black House.*

There in that setting of immemorial oaks, threaded by that broad, fast, knee-deep river ... there surely, where the masonry was crusty with age, was the setting above all settings for the Party.

It was now for Cheeta to discover someone who had been there on that faraway day. Someone who could find the place again.

Driving her fastest car, she was soon at the gates of the factory. At once she was surrounded by a dozen men in overalls. Their faces were all the same. One of them opened his mouth. The very act was obscene.

'Miss Cheeta?' he said in a curiously thin voice, like a reed.

'That's it,' said Cheeta. 'Put me through to my father.'

'Of course ... of course,' said the face.

'And hurry,' said Cheeta.

They led her to a reception room. The ceiling was matted with crimson wires. There was a black glass table of unnatural length, and at the far end of the room the wall was monopolized by an opaque screen like a cod's eye.

Eleven men stood in a row while their leader pressed a button.

'What's the peculiar smell?' said Cheeta.

'Top secret,' said the eleven men.

'Miss Cheeta,' said the twelfth man. 'I am putting you through.'

After a moment or two an enormous face appeared on the opaque screen. It filled the wall.

'Miss Cheeta?' it said.

'Shrivel yourself,' said Cheeta. 'You're too big.'

'Ha, ha, ha!' said the huge face. 'I keep forgetting.'

The face contracted, and went on contracting. 'Is that better?' it said.

'More or less,' said Cheeta. 'I must see Father.'

'Your father is at a conference,' said the image on the screen. It was still over life-size, and a small fly landing on his huge dome of a forehead appeared the size of a grape.

'Do you know who I am?' said Cheeta in her faraway voice.

'But of course ... of ...'

'Then stir yourself.'

The face disappeared, and Cheeta was left alone.

After a moment she wandered to the wall that faced the cod's-eye screen, and played delicately across a long row of coloured levers that were as pretty as toys. So innocent they looked that she pressed one forward, and at once there was a scream.

'No, no, no!' came the voice. 'I want to *live*.'

'But you are very poor and very ill,' said another voice, with the consistency of porridge. 'You're unhappy. You told me so.'

'No, no, no! I want to *live*. I want to *live*. Give me a little longer.'

Cheeta switched the lever and sat down at the black table.

As she sat there, very upright, her eyes closed, she did not know that she was being watched. When at last she raised her head she was annoyed to see her mother.

'You!' she said. 'What are you doing here?'

'It's absorbing, you know,' said Cheeta's mother. 'Daddy lets me watch.'

'I wondered where you got to every day,' muttered her daughter. 'What on earth do you do here?'

'Fascinating,' said the scientist's wife, who never seemed to answer anything.

A big arm came across the screen and thrust her aside. It was followed by a shoulder and a head. The father's face suddenly swam towards Cheeta. His eyes flickered to and fro to see if anything had been altered. Then they rested on his daughter.

'What do you want, my dear?'

'Tell me first,' said Cheeta, 'where are you? Are we near each other?'

'O dear no,' said the scientist. 'We're a long way apart.'

'How long would it take me to . . .'

'You can't come here,' said the scientist, with a note almost of alarm in his voice. 'No one comes here.'

'But I want to talk to you. It's urgent.'

'I will be home for dinner. Can't you wait until then?'

'No,' said Cheeta, 'I can't. Now listen. Are you listening?'

'Yes.'

'Twenty years ago, when I was six, an expedition set out to plot out territory in the south-west. We found ourselves bogged down and had to give up. On our return journey we came unexpectedly upon a ruin. Do you remember?'

'Yes, I remember.'

'I am questioning you in secrecy, father.'

'Yes.'

'I must go there today.'

'No!'

'Yes. But who will guide me?'

There was a long silence.

'Do you mean to have the party *there*?'

'Exactly.'

'Oh no . . . no . . .'

'Oh yes. But how to *find* him. Who was he? The man who led the expedition long ago? Is he alive?'

'He is an old man now.'

'Where does he live? There is no time to waste. The party is close upon us. Oh hurry father. Hurry!'

'He lives,' said the scientist, 'where the Two Rivers join.'

Cheeta left him at once, and he was glad, for Cheeta was the only thing he feared.

Little did he know that someone more to be feared was making his way, all unknowing, in the direction of the factory. A figure with a wild light in his eyes, a five day growth on his chin, and a nose like a rudder.

NINETY

IT was not long before Cheeta ran the old man to ground, and a tough old bird he proved to be. She asked him at once whether he remembered the expedition, and in particular the unhealthy night that the party spent at the Black House.

'Yes, yes. Of course I do. What about it eh?'

'You must take me there. At once,' said Cheeta, recoiling inwardly, for his age was palpable.

'Why should I?' he said.

'You will be paid . . . *well* paid. We'll go by helicopter.'

'What's *that*?' said the septuagenarian.

'We'll fly,' said Cheeta, 'and find it from above.'

'Ah,' said the old man.

'The Black House . . . you understand?' said Cheeta.

'Yes, I heard you. The Black House. South-sou'east. Follow the knee-deep river. Aha! Then west into the territory of the wild dogs. How much?' he said, and he shook his dirty grey hair.

'Come now,' said Cheeta. 'We'll talk of that later.'

But it was not enough for the dirty old man, the one-time explorer. He asked a hundred questions; sometimes of the airborne flight, or of the machine, but for the most part of the financial side which seemed to be his chief interest.

Finally everything was settled and within two hours they were on their way, skimming the tree-tops.

Beneath them was little to be seen but great seas of foliage.

NINETY-ONE

TITUS, drowsy in the arms of a village girl, a rosy, golden thing, opened one eye as they lay together on the banks of a loquacious river, for he had heard through the ripples another sound. At first he could see nothing, but lifting his head he was surprised to see a yellow aircraft passing behind the leaves of the overhanging trees. Close as it was, Titus was yet unable to see who was piloting the machine, and as for the village maiden, she neither knew nor cared.

NINETY-TWO

THE weather was perfect, and the helicopter floated without the least hindrance over the tree-tops. For a long while there was silence aboard, but at last Cheeta, the pilot, turned to look at her companion. There was something foul in the way his dirtiness was being carried aloft, through the pure air. What made it worse was the way he stared at her.

'If you keep looking at me,' she said, 'we may miss the landmarks. What should we be looking for now?'

'Your legs,' said the old man. 'They'd go down very nice,

with onion sauce.' He leered at her, and then all at once cried out in a hoarse voice; 'The shallow river! Alter her course to south'd.'

Three long cobalt-blue mountains had hoisted themselves above the horizon and what with the sunlight bathing the foliage below them, and dancing down the river, it was a scene so tranquil that the sudden chill that rose, as though on an updraught from below, was horrible in its unexpectedness. It seemed that the cold in the air was directed against them, and at the same moment, on looking down as though to see the cause of the cold, Cheeta cried out involuntarily ...

'The Black House! Look! Look! There below us.'

Hovering as they descended; descending as they hovered, the ill-matched pair were now no more than weather-cock high above the ruin ... for so it was ... though known (time out of mind), as the Black House.

Very little of the roof was left, and none of the inner walls, but Cheeta, gazing down, recalled immediately the vast interior of the building.

It had an atmosphere about it that was unutterably mournful; a quality that could not be wholly accounted for by the fact that the place was mouldering horribly; that the floor was soft with moss; or that the walls were lost in ferns. There was something more than this that gave the Black House its air of deadly darkness; a darkness that owed nothing to the night, and seemed to dye the day.

'I'm bringing her in,' said Cheeta, and as they came down to make a perfect landing in a grey carpet of nettles, a small fox pricked its ears, and loped away, and as though taking their cue, a murmuration of starlings rose in a dense cloud which coiled its way up, up into the sky.

The old man, finding himself on terra firma, made no immediate effort to get to his feet, but stretched out his withered arms and legs, as though he was a ragged windmill, and then, prising himself to his feet ...

'Hey you!' he cried. 'Now that you're in it, what do you *want* with it? An armful of bloody nettles?'

Cheeta took no notice, but made her way, quick and light as a bird, to and fro across what might have been the shell of an abbey, for there was a heap of masonry that might or might not have been some kind of altar, sacred or profane.

As Cheeta flickered to and fro over the moss and fallen leaves, with the pale sun above her and the surrounding forest breathing gently to itself, she was taking note of every kind of thing. To her it was second nature to remember anything that might prove to her advantage, and so today it was a case of absorbing into her brain and being, not only the exact lie of the land; not only the orientation and the proportions and the scale of this bizarre setting, but also the exits and entrances that were to fill with figures unforeseen.

Meanwhile, the old man, unabashed, made water in a feeble arc.

'Hey, you,' he shouted in that gritty voice of his, 'where is it then?'

'Where is what?' whispered Cheeta. It was obvious from her tone of voice that her mind was elsewhere.

'The treasure. That's what we've come for, ain't it? The treasure of the Black House.'

'Never heard of it,' said Cheeta.

A flush of anger spread itself over the old man's face so that the hot hue became reflected in the white of the beard.

'Never heard of it?' he cried. 'Why you . . .'

'Any more abuse from you,' said Cheeta in a voice quite horrible in its listlessness, 'and I will leave you here. *Here*, among a thousand rotting things.'

The old man snarled.

'Get into your seat,' said Cheeta. 'If you touch me, I will have you whipped.'

The return journey was a race against darkness, for Cheeta had remained longer than she had meant in the Black House. Now, sailing over the varying landscape that slid below them, she had time to make her calculations.

For instance, there was the problem of how the workmen, and later on, the guests, were to find their way through long neglected woodlands, swamps and valleys. Here and there, it is true, there were signs of ancient roads, but these could not be relied upon, as they were apt at any moment to go underground or lose themselves beneath the swamp or sand.

This problem was largely solved (in theory) by Cheeta, as she floated down the sky; for her idea was to have several scores of men dropped at regular intervals in a long line reaching from the known boundaries to the tundra of the south-east, and the forests of the Black House.

At a given time it was for these scores of isolated men to ignite the great stacks of timber that they had been collecting all day long. With the smoke from these great bonfires to guide him, the least intelligent voyager to the Black House would surely be able to make his way without difficulty, and in any fashion he chose, whether by air or on land.

The workmen, thought Cheeta, as she perused the landscape, must have at least three days' start, and must return before the first of the guests. They must work to plan and in silence, not one of them knowing the business of his neighbour.

They must come in every kind of vehicle, from great vans loaded with the most unlikely contents, to pony traps: from long cars to wheelbarrows.

At dawn, on the day of the Party ... there must be sounded across the land the voice of a gong. And Cheeta would have been prepared to stake a fortune that anyone near Titus at the time of the gong-boom, would see a shadow cross his face ... almost as though he were reminded of another world: a world he had deserted.

NINETY-THREE

FOR all her skill and speed, a time had come when it was impossible for Cheeta to be everywhere at the same time (a characteristic for which she was famous), and within a matter of minutes, she had stepped out of the helicopter and was on her way to the 'Making Shops', and within a few minutes more she was in rapid conversation with the more responsible of the 'makers'.

It was now impossible to carry on without a delegation of duties, for time was hard at their heels. Some part of the secrecy must inevitably be made less stringent for, unless the curtain were raised a little, there would be danger of chaos. As it was it was almost too late. For all the power that Cheeta held in her tiny, bow-string body, there was yet a murmur of discontent in the Workshops that grew louder every day.

Even among the gentry there were murmurings; and Cheeta was forced to take a couple of them into her confidence.

Apart from this there was her father. He had at last been partially won over.

'It won't be long, father.'

'I don't like it,' said the hollow wisp.

'You must do as you're told, mustn't you? Is your costume ready? And your mask?'

A fly settled on the horrible egg-shaped head. Twitching the skin of his cranium into a minor convulsion he dislodged the creature, and by the time he was able to answer, his daughter was no longer with him. Cheeta had no time to waste.

NINETY-FOUR

AT a muster of the executive, which numbered nine souls including Cheeta (if she can be called a soul) and which had among its numbers representatives of all social grades, it was agreed that everybody should be kept in suspense as to where the party should take place; the chosen nine alone being in some kind of mental half-light.

These nine alone were bribed. These nine alone had some kind of inkling as to what was being made in the shops, the barns, the warehouses, and the private houses.

Yet there was rancour among the nine. It is true that compared with the horde they were privileged, but compared with Cheeta they were in outer darkness, fobbed off with bits and pieces of knowledge; knowing only that out of the miscellaneous chaos, some kind of mammoth invention was at work in Cheeta's brain.

NINETY-FIVE

'I'VE got a feeling,' said Juno, 'that all is not well with Titus. I dreamed of him last night. He was in danger.'

'He's been in danger most of his life,' said the Anchor. 'I don't think he'd know what to do with himself if he wasn't.'

'Do you believe in him?' said Juno, after a long pause. 'I've never asked you before. I've always feared the answer, I suppose.'

Anchor raised his eyes, and studied the ceiling of a private lounge on the ninety-ninth floor. Then he leaned back against an indigo cushion. Juno stood by a window. She was as regal as ever. The fullness under her chin, and the tiny crow's-feet around her eyes in no way impaired her grandeur. The room was full of a pale blue light which gave a strange glint to the Anchor's mop of red hair. Far away there was a murmuring sound like the sound of the sea.

'Do I believe in him?' queried the Anchor. 'What does that mean? I believe in his existence. Just as I believe that you are shaking. Are you ill?'

Juno turned round and faced him. 'I am not ill,' she whispered, 'but I will be if you don't answer my question. You know what I mean.'

'His castle and his lineage? Is that what worries you?'

'He's such a boy! Such a golden boy! He was always sweet with me. How is it he could lie to me, and to everyone? What do you feel at the sound of that strange word?'

'Gormenghast?'

'Yes, Gormenghast. Oh, Anchor my dear. I have such a pain in my heart.'

Anchor rose to his feet in one quiet movement and moved with a faintly rolling gait towards her. But he did not touch her.

'He is not mad,' he said. 'Whatever else he is, he is not mad. If he were mad then it would be better for madness to thrive in the world. No. *Inventive* perhaps. He may be for all we know the last word in the realms of imagery, supposition, hypothesis, conjecture, surmise, and all that is clothed in the wild webs of his imagination. But mad? No.'

Anchor looked at her with a wry smile on his lips.

'Then you *don't* believe him, for all your long words,' cried Juno. 'You think he's a liar! Oh my dear Anchor, what has come over me? I feel so frightened.'

'It was your dream,' said Anchor. 'What was it about?'

'I saw him,' whispered Juno at last, 'staggering with a castle on his back. Tall towers were intertwined with locks of dark red hair. He cried out as he stumbled . . . 'Forgive me! Forgive me!" Behind him floated eyes. Nothing but eyes! Swarms of them. They sang as they floated through the air at his side, their pupils expanding or contracting according to the notes they were singing. It was horrible. They were so intent, you see. Like hounds about to tear a fox apart. Yet they sang all the while, so that it was sometimes difficult to hear the voice of Titus calling out, "Forgive me. For pity's sake, forgive me".'

Juno turned to the Anchor.

'You see, he *is* in danger. Why else should I dream? We must not rest until we find him.'

She turned her head up to his.

'It isn't love any more,' she said, 'as it used to be. I have lost my jealousy and my bitterness. Nothing of this is any longer a part of me. I want Titus for another reason . . . just as I want Muzzlehatch and others I have cared for in the past. The past. Yes, that is it. I need my past again. Without it I am nothing. I bob like a cork on deep water. Perhaps I am not brave enough. Perhaps I am frightened. We thought that we could start our lives again. But all this time I brood upon what's gone. The haze has settled like a golden dust. O my dear friend. My dear Anchor. Where are they? What shall I do?'

'We will away and find them. We'll lay their ghosts, my dear. When shall we start?'

'Now,' said Juno.

Anchor got to his feet.

'*Now it is*,' he said.

NINETY-SIX

HE only knew he was aloft and airborne: that no one answered him when he spoke: that he appeared to be moving: that there was a soft buzz of machinery: that the night air was gentle and balmy: that there were occasional voices from far below, and that there was someone near him, sharing the same machine, who refused to talk.

His hands were carefully tied behind him, so that he should suffer no pain: yet they were firm enough to prevent his escape. So it was with the silk scarf across his eyes. It had been carefully adjusted so that Titus should feel no inconvenience, save that of being sightless.

That he was in such a predicament at all was something to wonder at. Indeed if it were not that Titus was apt to throw in his lot with any hair-brained scheme, he would by now be yelling for release.

He had no sense of fear, for it had been explained to him that, this being the night of the party, he must expect anything. And he must believe that to make it a night of all nights, one element alone was paramount, and that element was the element of surprise. Without it, all would be stillborn, and die before its first wild breath was drawn.

It was for him, at a future moment, to have the silk scarf plucked from his eyes to behold the light of a great bonfire, a hundred bright inventions.

It was for him to await the quintessential instant and to let it flower. Under the star-flecked sky, under the sighing of the leaves and ferns, there lay the Black House. Here was a setting for a dark splendour, a dripping of the night dew. Here was the forlorn decay of centuries, which, were Titus to set his eyes upon it, could not fail to remind him of the dark clime he had thought to toss off like a cloak from his shoulders, but which he now knew he had no power to divest.

Without surprise, all else was doomed to falter, as Cheeta well knew. It mattered not how brilliant the concept, how marvellous the spectacle, all, all would be lost unless the boy, Titus, suffered the supreme degradation.

It was not for nothing that Cheeta had sat at the end of his bed hour after hour, while he raved or whispered in his fever. Over and over again she heard the same names repeated; the same scenes enacted. She knew to the last inch whom he loathed and whom he loved. She knew almost as though it were a map before her eyes, the winding core of Gormenghast. She knew who had died. She knew who were still alive. She knew of those who had stood by Gormenghast. She knew of an *Abdicator*.

Let him have his surprise. His golden treat. His fantastic party for which no expense was enough. This will be a 'Farewell' never to be forgotten.

Cheeta had whispered ... 'It will burn like a torch in the night. The forest will recoil at the sound of it.'

At a weak moment, all in the heat of it, when his brain and senses contradicted one another, and a gap appeared in his armour, he had said, 'Yes.'

'Yes,' that he would agree to it ... the idea of going to an unknown district, blindfolded, for the sake of the secret.

And now he was aloft in the evening air, sailing he knew not where, to his Farewell party. Had his eyes been free of the silk scarf he would have seen that he was supported in mid-air by a beautiful white balloon like a giant whale, tinted in the light.

Above the balloon, high up in the sky, were flocks of aircraft of all colours, shapes and sizes.

Below him, flying in formation, were craft like golden darts, and far, far below these, he would have seen, in the north, a great tract of shimmering marshland reaching away to the horizon.

To the south in the forest land he would have caught sight of smoke from the bonfire which gave them their direction.

But he could see nothing of all this – nothing of the play of light upon the silky marshes nor how the shadows of the various aircraft cruised slowly over the tree-tops.

Nor could he see his companion. She sat there, a few feet out of his reach, very upright, tiny and supremely efficient, her hands on the controls.

The workmen were gone from the scene. They had toiled like slaves. Rough country had been cleared for the helicopters, and all types of aircraft to land. The heavy carts were filled with weary men.

The great crater of the Black House that had until recently yawned to the moon was now filled with something other than its mood. Its emptiness gone, it listened as though it had the power of hearing.

There had, in all conscience, been enough to hear. For the last week or more, the forest had echoed to the sound of hammering, sawing and the shouts of foresters.

Close enough to observe without being seen, yet far enough in danger's name, the scores of small forest animals, squirrels, badgers, mice, shrews, weasels, foxes and birds of every feather, their tribal feuds forgotten, sat silent, their eyes following every movement, their ears pricked. Little knowing that between them they were forming a scattered circle of flesh and blood, they drew their breath into their lungs and stared at the shell of the Black House. The shell and the strange things that filled it.

As the hours passed, this living circumference grew in depth, until the time came when a day of silence settled down upon the district, and in this silence could be heard the breathing of the fauna like the sound of the sea.

Mystified by the silence (for the day had come for the workmen to leave, and the socialites had not yet arrived), they stared (these scores of eyes) at the Black House, which now presented to the world a face so unlikely that it was a long time before the animals and the birds broke silence.

NINETY-SEVEN

CASTING their wicked shadows, two wild cats broke free at last, from the trance that had descended upon the scores of spellbound creatures, and with almost unbelievable stealth crept forward cheek to cheek.

Watched by silent miscellaneous hordes, they slid their feline way from the listening forest and came at last to the northern wall of the Black House.

For a long time they stayed there, sitting upright, hidden by a wealth of ferns, only their heads showing. It seemed they ran on oil, those loveless heads, so fluidly they turned from side to side.

At last they jumped together as though from a mutual impulse, and found themselves on a broad moss-covered ledge. They had made this jump many times before but not until now had they looked down from their old vantage point upon so unbelievable a metamorphosis.

Everything was changed and yet nothing had changed. For a moment their eyes met. It was a glance of such exquisite subtlety that a shudder of chill pleasure ran down their spines.

The change was entire. Nothing was as it was before. There was a throne where once was a mound of green masonry. There were old crusty suits of armour hanging on the walls. There were lanterns and great carpets and tables knee-deep in hemlock. There was no end to the change.

And yet it was the same in so far as the mood swamped everything. A mood of unutterable desolation that no amount of change could alter.

The two cats, conscious that they were the focus of all eyes, grew progressively bolder until slipping down an ivy-faced wall, they positively grinned with their entire bodies and sprang into the air with a mixture of excitement and anger. Excitement that there were new worlds to conquer, and anger that their secret paths were gone for ever, and the green abodes and favourite haunts were gone. The overgrown ruin which these two had taken for granted as part of their lives, ever since, like little balls of spleen, they nuzzled and fought for the warmth of their mother's belly ... this ruin was now, suddenly, another thing, a thing to be assimilated and explored. A world of new sensations ... a world that had once rung with echoes, but which now gave no response, its emptiness departed.

Where was the long shelf gone: the long worn dusty shelf, festooned with hart's tongue? It had disappeared, and what stood in its place had never felt the impress of a wild cat's body.

In its place were towering shapes, impossible to understand. As their courage strengthened, the wild cats began to run hither and thither with excitement, yet never losing their poise as they ran, their heads held high in the air in such a sentient and lordly way as to suggest a kind of vibrant wisdom.

What were these great swags of material? What was this intricate canopy of bone-white branches that hung from the roof and over their heads? Was it the ribs of a great whale?

The two cats growing bolder began to behave in a very peculiar way, not only leaping from vantage-point to vantage-point in a weird game of follow-my-leader, but wriggling their ductile bodies into every conceivable position. Sometimes they ran alone along an aisle of hoary carpet: sometimes they clung to one another and fought as though in earnest, only to break off suddenly, as though by common assent, so that one or other might scratch its ear with a hind foot.

And still there was no movement from the ring of watching creatures, until, without warning, a fox suddenly trotted out of the periphery, leapt through a window in one of the walls, and running to the centre of the Black House sat down on an expensive rug, lifted his sharp yellow face, and barked.

This acted like a tocsin, and hundreds of woodland creatures rose to their feet, and a minute later were down in the arena.

But they were not there for long, for immediately after the two cats had arched their backs and snarled at the fox and all the other invaders, something else occurred which sent the birds and beasts back into their hiding places.

The sky above the Black House was, of a sudden, filled with coloured lights. The vanguard of the airborne flotilla was dropping earthwards.

NINETY-EIGHT

DELICATELY stepping from their various machines, the glittering beauties and the glittering horrors, arrayed like humming birds, passed in and out of the shadows with their escorts, their tongues flickering, their eyes dilated with conjecture, for this was something never known before ... the flight by night. The overhanging forests; the sense of exquisite fear; the suspense and the thrill of the unknown; the pools of dark; the pools of brilliance; the fluttering breath drawn in and exhaled with a shudder of relief; relief in every breast that it was not alone, though the stars shone down out of the cold and the small snakes lurked among the ruins.

As each dazzling influx tiptoed through the mouldering doorways of the Black House, their heads involuntarily turned to the central fire; a careful structure composed of juniper branches which when alight, as now, threw up a scented smoke.

'Oh my darling,' said a voice out of the darkness.

'What is it?' said a voice out of the light.

'This is the throb of it. Where are you?'

'Here, at your dappled side.'

'O Ursula!'

'What is it?'

'To think it is all for that boy!'

'O no! It is for us. It is for our delectation. It is for the green light on your bosom ... and the diamonds in my ears. It is bloom. It is brilliance.'

'It is primal, darling. Primal.'

Another voice broke in. . . .

'It is a place for frogs.'

'Yes, yes, but we're ahead.'

'Ahead of what?'

'The avant-garde. Look at us. If we are not the soul of chic, who is?'

Another voice, a man's; a poor affair. 'This is double pneumonia,' it wheezed.

'For heaven's sake be careful of that carpet. It sucked my shoe off,' said his friend.

With every moment that passed, the crowd thickened. For the most part guests made for the juniper fire. Their scores of faces flickered and leapt to the whim of the flames.

Were it not Cheeta's party there would undoubtedly have been many more than ready to criticize the lavish display ... the heterodoxy of the whole affair would have rankled. As it was, the discomfort of the Black House was more than made up for by the occasion. For that is what it was.

The babble of voices rose, as the guests multiplied. Yet there were many young adventurers who, tired of staring into the flames almost as much as having to listen to the shrill tongues of their partners, had begun to leave the warmth in order to explore the outer reaches of the ruin. There they came across bizarre formations reaching high into the night.

Here, as they moved, and there, as they moved, they came upon peculiar structures hard to understand. But there was nothing hard to fathom about the dusky table, dim-lit by candles, where a great ice-cake glimmered, with 'Titus, Farewell' sculpted in its flanks. Behind the cake, there arose tier upon tier, the Banquet, in half-light. A hundred goblets twinkled, and the napkins rose as though in flight.

Six mirrors reflecting one another across the sullen reaches of the Black House focused their light upon something which appeared to contradict itself, for, looked at from *one* angle, it appeared to resemble a small tower, yet from another it seemed more like a pulpit, or a throne.

Whatever it might be, there was no doubt that it was of some importance, for posted at its corners were four flunkeys who were almost abnormally zealous in keeping any odd guest who had strayed that far, from coming too close.

Meanwhile there was something happening, something – if not *of* the Farewell Party, yet close to it. Something that strode!

NINETY-NINE

HE was not entirely cut out to pattern, this strider. Barbaric to the eye, his silhouette more like something made of ropes and bones, he was nevertheless instantly recognizable as Muzzlehatch.

A little behind him, as he approached were the three one-time Under-River characters. Peculiar as they were, they paled into nothingness beside their eccentric leader whose every movement was a kind of stab in the bosom of the orthodox world.

They had searched for, and found, more by luck than wisdom (though they knew the country well), this Muzzlehatch, and had forced him to rest his long wild bones, and to shut for an hour his haunted eyes.

What they *had* hoped to do (Crabcalf and the rest) was to find Muzzlehatch, and warn him of Titus's danger. For they had come to the conclusion that some black force had been unearthed, and that Titus was in real peril.

But what they *found*, when at last they tracked him down, was not the Muzzlehatch they knew, but a man of the wilds. Of the wilds within himself and the wilds without. Not only this, but a man who had but recently been deep into the steel heart of the enemy: a man with a mission half complete. One eye had closed in satisfaction. The other burned like an ember.

Little by little, they drew out his story. Of how he came upon the factory and knew at once that he was at the door of hell. The door he had been searching for. Of how by bluff and guile, and later by force, he had found and forced his way into a less frequented district of this great place where he began to be sickened by the scent of death.

They listened carefully, the three followers, but for all their concentration they could barely make out what he was saying. Had their interpretation of his words been pooled and sifted so that it was possible to evoke a summary of all he whispered (for he was too tired to speak) then in the broadest way he told the three who hovered above him, of the identical faces: of how he slid down endless belts of translucent skin; and how, as he slid, a great hand in a glove of shining black rubber reached out for him so that Muzzlehatch was forced to haul at the creature; to haul it aboard upon the moving belt; a vile thing to touch it was and shrouded in white from head to toe; a thing that lashed out, but could not escape from Muzzlehatch's clench, and fell back at last, dead.

It seems that Muzzlehatch had ripped away the dead man's working-shroud before that cipher slid into a glass tunnel, and then, clad in white, had escaped from the belt and the empty hall, and loping away, had soon found himself in another kind of district altogether.

Strange as it seems (when it is remembered how horrible and multifarious are the ways of modern death), yet it is true that a jack-knife at the ribs can cause as terrible a sensation as any lurking gas or lethal ray. His knife was at the ready, and it was very sharp, but before he had any chance to use it, the light turned from a clear cool grey to a murky crimson and at the same moment the entire floor of the factory, like the floor of a lift began to descend.

So much could the three vagrants understand, but then began a long period of confused muttering which, try as they would they could not decipher. It was obvious that they were missing much, for the gaunt man's arms kept beating the ground as he fought to recover from his terrible experience.

At times the intensity grew less and his words came back again like creatures from their lairs, but almost at once the 'three' became aware of how, in spite of the increasing volubility, it spelt no certainty, for their master began more and more to drift away into an almost private language.

But this much they *did* discover. He must have waited almost to distraction; waited for the one opportunity when at the supreme moment he could single out a hierophant, and with his jack-knife in that creature's back, demand to be taken to the *centre*.

It came at last. The victim almost sick with fear leading Muzzlehatch down corridor after corridor. And all the time the gaunt man repeated . . .

'To the centre!'

'Yes,' said the frightened voice. 'Yes . . . yes.'

'To the centre! Is that where you're taking me?'

'Yes, yes. To the centre of it all.'

'Is that where he hides himself?'

'Yes, yes . . .'

As they proceeded, white hordes of faces flowed by like a tide. Then silence and emptiness took over.

ONE HUNDRED

Titus, where are you? Are your eyes still bandaged? Are your arms still tied behind you?

Through a gap in the forest the night looked down upon the roofless shell of the Black House studded with fires and jewels. And above the gap, floating away forever from the branches was a small grass-green balloon, lit faintly on its underside. It must have come adrift from its tree-top mooring. Sitting upright on the upper crown of the truant balloon was a rat. It had climbed a tree to investigate the floating craft; and then, courage mounting, it had climbed to the shadowy top of the globe, never thinking that the mooring cord was about to snap. But snap it did, and away it went, this small balloon, away into the wilds of the mind. And all the while the little rat sat there, helpless in its global sovereignty.

ONE HUNDRED AND ONE

TITUS was no longer in any mood for collaboration, party or no party. Up to an hour or so ago, he had been willing enough to join in what was supposed to be an elaborate game in his honour; but he was beginning to feel otherwise. Now that his feet were on terra firma he began to hanker for release. His blindness had gone on for too long.

'Undo my bloody eyes,' he cried, but there was no reply until a voice whispered . . .

'Be patient, my lord.'

Titus, who was now being led forward to the great door of the Black House came to a halt. He turned to where the voice had come from.

'Did you say "my lord"?'

'Naturally, your lordship.'

'Undo these scarves at once. Where are you?'

'Here, my lord.'

'Why are you waiting? Set me free!'

Then out of the darkness came Cheeta's voice, dry and crisp as an autumn leaf.

'O Titus dear; has it been *very* irksome?'

A group of sophisticates edging up behind Cheeta echoed her . . .

'Has it been *very* irksome?'

'It won't be long now, my love, before . . .'

'Before *what*?' shouted Titus. 'Why can't you set me free?'

'It is not in my hands, my darling.'

Again the echo from the voices, '. . . my hands, my darling.'

Cheeta watched him with her eyes half closed.

'You promised me, didn't you,' she said, 'that you would make no fuss? That you would walk quietly to the place of your appointment. That you would take three paces up and then turn about. That then, and only then, would the scarf be unknotted, and your eyes be freed. That is the moment of surprise.'

'The best surprise you could give me would be to rip these rags off! O lord of lords! How did I get mixed up in it all? Where are you? Yes, you in your midget body. O God for help! What's all the shouting for?'

Cheeta, whose hand had been raised in a signal, now dropped it again and the shouting died away.

'They want to see you,' said Cheeta. 'They are excited.'

'*Me*?' queried Titus. 'Why *me*?'

'Are you not Titus, the Seventy-Seventh Lord of Gormenghast?'

'Am I? By heaven I don't feel like it; not with you about.'

'He must be tired to be so *very* rude,' said a treacly voice.

'He doesn't know what he's doing,' said another.

'Gormenghast indeed!' said a third, with a titter. 'The whole thing's improbable you know.'

Cheeta's high heel came down like a hammer on the instep of the last speaker. 'My dear,' she said, as though to distract attention from his cry, 'those who have waited so long for the Party are drawing together. Everything is drawing together. And you will be our focus. A lord! A veritable lord!'

'Hell gripe all bleeding lords. Give me my home!' he cried.

The crowds were closing in, for there was something in the air; a chill; a menace; a horrible darkness that seemed to sweat itself out of the walls and the floor of the place. In the shuffling that followed the comparative silence, there was an undertone, almost of apprehension, unformulated as yet in their conscious minds, yet real in the prickle of their nerves. The banqueteers forsook their scented alcoves, and men of all stations withdrew from the outlying sectors, and drawn by an invisible agent, they drew ever closer to the roofless centre of the Black House.

It was not only these who were on the move. Cheeta had ordered a cluster of her personal friends to follow her (excluding her father, for he was in the forgotten room, where sat the star performers, biting their nails).

The band, with an imposing array of instruments swayed forward through the gloom, while Titus was borne forward on a human wave, struggling as he went.

It was a part of Cheeta's plan that Titus should suffer acute alarm, not to say fear, and her delicate mouth (pursed like a tiny vermilion bud) registered a certain satisfaction as to the way things were going. For she was bent on his discomfiture and shame, and even more. Now was the time for Titus to climb the three steps to the throne ... and he stumbled as he climbed. Now was the time for him to turn about; and now, for his wrists to be freed, and for the scarf to be plucked from his eyes and for Cheeta to cry ... 'Now!'

And now it was, for her voice, like a voice in a dungeon, awoke a string of echoes. Everything happened in the same split second. The scarves were whipped from Titus's wrists and eyes. The band crashed into dreadful martial music. Titus sat down upon a throne. He could see nothing except the vague blur of the juniper fire. The crowds surged forward as lamps blazed out of the surrounding tree-tops. Everything took on another colour ... another radiance. A clock struck midnight. The moon came out and so did the first of the apparitions.

UNDER a light to strangle infants by, the great and horrible flower opened its bulbous petals one by one: a flower whose roots drew sustenance from the grey slime of the pit, and whose vile scent obscured the delicacy of the juniper. This flower was evil, and its bloom satanic, and though it was invisible its manifestations were on every side.

It was not the intrinsic and permanent mood of the Black House, although this alone was frightening enough, with the fungi like plates on the walls, and the sweat of the stones; it was not only this, but was this combined with the sense of a great conspiracy: a conspiracy of darkness, and decay: and yet of a diabolical ingenuity also; a setting against which the characters played out their parts in floodlight, as when pre-destined creatures are caught in a concentration of light so that they cannot move.

Then came Cheeta's voice again, and this time it seemed to Titus that there was an edge to it he had never heard before.

'Flood in the heliotrope.' At this obscure demand the whole scene shuddered into another world of light; a weird and purplish suffusion, and for the first time, Titus, sitting bolt upright on his throne, felt a kind of palpable fear he had never experienced before.

Titus who had killed Steerpike in a war in deep ivy. . . . Titus who had been lost in the underground tunnels of Gormenghast now trembled in the face of the unknown. He turned his head, but he could see no sign of Cheeta. Only a great throng of heliotrope heads . . . a world of watchers who stood as though waiting for him to stand and speak.

But where were the heads he knew? Apart from Cheeta, where was her father, the nondescript man with no hair?

It seemed they formed a kind of foreign terrain, as though of all that multitude there was not one who did not know him, yet for Titus there was not one to recognize.

About him, beyond the crowd, the walls were draped with flags. The flags that he half remembered. Torn flags; flags out of limbo. What was he doing here? What, O dearest God, was he doing? What were these shadows? What were these echoes? Where was a friend to grip him by the shoulder? Where was Muzzlehatch? Where was his friend? What was that sound like the purring of the tide? What was it that was purring if not cats?

The voice of Cheeta rose again. It was harsher with every order. The light changed and yet another mood more sinister than ever settled down upon the place, changing the quality of everything down to the least minutiae; down to the smallest frond in acid green.

Titus, his hands trembling, turned his face from the crowd, meaning to rise from the insufferable throne directly his dizziness passed by. Not only did he turn his face but his body also, for the faked green world before him was revolting to the soul.

Having turned he saw what he might never have seen, for perched along the back of the throne were seven owls, and at the same moment that he saw them there came a long-drawn hoot. It came from beyond the throne both near and far away, but as for the birds themselves they were filled with straw. Beyond the owls the darkness was lit and intersected by a filigree of webs as green as flame.

Titus, who was about to have risen to his feet, remained immobile as he stared at the brilliant mesh, and as he stared another wave of fear took hold of him.

Something, somehow, when he saw the owls, began cutting at his heart. At first there had been a quickening of excitement; he knew not why ... a kind of thrill ... of remembrance or of re-discovery. Was he returning to a realm he could understand? Had he travelled through time or space or both to reach this recrudescence of times gone by? Was he dreaming?

But this did not last long, this quickening of hope. He had not been asleep. He had not dreamed.

The only time he had dreamed was in his fever. It was then that he gave himself unwittingly to Cheeta's mercy.

Powerless to find satisfaction, though brilliant in her power to organize, Cheeta began to issue orders to a small group of the élite. These gentlemen turned at once to their work, which was to clear a passage from the throne, to where, in a dark hall, there lurked the Twelve.

And then, all at once she was beside him, her inscrutable little head staring up at him. Her perfect mouth quivering as though she wished to be kissed.

'You have been so quiet and so patient,' she said. 'It is almost as though you were alive. I have brought your toys, you see. I haven't forgotten anything. Look, Titus ... look at the floor. It is covered with rusty chains. Look at the coloured roots ... and see ... O Titus, see the foliage of the trees. Was Gormenghast forest ever so green as these bright branches?'

Titus tried to rise to his feet, but a sickness lay over his heart like a weight.

She lifted her head again as a creature might do as it harkened. But the voice was no longer merely husky; it was grit ...

'Let in the night,' she cried, in this new voice.

And so the viridian died and the moon came into its own, and a hundred forest creatures crept up to the walls of the Black House, forgetting the horrible colours that had so recently appalled them.

And yet there was a quality about this lunar scene which was more terrible than ever. They were no longer figures in a play. There was no longer any artifice. The stage had vanished. They were no longer actors in a drama of strange light. They were themselves.

'This is what we planned for you darling! The light no man can alter. Sit still. Why is your face so drawn? Why is it melting? After all, you've got your surprise to come. The secret's on its way. What's that?'

'A message, madam, from the look-out tree.'

'What does he want? Speak up at once!'

'A great beggar with a group behind him.'

'What of it?'

'We thought ...'

'Leave me!'

The break in Cheeta's monologue had brought Titus to his feet. What had she said to him, that his fear should be redoubled? That terror; not of Cheeta herself nor of any human being, but of doubt. The *doubt* of his own existence; for where was he? Alone. That's where he was. Alone with nothing to touch. Even the flint from the tall tower was lost. What was there left to guide him? What did Cheeta mean when she said, 'It is almost as though you were alive'? What did she mean when she said, 'I have brought you toys to play with'? What was it that was breaking through the walls of his mind? She had said he was melting. What of the owls? And the purring of the cats? The white cats.

Whatever may have happened to his world one thing was sure: mixed with his homesickness was something else: the beginning beneath his ribs of a conflagration. Whether or not his home was true or false, existent or nonexistent, there was no time for metaphysics. 'Let them tell me later,' he thought to himself, 'whether I am dead or not; sane or not; now is the time for action.' Action. Yes, but what form should it take? He could jump from his throne, but what good would that be? There she was below him, but he no longer wished to see her. It seemed she had some power when he looked at her; some power to weaken and confuse him.

Yet he must not forget that this party was in his honour. Were the symbols that cluttered the floor of the Black House supposed to be a happy reminder of his home, or were the owls and throne and the tin crown there to taunt him?

Here he stood like a dummy while his limbs ached for action. He was no longer dizzy. He waited for the moment to advance into the heart of it all, and to do something, good or bad. As long as it was *something*.

But the expression in her eyes was no longer glazed with a deceptive love. The veil had been lifted or drawn aside, and malice, unequivocal and naked, had taken its place. For she hated him so; and hated him all the more when she realized that he was not so easily made to suffer. Yet superficially all had gone well for her. The young man was obviously in a state of grievous bewilderment, for all the affectation of his stance and the contemptuous tilt of his head. He was thus through fear. But the fear was not great enough yet to break him. Nor was it meant to. That was to come, and in assurance of this, she all but lost herself for the moment in a deadly orgy of anticipa-

228

tion. For it was soon to happen: and all Cheeta could do was to clench her tiny hands together at her breast.

A spasm caught hold of her face and for an instant she was no longer Cheeta, the invincible, the impeccable; the exquisite midget, but something foul. The twitch or spasm, short as had been its duration, had fixed itself so fiercely that long after her face had returned to normal it was there ... that beastly image ... as vivid as ever. What had taken a split moment now spread itself so that it seemed to Titus that her face had been there forever; with that extraordinary contortion of her facial muscles which turned a gelid beauty into something fiendish. Something almost ludicrous.

But what no one expected, least of all Titus or Cheeta herself, was that it should be on the ludicrous and not the terrifying that Titus should fix his attention.

Added to this there was another element that tipped the balance in favour of all that can become uncontrolled; for the spectacle of the sprite with her face turned up to his awoke the image of a dog sitting back on its haunches, waiting to be fed.

The icy Cheeta and the face that she unwittingly let loose were so at variance as to be comic. Horribly, inappropriately comic.

Such a sensation can become too powerful for the human body. It is as easy to control as a sliding avalanche. It takes a sacrosanct convention and snaps it in half as though it were a stick. It lifts up some holy relic and throws it at the sun. It is laughter. Laughter when it stamps its feet; when it sets the bells jangling in the next town. Laughter with the pips of Eden in it.

Out of his fear and apprehension something green and incredibly young took hold of Titus and sidled across his entrails. It shot up to the breast-bone: it radiated into separate turnings: it converged again, and, capsizing through him in an icy heat, cartwheeled through his loins, only to climb again, leaving no inch of his weakening body unaffected. Titus was half away. But his face was rigid and he made no sound: not a catch of the breath or a tilt of the lip. There was no penultimate stage of choking, or a visible fight for composure. It came

229

with extraordinary suddenness, the release of pressure: and he made no effort once he had started to laugh, to check himself. He heard his voice soar clean out of register. He followed it. He yelled to and fro to himself as though he were two people calling to one another across a valley. In another moment, in a seismic access, he tore the stuffed owls from their perch. He dropped them to the ground. He could hold them no longer. He gripped his sides with his hands and staggered back into the throne.

Opening one eye as his body ached with a fresh gale of un-controllable laughter he saw her face before him, and on that instant he was no longer the great belly-roarer: the cracker of goblets, the eye-streaming, arm-dangling, cataleptic wreck of a thing half over the throne, and all but crazed with the delirium of another world: he was suddenly turned to stone, for in her face he read pure evil.

Yet listen to the sweetness of her voice. The words like leaves, are fluttering from the tree. The eyes can no longer pretend. Only the tongue. She fixed him with her black eyes.

'Did you hear that?' she said.

Titus never having seen such an expression of loathing on any woman's face before, answered in a voice as flat as waste-land.

'Did I hear what?'

'Someone laughing,' she said. 'I would have thought it would have wakened you.'

'I heard the laughter too,' said another voice. 'But *he* was asleep.'

'Yes,' said another. 'Asleep in the throne.'

'What? Titus Groan, Lord of the Tracts, and heir to Gor-menghast?'

'The same. A heavy sleeper!'

'See how he stares at us!'

'He is bewildered.'

'He needs his mother!'

'Of course, of course!'

'How lucky he is!'

'Why so?'

'Because she's on her way.'

'Red hair, white cats, 'n all?'

'Exactly.'

Cheeta, furious, had had to change her plans. Just as she was about to bring on the phantoms, and by so doing, derange once and for all the boy's bewildered mind.

And so, with a sweet smile to those at her side, she began again to create an atmosphere most conducive to madness.

It was at this moment that, without knowing what he was doing, he picked up the flimsy throne with both hands and dashed it to the ground. The silence was palpable.

At last there came a voice. It was not hers.

'He came to us when he was lost, poor child. Lost, or so he thought. But he was no more lost than a homester on the wing. He searches for his home but he has never left it, for this is Gormenghast. It is all about him.'

'No!' cried Titus. 'No!'

'See how he cries. He is upset, poor thing. He does not realize how much we love him.'

A hundred voices, like an incantation, repeated the words ... 'how much we love him.'

'He thinks that to move about is to change places. He does not realize that he is treading water.'

And the voices echoed ... 'treading water.'

Then Cheeta's voice again.

'Yet this is our farewell. A farewell from his old self to his new. How splendid! To tear one's throne up by the roots, and fling it to the floor. What was it after all but a symbol? We have too many symbols. We wade in symbols. We are sick of them. It is a pity about your brain.'

Titus wheeled upon her. 'My brain,' he cried, 'what's wrong with my brain?'

'It is on the turn,' said Cheeta.

'Yes, yes,' came the chorus from the shadows. 'That's what has happened. His brain is on the turn!'

And then the authoritative voice rose again beyond the juniper fire.

'His head is no longer anything but an emblem. His heart is a cypher. He is a mere token. But we love him, don't we?'

'Oh yes, we love him, don't we?' came the chorus.

'But he's so confused. He thinks he's lost his home.'

'. . . and his sister, Fuchsia.'

'. . . and the Doctor.'

'. . . and his mother.'

At this moment, hard upon the mention of his mother's name, Titus, turning a deathly colour, sprang outward from the debris.

ONE HUNDRED AND THREE

IT might have been Cheeta: but it was not. She had made a sign, and in making it she had moved back a little to obtain a clearer view of the entrance to the forgotten room. Who it was that suffered the agonizing jab in the region of the heart will never be known; but that ornate gentleman collapsed upon the pave-stones of the aisle receiving, as though he were a scape-goat, the fury which Titus, at that moment, would gladly have meted out to all.

Panting, the sweat glistening on his face he suddenly found

himself gripped by the elbow. Two men, one on either side, held him. Struggling to free himself he saw, as though through the haze of his anger, that they were the same tall, smooth, ubiquitous helmeted figures who had trailed him for so long.

They backed him up the steps to where the throne once stood, when suddenly, as he struggled and tossed his head, he saw for an instant something in the corner of his eye that caused his heart to stop beating. The helmeted figures loosened their grip upon his arms.

ONE HUNDRED AND FOUR

SOMETHING was emerging from the forgotten room. Something of great bulk and swathing. It moved with exaggerated grandeur, trailing a length of dusty, moth-eaten fustian, and over all else was spattered the constellations of ubiquitous bird-lime. The shoulders of her once black gown were like white mounds, and upon these mounds were perched every kind of bird. As for the phantom's hair (a most unnatural red), even this was a perch for little birds.

As the Lady moved on with a prodigious authority, one of the birds fell off her shoulder, and broke as it hit the floor.

Again the laughter. The horrible laughter. It sounded like the mirth of hell, hot and derisive.

Were there a 'Gormenghast', then surely this mockery of his mother must humble and torture him, reminding him of his Abdication, and of all the ritual he so loved and loathed. If, on the other hand there were no such place, and the whole thing a concoction of his mind, then, mortified by this exposure of his secret love, the boy would surely break.

'Where is he? Where is my son?' came the voice of the voluminous impostor. It was slow and thick as gravel. 'Where is my only son?'

The creature adjusted its shawl with a twitch.

'Come here my love and be punished. It is I. Your mother. Gertrude of Gormenghast.'

Titus was able to see in a flash that the monster was leading

233

another travesty into the half-light. At that excruciating moment, Cheeta heard what Titus also heard; a shrill whistling. It was not that the sound of the whistle in itself puzzled her, but the fact that there should be anyone at all *beyond* the walls. It was not part of her plan.

Although he could not at first recall the meaning of the whistle, yet Titus felt some kind of remote affinity with the whistler. While this had been going on, there was at the same instant much else to be seen.

What of the monstrous insult to his mother? As far as *that* was concerned, his passion for revenge burned fiercely.

The guests, now lit by torchlight, were beginning, under orders, to sort themselves into a great circle. There they stood on the loose, grassy floor, craning their necks like hens to see what it was that followed on the heels of something preternaturally evil.

ONE HUNDRED AND FIVE

WHAT Titus could *not* see was the interior of the forgotten room where a dozen ill-tempered monstrosities had been incarcerated. But now there was a stir in the dungeon: the entrance had cleared itself of its first huge character, and close behind her, walking like a duck, was a wicked caricature of Titus's sister. She wore a tattered dress of diabolical crimson. Her dark dishevelled hair reached to her knees, and when she turned her face to the assemblage there were few who did not catch their breath. Her face was blotched with black and sticky tears, and her cheeks were hectic and raw. She slouched behind her huge mother, but came to a halt as they were about to enter the torch-lit circle, for she stared pathetically this way and that, and then stood grotesquely on her toes as though she were looking for someone. After a few moments she flung her head back so that her black tresses all but touched the ground. Now, with her blotched face turned pitifully to the sky she opened her mouth in a round empty 'O' and bayed the moon. Here was madness complete. Here was matter for revenge. It

234

took hold of Titus and it shook him, so that he wrenched this way and that against the grip of the helmeted figures.

So strange and terrible was what he saw that he froze within the grip of his captors. Something began to give way in his brain. Something lost faith in itself.

'Where is my son?' came the soft gravel throat, and this time his mother turned her face to his, and he saw her.

In contrast to Fuchsia's raddled, hectic, tear-drenched face was his mother's. It was a slab of marble over which false locks of carrot-coloured hair cascaded. This monster spoke, though there was little to be seen in the way of a mouth. Her face was like a great, flat boulder that had been washed and worn smooth by a thousand tides.

With the blank slab out-facing him, Titus let out a cry of his own; an inward cry of desolation.

'That is my boy,' came the gravel voice. 'Did you not hear him? That was the very accent of the Groans. How grievous, yet how rare that he should have died. What is it like to be dead, my wandering child?'

'Dead?' whispered Titus. 'Dead? No! No!'

It was then that Fuchsia made her gawky way across the rough circle, the perimeter of which was thick with faces.

'Dear brother,' she said, when she reached the broken throne. 'Dear brother, you can trust *me*, surely?'

She turned her face to Titus.

'It's no use pretending; and you're *not* alone. I drowned myself, you know. We have death in common. Have you forgotten? Forgotten how I sank beneath the frog-spawn waters of the moat? Is it not glorious to be dead together? I, in my way. You in yours?'

She shook herself and clouds of dust drifted away. Meanwhile Cheeta suddenly appeared at Titus's side.

'Let his lordship go,' she said to the captors. 'Let him play. Let him play.'

'Let him play,' came the chorus.

'Let him play,' whispered Cheeta. 'Let him make believe that he's alive again.'

THE helmeted figures let go their grip upon his arms.

'We have brought your mother and your sister back again. Who else would you like?'

Titus turned his head to her and saw in her eyes the extent of her bitterness. Why had he been so singled out? What had he done? Was the fact that he had never loved her for herself but only out of lust, was this so dire a thing?

The darkness seemed to concentrate itself. The torchlight burned fitfully, and a thin sprinkling of rain came drifting out of the night.

'We are bringing your family together,' whispered Cheeta. 'They have been too long in Gormenghast. It is for you to greet them, and to bring them into the ring. See how they wait for you. They need you. For did you not desert them? Did you not abdicate? That is why they are here. For one reason only. To forgive you. To forgive your treachery. See how their eyes shine with love.'

While she was speaking, three major things took place. The first (at Cheeta's instigation) was that a channel was rapidly cleared from the steps of the throne to the ring itself, so that Titus should be able to make his way without hindrance into the heart of the circle.

The second thing was the recurrence of that shrill and reminiscent whistle that Cheeta and Titus had heard some time before. This time it was nearer.

The third was that into the ring, fresh monsters began to arrive.

The forgotten room disgorged them, one by one. There were the aunts, the identical twins, whose faces were lit in such a way that they appeared to be floating in space. The length of their necks; their horribly quill-like noses; the emptiness of their gaze; all this was bad enough, without those dreadful words which they uttered in a flat monotone over and over again.

'Burn ... burn ... burn ...'

There was Sepulchrave, moving as though in a trance, his tired soul in his eyes, and books beneath his arms. All about were his chains of office, iron and gold. On his head he wore the rust-red crown of the Groans. He took deep sighs with every step; as though each one was the last. Bent forward as though his sorrow weighed him down he mourned with every gesture. As he moved into the centre of the ring he trailed behind him a long line of feathers, while out of his tragic mouth the sound of hooting wandered.

More and more it was becoming a horrible charade. Everything that Cheeta had heard during those bouts of fever when Titus lay and poured out his past, all this had been stored up in her capacious memory.

One of them after another reared or loomed, pranced or took mournful steps; cried, howled or were silent.

A thin wiry creature with high deformed shoulders and a skewbald face leapt to and fro as though trying to get rid of his energy.

On seeing him Titus had recoiled, not out of fear, but out of amazement; for he and Steerpike, long ago, had fought to the death. Knowing that all this was a kind of cruel charade, did not seem to help for in the inmost haunts of the imagination he felt the impact.

Who else was there in the rough ring towards which Titus was involuntarily moving? There was the attenuate Doctor with his whinnying laughter. As Titus looked at him he saw, not the bizarre travesty that faced him with its affected gait and voice, but the original Doctor. The Doctor he loved so much.

When he had reached the ring and was about to enter it he closed his eyes in an effort to free himself of the sight of these monster, for they reminded him most cruelly of those far-away days when their prototypes were real indeed. But no sooner had he closed his eyes than he heard a third whistle. This time the shrill note was closer than before. So close in fact that it caused Titus not only to open his eyes again, but to look about him, and as he did so he heard once more that reedy note.

ONE HUNDRED AND SEVEN

WHEN Titus saw the three of them, Slingshott, Crabcalf and Crack-Bell, his heart leaped. Their bizarre, outlandish faces fought for his sanity as a doctor fights for the life of his patient. But by not so much as a flicker of an eyelash did they betray the fact that they were Titus's friends.

But now he had allies, though how they could help he could not tell. Their three heads remained quite still throughout the commotion. Not looking at him but *through* him, as though like gun dogs they were directing Titus to turn his gaze to where, leaning against a fern-covered wall as rough as himself lolled Muzzlehatch.

As for Cheeta, she was scrutinizing her quarry, waiting for the moment of collapse; tasting the sweet and sour of the whole affair, when suddenly Titus swung his head away with a bout of nausea. She in her turn, followed his gaze and saw a figure who in no way fitted into her plans.

Directly Titus saw him, he began to stumble in his direction, though of course he could not hope to break through the human walls of the ring.

With Titus's eyes upon him and Cheeta's also, it was not long before an ever-growing number of guests became aware of Muzzlehatch, who leaned so casually in the shadow of the fern-hung wall.

ONE HUNDRED AND EIGHT

As the moments passed, less and less attention was paid to the mockers in the ring, and Cheeta, realizing that her plan was miscarrying, turned a face of concentrated fury upon this tall and enigmatic alien.

By now, according to plan, the cause of her heartburn and enmity, Titus, should have been in the last throes of subjugation.

With practically every head turned to the almost legendary Muzzlehatch, a curious silence fell upon the scene. Even the soughing of the leaves in the surrounding forest had died away.

When Titus saw his old friend he could not withhold a cry. ... 'Help me for pity's sake.'

Muzzlehatch appeared to take no notice of his cry. He was staring in turn at the apparitions, but at last his eyes came to rest upon one in particular. This nondescript figure crept in and out of the ring as though it were in search of something important. But whatever it was the glinting eye of Muzzlehatch followed it everywhere. At last the figure came to rest, his bald head shimmering, and Muzzlehatch was no longer in doubt of the man's identity. The creature was both repulsive and nondescript, in a way that chilled the blood.

Titus again cried out for Muzzlehatch, and again there was no reply. Yet there he stood, leaning in half-light, well within earshot. What was the matter with his old friend? Why, after all this time was he being ignored? Titus beat his fists together. Surely in finding one another again there should have been aroused some kind of emotion? But no. As far as could be seen Muzzlehatch made no response. There he lounged in the shadows of the ferny pillar, a creature who might easily be taken for a mendicant, were it not that there was no beggar alive who could look so ragged and yet, at the same time, so like a king.

Had Titus, or had anyone approached him *too* closely, he or they would have seen a lethal light in the gaunt man's eyes. It was no more than a glint, a fleck of fire. Yet, this fleck, a dangerous thing, was not directed at anyone in particular; nor did it come and go. It was a constant. Something that had become a part of him as an arm or leg might be. It seemed by his attitude that Muzzlehatch might be staying there forever, so seemingly listless was his pose. But this illusion was short-lived although it seemed as though the congregation had stood there watching him for hours. They had never before seen anything like it. A giant festooned with rags.

And then, gradually (for it took a longish while for everyone to transfer their gaze from the magnetic interloper to the object of his scrutiny), gradually and finally there was not one of the assemblage who was not staring at the polished head of Cheeta's father.

One could not help but think of death, so visible was the skull beneath the stretched skin. There was at length only one pair of eyes that were not fixed upon the head; and those eyes belonged to the man himself.

Then, quite gradually Muzzlehatch yawned, stretching his arms to their extremities, as though to touch the sky. He took a pace forward, and then, at last, he spoke, yet not with his *voice* but more eloquently, with a great scarred index-finger like a crook.

ONE HUNDRED AND NINE

CHEETA'S father, realizing that he had no choice but to obey (for there was something terrible and compelling about Muzzlehatch, with the crumbs of fire in his eyes) began to make his way willy-nilly in the direction of the great vagrant. And still there was no noise in all the world.

Then, suddenly, like something released, Titus beat his fists together, as a man might beat upon a door to let out his soul. Not a head turned at the sound, and the silence surged back and filled the shell of the Black House. But although there was no physical movement save for the progress of the bald man, there passed over the ground a shudder and a chill, where there was no breeze blowing, like the breath of a cold fresco, dank and rotting, filled with figures, so was this nocturnal array equally silent; when all at once, the ring of heads closed in upon the protagonists, and at the same time the two protagonists closed in on one another.

Muzzlehatch had dropped his index finger, and was approaching the scientist at a speed deliberately slow. Two worlds were approaching one another.

What of Cheeta? Where in this forest of legs could she be with her beautiful little face contorted and discoloured? Everything had gone wrong. What had been an ordered plan was nothing now but a humiliating chaos. She had been almost forgotten. She had become lost in a world of limbs. She had, more by instinct than knowledge, been making her way to where she last saw Titus, for to lose him would be for her like losing her revenge.

But she was not the only malcontent. In his own way, Titus was as fierce as she. The grisly charade had left him full of hatred. Not only this; there was Muzzlehatch too. His old friend. Why was he so silent and so deaf to his cries?

In an access of frustration he elbowed his way to the outskirts of the ring, and then, free at last, he ran at Muzzlehatch as though to endanger him.

But when Titus was close enough to strike out in his anger at the great figure, he stopped short in his tracks, for he saw what it was that had subjugated the bald man. It was the embers in the eyes of his friend.

This was not the Muzzlehatch he used to know. This was something quite different. A solitary who had no friends, nor needed any: for he was obsessed.

When Titus closed in upon Muzzlehatch in the semi-darkness he could see all this. He could see the embers, and his anger melted out of him. He could see at a glance how Muzzlehatch was bent upon death: that he was deranged. What was it then, in spite of this horror, that drew Titus to him? For Muzzlehatch had as yet taken no notice of him. What was it that urged Titus forward until he blocked the torn man's view of Cheeta's father? It was a kind of love.

'My old friend,' said Titus, very softly. 'Look at me, only look at me. Have you forgotten?'

At long last, Muzzlehatch turned his gaze upon Titus, who was now within arm's reach.

'Who is it? Let go my lemurs, boy.'

His face looked as though it were carved out of grey wood.

'Listen,' said the wanderer. 'You remind me of a friend I used to know. His name was Titus. He used to say he lived in a castle. He had a scar across his cheekbones. Ah yes, Titus Groan, Lord of the Tracts.'

'That man is me!' cried Titus in his desperation.

'Boom!' said Muzzlehatch, in a voice as abstracted as the night air. 'It won't be long now. Boom!'

Titus stared at him, and Cheeta also, through a gap in the crowd. He was shaking violently.

'Give me a clue, for God's sake. What are these "boom"s of yours? What is it that *won't be long*?' said Titus.

By now the scientist was only a few paces from Muzzle-hatch, as though propelled slowly forward by an unseen force.

Yet it was not only the scientist who was inexorably on the move. The crowds, inch by inch, began to shuffle in little steps; their heads closed in upon the protagonists.

Were it not that all eyes were transfixed on the sight of the three, someone would by now have noticed Juno and Anchor.

ONE HUNDRED AND TEN

No one had noticed their arrival. A great bell pounded in Juno's bosom. Her eyes were fixed on Titus. She trembled. A rush of memories filled her. She longed to run to him and to draw him to her. But Anchor restrained her, his hand holding her trembling elbow.

Unlike Juno, the Anchor, with his mop of red-black hair, stood by her with all the sang-froid in the world. He seemed to have come into his own.

He watched every move and then led Juno away to an inky alcove. She was not to stir until he called for her. He returned to the centre of potential violence. He saw a creature break loose from a wall of legs. It was as slender as a switch. A great blood-coloured stone winked at her breast as though it spelled out some secret code. But it was her face that chilled him. It was terrible because it had given up trying. It no longer *cared*. All femininity had gone out of it. The features had become merely physical additions to the head. The face had died behind them. It was an empty place through which the winds could blow, now hot, now cold, from hell or heaven.

As for the phlegmatic Anchor, he had noted the long line of aeroplanes that glimmered in the half-darkness. There, if nowhere else, was their escape route.

Now he was ready. Now, before the evening closed in, he

must strike when the moment came. Strike when? He had not long to wait for an answer.

Cheeta had by now seen not only Titus, but her father also. She had stopped as a bird stops in the middle of a run; for it was with amazement that she found herself so close to the huge stranger, who was even now picking her father up by the nape of his neck as a dog might lift a rat.

ONE HUNDRED AND ELEVEN

EVERYTHING seemed to be happening together. The light shifted like a gauze across the scene, almost as though the moon was making a return journey. Then something shone in the darkness. Something of metal, for there was no other substance that could throw out so strong a glint into the night air.

Titus, his gaze distracted for a moment by these flashes of light, turned his head away from Cheeta and her suspended father, and discovered, at last, what he was looking for. And while he watched, the leaping bonfire sent out a more than usually brilliant tongue, and this tongue, though it was far away, was strong enough to draw out of the darkness an expressionless face, and then another. Now they were gone again, though the light went on flashing above them. Plunged in their caves, their faces were no more, though their crests were alive with light. The helmeted men. Even without their helmets they would be tall. But with them, they stood head and shoulders above the crowd.

A shudder passed through Titus's body. He saw the crowds draw themselves apart so that the 'helmets' could pass through. He heard the assembly call out for them to deal with Muzzle-hatch.

'Take him away,' they cried. 'Who is he? What does he want? He is frightening the ladies.'

Yet not one of that crowd, save for the 'helmets' themselves, and Cheeta, who was trembling in a diabolical rage; not one dared to take a step alone.

As for Muzzlehatch; his arm was outstretched and the scientist was still dangling at the end of it. This was the man whom he intended to slay. But now that he had the bald creature at arm's length, he could not feel the hatred so strongly.

Titus was appalled at the scene. Appalled at the vileness of it. Appalled that anyone should have thought out such an idea as to mock his family in such a way. Appalled and frightened. He turned his head and saw her, and his blood ran cold.

Revenge filled up her system, and battled with itself in her miniature bosom. Titus had scorned her. And now there was the ragged man as well, for he was holding up her family to scorn. And now Juno, whom she saw out of the tail of her eye. Her hair rose at the nape. There was no forgetting so far as Cheeta was concerned. This was the Juno of his early days. This was she; his one-time mistress.

ONE HUNDRED AND TWELVE

THE bonfire of juniper branches had been replenished, and again a yellow tongue of fire had fled up into the sky. Its light lit up the nearest of the trees with a wan illumination. The scent of the juniper filled the air. It was the only pleasant thing about the night. But no one noticed.

The animals and the birds, unable to go to sleep, watched from whatever vantage point they could cling to. There was among them an understanding that they left one another alone, until dawn, so that the birds of prey sat side by side with doves and owls, the foxes with the mice.

*

From where he stood, Titus could see, as though on a stage, the protagonists. Time seemed to draw to a close. The world had lost interest in itself and its positionings. They stood between the coil and the recoil. It was too much. Yet there was no alternative either of the heart or of the head. He could not leave Muzzlehatch. He loved the man. Yes, even now, though the flecks of red burned in his arrogant eyes. Sensing the wide-

244

spread derangement all about him, Titus was becoming fearful for his own sanity. Yet there is loyalty in dreams, and beauty in madness, and he could not turn from the shaggy side of his friend. Nor could the scores of guests do anything. They were spellbound.

Now Muzzlehatch's boulder-like rolling of his own voice was repeated, and then immediately followed by a voice that did not seem his own. Something muted: something more menacing took its place,

'That was a long time ago,' said Muzzlehatch, 'when I lived another kind of life. I wandered through the dawn and back again. I ate the world up like a serpent devouring itself, tail first. Now I am inside out. The lions roared for me. They roared down my bloodstream. But, as they are dead, their roaring comes to nothing, for you, Bladder-head, have stopped their hearts from beating, and now it's about time for me to stop yours.'

Muzzlehatch was not looking at the living bundle at the end of his arm. He was looking through it. Then he dropped his hand and trailed the scientist in the dust.

'So I went for a stroll, and what a stroll it was! It took me to a factory at last. And there I met your friends and your machines, and all that caused the great death of my beasts. O God, my coloured beasts, my burning fauna. And there I lit the blue fuse at the centre. It can't be long to wait. Boom!'

Muzzlehatch looked about him.

'Well, well, well,' he said. 'What a pretty lot we have here! By heaven, Titus boy, the air is full of damnation. Look at 'em. D'you know 'em? Ha, ha! God's liver, if it ain't the "Helmeteers". How they do tread on our tails.'

'Sir,' said Anchor, moving up. 'Let me relieve you of the scientist. Even an arm like yours must tire at times.'

'Who are you?' said Muzzlehatch, leaving his arm where it was, like a signpost, for he had lifted it again.

'Does that matter?' said Anchor.

'Matter! Ha, that's ripe,' said Muzzlehatch. 'Ripe as your copper-coloured mane. How is it you have jumped from the ranks to join us?'

'We have a lady in common,' said Anchor.

'Who would that be?' said Muzzlehatch. 'Queen of the mermaids?'

'Do I look it?' It was Juno who, against Anchor's instructions, had crept out of the alcove, and now stood at his side.

'O Titus, my most dear!' She ran towards him.

At the sight of Juno, the air became electric and through this atmosphere a figure darted, rapid as a weasel. It was Cheeta.

ONE HUNDRED AND THIRTEEN

So *this* was Juno; *this*, the billowy whore. Cheeta bit her underlip until the blood ran over her chin.

She had long ago dismissed from her mind any thought of her own attractions. They had ceased to be of any interest to her, for something a thousand times more important filled her vision as a pit can be filled with fumes. But as the venomous midget slid with a dreadful intensity of purpose towards Juno, her rival, she was brought to an incongruous halt by an explosion.

Not only was Cheeta halted in her progress at the sound of the reverberation, but each in their own way found himself or herself rooted to the floor of the Black House; Juno, Anchor, Titus, and Muzzlehatch himself, the 'Helmets', the Three, and a hundred guests. And more than this. The birds and the beasts of the surrounding forests, they also froze along the boughs, until simultaneously taking wing a great volume of birds arose like a fog into the night, thickening the air, and quenching the moon. Where they had perched in their thousands the twigs and boughs lifted themselves a little in the bird-made darkness.

Seeing the others glued to the ground, Cheeta struggled against her own inability to close with them and to fight with the only weapons she possessed; two rows of sharp little teeth and ten finger nails. She had turned from Titus to Juno as the first of her enemies to dispatch, but like them, her head was turned in the direction of the sound, and she could not twist it back.

That her father, the greatest scientist in the world was hanging upside down from the outstretched arm of some kind of brigand did not, in itself, inflame or impress upon her passions, for there was no space left in her tiny tremulous body for such an emotion to find foothold. She could not feel for him. She was consumed already.

The first to speak was Anchor.

'What would that be?' he said. Even as he spoke a light appeared in the sky in the direction of the sound.

'That would be the death of many men,' said Muzzlehatch. 'That would be the last roar of the golden fauna: the red of the world's blood: doom is one step closer. It was the fuse that did it. The blue fuse. My dear man,' he said, turning to Anchor, 'only look at the sky.'

Sure enough it was taking on a life of its own. Unhealthy as a neglected sore, skeins of transparent fabric wavered across the night sky, peeling off, one after another to reveal yet fouler tissues in a fouler empyrean.

Then the crowd raised its voice, and demanded that it be set free from the ghastly charade that was taking place before its eyes.

But when Muzzlehatch approached them they drew back, for there was something incalculable about the smile that turned his face into something to be avoided.

They all drew back a pace or two, except for the helmeted pair. These two, holding their ground, leaned forward on the air. Now that they were so close it could be seen that their heads were like skulls, beautiful, as though chiselled. What skin they had was stretched tight as silk. There was a sheen over their heads, almost a luminosity. Nor did they speak from those thin mouths of theirs. Nor could they. Only the crowds spoke, while their clothes grew damp as the night fell, despoiling the exquisite gowns, and blackening their hems with dew. So with the medallioned chests of their tongue-tied escorts.

'I ask you sir, again. What was that noise? Was it thunder?' said Anchor, knowing full well that it was not. He watched the gaunt man while he spoke but he also watched Titus; and Cheeta. He watched the helmeted men who menaced Muzzlehatch. He watched everything. His eyes, in contrast to the shock of red hair, were grey as pools.

But above all he watched Juno. All eyes had by now been turned away from the direction of the sound and of the sick sky also, and formed between them a pattern in the darkness, and at the same moment the first twinge of sunrise in the forested east.

Juno, her eyes filled with tears, took hold of Titus by the arm at a moment when he longed from the bottom of his soul to get away, to leave for ever. But he did not by an iota tense or withdraw his arm from her, or do anything to hurt her. Yet Juno let go her hand from his arm, and it fell like a weight to her side.

He gazed at her, almost as though she belonged to another world, and his lips, though they formed a smile, had no life in them. Here they stood side by side, these two, with the loveliest section of their past in common. Yet they appeared to have lost their way. All this was in a flash, and the Anchor took it in.

He also took in something of another kind. The impersonal embers in Muzzlehatch's eyes appeared to have been fanned into life. The small, dull red light had now begun to oscillate to and fro across the pupils.

But in contrast to this grisly phenomenon, was the control he exercised over his own voice. It was perfectly audible though a little more than a whisper. Coming from the great rudder-nosed man it was a double weapon.

'It was not thunder,' he said. 'Thunder is purposeless. But this was the very backbone of purpose. There was no explosion for explosion's sake.'

Taking advantage of the fact that Muzzlehatch was engaged in his own oratory, Anchor moved around him, unseen, until he stood a little behind Titus, for from this position he was able to command a view of Cheeta and Juno at the same time.

The air was bristling, for they had seen one another. Without her knowing it, the initial advantage lay with Juno, for Cheeta's ferocity was almost equally divided between her and Titus.

The whole travesty had been planned as something to humiliate Titus. She had been to all lengths to insure its success; yet now it was over, and she stood among the wreckage, her little body vibrating like a bow-string.

'Dismantle them!' she screamed, for she saw out-topping the

crowd, the battered masks, the hanks of hair; the Countess breaking in half, dusty and ludicrous; the sawdust; and the paint.

ONE HUNDRED AND FOURTEEN

'TAKE those things down!' she screamed, standing on tiptoe, for she saw in the tail of her eye, a great wavering, semi-human bulk, that was even now as she watched it, breaking in half and turning as it collapsed, to show the long filthy hanks of hair, the mask with its dreadful pallor, lit by the flooding of the dawn, sink to the floor. Down came the others, that had so recently been the symbols of mockery and scorn. Some with their grease-paint dripping; the dusty remnants of blotched sawdust.

All at once a woman screamed, and as though this were a signal for release, a general cacophony broke out and a number of ladies grew hysterical, striking out at their husbands or their lovers.

Muzzlehatch, whose peroration had been interrupted, merely cocked an eye at the crowd, and then stared fixedly and for a long time at what was still dangling at the end of his arm. After a while he remembered what it was.

'I was going to kill you,' said Muzzlehatch, 'in the way you kill a rabbit. A sharp stroke at the nape of the neck, delivered with the edge of the hand. I was even going to throttle you, but that seemed too good for you. Then there was the idea of drowning you in a bucket, but all these things were too good for you. You would not appreciate them. But I'll have to do something about you, won't I? Do you think your daughter wants you? Has she a birthday coming? No? Then I'll take a chance, my little cockroach. Only *look* at her. Dishevelled and wicked. Look how she pines for him. Why, you'd take his nut for an onion. I must be rude after all, my sweet dangler, for you killed my animals. Ah, how they slid in their hey-day. How they meandered; how they skidded or leapt in their abandon. Lord, how they cocked their heads. Dear heaven! How they cocked their heads!

'Once there were islands all a-sprout with palms: and coral reefs and sands as white as milk. What is there now but a vast shambles of the heart? Filth, squalor, and a world of little men.'

At the same moment that Muzzlehatch drew breath, Cheeta was seen to speed across the last few steps that divided her from Titus, like an evil thing borne on an evil draught.

Had it not been that with an unexpected agility, Juno leapt in front of Titus, he might well have had his face cut over and over by Cheeta's long green nails.

Thwarted in her passion to leave her marks on Titus's face, she howled in an access of evil as tears churned down her cheeks in channels of make-up.

For, no longer than it takes to tell it, Anchor had dragged both Titus and Juno out of reach of the malignant dart. Trembling, she stood and waited the next move, rising and falling on her tiny feet.

The dawn was now beginning to pick out the leaves from the trees of the surrounding forests and glowed softly on the helmets of the agents.

But Titus did not want to be hidden away behind the stalwart Anchor. He was grateful but angry that he should have been plucked backwards. As for Juno who had disobeyed Anchor – she was doing it again. For she also had no wish to remain in the shadow of her friend. They were too restless, too on edge to stand still. Seeing what was happening, Anchor merely shrugged his shoulders.

'The time has come,' said Muzzlehatch, 'to do whatever it was we set out to do. This is the time for flight. This is the time for bastards like myself to put an end to it all. What if my eyes are sore and red? What if they burn my sockets up? I've bathed in the straits of Actapon with phosphorus in the water, and my limbs like fish. Who cares about that now? Do you?' he said, tossing the bundle who was Cheeta's father, from one huge hand to another. 'Do you? Tell me honestly.'

Muzzlehatch bent down and put his ear to the bundle. 'It's beastly,' he said, 'and it's alive.' Muzzlehatch tossed the little scientist to his daughter, who had no option but to catch him.

He whimpered a little as Cheeta then let him fall to the floor. Getting to his feet, his face was a map of terror.

'I must go back to my work,' he said in that thin voice that sent a chill down the spines of all his workmen.

'It's no good going *there*,' said Muzzlehatch. 'It has exploded. Can you not hear the reverberations? Can you not see how ghastly is the dawn? There's a lot of ash in the air.'

'Exploded? No! ... No! ... It was all I had; my science, *all* that I had.'

'And she was a lovely girl, I'm told,' said Muzzlehatch.

Cheeta's father, too frightened to answer, now began to turn in the direction of the foul light that was still angry in the sky. 'Let me go,' he cried, though no one was touching him. 'O God! My formula!' he cried. 'My formula.' He began to run.

On and on he ran, over the walls and into the dawn shadows. Immediately upon his words came a thick and curious laughter. It was Muzzlehatch. His eyes were like two red-hot pennies. While the echoes of Muzzlehatch rang out, Cheeta had manoeuvred herself so that she was again within striking distance of Titus, who, now that he was some way from Anchor, had turned for a moment to stare about him at the gaping throng.

It was at that moment, with his head averted, that Cheeta struck, breaking her nails as one might crunch sea-shells. The warm blood ran profusely down his neck. At once Juno was upon her.

How she could have moved with such speed it was impossible to say. But when she leapt forward and lifted her arm to strike, Juno recoiled from touching the febrile thing, for there was something horrible in the discrepancy in their sizes, and something pitiful about Cheeta's small bedraggled face spotted with blood, however evil.

But that was where the compunction ended, and Juno, trembling as much as her antagonist, was about to be grabbed by Anchor, when the shrillest scream of all tore its way through the body of the sunrise like a knife through tissue; and immediately upon this vent from Cheeta's lungs, the little creature turned upon them all and spat. This was the once exquisite Cheeta, the queen of ice; the orchid; brilliant of brain and limb. Now with her dignity departed forever, she bared her teeth.

What was she to do? She darted her glance along the half

circle. She saw how Juno was attending to Titus's wounds as well as she could. Between them and herself, stood Anchor. She looked about her wildly, and saw how the light in Muzzlehatch's eyes was directed upon her, and how there was no love in them; and how she was irrevocably alone.

She returned her gaze to Titus.

'I hate you!' she cried. 'I hate all that you think you are. I hate your Gormenghast. I will always hate it. If it were true I'd hate it even more. I'm glad your neck is bleeding. You beast! Bloody beast!'

She turned and ran from them crying out words that none of them could understand ... ran like a shred of darkness; ran and ran; until only those with the keenest sight could see her as she fled into the deep shadows of the most easterly of the forests. But though she was soon too far away for even the best of eyes, yet her voice carried all the way, until only a far, thin screaming could be heard, and after that no more.

ONE HUNDRED AND FIFTEEN

MUZZLEHATCH turned his great hewn face to the sky.

'Come here Titus. I am suddenly remembering you. What's the matter? Do you always go round with blood all over you, like a butcher's shop?'

'Leave him alone, Muzzle dear. He's very sick indeed,' said Juno.

But they were not destined for any slackening of the pressure. Cheeta had gone it is true, and her father also, but danger was now from another quarter. The crowd was beginning to surge towards them. There were cries of anger, for they were very afraid. Everything had gone wrong. They were cold. They were lost. They were hungry. And Cheeta, the centre of it all, had forsaken them. Who could they turn to? In their lost condition, they could do little else but fling abuse at the shadowy figures, and it was only after a particularly ugly bout that a thick voice called out ...

'And look at them,' it cried. 'Look at that fool in a bandage.

252

Seventy-Seventh Earl! Ha! ha! There's Gormenghast for you. Why don't you come and prove yourself, my lord?'

Why this particular remark should have got under Muzzlehatch's skin, it is hard to fathom, but it did, and he stalked to the border of the crowd in order to annihilate the man. In order to do so he passed, swaggering in his rags, between the two inscrutable Helmeteers. As he did so there was a kind of hush as they slid aside to let him through. Then, as though it had all been premeditated, they turned and, bringing out their long-bladed knives, they stabbed Muzzlehatch in the back.

He did not die all at once, though the blades were long. He did not make a sound except for a catch in his breath. The red had gone out of his eyes, and in its place was a prodigious sanity. 'Where's Titus?' he said. 'Bring the young ruffian here.'

There was no need to tell Titus what to do. He flung himself at Muzzlehatch, yet with tenderness, for all his passion, and he clasped his old friend with his hand.

'Hey! hey!' whispered Muzzlehatch. 'Don't squeeze out what's left of me, my dear.'

'Oh my dear Muzzle . . . my dear friend.'

'Don't overdo it,' whispered Muzzlehatch, as he began to sag at the knees. 'Mustn't get morbid . . . eh? . . . eh? . . . Where is your hand, boy?'

What had been diffused throughout the sunrise, had now contracted to a focus. What was atmospheric had become almost solid. As they looked at one another, they saw what some see under the influence of drugs, a peculiar nearness, and a vividness hardly to be borne.

ONE HUNDRED AND SIXTEEN

JUNO, though knowing herself to be an outsider, in spite of her devotion to them both, yet had no power to keep away from her one-time lover, and it is strange that they needed Muzzlehatch at this last moment more than vengeance. Vengeance was to come, and Anchor was on his way to dispense it.

By now the sun was clear of the eastern forests, and every

shape of form and colour would have shone clearly were it not for the omnipresent veil of the foul orange tint, that bastard hue, that was neither red nor yellow, but wavered on the brink of both. The only thing that burned with decision was Anchor.

Within a few strides he was beside them. The Helmeted Men. They were wiping their long steel blades upon the dock leaves that grew profusely on the floor of the Black House. For a moment his stomach turned with revulsion, for there was no expression on their faces. During the moment, too short to be called a pause, Anchor averted his gaze, and he saw on the other side of the two 'Helmets', the three characters from the Under-River.

Anchor knew nothing of these three, but he was not left long in doubt as to their intentions. Clumsy in movement, yet working in a crude unison they took the helmeted murderers from behind, snatching their long knives and pinning their arms to their sides. Yet the more they squeezed and pinioned them the stronger the sinister couple grew, and it was only when their helmets fell to the ground that a supernatural strength deserted them, and they were at once overpowered and slain by their own weapons.

Then a great hush came down upon the Black House, and over the wide and tragic scene. Titus could, only with difficulty, help the gaunt man down to his knees, inch by inch. Never for an instant did he cease from the fighting: never for a moment did he murmur. His head was held high; his back was straight as a soldier's as he slowly sank. With one hand he gripped Titus by the forearm as hard as he could. But the youth could hardly feel it.

'Something of a holocaust, ain't it,' he whispered. 'God bless you and your Gormenghast, my boy.'

Then came another voice. It was Juno.

'Let me see you. Let me kneel beside you,' she said.

But already it was too late. Something had fled from the sun-lit bulk on the floor. Muzzlehatch had gone. He had heeled over. His arrogant head lay upon its side, and Juno closed his eyes.

Then Titus stood up. At first he saw nothing, and then it was the swaying of the crowd. He saw a face . . . white as a sheet: an enormity. It was too big for a human visage. It was surrounded by crude locks of carrot-coloured hair, and there were stuffed birds perched upon the dusty shoulders. It was the last of the monstrosities to fall, Titus's mother. Turning from Muzzlehatch's side, Titus, with his eyes fixed upon this pasteboard travesty began to shake, for it reminded him of his own treachery when he left her; and the castle, his heritage.

But he was weak from loss of blood, and there came over him an absolute emptiness. It seemed that nothing mattered any more, so that when Anchor slung him over his shoulder, it was without any kind of argument. Titus had lost all his strength. Again there were cries from the congregation, which were stifled as soon as begun, for an owl the size of a large cat lolled through the air above the Black House, only to return to make sure whether what it had seen was true.

What did it see? It saw the dwindling of the juniper fire. It saw a long corpse lying by itself. Its head was turned on one side. It saw a dormouse under a bunch of couch-grass. It saw the glint of up-turned helmets, and a little to the west, their one-time owners. There they lay, sprawled across one another.

It saw Titus's bandages and Anchor's red hair in the foul morning light. It was a bangle glinting on Juno's wrist. It saw the living and it saw the dead.

ONE HUNDRED AND SEVENTEEN

OWL or no owl, it was essential to get Juno and Titus out of this sickening place, where in the full, if beastly light of the risen sun, objects that appeared mysterious and even magnificent during the night appeared now to be tawdry; cheap; a rag-and-bone shop.

Had Anchor been alone he would have experienced no great difficulty in making an escape from what was fast becoming an angry crowd. For he could handle most aircraft and had already selected one.

But Titus was weak with loss of blood, and Juno was trembling, as though she was standing in icy water.

As for Muzzlehatch, sprawled as though to take the curve of

the world; what could be done about him? That heavy body. Those prodigious limbs. Even were he to have been alive he would have had great difficulty in manoeuvring himself into the aircraft, built like a flying fish.

But now, a dead-weight with his muscles stiffening, how much more difficult!

It was then that the three vagrants ran from the crowd, Crack-Bell, Crabcalf and Slingshott. They had seen it all, and knew just as well as Anchor knew that their only hope was to jettison the dead giant and make for the planes where they stood in long lines under the cedar branches.

'Muzzlehatch; where is he?' whispered Titus. 'Where is he?'

'We cannot take him,' said Anchor. 'We must leave him where he lies. Come, Titus.'

But it was a little while (in spite of Anchor's peremptory command) before Juno could tear herself from what had been so much a part of her life. She bent down and kissed the cold craggy forehead.

Then at Anchor's second shout they left him in the pitiless sunshine, and stumbled towards the voice.

The noise of the crowd had become menacing. Was *this* Cheeta's party? The men were furious; the women tired and vicious. Their clothes were ruined. Was it not natural for the company to wish to revenge itself on something or other? What better than the remaining three?

But they had not reckoned with the men from the Under-River who, seeing how dangerously Titus and the others were placed, barred the obvious exits to the outside world.

But first they let slip through their fingers Juno, Titus and Anchor, and at that moment there began a most outrageous din. Those with a reputation as gentlemen were now forced to think otherwise for there was a great deal of scuffling and cursing before they had all fought their way out of the Black House, and into the open, where they began to mill around. Chivalry had apparently lost itself in a swarm of knees and elbows.

The Three were old campaigners and directly they saw how they had created sufficient chaos, they lost themselves in the irritable crowd.

The sky, curdled as it was, had now begun to look less ominous. A clearer, fresher stain was in the sky.

The vagrants, Crabcalf and the rest, joining up as planned in a rendezvous of branches, sat among the leaves like huge grey fowl.

Then Crabcalf lifted his head and whistled. It was the signal for Titus that all was clear as far as the making of their way was concerned, to where the long line of aircraft lay like frigates at anchor.

ONE HUNDRED AND EIGHTEEN

How beautiful they looked, those dire machines, each of a different colour, each with a different shape. Yet all of them with this in common; that speed was the gist of them.

Though it seemed to Juno, Anchor and Titus that they had been stumbling for ever, it was no more than eight or so minutes before they saw her: a lemon-yellow creature the shape of a tipcat.

As they began to clamber aboard, they could hear the angry voices growing louder every moment, and it was indeed a near thing, for as they rose into the air the first of the forsaken crowd came running into view.

But Muzzlehatch? What of that vast collapse? What of that structure? There it lay so still in the sunlight. What of the way his head lolled over in absolute death? What could they do about it? There was nothing they could do.

The machine rose into the air, and as it rose they saw him dwindle. Now he was the size of a bird: now of an insect on the bright earth. Now he was gone. Gone? Had they forsaken him? Had they lost him forever? Lost him, where he lay, depth below depth, as though fathomed under water; Muzzlehatch . . . silence forever with him; one arm flung out.

For a long while, as the aircraft rose, and moved at the same time into the south, they took no heed of one another; each of them bemused: each in a wilderness of their own.

Anchor, perhaps, his fingers moving mechanically across the

257

controls, was less far from reality than Titus or Juno, by reason of his watchfulness, but even he was hardly normal, and there was upon his face a shadow that Juno had not seen before.

From time to time, as they sped through the upper atmosphere, and while the world unveiled itself, valley by valley, range by range, ocean by ocean, city by city, it seemed that the earth wandered through his skull . . . a cosmos in the bone; a universe lit by a hundred lights and thronged by shapes and shadows; alive with endless threads of circumstance . . . action and event. All futility: disordered; with no end and no beginning.

ONE HUNDRED AND NINETEEN

JUNO was motionless. Her profile was like that of an antique coin. A fullness under the chin; her nose straight and short; her face floated it seemed, unattached against the sky. A planet lit a cheekbone and revealed a tear. It hung there. It could not roll. The sweet down of her cheekbone held it where it was.

As Titus turned and saw her, he recoiled from her pathos. He could not bear it. He saw in her a criticism of his own defection. He suddenly hated himself for such a thought and he half rose from his seat in an agony of confusion. He loathed his own existence. He hated the unnatural from whose platter he had supped too often. The face of Muzzlehatch grew large in his mind. It filled him. It spread deeper. It filled the coloured plane. It filled the heavens. Then came a voice to join it. Was it *Muzzlehatch* with his eyes half closed upon his rocky cheekbone?

Titus shook his head to free his brain. Anchor glanced at the young man and tossed a hank of red hair from his eyes. Then he stared again at Titus.

'Where are we going?' he said at last. But there was no reply.

THE darkness fell and the little craft sped on like an insect in the void. Time seemed to be a meaningless thing; but dawn came at last, its breast a wilderness of feathers.

The red-headed pilot seemed to be slumped over the controls but every now and again he shook himself and adjusted some device. All about him were the intricate entrails of the yellow machine; a creature terrible in its speed; lethal in its line; multitudinous in its secrets; an equation of metal.

Juno was fast asleep with her head on Titus's shoulders. He sat in stony silence while the slim plane whistled through the air.

Suddenly he sat forward in his seat, and clenched his hands. A dark flush covered his brow. It was as though he had only just heard Anchor's question.

'Did someone ask where we were going? Or am I dreaming? Perhaps it is all a figment of my brain.'

'What is the matter, Titus?' said Juno, lifting her head.

'What is the matter? Is that what you said? So *you* don't know either? Neither of you know. Is that it? Have we no destination? We are *moving*, that is all; from one sky to the next. Is that what you think? Or am I mad? I have drowned my birthplace with rant until its name stinks to heaven. Gormenghast! O Gormenghast! How can I prove you?'

Titus banged his head down upon his knees over and over again.

'Dear God! Dear God!' he muttered. 'Don't make me mad.'

'You are no more mad than I am,' said Anchor. 'Or than any other creature who is lost.'

But Titus went on banging his head on his knees.

'Oh Titus,' cried Juno. 'We will search until we find your heart's home. Have I ever doubted you?'

'It is your *pity* for me. Your damnable *pity*,' cried Titus. 'You do not believe. You are gentle, but you do not believe. Oh God, it is your terrible, ignorant pity. Don't you see it is the grey towers that I want? It is my Doctor; it is Bellgrove. If I

shout will she hear me? Turn off the engine, Mr Anchor, and I
will call her out of the air.' Juno and Anchor exchanged glances,
and the engine was switched off. The slithering silence filled
them. Titus raised his head to cry, but no sound came. Only
within himself could he hear a faraway voice calling out. . . .
'Mother ... mother ... mother ... mother ... where are you?
Where ... are ... you? Where ... are ... you?'

ONE HUNDRED AND TWENTY-ONE

NEVER knowing where they were, for they could see nothing
but alien hills and a great unheard-of sea, yet, nevertheless,
they had no option but to cruise ever deeper into the unknown.

They took it in turn to guide the sleek machine, and it was
well that Titus took his share of the responsibility. To some
extent it kept him from brooding.

Yet even then his mind was half aware. Childhood and rebel-
lion ... disobedience and defiance; the journey; the adventures
and now a youth no longer – but the *man*.

'Good-bye, my friend. Look after her. She is all heart.'

Before Anchor and Juno knew what was happening he pressed
a button, and was a second or two later alone, falling through
the wilds of space, his parachute opening like a flower above
him.

Gradually the dark silk tent filled up with air, and he swayed
as he descended through the darkness, for it was night again.
He gave himself up to the sensation of seemingly endless des-
cent.

For a little while he forgot his loneliness, which was strange,
for what could have been a lonelier setting than the night
through which, suspended, he gradually fell? There was nothing
for his feet to touch and it was right for him to be, for the time,
so out of touch in every kind of sense. And so it was with composure that he felt and saw the bats surround him.

Now lay the land below him. A vast charcoal drawing of
mountains and forests. There was no habitation to be seen, nor
anything human, yet the stark geology and the crowding heads

of the forest trees were redolent of almost human shapes. It was among the branches of a forest tree that Titus eventually subsided, and he lay there for a little while unharmed, like a child in a cradle.

When he had freed himself of his harness, and had cut away the deflated silk, he lowered himself branch by branch, and by the time he had reached the forest floor the sunshine was threading its way through the trees.

Now he was really alone and in making for the east he had no better reason than that it was out of there that the sunbeams were pouring.

Hungry, weary, he made his solitary way, eating roots and berries and drinking from the streams. Month followed month until one day, as he wandered through the lonely void, his heart jumped into his throat.

ONE HUNDRED AND TWENTY-TWO

WHY had he stopped to stare at the shape of a rock, as though it were in any way unusual? There it stood, perfectly normal, a great lichened boulder of a thing, pock-marked by time, its northern side somewhat swollen like the sail of a ship. Why was he staring at it as though struck by recognition?

As his eyes raced over the triturated surface of this dead yet evocative thing he took a step backwards. It was as though he was being warned.

There was no getting away from it. He had seen this rock before. He had stood upon its back, a 'king of the castle', in his childhood. He now remembered the long scar, a saw-toothed fissure down its crusty flank.

He knew that if he scaled it now and stood, once again, as in the old days, a 'king of the castle', he would see the very towers of Gormenghast.

That was why he trembled. The long indented outline of his home was blocked away from his sight by the mere proximity of a boulder. It was, for no reason he could see, a challenge.

A flood of memories returned; and as they spread and interspread and deepened, another part of his brain was wide aware of closer manifestations. The recognized existence, the very *proof* of the stone, there before him, not twenty feet away, argued the no less real existence of a cave that yawned at his right hand. A cave where an infinity ago he had struggled with a nymph.

At first he did not dare to turn his head, but the moment had come when he must do so, and *there it was* at last, away behind his right shoulder, and he knew for very proof that he was in his own domain once more. He was standing on Gormenghast Mountain.

As he rose to his feet a fox trotted out of the cave. A crow coughed in a nearby spinney and a gun boomed. It boomed again. It boomed seven times.

There it lay behind the boulder; the immemorial ritual of his home. It was the dawn salvo. It boomed for him, for the seventy-seventh Earl, Titus Groan, Lord of Gormenghast, *wherever* he might be.

There burned the ritual; all he had lost; all he had searched for. The concrete *fact* of it. The proof of his own sanity and love.

'O God! It's true! It's true! I am not mad! I am not mad!' he cried.

Gormenghast, his home. He could feel it. He could almost *see* it. He had only to skirt the base of the great rock or climb its crusty crown, for his eyes to become filled with towers. There was a taste in the air of iron. There was a quickening it seemed of the very stones and of the bridgeless spaces. What was he waiting for?

It would have been possible, had he wished it, to have reached the mouth of the cave without a glimpse of his Home. Indeed he took a step or two towards the cave-mouth. But again a sense of impending danger held back his feet, and a moment later he heard his own voice saying . . .

'No . . . no . . . not now! It is not possible . . . now.'

His heart beat out more rapidly, for something was growing . . . some kind of knowledge. A thrill of the brain. A synthesis. For Titus was recognizing in a flash of retrospect that a new phase of which he was only half aware, had been reached. It was a sense of maturity, almost of fulfilment. He had no longer any need for home, for he carried his Gormenghast within him. All that he sought was jostling within himself. He had grown up. What a boy had set out to seek a man had found, found by the act of living.

There he stood: Titus Groan, and he turned upon his heel so that the great boulder was never seen by him ever again. Nor was the cave: nor was the castle that lay beyond, for Titus, as though shaking off his past from his shoulders like a heavy cape began to run down the far side of the mountain, not by the track by which he had ascended, but by another that he had never known before.

With every pace he drew away from Gormenghast Mountain, and from everything that belonged to his home.

MORE ABOUT PENGUINS
AND PELICANS

For further information about books available from Penguins please write to Dept EP, Penguin Books Ltd, Harmondsworth, Middlesex UB7 0DA.

In the U.S.A.: For a complete list of books available from Penguins in the United States write to Dept CS, Penguin Books, 625 Madison Avenue, New York, New York 10022.

In Canada: For a complete list of books available from Penguins in Canada write to Penguin Books Canada Ltd, 2801 John Street, Markham, Ontario L3R 1B4.

In Australia: For a complete list of books available from Penguins in Australia write to the Marketing Department, Penguin Books Australia Ltd, P.O. Box 257, Ringwood, Victoria 3134.

In New Zealand: For a complete list of books available from Penguins in New Zealand write to the Marketing Department, Penguin Books (NZ) Ltd, P.O. Box 4019, Auckland 10.

KING PENGUIN

Bringing together the very best in international writing, King Penguin, a new series, will include the most exciting new and contemporary works, as well as books of established reputation, and rediscoveries. It is altogether a series to be enjoyed, in the finest tradition of Penguin Books.

A selection

THE VIRGIN IN THE GARDEN
A. S. Byatt

As a Yorkshire community prepares to celebrate the Coronation, A. S. Byatt paints a rich and elegant portrait of the new Elizabethan age – seen as a curiously distorted image of the old.

A CONFEDERACY OF DUNCES
John Kennedy Toole

Outrageous, grotesque, superbly written, the critics acclaimed this great comic novel as one of the most exciting discoveries in current American fiction. Its Falstaffian hero is Ignatius J. Reilly, a self-proclaimed genius in a world of dunces.

THE YAWNING HEIGHTS
Alexander Zinoviev

Clive James has called this larger than life satire on contemporary Russian society 'a work vital to the continuity of civilization'.

LAMB
Bernard Mac Laverty

This story of a priest and a boy from the Dublin slums who attempt to live by an ideal of love becomes an image of piercing simplicity. Bernard Mac Laverty's brilliant first novel is the work of 'a born writer with a manifest destiny' – *Sunday Times*

Vladimir Nabokov in Penguins

THE GIFT

Life and memory, tradition and heritage all intertwine
in the shimmering tapestry of the writer's mind.

Fyodor Godunov-Cherdynstev is an impoverished writer
living in Berlin after the First World War, and it is through
him that we see art and life converge: his childhood in Russia,
recaptured in a volume entitled 'Poems'; Pushkin
entering his blood, and with Pushkin's voice merges the voice
of his father; while all the time Zina's vibrant presence
continues to influence his work. As Nabokov unfolds
his phantasmal tale, the threads gather together to foreshadow
the book Fyodor dreams of writing: *The Gift*.

LOLITA

'Massive, unflagging, moral, exquisitely shaped, enormously
vital, enormously funny' – Bernard Levin

Nabokov's novel of a middle-aged Englishman's passion
for a honey-hued, twelve-year-old American girl
has become one of the world's great love stories.

'No lover has thought of his beloved with so much tenderness, no
woman has been so charmingly evoked, in such grace
and delicacy, as Lolita' – Lionel Trilling

and

BEND SINISTER
DESPAIR
GLORY
INVITATION TO A BEHEADING
A RUSSIAN BEAUTY
TYRANTS DESTROYED
LAUGHTER IN THE DARK
LOOK AT THE HARLEQUINS
THE REAL LIFE OF SEBASTIAN KNIGHT
ADA
PNIN
SPEAK, MEMORY: AN AUTOBIOGRAPHY
NABOKOV'S DOZEN
PALE FIRE

Angela Carter in King Penguin

THE BLOODY CHAMBER

From the lairs of the fantastical and fabulous and from
the domains of the unconscious's mysteries lie the brides in the
Bloody Chamber, hunts unwillingly the Queen of the Vampires,
slips Red Riding Hood into the arms of the Wolf, pimps
our Puss-in-Boots for his lustful master . . .

In tales that glitter and haunt – strange nuggets from a
writer whose wayward pen spills forth stylish, erotic,
nightmarish jewels of prose – the old fairy stories live and
breathe again, subtly altered, subtly changed.

'A classic of short fiction, literally aglow with lyrical
intensity, comic ingenuity . . . few forests are so deep, so
seductive, as these magical entanglements' – Robert Coover,
author of *The Public Burning*

THE INFERNAL DESIRE MACHINES OF
DOCTOR HOFFMAN

The story of a war fought against the diabolic
Doctor Hoffman who wanted to demolish the structures
of reason and liberate man from the chains of the reality
principle for ever.

Doctor Hoffman chose the human mind and the human heart
for his battleground – and it was left to Desiderio to stop him.

'Angela Carter is one of my favourite drugs' – Tom Robbins,
author of *Another Roadside Attraction*

'Combines exquisite craft with an apparently boundless reach'
– Ian McEwan, author of *First Love, Last Rites*

Also published

HEROES AND VILLAINS

Jorge Luis Borges in Penguins

'A great writer who has composed only little essays or short narratives. Yet they suffice for us to call him great because of their wonderful intelligence, their wealth of invention and their tight, almost mathematical, style' – André Maurois in his introduction to *Labyrinths*

LABYRINTHS

The twenty-three stories in *Labyrinths* include Borges's classic 'Tlön, Uqbar, Orbit Tertius', a new world where external objects are whatever each person wants; and 'Pierre Menard', the story of the man who rewrote parts of *Don Quixote* for the twentieth century in Cervantes's words.

The ten essays reflect the extraordinary scope of Borges's reading – the ancient literatures of Greece and China, the medieval philosophers, Pascal, Shakespeare, Valéry, Shaw and Wells – while the seven parables are unforgettable exercises in the art of astonishment.

A UNIVERSAL HISTORY OF INFAMY

This book includes the popular 'Streetcorner Man', Borges's very first short story, and a final selection of brief tales in which human villainy becomes the victim of fate, enchantment or its own perversity. Here, as well as chronicling the lives of such famous villains as Billy the Kid and the Tichborne Claimant, Borges perpetrates a hoax or two – a technique for which he later won acclaim – by inventing stories and ascribing them to other authors.

Also published

THE BOOK OF SAND
DOCTOR BRODIE'S REPORT

MR PYE

Mervyn Peake

Mr Pye comes to the Island of Sark with
a mission, to convert the islanders into a
crusading force for the undiluted goodness
that he feels within.

Mr Pye, however, is prone to excess, and
excess is very nearly his downfall.
For when the struggle between good and evil
becomes embarrassingly personalized
Mr Pye finds it impossible to maintain the
delicate balance, and finds that evil
can only be defeated by complete surrender
to goodness, the outcome of which
is truly miraculous.

In his fight he finds invaluable help from
Miss Dredger, his aggressively robust landlady,
Thorpe the archetypal seaport painter, and
Tintagieu, wanton, blackhaired, five foot
three inches of sex, but who still retains the
perfect innocence of a child, the same
innocence that is to provide Mr Pye with the
courage to face the inevitable.

Mervyn Peake captures the essence of the
closeknit community in the same masterly way that
he created the Gormenghast trilogy, and
leads us to an understanding of the paradox
of good and evil.

The Gormenghast Trilogy by Mervyn Peake

TITUS GROAN

Stranger than fiction, larger than life, full of shades and echoes, *Titus Groan* is not merely one of the most brilliantly sustained flights of the imagination in modern English fiction, it is also a sustained piece of deadly irony. The characters are weird; the setting fantastic; everything about Mervyn Peake's masterpiece seems eccentric but for the stringent sense of reality which always seeps through the farcical, frightening antics in the mad castle of Gormenghast.

GORMENGHAST

Gormenghast is the second book in Mervyn Peake's Titus trilogy: a magnificent flight of Gothic fantasy which ranks as one of this century's most remarkable feats of imaginative writing.

Titus, 77th Lord Groan of Gormenghast, is restless in his cobwebbed kingdom of crumbling towers and ivied quadrangles, dank passages and battlements elbow-deep in moss. The castle is instinct with spreading evil. Titus's father, his twin sisters and several castle officials have met terrible and secret ends and Titus feels that, if he isn't destined for a similar fate, his life can only ever be an endless round of pre-ordained ritual. Somehow he must cut off the evil at source – or escape into the unknown world beyond Gormenghast.